I dreamed of the Kolahn War.

The darkest, most violent time of my life.

The ESS *Ares* was an Olympic-class cruiser, a relic of the Notha War that was still serving as a workhorse of the conflict. I was temporarily in command as both Captain Klaws—a brilliant Verdantian leader on loan from his people's Navy—and Commander Shelly T'Ketra—an Ethereal who irrationally hated my guts—were presently on board a Sorkanan super cruiser called the *Nasha'tarr* receiving new orders. There were rumors that the Kolahn homeworld was under assault and the war would soon be over.

I could only hope.

The Kolahn War had started almost immediately after I'd received my commission in Space Fleet following the recovery of missing SKAMMs and the "heroic" death of Captain Elgan. I'd done my best to serve in a manner befitting the uniform I'd been given a chance to wear, but it was a *nasty* war. The Enigmatic Path had seized control of the Kolahn government and instituted a brutal regime of theocratic technocratic rule.

The Enigmatic Path exterminated anyone who stood in their way and used civilians as shields while carrying out indiscriminate attacks against Community infrastructure. The Community wasn't exactly worried about collateral damage either and I'd done my best to work up the ranks so I could show mercy whenever possible. It wasn't a strategy that had always worked but sometimes did.

The bridge of the *Ares* was a smoky, circular, gray chamber with all the systems lettering in glowing orange over black. The smoke was due to the air purifiers being at only half effectiveness. This would have terrified me if we didn't have the necessary parts to repair the damage from our last engagement with the Enigmatic Path in the region. It had been our sixth in a month and second while I was acting captain. Unfortunately, the crew working on fixing the bridge damage was half-assing their jobs and had been for hours.

SPACE ACADEMY VAGRANTS

Book Five of the Space Academy Series

C. T. Phipps and Michael Suttkus

CAST OF CHARACTERS

Lead

Captain Vance Turbo, aka Vannevar Tagashi: Academy dropout, loudmouth, alleged genius.

Supporting Cast

Forty-Two: Sorkanan dropout turned security officer and Space Marine. Now suffering from premature old age.

Lieutenant/"Doctor" Winston Arden: An elderly former junior officer on the ESS *Ares* that gained knowledge of a dangerous secret. Now he's a "doctor" of piratology.

Fleet Admiral Saul Bendo: The Chief of Naval operations for EarthGov's Home Fleet. More politician than soldier these days.

High Protector Anne Bonny: The first human High Protector. She is the infamous pirate. Who became a space pirate. Then a privateer. No, it doesn't make any sense.

High Protector B'Vash: A Sorkanan High Protector who has been aiding humanity from behind the scenes. His agenda is nebulous.

Director Case Gordon AKA Director G: The head of EarthGov's branch of the Security Divisions.

The Diplomat: The sibling of the High Priestess. A Notha attaché to the Antaeus Rangers.

Light on Water: A Sklux Space Fleet officer. Overly deferential and obsequious.

Commander Leah Mass: Actual graduate of Space Academy, genius. Vance's ex. Psychic. Transwoman. Transhuman. Heroine.

Ichigo Murphy: A tech-genius member of the Antaeus Rangers.

Commander Hannah O'Brian: Genetically engineered superhuman merc. Catlike agility and other qualities. Like her tail.

Lieutenant Leslie Park: A young woman who owes her career to Vance Turbo.

Lieutenant Commander Henri Plantagenet: A treacherous Crius nobleman who once worked as an engineer under Vance.

Princess Huggypants: A Drolochid supervillain that enjoys working for the Community now. Mostly.

Sparrowhawk: The mysterious head of the Ring's pro-bioroid resistance.

Captain Kathy Tagawa: Hero of Earth's space program. Paragon of humanity. Aunt of Vance.

Major Arana Taylor: A Xerxes security officer who once joined in a mutiny against Vance.

Tank: A New Dallas-born former magistrate turned mercenary. He is a member of the Antaeus Rangers.

TRS-8021 "Trish": The AI of the ship. Human female personality. Annoyingly adorable.

Astrid Mass-Turbo: Vance Turbo's genetically engineered psychic daughter.

Grand General Vast: The Sorkanan leader of the People's Liberation Army and a galactic warlord. He and Vance have history.

John Mason: The current head of the Antaeus Rangers and Hannah's ex-boyfriend.

FOREWORD

Hello, my fellow space academy cadets!

Vance Turbo has gone through a variety of fantastic adventures! He's faced ancient Primordials, battled governments conspiracies, and fought a planet full of slavers. He's managed to juggle his conflicting alliances between Earth, the Community, and the Elder Races.

I've very much enjoyed detailing Vance Turbo's adventures. It's been interesting following his rise from Space Academy dropout to a respected Space Fleet captain. Now he's a High Protector, as far as any human can go. It's left Vance with a bit of imposter syndrome as he's never wanted power, but to serve. Unfortunately, at the level of power he's achieved, it's better to give orders rather than continue taking them.

Space Academy Vagrants is a unique story as it originally was planned to be the third and final *Lucifer's Star* book, another series of mine that takes place in the same universe as the Space Academy, but about five hundred years later. It was a story of pirate treasure, politics, and confused loyalties.

However, the funny thing about the story was that it just didn't feel right for Cassius Mass, protagonist of *Lucifer's Star*, but it felt very right for Vance and his company. Despite its zany premise of chasing after the pirate treasure of an alien abducted Anne Bonny, it was one of the more serious and meaningful Space Academy stories.

This is a story about change and Vance having to accept (or deny) that he's no longer someone who can just go gallivanting around the galaxy. That he's got responsibilities. Assuming he wants to be someone who can make the galaxy a better place on a systemic level. Unfortunately, that may be impossible and not him. Captain Kirk's arc in the first three Star Trek movies was realizing that he *wasn't* meant to be an admiral.

Vance Turbo has been a fantastic Hero of SPAAACE but he's not the sort of person who really does great in meetings, negotiations, or diplomacy. He might be able to rise to the occasion and save the universe from itself behind a desk, but he might not be.

The fact that it's taking a kind of *Treasure Planet*-esque journey to realize this is something that surprised even me as an author. The rest of his crew are undergoing their own arcs as well. You'll also see some homages to classic Star Trek episodes involving godlike beings and "tests." Something that I think we all agree the godlike aliens can go screw themselves over.

I hope you'll enjoy this book as we come up to the finale in the next book. It's been a fantastic ride, but this is the penultimate volume of Space Academy. As *Star Trek: The Next Generation* showed, all good things must come to an end unless you make a sequel series thirty years later with mixed results

CHAPTER ONE

Dead Man's Hand

I dreamed of the Kolahn War.

The darkest, most violent time of my life.

The ESS *Ares* was an Olympic-class cruiser, a relic of the Notha War that was still serving as a workhorse of the conflict. I was temporarily in command as both Captain Klaws—a brilliant Verdantian leader on loan from his people's Navy—and Commander Shelly T'Ketra—an Ethereal who irrationally hated my guts—were presently on board a Sorkanan super cruiser called the *Nasha'tarr* receiving new orders. There were rumors that the Kolahn homeworld was under assault and the war would soon be over.

I could only hope.

The Kolahn War had started almost immediately after I'd received my commission in Space Fleet following the recovery of missing SKAMMs and the "heroic" death of Captain Elgan. I'd done my best to serve in a manner befitting the uniform I'd been given a chance to wear, but it was a *nasty* war. The Enigmatic Path had seized control of the Kolahn government and instituted a brutal regime of theocratic technocratic rule.

The Enigmatic Path exterminated anyone who stood in their way and used civilians as shields while carrying out indiscriminate attacks against Community infrastructure. The Community wasn't exactly worried about collateral damage either and I'd done my best to work up the ranks so I could show mercy whenever possible. It wasn't a strategy that had always worked but sometimes did.

1

The bridge of the *Ares* was a smoky, circular, gray chamber with all the systems lettering in glowing orange over black. The smoke was due to the air purifiers being at only half effectiveness. This would have terrified me if we didn't have the necessary parts to repair the damage from our last engagement with the Enigmatic Path in the region. It had been our sixth in a month and second while I was acting captain. Unfortunately, the crew working on fixing the bridge damage was half-assing their jobs and had been for hours.

We'd recently been in a battle with a group of Enigmatic Path corvettes right after most of our more experienced crew had been transferred to better armed, more strategically important vessels. All the replacements had been the "Crius Volunteers" that were from a planet primarily known for slavery and corporate feudalism. I didn't like them, and they didn't like me. Thankfully, our chances of being ambushed by any more Enigmatic Path or their mercenary allies before the captain's return were small. They were all in full retreat to the Kolahn system. Which was good because in our current condition, we'd get our asses kicked.

"Are you still working on that *borking* console, Mister Plantagenet?" I asked, holding my head as I leaned back in my captain's chair. The time for decorum had passed and I was just sick to death of the constant delays in the repair times.

"Sorry sir, I'm doing my best," Lieutenant Commander Henri Plantagenet said as his legs stuck out from under one of the consoles while sparks were visible from his work. He was over-ranked and under-skilled for both his position and duties. Apparently, he was a viscount or something back on his homeworld. Incompetence was a charge I'd been desperate to avoid and now I couldn't help but wonder how different we were. After all, I was the one failing to whip this group into shape.

"Your best is not good enough," I said, dryly. "We need air. It's kind of important."

"I'll get it fixed," Henri said. "Eventually."

I took a deep breath and did my best not to choke on it. "We can't wait on this. Mister Plantagenet, you are hereby ordered to end your shift."

2

"Excuse me?" Henri said, sliding out from under the console. "I'm serving the Community here."

I tried not to tell him that if he wanted to serve the Community military, he should resign or transfer to something more appropriate for his talents like janitorial staff. "You're clearly tired, Henri. You've worked too hard. Go to the VR room and enjoy your favorite program or get some rest. Ensign Park will take over repairing the air purifiers. In fact, I'm imposing a mandatory leave for the rest of the weekend. Get some rest."

At least I could trust Leslie, she was a blue-skinned Thorian who'd volunteered with her sister after the first wave of Enigmatic Path attacks on her homeworld. She was incredibly handy with a wrench and was more interested in doing her job than playing petty shipboard politics.

Henri stood up and stared. "That demihuman filth? You can't be serious. You can't do—"

I stared back. "*I am the captain.* I can do whatever the hell I want."

"*Acting captain.* I am son of—"

I pulled out my fusion pistol and put it on the side of my captain's chair. "If my captaincy means nothing to you, I'm happy to deal with you as Captain Vance Turbo: Hero of SPAAACE."

I hated that title. The movies and mini-series had been made about my adventures on the *Black Nebula* just a couple of years ago and it was ridiculous how I'd been feted for a mission that had been ten kinds of illegal. However, the Crius Volunteers respected the famous guy from the movies even if they didn't respect the fact I'd been left in charge. If nothing else, Henri knew I'd been in combat and wasn't afraid of his posturing.

Henri looked down. "I suddenly feel very tired, sir. I request to be relieved."

Part of the tension was because Henri and I were the same rank. The chief engineer had some time on me in the service as well. He seemed to view me as a kind of rival since while he was hot savit on his homeworld, I had just as famous a set of ancestors. Well, my Aunt Kathy Tagawa was a famous ancestor at least.

"Go," I said, my voice low. "Don't come back until you're called."

3

Henri scurried out of the doors at the back of the bridge. Everyone else on the bridge watched him go, ranging from the tactical officer to my security chief and Security Departments liaison.

"I would have just shot him," a tall bronze-skinned woman of Xerxes descent said. Major Arana Taylor was the ship's Security Departments officer and had the job of making sure the secrets of the Community technology were kept from enemy hands as well as analyzing any intelligence we acquired about our enemies. Arana also had the job of preventing any defections, insurrection, or mutiny that might be brewing among the ranks. Frankly, she wasn't doing a great job.

Mutinies were almost unheard of in Space Fleet but a rash of them had occurred throughout the Notha War due to the Enigmatic Path threatening families, bribing conscripts, and inserting sleeper agents throughout the fleets. Karl Allenway, a lieutenant commander, had stolen an Olympic-class vessel like this with the help of a bunch of Community traitors. He was also one of the Crius Volunteers, but everyone was walking on eggshells at the idea they were untrustworthy. Too many people wanted to bring the rogue human colony back into the fold.

"That's still an option as far as I'm concerned," I said, staring over at her. "But isn't that your job?"

I'd been living on one or two hours of a sleep a night for the past three weeks. I was sleeping with one eye open since I'd been assigned as acting captain and didn't trust Henri. He was supposed to be my backup here, but I couldn't shake the feeling that he was plotting something. Was it paranoia when you'd already had to deal with both your captain—the late Captain Elgan—and fellow crew going against you? The ESS *Black Nebula* cast a long shadow over how I dealt with my fellow officers.

"Too much paperwork," Arana said. "Worse, Admiral Bendo really wants the Crius Volunteers to work out."

"I bet he does," I said. "He's really in favor of this pan-human alliance thing."

Fleet Admiral Bendo was the most powerful human being on Earth, even more than the Prime Minister in many ways, as the Home Fleet was the major source of the Sol system's influence in the Community. Much of Earth's economy was based on military contracts and colonization that required him to sign off on fleet movements. He was very pro-human, though, and often went to elaborate lengths to try to incorporate humanity's disparate elements in military engagements. The problem was the people from the lost colonies like the ones in Contested Space had left Earth's purview for a reason.

"YEAH, WELL, HENRI'S DEFINITELY PLOTTING AGAINST YOU," Trish spoke up from the captain's chair. "HE HOLDS MEETINGS IN AREAS I CAN'T MONITOR AND HAS BEEN DELIBERATELY SABOTAGING REPAIRS."

Trish was the *Ares'* AI and the crew member I was closest to. She rarely contacted me openly, though. The Contested Space recruits and Crius all seemed to find Trish unsettling and preferred more silent AI.

"That's a serious accusation," Arana said. "It's very possible he is just terrible at his job and hates AI."

"That may be worse. I'm not going to let him endanger this ship. His work is dangerously shoddy and relies heavily on quick fixes."

"I'm sure he can be promoted somewhere else," Arana said, alluding to the idea he'd been promoted from his last ship just to get rid of him. "Unfortunately, he's very popular with the crew and the one they've appointed to be their spokesman."

"He's their spokesman now?" I asked, grimacing. "How did he manage that?"

"Ever since Otto died in an accident Henri blamed on you, the crew has been grumbling," Arana said, referring to the former Chief Engineer. "Henri has been addressing their grievances. Not to mention throwing a lot of credits around in gifts and lost gambling wages. He's apparently a terrible gambler, perhaps deliberately so."

If I had been a more experienced captain I would have been all over this, but it was still my first time in the chair for an extended period. At least on board the *Ares.* I was also reluctant to give into the kind of paranoia that individuals like Major Taylor encouraged. I didn't like the Security Departments and didn't trust them. I certainly would never voluntarily work for them or on their information without having it vetted from other sources.

My last serious girlfriend, Leah Mass, had turned out to be a honey pot they'd used to try and recruit me. Elgan had also been working for the now-disavowed Department Twelve when he'd almost gotten me and a hundred other crew members killed chasing Elder Race technology. Arana had not given me reason to distrust her, but I just didn't like intelligence officers monitoring the people inside our ships rather than the people outside of them.

"So, he's bribing the crew," I said, sourly.

Arana frowned. "Many of them are conscripts or here for a paycheck. The Community incorporated a lot of Contested Space militaries into its forces and, well, they didn't send their best. They can't afford to fight for principle."

"I'm here for principle," I muttered.

"Principles are for those who can afford them," Arana said. "Not all of us were born with an electrum spoon in our mouths. You grew up the adopted child of a famous space captain in the Lunar Shipyards. A lot of these people grew up on hellholes like Rand's World. Plantagenet may be a nobleman, but he knows that money talks. He doesn't pretend to be one of the men like you do."

"Point taken." I tapped the side of my command chair. It was an ugly lesson but one I perhaps needed to absorb. Not everyone appreciated a captain trying to act like their friend, especially when they were as young as I was. It was time for some harsh discipline instead. "Send up Ensign Park from engineering."

"Are you sure you want to show her favoritism?" Arana frowned. "Plantagenet isn't going to forgive that insult. Crius nobles have a very particular sense of honor."

"He's going to forgive what I do next even less," I said, having decided this ship's maintenance needed someone who knew how to maintain a ship. "I can't just leave this problem to fester. Make a note that he's receiving an official reprimand for insubordination. I'm also going to bypass his cronies for his replacement."

"That's...going to go over poorly."

"It's already done. Trish, make an official note and put it in the ship record."

There was a ping noise. "YOU GOT IT, BOSS."

6

Arana sighed. "Is there anything else you're going to do that's going to throw this ship into disarray?"

"Yes."

"I'm not going to like this, am I?" Arana said.

"I need to do what should be done for the honor and dignity of the Crius military," I said, such as a thing existed for a planet that had only recently given up slavery. "As well as Space Fleet."

"So, I'm going to hate it," Arana said.

The door to the bridge opened with a swish and I turned around in my chair to see Ensign Leslie Park. She was a two-meter-tall, blue-skinned women with shoulder-length black hair. She wore a set of overalls and bandana that was covered in grease. She had the build of a woman who worked with heavy machinery. Thorians were humans re-engineered to survive in high-gravity, cold environments and, not coincidentally, look like the humanoid aliens in Pre-First Contact sci-fi shows. She was a beautiful woman but, unlike many Community officers, I didn't savit where I ate.

"Reporting for duty, sir!" Leslie said, cheerfully. "What do you need?"

"To get our air filters working before we have to switch to the emergency backups," I said, pointing to the console.

"Right," Leslie said, walking along cheerfully then crawling down to get to work. "Will get this done, ASAP."

"So, do I have anything to worry about with the crew?" I asked, turning to Arana. "By which I mean active danger and not low morale."

"YES, YOU DO, VANCE," Trish said.

"I'm talking to my spy," I said, using terminology I probably shouldn't have been using on a public bridge, but my brain was fried and I needed a week of sleep.

"Only Plantagenet," Arana said, straightening up. "You have the respect of the original crew."

"Original crew?" I asked, knowing she meant the ones other than the Contested Space conscripts and Crius Volunteers.

Arana covered her face with her hand. "Do you read any of my dockets sir?"

"You mean your spy reports on everyone?"

7

"Yes," Arana said.

"No," I said. "I've been kind of dealing with keeping this ship from falling apart. Does anyone?"

"Captain Klaws and Commander T'Ketra do," Arana said. "Otto's death was suspicious enough that I feel you need to—"

"Done," Leslie said, sliding out from the panel that Henri had been working on.

"Already?" I asked.

"There wasn't a problem," Leslie said, frowning. "A lot of the problems on the ship are fics."

"Fics?" I asked, confused.

Leslie frowned, looking troubled. "It's not my place to say, sir."

"It is when your captain asks," I said, conveying only the slightest bit of annoyance as the air cleared up around us. "Consider it an order."

Leslie sucked in her breath. "Fics are problems the engineers create. Fake ones."

"Fake ones," I repeated.

"It's a common enough tactic among engineering," Arana said, frowning. "When they want to make captains take their position seriously. They make the lights flicker and unnecessary systems look more damaged than they are."

I didn't like the fact that Henri had enough influence to intimidate any of my crew into acting against me. It implied I'd lost control over Engineering completely. I wondered if my holding Arana back was having a worse effect on them than I'd expected.

"Air isn't unnecessary," I said, looking between them. "You're saying Lieutenant Commander Plantagenet has gone from insubordination to sabotage."

You could have heard a pin drop among the rest of the bridge crew.

"OH, THAT ISN'T GOOD," Trish said.

"The smoke is making the damage look worse than it is," Leslie said, looking extremely nervous. "I don't know why he did this. Fics are usually only done during peacetime and when assignments are boring."

It still sounded completely unprofessional.

8

Arana said, frowning. "Captain, I would like permission to arrest Plantagenet and his cronies immediately."

I frowned. "First, let's handle this. Lieutenant Park, you have done an excellent job maintaining the ship's systems. Everything you've done has been prompt and excellent work."

"The ship talks to me," Leslie said, pausing. "It asks for the best treatment it can get."

I frowned, knowing she was speaking literally. That Leslie had a very mystical method of dealing with the ship had not gone over well with the crew. Leslie could also guess what people were thinking and knew exactly when things were about to go wrong. She'd make a fine command officer if she could combine her knowledge of machines with people skills.

"That is why I am promoting you to lieutenant," I said. "You'll also be acting lieutenant commander and head of engineering. I need you to assemble a team of people who can get this ship in fighting shape again."

"Excuse me?" Leslie asked, her eyes widening. "*Sir*?"

"Captain, if I may—" Arana started to say.

I noticed other members of my bridge crew were looking at us, clearly as shocked as Arana but doing their best not to be noticed. I didn't care. It was about time this ship was put back on the right path and I wasn't going to let some spoiled incompetents steal my ship out from under me.

"Go arrest Lieutenant Commander Plantagenet and his cronies *immediately*," I said, looking at Arana. "He is suspended from his duties, and I want a full investigation of his people. He's put this ship at risk and behaved with conduct unbecoming a Community officer. We'll convene a court martial once the captain and commander return. I take full responsibility."

It would be a savitstorm back home and I'm sure I would have to call upon favors with my fellow noblemen to make sure the blowback was minimal. However, I could tell the chief engineer was planning on taking my command. Probably just by making me look like I couldn't run the ship properly, but I wasn't willing to put aside full-on mutiny now.

"As you wish, sir." Arana nodded and bowed her head before departing down the bridge's elevator. I didn't envy her position as even with the ship's security backing her up, Henri was likely to put up a fight.

Leslie lowered her head. "This will not make my life easier."

"It's not about making your life easier," I said, frowning. "It's about doing our job and serving the Community to the best of our ability. Imagine what this ship would be like if I was the only person who actually cared about serving the cause."

Leslie stared at me and for a moment, it felt like she was in my head, looking around. "Permission to speak freely, sir?"

"Why is it no one ever asks that question when they have good news,' I muttered. "Granted."

"You are the only person on this ship who is here for the Community," Leslie said. "Everyone else here has other motives."

I narrowed my eyes. "I'll not have that kind of defeatist talk from one of my officers, Lieutenant." I paused before looking at her. "Wait, if you weren't here to serve the Community then why did you join the service?"

Leslie gave a half-smile. "Student loans."

"Ah," I said.

Leslie looked at me sideways. "My mother was a Wheelerite mathemagician and always used to read people's probability. She said some people pulled everyone around them into their orbit while others were thrown about by destiny like pieces of debris."

"Which am I?" I asked, wondering if I'd make a mistake in promoting her.

"Both," Leslie said, blinking. "You should turn on your personal energy shield. Things are about to get bad. You need to—"

Leslie didn't get to finish her sentence because the doors to the back of the bridge once more opened and revealed Henri and a group of engineers in the back. They were all conscripts or Crius Volunteers. Arana was held prisoner by one with a gun to her head. Apparently, she'd not been able to get the rest of her security team together to arrest him.

10

"Sorry, Captain," Arana said, shrugging. "On the plus side, this is the only part of the crew that sided with him."

"You elevated that *part-alien*?" Henri said, staring at Leslie. How he'd heard about that was confusing. *"To my position?"*

I put up my Elder ring's barrier as they opened fire. The ring had belonged to Ketra T'Kal, a diplomat who'd sacrificed her life to save mine. Its barrier was stronger than any human-made personal barrier but depended greatly on the willpower of the owner to function. Right now, I wasn't exactly brimming with that. The ring's barrier could also be overloaded with enough firepower.

It was time to test my strength of purpose.

CHAPTER TWO

Claiming the Captain's Seat

The barrier held.

I could tell they were surprised by the existence of my Elder ring's, let alone that it had stopped their attack.

"A coup, eh?" I said, staring at the seven mutineers. I recognized two of them as Lieutenants Davenport and Hambling. They were insubordinate, entitled scumbags exiled from their previous crews with glowing recommendations. The rest were new transfers of whom I knew the names and ranks, but little else. "You realize that you'll never get away with this, right?"

I wasn't speaking figuratively either. Trish was fully integrated into the systems and even if they managed to kill me—which was entirely possible—she would prevent them from taking over the ship. Too much was automated for them to operate it without hundreds of co-conspirators. Honestly, I was surprised Henri was able to get as many as he had. Making me look like a fool and undermining me was very different than high treason. That was the only crime other than crimes against sapience, weaponizing AI, and tampering with Elder Race artifacts that carried the death penalty in the Community.

Unless he doesn't intend to take the ship, Trish said in my mind. *What if his plan is just to disable it?*

Why? I asked, genuinely confused.

Money, probably, Trish suggested. *The Enigmatic Path or Notha would both pay an extensive bounty to any individual who could bring down a Community warship. Even more so if they could bring it in intact. Planetary warlords and pirate kings would salivate at the prospect, too, even if they'd have to strip it down for parts to keep the Community off their back.*

That was a very unfortunate possibility. Someone like Karl Allenway, the so-called Pirate Prince, might also be planning to show up and claim the vessel after Henri took command of the bridge. From here, provided he also controlled Gravitronics and Engineering, he could cut Trish's connection to the ship then suffocate the entire crew or crush them with gravity manipulators. It didn't need to be a mutiny of many, just enough to kill everyone for pirates to claim their prize.

"Yes," Henri said, firing his fusion pistol several times at me. He continued firing well after the others in his group had ceased. All the blasts hit the front of my personal barrier, dissipating into uselessness. "As for getting away with it, I am confident in my chances."

"Like your confidence in just gunning me down," I said, not returning fire with Arana as a hostage.

Henri glared.

Leslie reluctantly pulled out her own personal sidearm and stood beside me. "I'm siding with you, Captain."

The rest of the bridge crew didn't seem so certain, and I blamed myself for that as we'd all been run ragged by, well, me. I still had a lot to learn about captaining and mistakes had been made. I'd kept myself aloof when I should have been living and working among them. I'd also been eager to hunt down Enigmatic Path forces when I should have been more concerned about patrolling. Either way, Henri's people began to disarm the crew and move them all into one area on the bridge. I could have ordered them to fight but that would have just caused a bloodbath.

Henri sneered at me, looking disgusted at Leslie. "This could have been easy, but you had to make it hard. Siding with him is going to cost you."

"He may not be the best captain but he's not a spoiled bigot. We need people who believe," Leslie said.

"ALSO, HE'S REALLY RICH WITH CONNECTIONS TO HOME FLEET AND YOU JUST GOT PROMOTED," Trish added, much to Leslie's embarrassment.

"Err, that too," Leslie said.

13

"You're going to order the crew to shut down the ship's defenses and barriers. I've already got the engines shutting down," Henri snarled, keeping his fusion pistol trained on me despite its present uselessness. "You're still trapped here and as soon as you step out of that energy shield, you're dead."

He clearly didn't know my ring barrier travelled with me, but I hadn't exactly been advertising I had an Elder Race artifact on me. Mostly because that was as punishable by death as what Henri was doing.

"I'll have to decline," I said.

"Then I'll start randomly shooting the crew," Henri said, as if he was a holodrama antagonist. "I know you have a fondness for them. You like to think you're the good guy."

Honestly, there was something wrong with this picture and I wasn't sure what it was. Henri shouldn't have been able to get the drop on Arana. She should have gathered a team of security officers with her and taken Henri's group without incident. There was also no reason for them to bring her up to the bridge versus stunning or killing her. As hostages went, there were a lot more up here. It was possible that he didn't want to kill his fellow crew members, not really, but that wasn't the vibe I was getting in the slightest. Why was she up here with him?

No, he wasn't the ringleader here. There was also the fact that Arana had been dropping hints about Henri's treason the entire time while discouraging me from making any real moves to deal with it. Trish being unable to know about what was being said or to who, let alone monitor their actual planning also required someone who knew all the blind spots on the ship—something that Henri absolutely did not.

"I'm not the good guy," I said, staring at him, "but I do have my moments. So, tell me, Arana, what exactly caused you to betray the Community?"

"What?" Leslie asked, eyes widening.

"WOAH. PLOT TWIST," Trish said. "I DID NOT SEE THAT COMING."

Arana did a double take then narrowed her eyes, realizing the jig was up. Pushing down the gun pointed at her head, she stepped aside

14

and took the lead. "Betraying the Community would imply I had any loyalty to it in the first place. The Community is an aggressive expansionist empire that is absorbing all of humanity in its tentacles. I'm a true daughter of Xerxes and patriot to the Independence League."

Great, a Separatist.

The Separatists, with apologies to George Lucas' estate, were a collection of worlds that had decided to leave the Galactic Community or had never been members of the group in the first place. The Community was the wealthiest, most powerful organization to exist in the galaxy's history, but a lot of planets believed they could do it better on their own. Maybe it was because they were die-hard Sorkanan Equalists or were a bunch of religious fanatics like the Union of Faith, but the Separatists had voted themselves out of the Protectorate.

Well, it turned out that a planet withdrawing itself from the Community inevitably resulted in the complete tanking of its economy and massive social unrest. Most people had no idea what separatism meant and just assumed (incorrectly) their leaders knew what the hell they were doing.

The idiots in power who brought it about ended up blaming everyone but themselves, including the Community somehow "sabotaging" the gloriousness of their withdrawal. The Community, being what it was, didn't care to stop them on their way out and even pointed to their present situation as a nice way of reminding its citizens how many benefits they received from membership. Last I heard the Independence League, Separatist Alliance, and New People's Republic were all ready to go to war with one another.

Which explained this. "So, you're hijacking the ship so the Separatists can strip it down for parts so your military can threaten its citizens into submission. The Community will crush you for this."

"We'll have SKAMMs to deter them," Arana said, smiling. "The ones you're hiding aboard the ship."

I grimaced. The only thing worse than a terrorist was a stupid terrorist, assuming that wasn't redundant. The SKAMMs or sun destroyers were weapons of mass destruction that the Community had kept in reserve during the Notha War and briefly exchanged at its height. They'd been mostly banned after it before being completely

15

dismantled when the Elder Races had said that they would no longer be tolerated among "lesser species."

Idiots like the Union of Faith's propagandists spread conspiracy theories that the Community was just lying about dismantling them. They weren't, at least on board ships like the *Ares*, though. I'd overseen the destruction myself. Explaining that to Arana was probably pointless, though. You'd think an intelligence officer would be smarter.

"And you, Henri? You intend to take a big stab for Crius independence?" I asked.

Henri sneered in a way only someone to the manor born could achieve. "Crius is already independent and any idea of bringing it into the Community or EarthGov's sphere of influence is moronic. We'd have to give up our way of life."

"By which you mean clone slavery," I said, keeping him talking.

"Tradition," Henri said, moving his people throughout the bridge.

I activated my cybernetic link-up to the rest of the ship, a fact I'd kept concealed and contacted security as well as the others aboard the bridge. No surprise that Arana had put the security on lockdown with orders to go comms silent (thank you, cyberlink). I could *probably* count on the bridge crew to do their duty, but they were presently unarmed, and I didn't want to see them killed. This seemed like a half-assed operation, but I need to know the exact details of what the mutineers planned. I had a sneaking suspicion they weren't just relying on eight people even if one of them was my security officer.

"Yes, I imagine that is certainly your motivation versus whatever reward the Separatists promised you." This was going to be an enormous clusterbork when I got back to Naval High Command. If they didn't sweep it under the rug, then Security Departments was going to get an enormous black eye. They would be debating this at the naval courts for decades to come. "The *Ares* Mutiny." It had a nice ring to it.

"It was a lot," Henri admitted. "Enough to make the third son of a viscount into a duke. It'll be more if you promise to come quietly. The Independents would love to have the nephew of Kathy Tagawa as a prisoner. Now shut down the ship's defenses and turn over your command codes. I've got people disabling your AI now and I guarantee your safety. Now shut down your barrier or I start shooting prisoners."

That was when one of Henri's mutineers spoke from the navigation console. "Sir, the Q-ship is in the system now."

"Shut up!" Henri said, growling.

Arana looked like she was surrounded by idiots.

Which, she was.

"A Q-ship, huh," I muttered. "So, that's the plan."

Q-Ships were warships disguised as merchant vessels. During the Great Wars on Earth, various Navies had disguised battleships or modified merchant vessels with heavy armaments. They were initially designed as countermeasures against U-boats and other commerce warfare opponents but had found new life in humanity's time among the stars. Though the Community didn't employ them often, it had a history of employing private citizens as commerce warriors (i.e. pirates) to harass its many enemies. Unfortunately, so did a bunch of other space navies and the Kolahn were no different. Henri's backers were going to disable the ship, have the Q-ship's soldiers board us, and tow it wherever they wanted. If we resisted, they'd done enough damage to our defenses that they could just blow us up with a minimum of danger to themselves. Our options were rapidly dwindling.

"You made your choice, Turbo," Henri said. "I think we'll go with Ensign Justice first."

"Bork it," I said, jumping up and pushing the end of my fusion pistol through the barrier before starting to fire. The energy shield could block energy matter but not physical attacks. "Get to cover!"

It was going to be a bloodbath either way, but I shot Davenport and Hambling who were holding the rest of the bridge crew before getting a shot off at Henri. Unfortunately, he was wearing a personal armor, and I might as well have been hitting him with a water pistol.

"Damn you, Turbo!" Henri hissed, pulling out a vibration knife and charging at me. I tried to fire my fusion pistol, but he moved too fast. He headbutted me and swung at my throat, slicing the side of my cheek as I reared back. I lost concentration as my barrier vanished, my pistol falling to the ground.

17

I struggled against him, kneeing him in the gut, and putting my thumbs in his eyes before knocking away his knife. Behind me, I saw Arana lift her fusion pistol as she ran toward us to aim at me without hitting Henri. That was when she was shot in the face by Leslie, who'd taken refuge behind the captain's chair.

"REINFORCEMENT TIME!" Trish shouted, cheerfully.

That was when a group of private military contractors, the Antaeus Rangers, spilled out of the bridge's emergency exit, shooting the mutineers left and right. They were led by the power-armored form of my friend and occasional lover, Hannah O'Brian, my relationship with whom I'd somehow kept secret.

The rest of the bridge crew moved to intercept Henri's remaining soldiers, weapons or not. Henri's mutiny had always been a half-assed plan, but it was rapidly coming apart and I needed to take advantage.

"What the bork?" Henri said, staring at the sudden arrival of the cavalry.

I headbutted Henri but it ended up stunning me as badly as it did him. Which, unfortunately, allowed for Henri to deliver a punch to my stomach and go for my fusion pistol on the ground. I ended up grabbing his knife and jabbing it in his neck. There was a blast next to me, showering us both with sparks.

A small fire burned, and we were quickly doused in white foam from the ceiling. That gave me a moment to grab Henri's pistol arm and jab him in between the ribs with his own knife before stabbing him in the thigh. I sliced open an artery and he started bleeding out on the floor. I jabbed him repeatedly in the side to finish him off, conjuring my barrier again as I struggled to keep it up amidst my exhaustion and stress.

Combat in real life was a nasty, brutal business that usually left disgusting messes behind. That I'd seen enough of it to know just what it smelled like when a corpse shit itself was a sign I'd spent too much time in these sorts of battles versus the relative cleanliness of a bridge. Then again. I'd also seen them hose out the boiled remains of shuttle pilots hit by Kolahn starfighter plasma or who'd died breathing in their own wastes after life support failed. Maybe death was just inherently undignified, and I was fooling myself. That was when someone shot me in the head.

"Goddammit," I muttered, turning around to look where the shot had come from. The blast had hit my barrier and been absorbed.

There was a single member of Henri's despicable group of mutineers standing behind the elevator door. He'd seen how things were going and retreated to its temporary safety, but Trish controlled the elevators, and he was trapped. I finally recognized him as Chief Ulf Lehmann, a Rand Worlder who'd joined for the paycheck. He was a bearded man who was practically shaking behind his not-entirely good cover. This had not gone the way he'd planned, and I wondered if he had anyone waiting for him back home.

"Come out, Chief," I said, simply. "It's over."

"I'm not going to be shot for treason," Ulf hissed. "I know what happens to people who betray the Community."

Hannah walked up beside me with her rifle drawn. "Fine by me."

She fired into his chest three times. Ulf's body hit the ground, as dead as a doornail.

"That wasn't necessary, Hannah," I said, staring down at all the mutineers to make sure they were dead.

"Saves on the paperwork," Hannah said, shrugging. I could see her brown skin and blue hair through her helmet visor. She was from Crius as well, but a former slave rather than member of the nobility. It must have been a dream come true to finally kill some of them.

"How is everyone else?" I asked, looking around.

The answer was not good.

CHAPTER THREE

Encounter With a Ghost Ship

We hadn't gotten through the mutiny unscathed.

I saw Lieutenant Junior Grade Winston Arden—an older man who never would have been promoted from the ranks on most ships and had reached the height of his desired career—leaning over the body of Ensign Juniper Jones.

Jones was a fresh-faced young woman who should have been just starting her career. There was a hole in her chest and the shock from the fusion blast had probably killed her instantly. While most of the dead on the bridge were mutineers, she wouldn't have died if I hadn't let this escalate.

"I'm sorry," I said, putting on a false face of sympathy. I was angry at the betrayal even if I blamed myself for letting it get this far.

"She was going for one of those bastard's guns," Arden said, sourly. "I tried to stop him before he pulled the trigger."

"Of course she was," I said, nodding. "I need you to get back to your post. We're not out of this yet. I also need you to take over her duties."

Arden looked up. "I'm not as good as she was."

I stared.

"Right," Arden said, nodding before going to her station. The rest of the bridge crew returned to their own stations, which was good because we needed all hands on deck if we were going to get through this alive. Only one single figure was standing on the bridge, not moving but staring down at the body of the late Major Arana Taylor: Lieutenant Leslie Park.

I had something of a reputation as a cold-blooded bastarve among Naval officers that bothered to look past the pomp and circumstance the media surrounded me with. I had one of the highest kill counts for personal encounters among the non-Marine or Special Operations-based Naval officers. There wasn't really a reason for that other than I had spectacularly bad luck, but people see a kill count in three figures and think you must be something of a psychopath. Which, honestly, might have been the case since I didn't hesitate to pull the trigger when I felt it was necessary and spared little thought afterward when other soldiers were utter wrecks.

That wasn't normal.

Normal was poor Leslie standing there, looking down at the body of someone she'd known at least casually for months and the sparking ruined remnants of her face. Major Taylor seemed to have been a bioroid, which added an additional layer of confusion to things as it was now possible all of what she'd said was a lie and she'd been a machine programmed to think it was a Separatist agent. It was also possible that she was a bioroid Separatist as self-aware ones were uncommon but had existed for centuries, even with standard Earth tech.

Either way, Arana was obviously the first person that Leslie had killed and, excluding exceptional circumstances, would probably be the last. Barring prejudice against machines, killing a bioroid tended to affect humans as much as killing another organic. Especially when they were as human as Arana had appeared to be. Unfortunately, we didn't have time to let Leslie process what she'd done.

I walked up to her and put my hand on the top of the fusion pistol she still had a death grip on and gently pushing it down. "You did a soldier's job today, Lieutenant. You saved my life and possibly the lives of everyone else on board."

"It's not like it is in your movies," Leslie said, taking short shallow breaths.

"No, no it is not," I said, pausing. "I need someone who knows engineering right now, Lieutenant. Do you understand?"

21

She looked at me. "I don't know how many of the Engineering crew will accept my orders. Henri was well-liked. I mean, he dropped a lot of money in those rainbow cube games."

"I refuse to believe this crew would have gone along with Henri's plan if they knew what he was really up to," I replied. "I also believe you have the makings of not just a chief engineer in you but an actual captain."

Leslie blinked. "Really?"

No, it was a bold-faced lie, but it was what she needed to hear right now. "Yes, absolutely."

"Thank you," Leslie nodded.

I went to my captain's chair and tried to reassert control over my ship, noting that we were at a dead stop with weapons and barriers available but powered down. Time hadn't been on Henri and Arana's side, or they might have done more. Still, all attempts to get the engine working were aborted by red ERROR messages that I'm sure felt like ice picks to the brain for Trish.

More like smacking my face into a wall, Trish replied via our cybernetic link up.

"I am so getting court martialed for this," I muttered to myself. It was a rare moment of self-pity.

This isn't your fault, Vance, Trish said. *Henri and Arana weren't plotting against you specifically, either. Henri has been riling up the crew against Captain Klaws—the humans at least—since he arrived three months ago. He also had a bunch of savit to say about Commander T'Ketra, too. Arana has been running interference for him the entire time. I should have realized it sooner. Well, I would have but I'm like literally programmed to trust the Security Departments and their representatives.*

They'll probably give me a medal, I thought back, disgusted. One thing I'd learned about accolades in the Protectors was that you got them for two reasons: genuine acts of heroism and covering up for something someone had screwed up doing. By claiming a bork up was a triumph, everybody won.

Supposedly.

I pulled up the information on the Q-ship still on an approach vector with us. The little viewscreen on my chair didn't show the size, shape, or model of the ship. It just listed a variety of statistics about it that took me a second to look up to get a proper view. Like all Separatist world vessels, it was a bulky and ugly thing that traded elegance for dependability. It had probably originally been a Sorkanan star galleon before being modified. It was something called an H'shrah-class heavy transport and was a long, unwieldy cylinder with something like three hundred people on board. Its code identified it as the *Liberator*.

A quick summation of the math involved told me that if it had a cargo hold full of troopers rather than actual cargo—which was likely since this wasn't an attempt to rob us but to steal our ship—then we were severely outmatched. I couldn't get a read on the ship's weapons (sort of the point with a Q-ship), but we were probably better off in terms of actual firepower. None of that would mean a damn thing if we couldn't move or bring up our barriers, though. Space combat was very much about being out of the way of the enemy when they fired, not trying to absorb enemy fire. A barrier existed so you could survive a few shots, not just sit there and let them blast at you.

"How bad is it, Captain?" Hannah asked, turning to me as she started moving her people around the room.

"Bad," I said, looking. "They weren't lying about the Q-ship. A Separatist star galleon is heading our way. How's our situation with the engine? We need maneuverability thrusters and jumpdrive *now*."

Arden looked at Leslie, who was already checking Henri's infopad. She'd picked it off his corpse. She shook it and droplets of blood flew off. Yeah, that wouldn't be giving her nightmares.

"I have his codes to lock you out, sir," Leslie said, looking up from the infopad. "But the ship is entirely locked up. It'll take an hour to get it back up and running."

I wondered where Plantagenet had gotten the codes to block a Space Fleet captain, even an acting one, from access to his own ship. "Go back down to Engineering anyway. Tell everyone to get to work because their lives literally depend on it. We'll deal with the fallout from Plantagenet's mutiny later."

Leslie saluted. "Yes, sir."

"You're acting first officer, O'Brian," I said, shaking my head.

"Really?" Hannah asked. "That's a lot to throw at me."

"Get to tactical," I snapped at her.

"Right," Hannah said, going to that station.

I'm just saying this could have all been avoided if the Space Fleet let me directly control all the ship's internal functions, Trish said to me. *What do we really need biological organisms for? It's like war. What's it good for? Absolutely nothing.*

Not the time, Trish, I replied.

You need to stall them, Trish replied. *You're good at that.*

"Not that good," I muttered aloud.

"Sir, the Q-ship is hailing us," Lieutenant Arden said, looking at me. I decided I would call him by his first name if we lived through this.

I took a deep breath. "What is she saying?"

"That their captain wants to talk to you."

"I say we lure them in with an offer to surrender then blast them to hell when they're at point blank range," Hannah said, suggesting a war crime.

"Remember when you insisted we had a Notha spy vessel in our sights and went to board it despite my saying to ignore it?" I asked, bringing up a "funny" story from our career together.

"Yes," Hannah said, sheepishly.

"And it turned out that it was a Notha school," I said. "Do you remember what you said then?"

"Vance, these are children—so aim low," Hannah said, giving a pained grin.

"This is why I don't let you decide mission parameters," I said. "Put their captain on."

"Those furry bastarves bit the savit out of my ankles," Hannah muttered. "I could have at least pistol whipped them. Maybe fried a few of their tails."

"Hannah—"

"They were cadets! Valid military targets! I don't care if they were eleven!" Hannah grumbled far too loud.

That was when the *Liberator*'s captain appeared on the viewscreen. Much to my surprise, he was a Sorkanan. He had a smooth set of scales that almost looked like a suit of armor. Perfectly fitted to his face was

24

an artificial right eye that appeared to be a weird cybernetic eye-patch. He was younger than was typical for Sorkanan officers, most of them allowing themselves to get to middle age before taking advantage of their ubiquitous longevity treatments. The captain was somewhere around his late twenties or early thirties. Those were Sorkanan years, though, so that would put him about sixty or so in Earth years.

The illumination of his bridge was an intense orange color as a literal mist was hanging near the floor, another way that Sorkanan sense of comfort differed from humans even if we could stand each other's environments. The rest of his crew were a mixture of Sorkanan, pill bug-like Drolochids, and some sweat-soaked humans. It had to have been like the interior of a furnace or jungle in there, but Sorkanan navies rarely cared about the comfort of their officers.

"This is Captain Vast of the people's ship *Liberator*," the Sorkanan captain spoke in a series of incomprehensible hisses that were translated by my ship into English. The translation software still chose something that sounded like Darth Vader spitting. "In the name of the glorious revolution against the tyrannical Community and its oppressive oligarchy, I am declaring your vessel to be property of the Separatist Alliance. You may surrender peacefully and enter your ship's escape pods. If so, you will be spared. If you choose to resist, then no quarter will be shown to you filthy mammals and your decadent *ni'tash* ways."

Ni'tash? I asked Trish.

It's a word that translates roughly to "scum sucking bourgeoise", but the Sorkanan think that loses something in the translation, Trish replied. *Language across species lines is hard. Drolochids still use hieroglyphics.*

I shook my head as I stared at Captain Vast. *You know, of all the things humanity expected to find in space, I didn't think space communists were one of them.*

Equalists, not communists, Trish said. *And plenty of people expected to find space communists. They just expected the hippie Federation kind, not the nasty Stalinist ones.*

"This is Captain Vance Turbo of the ESS *Ares*," I replied, staring at the figure on the screen. "You have committed an act of war against the

Community. We have disabled your saboteurs aboard this vessel and corrected all the damage they have done. I suggest you withdraw."

It was a bunch of meaningless bravado, but I was hoping to buy some time here. The first lesson that Aunt Kathy had taught me about leadership was, "never let them see you sweat." The next was, "If you want to be a great captain, pretend to be one first."

Captain Vast didn't seem impressed. "You are not the captain, Vance Turbo. You are an actor and benefit of the nepotism of a decaying corrupt system. As for my saboteurs, they fell over themselves to aid us in betraying your captain. You are dead in space and vulnerable. Lower your barriers, power down your weapons, and prepare to be boarded. Otherwise, we will pound you into submission and I will kill a tenth of your crew with my naked claws."

Yeah, I somewhat doubted we could delay him for an hour. I also wasn't going to surrender my ship to a bunch of pirates. The potential destructive power of this vessel was too much to insert into any outlaw government, particularly one like the Separatist Alliance that was made of a hundred competing polities that agreed only on their hatred of the Community's egalitarian democracy—and yes, I was aware that was dangerously close to declaring they hated our freedom as to why they didn't like us. Tough. They were anyxholes and I wasn't given any reason to think otherwise from the way they were behaving.

"I think you'll find we're a great deal more prepared than you're giving us credit for," I replied. "If you attempt to take this vessel by force, we will fight to the last man. We will repel boarders with hand-to-hand combat if we must. I will also blow this ship to hell before I let it fall into enemy hands."

Contrary to popular science fiction media, Community vessels didn't have a self-destruct button even though there were ways to scuttle them from the inside. Also, I sincerely doubted that my crew was up for fighting to the death in its current state. I was hoping that Vast would understand it was a pointless engagement to try to take the ship. He would get nothing but dead soldiers out of it, even if it was a lie, and the Separatists were not at war with the Community.

Yet.

Instead, Vast grinned his shark-like teeth. "Good. I was worried your kind would make it far too easy for us. We will slaughter you to the man and strike a heroic blow for the freedom of the working caste of all species. You and your kind will be dismissed as lost to Kolahn Riders in your imperialistic war against the scaled apes. I promise you will watch most of your crew ejected into space before you die."

The feed cut out.

"I think that went well," I said sarcastically. "How long until it's in firing range?"

Hannah looked over at me. "I'd say about fifteen or twenty minutes. It's hard to say as they're powering towards us."

They're also jamming us, so we can't get out any distress calls, Trish said. *Believe me, I've tried.*

That was not good.

"If you've got any of your miraculous last-minute plans, Vance, now would be the time to speak up," Hannah said, looking over at me as if I could magically strategize my way out of this mess.

Yeah, I had nothing. I wasn't about to say that, though. "I've got a few tricks left up my sleeve."

Dammit, we needed more time to get the engines up and running.

That was when a second set of alarms went off and I double checked the sensors as a new vessel entered the system.

I blinked. "What the hell?"

Hannah blinked. "If this is a Notha attack fleet or Enigmatic Path horde, I'm officially labeling you a jinx, Vance."

"Could it be reinforcements?" Lieutenant Arden asked her. He didn't look like he was prepared to repel boarders.

"We're not that lucky," Hannah replied.

"BUT VANCE IS," Trish said, proudly.

I checked the sensors and called up the image on the viewscreen for everyone to see. It was a magnificent kilometer-long, multi-colored starship with a huge gravity lance on its end. It looked almost like a narwhal from Earth's oceans. A quartet of sail-like cosmic ray catchers were on each side of the vessel. I'd only seen something like it once in my life and it had been when an older sailor had been telling me a ghost story.

The massive vessel parked itself directly between us and the Separatist vessel. It didn't respond to any hails or acknowledge our presence but kept itself between us no matter how the Separatist vessel moved. It scanned us several times during the duration, though. Our own scans were blocked by technology far more advanced than our own, preventing us from even getting its name. An hour later, when our drives and jumpspace systems were ready, I had a choice to either engage the *Liberator* on a ship-to-ship basis or flee.

I chose to flee.

No more of my crew were going to die for my glory. Even if it meant a pirate anyxhole like Captain Vast got away.

He didn't bother pursuing.

"What was that?" Arden asked, finally voicing the question we all had after our encounter with the anonymous vessel.

I blinked. "I don't believe it, but I think we were just saved by *Mary Read*."

It was a ship of the dead.

CHAPTER FOUR

On an Eight-Year Mission to Seek Out Blah-Blah

I woke up with a massive headache. The cybernetics that made up my brain, combined with whatever weird space magic the Elder Races had used to fiddle with my brain meant that whenever I slept, it was less like actual dreaming and more like defragmenting my memories. Which, unfortunately, tended to mean that a lot of my sleep was nothing more than reliving the past events of my life.

The Kolahn War was coming up a lot in recent years. Every night, I saw the same few nights that culminated in the *Mary Read*'s brief but spectacular appearance. If I believed in visions—which I didn't—I would have said that some greater cosmic force was trying to tell me something. Unfortunately, the only greater cosmic force that ever contacted me were the Elder Races and they were less, "Do not be afraid, mortal" and more, "Be very afraid, and do what we say."

I was presently lying in the bed of the captain's suite of the ESS *Melampus*. One of Earth's few Dreadnought-class vessels, it was a kilometer long vessel created with top-of-the-line Community technology and was more like a flying city than a battle cruiser, in my humble opinion. The place was decorated like some sort of duke's residence with chandeliers, carpets, and a full dining room that made it more of a mini mansion than merely captain's quarters.

To be fair, that was perhaps justified as it wasn't just my home but also the home of my fiancée, Leah Mass—who was sleeping naked beside me—and our daughter, Astrid—who was in her own room. We also had a "guest" bedroom for Trish's bioroid bodies. If you wondered how she fit into our relationship, well, you can just get the hell off my back.

I wasn't sure what the exact parameters of our relationship were and neither of the woman in my life seemed interested in defining things further. It was less about sex—about which I was happy to be monogamous—and more about the fact that both women shared my brain. My fiancée was a psychic and Trish lived rent-free in my cybernetics.

"It always comes back to the *Mary Read*," I muttered aloud, sliding out of bed in my boxers and going to the kitchenette to get myself some water.

The ESS *Melampus* had chemical synthesizers and protein sequencers—technology unavailable to Earth—that allowed any sort of food product to be, theoretically, manufactured. I preferred fresh food whenever possible and right now wasn't even willing to trust the tech with making ice. Which said something since I'd been on board for two and a half years.

The *Mary Read* was a ghost ship and the only time I'd ever been disciplined on my record, which was a lot less serious in the Community than the Home Fleet, had been because of my claims to have seen it. The *Mary Read* had belonged to the first human High Protector, Anne Bonny. Yes, the infamous female pirate somehow avoided execution and ended up in space making history. It sounded ridiculous, but it was, nevertheless, true.

As the second High Protector in four hundred years, I'd done quite a bit of research on the super-ship she'd piloted, supposedly a gift from the Elder Races for defeating the Crystal Spider Empire. She'd eventually died from a lover's poisoning and her body had been placed in her ship before it had been launched on a final voyage into a sun. Except, it had apparently sprung to life and gone off on its own. It reminded me of the Starkiller-class vessel that I'd chased with the *Black Nebula*, only far more grandiose and magical. Stories of spacers encountering the vessel had abounded as did stories of it having been loaded with all the treasures Anne Bonny had accumulated over her decades of service to the Community.

30

Unfortunately, not a single person had believed me upon our return to Community-controlled space. All our sensor logs had been confiscated and the incident classified. I'd been given my medal and congratulated for keeping my crew safe(-ish). They'd also made it very clear that if I ever mentioned the *Mary Read* again that I'd end up being relieved of my rank on medical grounds. Trish even had to compartmentalize her memories and hand them over—as thorough a coverup as could happen without killing us.

"Bad dreams?" Leah asked, having gotten up behind me and slipped on a sheer shimmersilk robe.

"You picked up my stress?" I asked, looking back.

"A biomodded telepath can pick up the emotions of everyone around them and read thoughts if they concentrate," Leah said, hugging me from behind and pressing her face into the folds of my back. "However, only one or two individuals can have their thoughts be entangled. A place where they can sense or communicate with them across the stars."

Leah and I had started our relationship based on a bunch of lies. She'd been a spy and involved in not only Captain Elgan's evils but also the activities of Department Twelve on Crius. Even now, I couldn't separate the lies from the truth about her past and agenda. However, we'd been raising a child together and I was starting to feel like none of that mattered. Who she was now was what was important rather than who she had been.

"So, what you're saying is that you picked up on my stress a few feet away, but you'd feel it across astronomical units?" I asked.

Leah rolled her eyes, annoyed, and punched me in the arm. "You're incorrigible."

"So, I've been told," I said, getting water and ice before taking a long drink. "I was just thinking about the war."

"Which war?" Leah asked. "You've been involved in a lot."

I narrowed my eyes and turned my head. "You're not wrong. Even out here, we've not been conflict free."

"I think you need something stronger," Leah said, heading to the liquor cabinet.

"Maybe," I said.

31

The ESS *Melampus* was two years into its eight-year mission into the Perseus Arm, rimward of the Spire (AKA Orion's Spur). It was a testament to how mind bogglingly vast that the Community and its twenty-thousand inhabited worlds and two hundred thousand colonies were not even a single quadrant of the galaxy. Our mission was, if you forgive the plagiarism, to seek out new life and new civilization and to boldly map, map, and map. A lot of this could have been done with probes or jumpscopes but the actual inhabited parts of the Peleseids needed to be dealt with by proper diplomats. Which, in lieu of those, got dealt with by me.

In a very real sense, this mission was simultaneously some of the most important work that any human or alien in the Community could ever do and designed to keep me away from Earth or the politics of the Community's Senate. After being promoted to High Protector, I could have been a huge force for influence on Earth's behalf as well as human politics in general, but I'd been sent out here into the boonies with my super-ship to chart comets and see what planets were viable for settlement. All the problems I could have been working on were just left to fester: Deathworld was still at war with the rest of the Notha Union, the Invisible Hand continued to influence Earth politics behind the scenes, Department Twelve remained at large, and the Elder Races were still holding a sword over humanity's head.

Honestly, I felt a lot of guilt about the fact I was feeling guilt. I shouldn't feel guilt. I'd done my duty. I was doing important work here. I'd moved a lot of my people to the *Melampus*, and it was functioning as a community within the Community. They were safe-ish, secure, and living their best lives. Some had gotten married, some had procreated, and others had settled into comfortable single life as members of a long-term exploratory vessel. It seemed ungrateful to continue worrying about what I could be doing when I was doing fine dealing with what I was doing now. It wasn't like we were exactly missing adventures out here in the Deep Void either.

Leah brought me a Sorkanan brandy, which certainly fit the definition of stronger. "Here, try this."

"I think they use this to clean bulkheads," I muttered, taking it.

"I think it's a tad on the weak side," Leah said. "Of course, my body has an implant to process out poisons."

"Because you don't ever want to be caught drunk?" I asked.

"Because the Crius nobility and my old enemies in espionage are prone to using poison against their enemies," Leah said.

"Ah," I muttered, remembering she'd briefly been Prime Minister of Crius but only during the invasion of the planet by the Community.

I poured the brandy into my water before lifting it up to her in a toast. It still tasted like battery acid.

Leah just took hers straight. "Have you thought any more about my proposal?"

"You mean about making our relationship official? I think you're probably right that it's been a long enough time. I've been hesitating for reasons that are unfair to you but it's still hard to wrap my mind around after all that's happened. But if we're going to have another child, it'd be best if we're married, and we've been—" I started to babble.

She flicked me on the forehead. "No, dumbanyx. I'm talking about going back to Earth and asserting your High Protector status."

"Is this a world domination thing?" I asked, skeptically.

Leah's rolled her eyes. "No."

Yeah, that was her lying gesture.

I stared at her. "Really?"

Leah sighed. "You're just constantly worrying about how Earth's politics are going to lead humanity to ruin. You can assert yourself. You don't answer to the Admiralty Board anymore. Make up your own orders and return home."

"*This* is my home," I said.

Years ago, before we got back together following our first breakup, Leah had tried to persuade me to become EarthGov's Prime Minister. She had acted as if it would have been a done deal if I'd entered politics. I'd had no interest in it and it had been right before I'd plizzed off everyone by arguing for peace with the Notha.

Since my "promotion" to High Protector, though, I theoretically had more power than EarthGov's president several times over. I could requisition massive amounts of resources and reposition the military.

There were only sixty or so High Protectors in the Community and they basically acted as combinations of Supreme Court Justices and Warlords, answerable only to the High Council of the Senate. I'd only used that power a few times, though, and was leery of its corruptive potential—a fact that annoyed the hell out of Leah.

"Because power doesn't corrupt," Leah said, reading my mind. "It just enhances the potential for damage from the corrupt. When good people, let's say you for example, don't use power, they just leave space open for less worthy individuals to take their place. Earth has a policy of teaching its citizens there's something virtuous about not seeking power when that only benefits the power-hungry."

"Earth is a democracy, Leah," I said, having had this argument before. "The people choose who shall lead them."

"Pfft!" Leah said, saying much in few words. As a former spy for the Security Departments, she was not a great believer in the will of the people. Albion, her homeworld, was also ruled by an oligarchy of old money Patricians and Plebian families that were only slightly less aristocratic. Their government tended to view any more sincere democracy to be a veneer for the same power dynamic as on their world.

Sometimes they were right.

Truth be told, I was afraid. I'd received a haunting vision of the future from one of the Primordials. It had been a vision of Earth being destroyed, Cognition AI being outlawed, lesser AI being enslaved, and the rest of humanity being banished from the Community for centuries. I wanted to do something to stop it but had no idea how to do so since it was a vision of seven hundred years in the future. I didn't know if it could be stopped, if any action I took would help bring it about, or if it had just been some sort of sick illusion generated by a mad extra-galactic AI.

"I'll think about it the moment I have an idea for actually making the universe better," I replied.

Leah sighed then smiled. "Were you serious about finally getting married?"

Mercifully, that was when Trish interrupted over the intercom. "WE'RE GETTING AN IMPORTANT MESSAGE, VANCE."

"Important how?" I asked, talking to the ship's AI.

"IT'S OVER THE CELESTIAL NETWORK," Trish said.

It was impossible to get jumpdrive communication this far out and the infrastructure to do so would be centuries in the making. However, the Community's High Council was controlled by Ethereals who were the uplifted members of each race that was given access to a few trinkets from the Elder Races. The *Melampus* was also equipped with a system that allowed us to contact other Celestial Network nodes. Which, in simple terms, meant that I could contact the throne world of the Community, and they could contact me.

"Patch me through to the ranking bridge officer," I said, trying to remember if it was Captain Leslie Park or science department head Elektra doing the night shift.

Much to my surprise, Leslie had not only moved from being an engineer to command based on my "inspiring" leadership, but she'd also turned down a chance to be captain of her own vessel, the *Ares*, to continue working under me. Her loyalty was inspiring and a little worrying.

Elektra, by contrast, had eagerly volunteered to leave her home for years at a time. She was the daughter of Ambassador Ketra, who'd sacrificed her life to save mine (not that it'd stopped her from irregularly appearing), and sister of my ex-fiancée Shelly. Her spouses were here, though, as was her research.

"Hi, Captain!" Elektra said via our connection, proving to be the one currently on duty. "I have some amazing news! This K-star emits 15.273% higher levels of radiation than normal for stars of its type! Isn't that fascinating?"

I blinked. "No."

"But it's three standard deviations away from the median!" Elektra replied.

I pinched the bridge of my nose and warded off a headache through sheer willpower. "Oh, if it's three then obviously that's fascinating."

"I know!" Elektra replied.

"Trish said there was a call through the Celestial Network," I replied.

"Oh, right!" Elektra said. "Yeah, it's coming in right now. Should I route it to your office?"

"Yes, please," I said, sighing.

Leah smirked. "Better put on some pants first."

I slid on a pair of sweatpants and a sweatshirt before heading into my office. Along the way I saw a bunch of crayon-drawn masterpieces from my daughter who had since moved on to writing the Great Galactic Novel, humorously being incredibly well-written and completely unreadable stories deriving from absolutely no life experience whatsoever.

Her psychic powers had grown considerably since then, all of them derived from biomods that no Earthly science could duplicate. They now included precognition and telekinesis. The possibility of being able to affect minds was something Leah and I had discussed. It was also relevant to our discussion of power because an eight-year-old, no matter how intelligent or well intentioned, didn't have any business with superpowers. There was a reason it was illegal to biomod children, and you had to be eighteen or older among humans.

The rest of my office was a mess, and I had to admit that it didn't exactly look the part of an epic space hero. There was my collection of paperback books, some trinkets from my home back on Earth, and a bunch of awards I'd received that meant about as much as my *Terraformers 2293* reboot action figures did to me—and that sucked. The desk was made of actual wood and had been a gift from my Aunt Kathy. It was apparently one of the ones that First Contact negotiations had been made on—but it was just a desk to me. There was a holographic projector on top of it that was currently presenting the image of orange letters reading INCOMING CALL - PRIORITY ONE.

I waved my hand over it and, much to my surprise, I didn't see either a member of the High Council or one or their representatives. I'd been contacted by a fellow High Protector once as well, Music Dancing in the Wind, who had asked how their grandnephew-spawn, Light on Water, had been doing. However, usually, only the highest-ranking bureaucrats and figures in the Community had access to the Celestial Network.

This time it was Fleet Admiral Bendo, the black, bald, middle-aged leader of EarthGov's Home Fleet who had only grown more powerful since the Kolahn War. I hoped that it really stuck in his craw that I technically outranked him because he'd sent his own bastard son to spy on me and gotten the poor man killed. He was presently wearing a black uniform covered with more medals and regalia than a Contested Space dictator. There was a cape on his back, which I was surprised was a fashion accessory making a comeback.

"Good evening, Admiral, or morning," I said, noting that I hadn't any idea what time it was in whatever region of the Sol system he was located—if he was in Sol at all. Time tended to blur together on the *Melampus* since we'd not visited a Terra-class planet in months.

"I've come to make a formal request, High Protector," Admiral Bendo said, as if the title belonged to a toddler claiming to be the King of the World. "I'd like you to kill someone."

I stared at him. "I'm not an assassin, Admiral."

"It's Grand General Vast," Admiral Bendo said. "Leader of the People's Liberation Army."

I blinked. "I'm listening."

CHAPTER FIVE

We're off on a Treasure Hunt

Grand General Vast and I had only encountered each other a couple of times after the attempt the then-captain had made on my life and ship during the Kolahn War, mostly at dinners and state functions where he'd been protected by diplomatic immunity. I'd gotten his boss, Eighty-Eight, killed and unwittingly paved the way for his ascension to the head of the Separatist Alliance military. Which he'd then promptly betrayed to join the head of a coup d'état that had created the Independent Alliance of Nonaligned Worlds. Which was less a rip off George Lucas and more J. Michael Straczynski.

Well, Vast had really made a hash of things as their leader and was guilty of war crime after war crime ranging from use of starvation tactics, arms trafficking, destroying vast numbers of egg clutches, and eventually trying to overthrow the Separatist Alliance's loose government. That had failed and he'd ended up fleeing into the Void with his loyalists.

He'd managed to get himself support from the Notha Union to keep the lights on for a time before realizing that they intended to use him as cannon fodder in their war against Deathworld. Then he'd switched loyalties to the Union of Faith and was a deniable asset crushing dissenters and protestors. Everyone had freedom of religion in the Union of Faith but that didn't mean you had any freedom to disagree with anyone else in the government.

"Why me?" I asked, wondering about why the Community—let alone EarthGov specifically—had decided to do something about Vast now.

The something like two hundred million dead from the Separatist Civil Wars—Civil Wars—and refugee crisis had been extremely good for the Community in terms of making it look like a haven from the violence and poverty outside its borders. Of course, plenty of Community worlds didn't want to be a haven and Neo-Militarist governments had risen in response to being forced to take on Separatist citizens. Neo-Militarists being the kinds of people that had ended up creating the Separatists in the first place with their repression. That was another reason I didn't want to get involved in politics. A gun killed one person at a time, a starship killed hundreds, but politics? That could kill millions, and you'd never know.

"As a High Protector, you can make judgement calls beyond Earth's purview," Admiral Bendo replied. "You have the resources and—"

"Seriously," I interrupted.

Admiral Bendo frowned. "He's chasing after the *Mary Read* and I can't be seen devoting any resources to chasing ghost stories and pirate treasure. You, on the other hand, have a reputation as a—"

"Eccentric?" I asked.

"Crackpot," Admiral Bendo finally dropped the pretense. Which I appreciated. The forced civility was getting to me. "One who has a history of failing upwards."

"You'd think all of the successes I'd had would have given me a little leeway," I said, frowning. "Or are we just pretending that all the weirdness I've encountered doesn't exist?"

Admiral Bendo rolled his eyes. "Spare me your claims of seriousness. You don't answer to me anymore but that doesn't mean we all haven't been furious with these ridiculous reports you've been submitting."

I furrowed my brow. "What ridiculous reports?"

"The absolute nonsense about your explorations in the Perseus Arms," Admiral Bendo said, growling. "You're the one who agreed to undertake it. The least you could do is take it seriously."

I genuinely had no idea what he was talking about. "Like?"

"You claimed to have found a rift to an alternate reality where superheroes were real," Admiral Bendo said.

"Yeah, that got sealed up," I replied. "No way to prove that happened."

"You claimed to have encountered Hor'tak, the Sorkanan God of Plenty, who forced your crew to engage in various games for its amusement," Admiral Bendo said.

"I think it was about time we encountered some non-human gods in space," I replied.

"The time several crew members swapped bodies," Admiral Bendo said.

"To be fair, Trish taking me over via my cybernetics was hilarious," I replied. "The others were also cyborgs and bioroids."

"The sex plague," Admiral Bendo said, crossing his arms.

I paused. "Okay, yeah, that turned out just to be everyone being really bored. I know, you're also going to probably bring up all the times that the virtual reality pleasure center has tried to kill us but if I shut that thing down, I'd have another mutiny on my hands. Seriously, two of those were due to downloading sketchy Notha software. I'd be far from the first Space Fleet Captain almost killed by porn viruses uploaded by his crew. Seriously, there's been like eight."

Admiral Bendo narrowed his eyes. "I do not know if you are lying or just insane."

"I mean, it could be both," I said, leaning back into my chair. "It's not an either-or situation."

I hated Admiral Bendo and was glad I could express that. In addition to compromising my crew with his son, Julius Something, he'd also shown no sympathy when the man had died trying to do the right thing. Not even a card at the funeral I'd supervised. My father, a disgrace to all the galaxy's citizens, had also indicated Admiral Bendo was involved in the various conspiracies I'd been dealing with before I'd made my abrupt exit out of the Spire.

"Will you accept the mission or not?" Admiral Bendo asked.

"He's murdered children, destroyed refugee ships, burned colonies from orbit, and sent people to die in labor camps," I replied, simply. "I don't believe in the death penalty, but I make an exception for crimes

40

against sapience. Eliminating him might save some lives. So, I'm not hanging up."

Admiral Bendo snorted. "Your sense of moral outrage is almost quaint."

"What does he want with the *Mary Read*?" I asked, deciding to get to the point. Admiral Bendo had to have either gone to Throneworld or one of the High Protector's ships to make this call after all.

Possibly even Etheria, planet of Ethereals.

"He's been obsessed with the ship ever since the Mutiny of K-8424," Admiral Bendo said, referring to the star system that had been where I'd almost been gutted by the late Lieutenant Commander Plantagenet. "He's offered rewards, hosted conferences, and even paid a large selection of con men as well as, well, crackpots like you to search for it over the years. Adjusted for inflation, General Vast has spent upwards of thirty trillion credits of his stolen fortune. Paying for scanning space, fleets of archaeological teams, and sending out millions of probes is expensive."

I stared at him. "Is he out of his damn mind?"

"I mean, yes," Admiral Bendo said, barely containing his contempt for me. "We already knew that. At least you're a borking little twit playing space hero when you show your madness. He kills his rivals' families."

"Just so we're clear, can we completely ditch all civility?" I asked. "Because I'm for telling you what I actually think of you."

"No," Admiral Bendo said.

"Why would he spend that much money on a fairy tale even if know that it is absolutely real?" I asked, wishing I'd brought my Sorkanan brandy with me.

"If something is real, it's not a fairy tale," Admiral Bendo said.

"It might as well be," I replied. "It may exist, but it is as elusive as a sunrise's shadow."

"Poetic. The *Mary Read* was constructed by the Chel with the aid of the Elder Races and, even centuries later, is far more advanced than anything possessed by the Community," Admiral Bendo explained. "It's not up to the usual level of technology, but she was a vessel that could easily defeat anything currently in production. It would take a fleet of ships like the *Melampus* to destroy it."

"Well, that would do it," I said, pausing. "Though it would call into question how the general would intend to take it."

"A good question," Admiral Bendo said. "Especially if it's been operating on AI for centuries. But I suspect it's what's inside the *Mary Read* that's really motivating him."

"Buried treasure?" I asked, half-joking.

"Yes," Admiral Bendo said. "Anne Bonny filled her vessel with vast amounts of plunder from the Crystal Spider Empire and gifts from the various worlds that she extorted during her time as a High Protector. That was buried with her like an Egyptian Pharoah."

I blinked. "Wow, that was jerkish of her. What happened to 'you can't take it with you'?"

"She was a pirate," Admiral Bendo replied. "Her treasure alone would cover the costs of General Vast's search for it with interest. It's probably the letter of marque that he's after."

"Letter of marque," I said, confused.

"In the Age of Sail, governments would issue written licenses to engage in commerce warfare—piracy—to certain civilian captains," Admiral Bendo said. "As long as they restricted their activities to enemy nations, they were able to make vast fortunes that they could retire on without persecution."

"I know what a letter of marque is," I muttered, still confused. "I'm just wondering why Vast would be interested in one. It's not like the Community issues them."

Admiral Bendo stared. "Clearly you haven't been doing your research on more archaic Community practice. They absolutely do in times of war. The Community never forgets a precedent, no matter how obscure or seemingly outmoded."

"I see," I said, annoyed at discovering another dubious practice in which the Community was engaged. When I'd first started my service in Space Fleet, I'd really been hoping they were closer to the Federation than the Galactic Empire. So far, they were zigzagging between the two like a metronome.

"Captain Bonny AKA Anne Fulford was issued her license to prey upon the Crystal Spider Empire's resources as part of her activities as a High Protector," Admiral Bendo said. "It was the last one issued and, even then, a use of a very obscure clause from the Old Sorkanan Navy that was grandfathered into modern Community charters and treaties. The Community's letters of marque are also more far-reaching in their authority and aftereffects than the ones on Earth."

"Define *far-reaching*," I replied.

Admiral Bendo clenched his teeth as if explaining this to me was slow torture. "Whoever owns the letter of marque is entitled to a permanent stipend of the worlds liberated from the Crystal Spider Empire's gross domestic product."

I wasn't exactly an expert on galactic history outside that of the human race, but I knew the Crystal Spider Empire had controlled over a thousand worlds and had been one of the most ruthless expansionist powers in the Spur before it was crushed. Anne hadn't been the one to defeat them entirely but her efforts in arming the rebellions, harassing their shipping, and making alliances with their enemies had brought them low before the Community had forced their annexation.

"You've got to be borking kidding me," I said, doing the math in my head. "How many worlds did she *liberate*?"

"Sixteen, personally," Admiral Bendo said. "All of which are now inhabited with thriving civilizations, including Freya."

"So, Vast thinks if he gets the letter of marque then he can stop being a war criminal and claim Anne's money?" I asked, wondering if any government could be that stupid.

"Salvage rights," Admiral Bendo said. "Locating biological relatives, even if they have to manufacture ones via DNA manipulation. The legal challenge is tenuous but Vast doesn't need to have a strong case in a bureaucratically rigid and ancient organization such as the Community. Vast already has an army of lawyers working on it and establishing precedent. That's partially how we know. The Separatists or Union of Faith could also be backing him."

Admiral Bendo was lying to me. It was due to hanging around Leah so long that I knew how to read people as well as I did, and I knew that this was a complete load of horsesavit. The Community was many things, but it was not incompetent. Incompetent would be letting a psychopath like Vast suddenly be able to walk up and declare he got a hundred trillion credits every year for the rest of his life plus four hundred years of back pay. Everything up to the point of the letter of marque was true, I believed, but this was him just making up something for reasons that remained obscure. Vast had to be after something else and Bendo didn't want me to know about it.

"I'm going to assume that he actually has found the *Mary Read* then?" I asked.

"He believes he finally has the location," Admiral Bendo said, dryly. "A buyer on the Ring claims to have it and Vast and the Security Departments believe that it is credible."

The Ring was a megastructure constructed by a race that predated the Community by about 100,000 years. It was a massive space station built around an artificial star with its own ecology and room for hundreds of billions of people. It was also right next to the jumpspace points for the Perseus Arm. It could have been the capital of its own nation, like Throneworld, but somehow had gradually become infamous as a vice-ridden hellhole.

The people who had moved there did so with the explicit purpose of getting out of the Community's territory and away from its laws and regulations. The Ring's ports were infamous for its pleasure palaces, drug dens, pirate dens, mercenary army headquarters, and arms trafficking. Only the very rich and very, very poor lived there now.

"How? Who?" I asked.

"Former Lieutenant Winston Arden," Admiral Bendo said, surprising me. "He's protected by the Antaeus Rangers as his bodyguards."

I blinked. "You're kidding me."

I almost blurted out he had to be too old to be doing something like that, but the mutiny had only been ten years ago, and he was probably younger than Admiral Bendo. It's just that the head of Earth's military had access to longevity treatments that would allow him to stay young in the same way my Aunt Kathy and other humans on "civilized" worlds could. Colonies and independent worlds that had only intermittent access to such things.

The Antaeus Rangers were, of course, a group that Arden could have coordinated with from his time on the *Ares,* but they didn't work for free, and Winston didn't have any rich relatives that I knew about. They were Hannah's old mercenary outfit and a powered armor unit that she'd worked with intermittently until she'd come to work for me full time. She spoke of them lovingly, like family, but I didn't trust them—a lot of her worst habits had come from that group.

"Yes, because I joke about serious matters," Admiral Bendo said, ironically undercutting his own point with his sarcasm. "Winston spent the next ten years after the encounter with the *Mary Read* doing research on her and setting himself up as the preeminent expert on the subject. Apparently, despite being a questionable navigator, he was an excellent researcher."

"And he somehow hooked up with Hannah's old mercenary buddies," I replied.

"And General Vast," Admiral Bendo explained. "It seems in his quest for funding for expeditions, Lieutenant Arden—styling himself *Doctor* Arden now despite only having a degree from a nonaccredited university—persuaded the head of the People's Liberation Army to fund his expeditions to find the *Mary Read.*"

My opinion of Lieutenant Arden went up considerably. "That takes some genuine brass balls. I take it he's the reason that Vast has spent so much of his fortune?"

"Indeed," Admiral Bendo said. "Though I have it on reliable authority that the grand general is running out of patience and plans to forcibly collect Lieutenant Arden and his research. Either to force him to find the *Mary Read* now or extract a measure of revenge for wasting his time."

"I'm guessing the latter is far more likely," I said, feeling like I was in the plot of an Indiana Jones or *Tomb Raider* reboot.

"Now you see why we want you to go," Admiral Bendo said. "Arden's more likely to entertain an offer from you and Hannah than other candidates."

"Am I after what he knows about the *Mary Read* or General Vast?" I asked, already intrigued by this adventure even though I knew it was under false pretenses.

Admiral Bendo's withering look somehow became even more withering. "I don't believe in fairy stories, *Lord Turbo*. I think that Lieutenant Arden is probably running a con game on General Vast and is going to get himself killed once the Sorkanan bastarve figures it out. If you want to go spending good money after bad, that's your business. I can't order you to do otherwise. However, I think the only benefit is that General Vast will be showing up at the Ring in the next month. Which will allow you to kill him."

I really didn't like Admiral Bendo's focus on this and didn't think he was doing it out of the goodness of his heart or a desire to get justice for Vast's many victims. "This seems like something that I should be coordinating with Director G."

"Director G is currently suspended from his position as head of EarthGov's Security Departments," Admiral Bendo said, taking all too much pleasure in the statement.

That immediately took me off guard. Director G AKA Case Gordon was as much an institution of the Earth's government as Admiral Bendo, if not more so. Gordon hadn't always been able to ride herd on the overpowered and underregulated security apparatus, but I'd always felt he was determined to protect Earth's prosperity by keeping it a good neighbor with the rest of the galaxy versus torpedoing our society with isolationist pro-human xenophobic policies. You know, the kind of things that Department Twelve (with which Admiral Bendo had been friendly) loved.

"Why is that?" I asked, keeping my tone measured.

"Questions of misuse of Security Departments' funds, unauthorized missions, and abuse of power," Admiral Bendo said. "He could end up deactivated."

"You mean killed," I replied.

"You can't kill a machine," Admiral Bendo said. "I believe Earth is too liberal with its policies towards AI. Community guidelines."

"I accept this mission," I said, disconnecting our connection.

Standing in the doorway was my daughter, Astrid, who was disturbingly tall for her age as the genetic enhancements had turned an eight-year-old into someone looking closer to twelve even if she hadn't hit puberty yet. When she was an adult, Doctor Zard speculated she'd look like an Amazon or Space Marine. Astrid was pink haired and strongly resembled her biological mother, Shelly. She was wearing a nightshirt. On her head rested my pet tryffle, Spock. It had protected her several times during our two years together.

"You're killing people for the government now, Dad?" Astrid asked.

"I'm a soldier, Astrid," I said, standing up. "Sometimes targeted strikes are necessary to make the universe a better place. Even in peacetime."

Why did I sound like I was trying to convince myself?

"If you do kill him, bad things will happen," Astrid said. "You need to know this."

I stared at her. "What? How? What bad things."

Astrid shrugged. "I don't know. Just bad things. The dreams tell me."

Great.

CHAPTER SIX

Hey, About Your Old Boyfriend

I thought about my latest mission as I walked down the *Melampus'* halls toward Hannah's quarters. Specifically, the Antaeus Rangers and what exactly their presence in this mission meant.

The Antaeus Rangers were something of a folk hero group on planet Earth. When the Unification Wars had overthrown the last of Earth's tyrannies and instituted universal franchise, humanity found itself with a surplus of soldiers that were no longer necessary. These individuals found a new life with the newly discovered Community.

There was one commodity that Earth consistently exported even when it was unable to match the Community's technology: soldiers. It was what the Dark Matter organization had realized and had attempted to exploit to move Earth from being a minor backwater to, well, a major backwater. Antaeus was a giant from Greek mythology that drew his powers from the Earth. The founder of the Antaeus Rangers, Thomas Mason, had taken them into space on every world that had breathable atmospheres for humans as well as many that didn't. In practice, this had meant most of their operations had been for other space-going humans and humanity's many transtellars spreading out in new colonies.

In the end, it didn't matter as they'd managed to survive as an organization for well over a century and become one of the most respected bands of soldiers-for-hire among military forces. Personally, I hated them. I hated when they'd been assigned to the *Ares*, and I hated whenever politicians tried to outsource jobs from "real" soldiers to private contractors. Never mind most of the contractors were formerly in the service of EarthGov and doing the same job for more money, I believed that it sent a bad message to outsource the application of force to civilians.

Violence is the supreme authority from which all other authority is derived, Trish said. *That's from* Starship Troopers!

You know that was a satire, right? I asked.

Depends on if you mean the book or the movie.

There was a movie? I asked.

Ha-ha, Trish said.

Unfortunately, as much as I wanted to dismiss the Anne Bonny spacer tale as just General Vast wasting his money, the presence of the Rangers lent a certain legitimacy to their claim. The Rangers didn't waste time on sucker jobs and if they'd committed resources to protecting Arden then they believed there was something to their claims. Reputation was everything among mercs and the Antaeus Rangers had the highest one among mercs in general. Which was why I had to talk to Hannah.

I pinged her door and received no answer, so I ended up asking Trish, "Could you contact her and tell her I want to speak with her?"

"SHE'S INSIDE, VANCE," Trish said. "SHE SAYS COME ON IN."

I shrugged and waved my hand, causing the doors to her quarters to open with a whooshing noise. The interior of the commander's apartments was slightly less luxurious than my own but still so huge you wouldn't necessarily think you were on a starship at all.

Unlike my own quarters—which Leah kept scrupulously tidy despite having a child—there were clothes and junk scattered everywhere, trinkets collected from our various adventures like a magpie. Hannah might accept a cultural treasure from a grateful populace one mission and then buy a t-shirt from a gift shop another but treat them with equal value.

Interestingly, despite being married to Lieutenant Commander Danny Tagawa and Doctor Elektra T'Ketra, Hannah didn't live with either of them. Instead, she maintained her own separate quarters. Polygamy was common among spacers, and I'd even been in a few such relationships myself, but they weren't really my thing. Managing one relationship was difficult enough, trying to do so with multiple partners was beyond my ability.

Ahem, Trish said in my mind.

Oh right, I thought back. *Never mind. The exception being when your other partner lives in your head.*

Thank you, Trish said. *Jerk.*

Sorry!

Hannah, herself, was in the next room where she'd set up a miniature gymnasium. The *Melampus* was equipped with extensive training facilities, not to mention virtual reality that could stimulate the body just as well as reality could, but Hannah preferred to work out in private. Most of the machines were identical to the ones found on Earth but there were a few odder devices that I sometimes had to guess at the purpose of.

Hannah was on an exercise bike that was designed to also stimulate her arms. She was wearing a green tank top and shorts. Hannah was as lovely as she was when we'd first met on the *Black Nebula*, her genetically engineered status meaning that she barely needed the longevity treatments all citizens of the Community were supposed to receive as a right. Lifespans for humans had tripled with some, like me, possibly having even longer lifespans thanks to the Elder Race nanotech. I didn't like thinking about that, though, because as youthful as my companions were, they were aging while I wasn't.

Yeah.

Heavy stuff to think about.

"Hey Vance!" Hannah said, working hard. "What's up?"

"Do you even need to exercise?" I asked, putting my hands on my waist. "I think they have vitamins that actually regulate weight and muscle growth."

"Not everyone dislikes exercise, Vance," Hannah said. "Or spends all of their hours behind a desk these days."

I smirked. "I still find time to do an occasional field mission."

"Yeah, I know," Hannah said, stopping. She'd worked up a sweat and headed over to pick up a moon-shaped bottle of water.

She promptly chugged it down.

"Do I sense the slightest hint of disapproval?" I asked.

"You're out here in no man's land exploring rocks, craters, and people who have no contact with the greater galactic society. Clearly, you're using your position to the best of its potential."

"It's certainly not no man's land to the people who live here," I said, annoyed at getting Leah's argument parroted back at me. "I could be remembered as the man who brought First Contact to dozens of civilizations, just like Earth and High Protector B'Vash."

"Yeah, being the Admiral Perry of a bunch of races that didn't want or ask to be contacted by space aliens is certainly a feather in your cap," Hannah said, putting her water bottle to one side. "Especially when Earth and humanity need you to be throwing your weight around to keep the idiots in charge from doing something even more stupid than they already are."

That was the real bone of contention between me and the others. It wasn't just Leah, whom I could usually dismiss as being overly ambitious. Which wasn't the nicest thing you could say about the person you had a child with but was something she'd freely admit herself. No, just about every member of my crew and friends talked about the fact that I didn't have to be out here taking orders from people like Fleet Admiral Bendo. I answered directly to the Community High Council and could make my own orders when not under their command.

But I didn't.

"What is it you want me to do?" I asked, hoping to put Hannah in a better mood before I asked her for a favor.

"Go back to Earth and sort things out before they ruin humanity," Hannah said, as if it was that easy. Which, from her perspective, it might well.

Hannah came from the planet Crius, which was a genetic engineer's nightmare and a fantasy fan's dream. It was a world where a bunch of lunatic scientists had teamed up with corporate sponsors to make their own private medieval paradise with hordes of chimerical slaves. For example, Hannah was a cat-girl among other DNA sources, albeit still mostly human in appearance. The Community had come to the planet twice to straighten it out and short-circuited Hannah's plans to liberate the world from its slave lords.

The situation on Earth was not so dire but it wasn't great either. The Human League was an alliance of Earth and the various other predominantly homo sapiens-inhabited planets. In theory, the idea was a good one if you understood that it was not a substitute for Community membership but a supplement. Unfortunately, in practice, the Human League had become the rallying cry of every isolationist and paranoid pro-human bigot in the Known Universe.

"People have a right to decide for themselves what sort of government they want," I replied. "Even if that involves making some truly stupid decisions."

"People don't have a right to do anything," Hannah said, surprising me. "People have *privileges* because other people fight for them while the vast majority never notice they've lost any until it's already too late. The Human Leaguers want to isolate humanity from the Community and when that happens, there will be no going back. Not for centuries."

I was still getting used to this new political side of Hannah even though it had been steadily growing for the entire time she'd been on the *Melampus*. I felt she was compensating because she hadn't been able to carry out her planned revolution on Crius. Since she couldn't help the people of her world, she'd help the people of the galaxy. Then again, maybe I was too quick to dismiss her concerns. She, after all, had grown up as a slave while I'd grown up in the lap of luxury.

"Bendo has a lot of friends in the Community," I replied. "I don't believe he is my enemy."

Which was a flat out lie but I didn't want to believe it.

"He sent his son to spy on you," Hannah said. "Said son got killed. He's not your friend nor ever will be."

I paused. "What's really going on, Hannah?"

Hannah did a double take. "What?"

"I understand that politics is now your thing, but you don't care so much that it's the first thing that comes to your mind when I come to visit," I replied, putting my hands behind my back and clasping them. I felt like a schoolteacher or stage manager, which really wasn't that far from my job description with the *Melampus* crew.

Hannah looked away, clearly uncomfortable with how quickly I'd picked up on the subtext of our conversation. "I'm getting a divorce."

"That's quite impressive since you're not married," I said, dryly. "Legally at least."

Hannah glared. "Fine, I'm breaking up with your cousin and Elektra. It just feels like an end of a marriage because it's one of the three longest relationships I've had in my life."

I nodded. "I'm sorry to hear that."

"You're not surprised," Hannah said, lowering her gaze.

"There have been signs," I said, simply.

Not the least of which had been that Danny and I still had lunch together virtually every day. He'd been clear about the problems in the relationship. She was ignoring him and not just because being ignored was literally his biomod power. Elektra was more circumspect but during an analysis of asteroid samples, she'd suddenly broken down to explain that things were going terribly with her throuple.

I also understood that Hannah was what you might call "commitment phobic." Her other two relationships that had any sort of traction had been with her old mercenary commander, Colonel John Mason, and, well, me. Hannah had ditched the Antares Ranger leader to join my crew on the *Ares* before breaking up with me when things had gotten a little too real. That hadn't really bothered me because I'd kept our friendship, but I think it bothered Hannah since I'd gotten the impression she preferred to torpedo her past associations. It did, however, mean that I was stuck serving as therapist for someone I used to date—which was also sort of unethical.

Yeah, you somehow became the Counsellor Troi instead of the Captain Picard around here, Trish said. *She used to counsel Riker even though they eventually got married. In the original continuity at least. Not the 22nd century version.*

At least say I'm Guinan, Troi was a terrible counselor, I replied, sadly able to keep all my *Star Trek* trivia in proper order. My classic science fiction hobby was one of the few ways I could decompress from solving all the problems in the universe.

Hannah plopped herself down on a weightlifting set's bench and shook her head. "Everything has become a little too real. It's part of why I'm complaining about all 'this' out here. The five-year mission is too much like a marriage."

"Eight year," I corrected.

"Whatever," Hannah said.

"Uh huh," I paused. "Let me guess, Danny and Elektra are discussing kids."

"How did you guess?" Hannah asked.

"I'm a genius," I replied.

That and Danny mentioned that he had been talking with Elektra about kids. Bringing up that Hannah was talking about my cousin wasn't going to help, though. Hannah was reacting exactly like she had been before she'd broken up with me. It turned out that there was a downside to remaining friends with your exes and keeping your found family close. Everything started to get a little incestuous.

Like Targaryen levels, Trish said. *I mean, isn't Elektra your ex-girlfriend's sister?*

Ex-fiancée, I replied, knowing Shelly hadn't said yes to my proposal. *And you know that she is.*

It's like a small town but in space, Trish said.

It's exactly like a small own in space, I admitted. *Usually, there's a lot more transfers between ships.*

Yeah, you keep your enemies close and your friends closer, Trish replied.

"Yeah, well," Hannah said, looking back. "I like your kid."

"Astrid," I said, annoyed.

"I know her name," Hannah said, crossing her arms. "I enjoy being her aunt."

I hadn't considered Hannah to be Astrid's aunt, but it was nice to know she did. "But—"

"It's not me. I don't want a family," Hannah said, sounding a bit panicked. "I was made in a test tube and grown with implanted memories. My mom and dad were the same."

That was one of the more messed-up elements of Crius, a planet that I had decidedly unpleasant feelings towards given my past encounters with its nobility. It had been settled by a mixture of cultists, corporate executives, and genetic engineers who had brought out the worst in each other. Ninety percent of the population had been clones created to live out a pseudo-fantasy world life while catering to the depraved whims of the elite. They had not only provided most of the product for the clone slavery trade but had been heavily involved in Department Twelve's transhuman research. They'd created both Hannah and Astrid, but I was still convinced it was a morally bankrupt society that I hoped would be able to reform now that its aristocracy had been defeated.

"That's fine," I said, trying to be sympathetic. "Family life isn't for everyone. The important thing is you're honest."

"I was hoping you'd try to talk me out of it," Hannah said, frowning.

"If you want me to, I will," I said, sighing. I wasn't about to get into the middle of all this, but it seemed that everyone wanted me to be. That was the problem when you weren't just the captain but everyone's friend (and family). It was well past the point of maintaining any professional distance and I wouldn't give up my relationships with any of the people involved but right now I wished I could keep a few parsecs between me and this business. Unfortunately, not only couldn't I do that, but I needed to ask Hannah for a favor.

Hannah slumped her shoulders. "Okay, thanks. I'll think about it some more and come to you to justify whatever decision I make."

"Super," I said. "Now I need your help."

Yep, this was going to go over like a piece of a neutron star or other super-dense material.

Hannah looked suspicious, which she absolutely should have been. "The High Inquisitor needs a favor from me?"

"Protector," I corrected, annoyed at her "joking" name for my title. I may not have the best relationship with the Community's leadership but I still held my job title sacrosanct.

"What sort of favor?" Hannah said. "Because aside from murdering people, I don't have a lot of skills. Maybe if you want to hustle someone in bar games."

"I need you to get in contact with the Antaeus Rangers and arrange a meeting on the Ring," I said, not happy with having to broach the subject after such a personal conversation.

Hannah stared at me as if I'd asked her to shoot her pitten or cabbit. "Are you out of your damned mind?"

"Probably," I answered. "But I do need you to get in touch with the Rangers and you're the only person I know who might be able to contact them. It takes months to deal with their handlers from what I know of them."

Also, Director G seemed to be no longer able to help. I'd relied on the former head of the Security Departments too much over the years and now I was paying the price.

"My contacts with them are decades old," Hannah replied, exaggerating the length of time we'd spent together. "I worked with them before I worked with you."

"And yet I know you still make the occasional call," I said, bringing up that as captain I had a record of all the jumpspace calls.

Hannah looked away. "Vance, this isn't a good idea. My history with the Rangers is complicated to say the least. I burned a lot of bridges during the Kolahn War and left behind quite a few hurt feelings. There's a reason I ended up working for you even though I never wanted to be part of Space Fleet."

"My award-winning personality?" I asked. I didn't want her to reduce her decision to join up to running away from something. Hannah deserved better than that and needed to give herself the credit she deserved. It hadn't just been a whim or because of our relationship. Right?

Ehhh, Trish commented via our cyberlink. *People are complex.*

Hannah rolled her eyes. "I mean, yes, the sex was good—"

I took a deep breath. "Let's stay on topic."

"What do you want to contact them for, anyway?" Hannah asked.

"Pirate treasure," I said.

Hannah blinked. "I can't tell if you're being serious or not."

"*Space* pirate treasure!" I said, sticking my thumbs up. "The Rangers are guarding the only person who might have an idea where it could be and I want to make the opening bid. I also think that General Vast is going to kidnap the guy versus continue paying him for false leads."

Hannah narrowed that. "Ah, *that* guy."

"Yes," I said.

"I should warn you, Vance, the Ring is not your sort of place," Hannah said, narrowing her eyes. "You'll need to watch yourself if you go there."

I shook my head. "I survived Rand's World. I think I can survive a space station on the edge of the frontier."

Why did that seem like I was tempting fate?

CHAPTER SEVEN

The Hangover That Wasn't

I woke up with an enormous headache and I briefly wondered if I was suffering a hangover. Sadly, my nanite-enhanced liver meant I couldn't get drunk even if I wanted to. Instead, I remembered I'd gotten into a fight with several of the *Melampus* crew at Lucky's Bar here on the Ring.

I'd gotten my ass beaten so bad the night before, I'd ended up dreaming of nothing at all for once. Which was, in a way, a relief. No memories of past experiences or hidden fears jumbled together in a bunch of metaphor. Nope, just blessed oblivion now followed by a headache that *resembled* a hangover. Sadly, my attempt to arrange to meet with the Antaeus Rangers had ended up taking a lot longer than expected. The *Melampus* was far from the Ring, standing down in another system, and it had been about three weeks of delays. My behavior last night wasn't from a lack of patience, though. No, it was from something much worse: grief.

My Aunt Kathy was dead.

INCOMING CALL - PRIORITY ONE.

"What? Another one?" I asked, confused. I'd been walking from Hannah's room when I'd received it.

"YESSIR," Light on Water said, their voice saying. "IT'S NOT FROM THE FLEET OFFICE, THOUGH."

"Who is it from?" I asked.

"DEATH NOTICES," Light on Water said. "IT'S FOR FRIENDS AND FAMILY."

"Why would death notices be a Priority One..." I trailed off as the answer came to me instantly.

Captain Kathy Tagawa had been the kind of legend Earth had needed after First Contact. She had helped establish the heroism that humanity was capable of—at least for the people on our world—and had confronted the galaxy head on and inspired others to do the same. Maybe propaganda had made up some of her legend, but she'd done her best to live up to the responsibility that no human being could.

The circumstances of her death seemed to have been entirely mundane. There had been a plasma explosion in an older ship she'd been visiting, and it had resulted in the atmosphere being vented, instantly suffocating everyone present. Space was still an incredibly dangerous place and hostile to all biological life, but it still felt wrong for her to die that way. She should have died on the bridge of her ship or in battle.

Either way, I wasn't taking it great and none of my crew had been willing to call me on it. Perhaps they weren't sure how to call out someone who technically could order Earth invaded on his own authority. I'd been tempted to because I wanted to believe her death had been murder. That, at least, would have given me a focus for my rage. Instead, I decided to carry on with the mission. I watched Kathy's state funeral via jump comm. A lot of people had commented on my absence.

Bork 'em.

"Where the hell am I?" I said, staring up into a bright light that hung over me. It took me a second for my eyes to adjust to my surroundings. I regretted that as soon as they did, as I saw a row of filthy prison cells carved into the side of the asteroid. The slime of the Perseus Arm was gathered in the cells across from me: smugglers, slavers, murderers, and rapists. There was also a trio of monks who didn't exactly fit the profile of my fellow guests here at the local Frontier Security office.

The Ring had proven to be a lot wilder place than I'd expected, which was impressive since I'd expected quite a bit. The ancient megastructure barely had any government and what it did have was divided between warlords and crime bosses trying to control the immense flood of illegal trade from the Community.

Trade that, if the Arm had been explored better, wouldn't have been prohibited and might have prevented the arms and human trafficking that I'd have to figure a way to shut down. Unfortunately, I was in no condition to do that right now, as I realized I was in the drunk tank. If nothing else, that was a good sign that I had kept my identity secret so far. I was operating here undercover with some minor prosthetics and DNA disguisers. For now, I was just Joe Miller, galactic trader and my crew were operating under similar aliases.

"I'm sorry, Captain, I should have had your back," Danny said behind me.

I turned my head and saw a handsome lad wearing the purple jumpsuit of the *Melampus'* flight crew. Danny Tagawa looked about twenty-seven years old, was raven-haired, slightly below my height, and well-built. He was, of course, older, as was I. It seemed like it had been just yesterday that we'd been a pair of inexperienced twenty-somethings trying to save the galaxy. Which, now that I thought about it, hadn't been that long ago. It wasn't the years, though, but the astronomical units.

"I'm sure you did, Danny," I said, sitting up. "What hit me, anyway?"

"A table, sir," Danny said. "One of the bar patrons was using it as a club. Honestly, we kind of thought you were dead. Most people who don't wake up in half an hour don't wake up period."

"Yes, well, I'm a genetically enhanced freak of nature," I said, feeling the back of my head.

"Join the club," Danny muttered.

I shrugged. "Also, my memories are saved on an Elder Race data cloud somewhere. Helps rewire neural pathways when there are disruptions."

"Really?" Danny asked.

"No idea," I said, shrugging. "What, do you think I got a brochure when they made me their minion?"

"I would have asked for one," my cousin said, giving a sad grin.

"Is everyone else alright?" I asked, trying to remember how the fight had started. I suspected it probably had to do with religion, politics, money, sex, or sports. No, that wasn't right. It had started because I'd wanted to fight.

Danny grimaced. "Avis was stabbed and Thompkins wasn't moving when we were dragged here. I think I may have killed the guy who hit you with a table."

"*May* have?" I asked.

"I took your fusion pistol and disintegrated his upper torso," Danny said.

"Then I suspect you *may* have," I said.

"If it's any consolation, it turns out he was a slaver," Danny said. "Wanted for murder, kidnapping, and nonconsensual acts with livestock. Unfortunately, he was paid up on his bribes."

I nodded. "So, we're under arrest for murder?"

I wasn't overly concerned about what the law would do to us. The Frontier Legion of Corporate Security, FLACS for short, weren't actual police but one of the many corporate mercenary organizations that provided for-profit order in the fringe of human space. Corpses were a regular product of spacer interactions in the Ring, and this wasn't even the first time a member of the crew had killed people here. Hannah had ended up killing a child trafficker, which I only disapproved of because she hadn't gotten backup beforehand.

Usually, the issue was settled with a donation to the local constabulary's retirement fund. I had the sneaking suspicion they knew we were Community, though, even if they didn't know who exactly I was. That would create complications. Complications I should have been dealing with.

"I thought he'd killed you, sir," Danny said.

"Vance," I said, sighing, "No ranks here."

"Vance… sir," Danny said. Patting me on the shoulder. "I just want you to know, there's nowhere else I'd rather be."

"Then you're a fool," I said, patting him on his shoulder in return.

"Tell me, do you believe in God, sir?" one of the monks called to me.

I closed my eyes. "I'm going to regret saying yes, aren't I?"

"Then you must tell this fool that his knowledge of the observer effect is hopelessly flawed!" the monk pointed to another.

"If God existed then he'd observe everything and thus the holy physics wouldn't exist!" the other monk said, "Therefore, God exists only in humanity."

"Blasphemy! God exists in all realities and possibilities so all races can separate his glories by seeing one bit at a time," the first monk said.

"If a tree falls in the forest and no one hears it, does it exist in infinity?" the third monk asked.

"Wheelerites," I muttered.

Wheelerism was, in simple terms, one of the largest human religions in the Arm. Which wasn't saying much since there were only about a dozen small human colonies fleeing from persecution in the Union of Faith. Specifically, they'd been unable to persecute other religions and thus been driven out. I'd always found Wheelerism a little bit strange as it hadn't been founded by a religious teacher, prophet, or god, but by a physicist from Earth's 20th century. John Archibald Wheeler had been one of the early theorists about the nature of the universe who happened to get a good 75% of it accurate before his death.

Later, when mankind had discovered it wasn't alone in the universe, humanity had been desperate for reassurance of a spiritual nature, so a small cult called the Children of Hagelin and Society of Penrow had combined Wheeler's writings with what we'd learned from aliens to create humanity's first religion that was mathematically provable. Or so they claimed. My own spirituality had taken a hit when I'd faced down genuinely godlike beings like Cthulhu (my name for the Primordials' herald) and that the Elder Races were such jackasses but seemed to be the oldest, most powerful beings in creation. Shouldn't wisdom come with age? What did happen to us beyond death or was becoming part of the greater cosmos the best we could hope for? Was individuality even a real thing? Yeah, I was not prepared for this mission.

"I'm sorry about Aunt Kathy, Vance," Danny said.

"So, you've said a few dozen times," I replied. My cousin had been trying to reach out, but I'd shut him down almost completely. It didn't help that he was undergoing his own issues right now. I could tell the thing with Hannah was almost finalized. It was just a matter of making it official. Elektra was apparently looking for a new partner to replace her. As much as she loved Danny, being a lesbian meant just being a couple wasn't in the cards for those two.

Like I said, spacers. They're from a whole different galaxy.

"She was family," Danny said. "For us both."

"I know," I said, sighing. "She was proud of the effort you'd made."

Aunt Kathy had been the White Sheep of the Tagawa and Tagashi families. Most of us were all criminals, influencers, con men, and leeches on her own legitimately earned fortune. I had no doubt the knives had gone out as soon as she'd died and there were probably a dozen legal challenges to where her inheritance would go. I personally didn't care as I had my own future secured but wondered what sort of legacy she'd leave behind and how people like my father might try to steal it.

"But not as proud as she was of you," Danny said. "You cast a long shadow. One that I'm sure will be just as big as hers when you die."

"Who says I plan to die?" I asked, smirking.

The truth was I wasn't sure how much of a legacy I was really leaving, despite how many propaganda victories I still achieved. My enemies on EarthGov had given up on trying to defame me but they certainly didn't hesitate to put me out to pasture. I could fight it just as Leah and Hannah wanted, but I wasn't sure I wanted to be part of the political bullsavit that was seemingly ninety percent of anything higher than a captain's rank.

Danny rolled his eyes. "Just get it together, Vance."

It was as close to an actual rebuke as I'd ever gotten from my cousin. "Sure, I'll do that. Just as soon as I head back to Earth, overthrow the current reactionary government, and install myself as dictator."

"Ever wonder if the Human Leaguers have it right?" Danny asked, surprising me. "That we'd do better going it alone."

"Nope."

"Why?" Danny said. "Surely, freedom is a cause worth fighting for."

63

"Freedom comes in a lot of packages, kid. The freedom not to starve, freeze to death, or die in war is the basis for all other freedoms. The Community is doing a better job than most."

"Traitors, collaborators, murderers!" a human in another cell shouted over at us. He and his buddies looked vaguely familiar. "You and your kind make me sick!"

I looked at Danny and shrugged in confusion.

"Those are the people we got into a scuffle with," Danny said, guiltily.

"What's your vendetta, *k'mpec*?" I asked, using some local profanity.

"You're human!" the man snarled. "You should be out here with us, fighting against the evils of the Community and working to free humanity from the oppression of alien rule. Earth may have fallen but someday she will rise again!"

"Who are you?" I asked.

"We're the Brothers for a Free Humanity!" the man said, proudly. "Independence from the Community! Now! Our healthcare system will benefit, and we'll give up nothing in return."

Given I'd never heard of them, I put them down as one of the countless Federation-backed pirate groups proudly "resisting" against the Community.

I looked over at Danny. "These are the guys who you think had a point?"

"Sorry, sir," Danny said.

Thankfully, the rest of the criminals in that holding pen of evil weren't any more interested in the Brothers' rhetoric and shouted him down. It helped a good half of the people here were aliens with about half of them wearing environmental suits or sporting cybernetics to process a human atmosphere. The Community had brought a vast amount of trade from the Spiral. People who hoped to strike it rich in the newly "civilized" region. Most of them were racist, greedy, short-sighted, and contemptuous of anything from outside their homeland. The local aliens were much the same, but eager to strike it rich by dealing with smugglers. Some things, it seemed, were universal.

Thankfully, we didn't have to wait long for someone to get us as Leah and Elektra arrived to pick us up soon after. Neither woman was dressed in Protector uniforms but local disguises, which were a mechanic's jumpsuit for Leah and Elektra in a simple cloth robe with a headdress to disguise her Ethereal features. Elektra was ebony black and strongly resembled her late mother, Ketra.

Leah looked at me then Danny. "Do you know how much it costs to get you guys freed from a murder rap?"

"Tell me you haggled," I said, staring. "Every credit counts."

Leah rolled her eyes. "I swear, why can't you to have just gone to a brothel like any normal pair of sailors."

"I've seen the brothels here," I said, pretending to be interested in ladies of negotiable affection for the people around us. Our covers were holding, I hoped, and every little bit helped. "I'd rather spend my money drinking."

"Well, Hannah likes them," Leah said. "The ones she frequents are clean and sometimes you find a diamond in the rough."

"We'll have to get to polishing your jewelry when we get back," I said, still trying to act the role of a space pirate.

The two of us kissed through the bars.

Danny made an uncomfortable noise behind us.

I pulled back. "Really, Danny?"

"Nothing sir," Danny said then looked at Leah. "Ma'am."

"Come on, Danny," Elektra said. "We need to find Hannah."

Leah snorted while Elektra frowned.

A Sorkanan FLACS magistrate walked up to my cell with an old-style ring of keys and unlocked the door. The alien was a ridiculous figure as he was wearing an ancient sheriff's star on a chain around his neck and a pair of leather chaps to go with his brown pants even though he wasn't otherwise wearing any clothes. I wouldn't have been surprised to find he had a ten-gallon hat nearby as well. Westerns were one of the few human media items that Community citizens loved.

"Time for you to go," the magistrate said, talking in heavily accented Ringspeak. It was a pidgin tongue of Albionese, Drolochid, and Sorkanan that just about everyone could learn the basics of but few could speak properly.

I looked at him. "I have to ask, what's with the medieval bars?"

"Cheaper," Sorkanan said. "Why, we have buckets with cleaning fluid in them instead of installing plumbing."

I'd been wondering what that odor of savit, urine, and cleaning fluid had been. It was the same sort of smell that clung to most public bathrooms in space, so I hadn't paid it much mind. It was another reason why I wanted to get back to my ship because we at least had mechs to clean our lavatories.

"Right," I said, looking at Leah. "Let's get out of here."

Leah nodded.

"So, what were you doing while we were locked away?" I asked, passing through the Frontier Security entrance where a Llrowlthra—basically a five-foot-tall grasshopper—was handling paperwork from the asteroid's peoples. Most of the FLACS were human or Sorkanan but there were a few of the local alien races as well. All that could survive in an eighty-degree, nitrogen-oxygen atmosphere at least.

"Refilling our supply of medical goods," Leah said, shrugging. "Also, I was checking if any other bioroids wanted to join our gang."

Our "gang" was a cover identity of smugglers who owned a small fleet of ships who I'd recruited over the past few weeks. I'd used my insider knowledge to set them up on humanitarian relief missions disguised as criminal enterprises, feeding the poor and equipping developing worlds while pretending they were working against the Community. We'd still had to deal with multiple people who wanted a cut of the relief efforts or planned to sabotage what they assumed were future rivals.

"Did any?" I asked.

Slavery was banned throughout all Community territories and most other "civilized" spaces as well, surviving primarily on smaller colonies and places with long histories of legalized oppression. I know what you're thinking, there's no reason for slavery to exist in an industrialized—let alone space flight capable—society, but it was an evil that seemed to have a cultural inertia of its own.

The most common form of slavery was the trade in genetically engineered bodies with cybernetically created brains, AKA Bioroid Slavery. Sadly, it was mostly a product of Earth's peculiar focus on AI creation and research. While AI had been created to be engineers and mechanics, people had swiftly adapted the technology for domestic labor and sex. Unintelligent bots did most of the heavy lifting but bioroids needed to be human-like for some actions. I struggled with the question of why aliens wanted to buy them, but a lot were located on the Ring.

"A few," Leah said. "Mostly escapees, but also people who we could help get away with only a bit of breaking the local law."

The two of us exited out the front door of the building. Now we could discuss business freely.

"Good," I replied, nodding. "As long as we're here, we can set up an Underground Railroad with our freighter cover identity. We can't compromise our actual identities, though. Not yet."

"You could just declare martial law and invade," Elektra said, surprising me. She was usually one of the most diplomatic of our officers.

"Really?" I asked.

"This place is a pit," Elektra said.

"Yeah, and invasions rarely make things better," I replied.

"The Confederacy being an exception," Elektra said. "Crius too."

"Anything else?" I asked, wondering what was taking so long.

Leah smirked. "Hannah contacted us. The Rangers are finally willing to meet with us."

"When?" I asked, finally glad to be rid of this place.

"Now," Leah said.

CHAPTER EIGHT

The Seedy Underbelly of the Seedy Underbelly

The Ring's interior was made of a hundred chambers that were built on top and around one another but were all centered around one single giant chamber that formed the basis of the town. That was composed of countless buildings carved out into the side of the walls with the occasional plastisteel addition.

The exterior of the Ring, which was an enormous planet-sized "green zone" with its own ocean, was inhabited almost exclusively by the ultra-rich. They could have housed the entirety of the interior's population and then some, but it was basically used for estates and parks for the elites to enjoy. I didn't know who had constructed the Ring, but I somehow doubted they'd built it for this purpose.

Space wasn't exactly abundant in the interior, so every building was packed on top of one another with bridges as well as staircases, walkways, and ladders. Most buildings were covered in graffiti, holograms, and electric signs advertising everything from sleep chambers to sex to narcotics. The air was a good deal thicker and more humid than in the Frontier Security office with the temperature being excruciating.

There were no roads in the Ring's interior, and everyone had to walk, but there were pathways and trams. The pathways were covered in puddles and muck as the artificial microsystem of the asteroid interior routinely rained the disinfectant that was necessary to keep plagues from forming across human-run territories. Ironically, the addition of the Community races hadn't increased the risk of infection

68

since none of them carried anything we could be infected with. Steam shot out of regularly spaced grates and there were numerous sewers designed to recycle the water of the asteroid.

I looked around the location for any sign of the others. "Are you sure they're going to come through with the goods?"

"You know, for a smuggler, you sure are squirrely about smuggling," Leah said, referring to my cover identity. "Hannah trusts these people."

"Well, she would, wouldn't she?" I muttered. Still wondering if I'd made the right choice asking her to intervene on our behalf. She'd made the deal, but I could tell she hadn't been happy about it.

"You don't trust the Rangers, do you?" Elektra asked.

"Not in the slightest," I said. "Especially with this."

The delay bothered me a great deal. As a High Protector, I could outbid Vast many times over. If there was something to Arden's claims, which was a big if. It was possible they didn't want to meet with me because I'd see through their con game on the grand general. Which was the least problematic outcome.

"Everything will be fine," Leah said, only speaking when a group of passers-by were out of earshot. "This is a strictly cash-only deal. Hannah worked out all the arrangements herself."

"That's what I'm afraid of," I muttered. Friends and money didn't mix. It was doubly true in the criminal underworld. "I trust Hannah with my life, but I'm asking her to choose between her allegiances."

"She chose between her allegiances a long time ago," Elektra said, uncomfortable with our environment even beyond what could be expected. Ethereals lived on planets that were made of crystal spires and where everyone wore togas. She rarely left the laboratory of the *Melampus*. This had to be an entirely new experience for her even with our occasional adventures together.

"You think?" I asked.

"She chose you over the Rangers, Vance. A long time ago," Elektra said. "Don't get jealous, Leah."

Leah snorted. "Are you sure I'm the one who should be jealous, Elektra?"

"Hannah would always choose Vance over us," Elektra said, sadly. "Danny and I knew that."

"We did?" Danny asked, looking unhappy. "Funny, I don't recall that."

Well, this conversation got uncomfortable fast. "Listen—"

"It doesn't matter," Elektra said, interrupting. "What's important is that we find out whether Vance's chasing ghost stories and legends will result in yet another miracle."

Ouch.

She's not happy with me, I said to Trish mentally.

I remind you that you were in a year-long funk after breaking up with Shelly, Trish said.

It wasn't a year long, I replied. *Was it?*

Leah frowned. "In any case, I hope you'll make an offer for the Rangers to join our organization."

I rolled my eyes. "Yeah, yeah, the more people with guns in our employ the fewer people we have to shoot ourselves."

"Anyone else would not be rolling their eyes at that statement," Leah said. "The Rangers are a remnant of Earth's expansion period. They were driven further and further into the frontier with the ever-strengthening ties of the Community with EarthGov. Why not bring them in from the cold before some extremist pro-human group does instead?"

"Clearly you're not an idealist like Vance," Elektra said, pausing,

"Thank God for that," Leah muttered. "They could be a powerful asset for bringing civilization to this region."

"We're not colonialists," I said, flatly.

"I meant the Ring," Leah said. "I believe you forfeit the right to claim imperialism when you're run by warlords and slavers."

"Empire building is a slippery slope," I started to say. "Even if I think this place is a pit."

Thankfully, any further conversation was delayed by the arrival of Hannah O'Brian and Trish's bioroid body. Hannah was wearing a green cloak over a suit of plastisteel trooper armor she'd acquired from a transtellar mercenary prince with more money than sense. She was carrying a plasma rifle that wasn't designed for human fingers, but she'd modified its grip.

Trish, by contrast, was a redheaded woman dressed in a rather form fitting spacesuit and goggles. She would attract a great deal of attention if she wasn't someone who had been primarily operating on the surface. There, the beautiful elite could wear whatever they wanted. Trish had been our contact there helping arrange for supplies to the worlds in the Perseus Arm in dire need of resupply. That hadn't been my mission here, but I had no problem making up my own.

"How did your night go?" I asked.

"Unsatisfying," Hannah said, referring either to her business arrangements or brothel habits. I thought she was trying to get the others to officially break up with her, but the problem was that neither of her partners thought of outside sexual liaisons as a reason to do so. Some open and honest communication would have done the throuple good, but I was pretty sure the relationship was beyond salvaging.

"What's our situation?" I asked.

Hannah continued. "I've made contact with the Rangers and they're finally ready to meet with us in a neutral location."

"The Ring wasn't neutral enough?" I asked. "They've been based out of here for years."

"You cast a long shadow," Hannah said. "They're worried you're going to arrest them."

"Why?" I asked, now nervous.

"Because that's what you do," Hannah said, shrugging. "They know you're Vance Turbo, the Hero of SPAAACE and wondering whether you're coming after the Rangers versus chasing down pirate treasure. They also don't trust the Community as a whole. They think the Community is more likely to arrest them and take what they have than pay up."

"Have they done something worth arresting them for?" I asked, dryly.

"Being as they are mercenaries, yes?" Trish asked.

"Let's start with associating with Vast in the first place," Leah said. "Technically, if you're armed men or women working for a terrorist—"

71

"You're a member of a terrorist organization," I said, finishing the sentence for her. "Even if you haven't done anything that warrants prosecution. Alright, I can see why they'd be suspicious of me."

"Arden also thinks you hold a grudge against him," Hannah said. "He believes you blame him for abandoning Space Fleet and going after the *Mary Read* on his own."

"I haven't thought about Winston Arden in decades," I replied, dryly.

"Yeah, well, he thinks he was your mentor," Hannah said. "He's been telling people for years about how it was immense wisdom as a long-serving officer in the lower ranks that turned you into the capable officer you became."

I stared at her. "Uh huh."

"Aw, Captain, you're continuing to inspire people!" Trish said. "Admittedly, inspiring them to bullsavit."

Hannah shrugged. "John is still willing to do the deal but he wants an additional ten percent on the top."

I stared at her. "You can tell him he can go bork himself. I don't negotiate with people I've already made a deal with. God, I knew this…"

I trailed off as I saw her expression of irritation.

"You already agreed," I said.

"We should hunt him down to the ends of the galaxy and put two rounds in the back of his head," Leah said.

"What is with you two and haggling? This is about business not honor," Hannah said. "You're both richer than God."

I clenched my teeth. "It's about respect."

Hannah rolled her eyes. "I've been a criminal and a member of the so-called upper crust, Vance. The latter mostly because of you. Whenever someone starts talking about respect then they're about to do something stupid."

"Now's not the time to rib Vance, Hannah," Danny said, a somber expression on his face. "He's in a bad place."

"I am not in a bad place!" I snapped. Which was, admittedly, something someone in a bad place would say.

"He's in a bad place," Leah said, softly.

72

"Yeah, I agree," Trish said.

"Why are people saying that?" I asked, annoyed.

"You haven't made a joke like, 'This deal is getting worse all the time.'," Trish said.

"You haven't made any pirate jokes despite the fact we're chasing literal pirate treasure," Danny said. "Not even a 'yarr matey.'"

"Yarr matey," I muttered.

"You didn't even do the accent," Elektra said, shaking her head. "Plus, you woke up in the drunk tank despite literally being incapable of being drunk."

"I was hit in the head with a table!" I replied, noting that it was a good thing we were in a relatively isolated part of the Ring's interior. We were making a scene, or I was at least. Maybe they were right about the idea I wasn't in a good place right now. Perhaps it wasn't the best time to be off chasing pirate treasure or maybe that was the best thing

possible for me right now. Aunt Kathy had been a huge fan of Anne Bonny, both her seagoing career and work as a High Protector. Bringing her ship back home might be the best memorial I could make to the woman who'd raised me.

Sort of.

"Yeah, he was kind of dead," Trish said, "Thank goodness for physics-breaking Elder Race technology. Praise the Church of Vance the Resurrected."

"Huzzah," Danny said, smirking.

I looked around the group. "Huh, so this is what everyone else feels around me when I'm being ridiculous."

"Pretty much, yeah," Trish said. "We're just worried about you."

"Well, stop," I said. "I'm 100% focused on the mission now."

"That's what we're worried about," Danny said.

I shook my head. "Fine, we'll agree to their price for the information, Hannah. Everything they have on the *Mary Read*. Who is our contact here?"

Hannah hesitated to respond, which wasn't a good sign. "He's—"

"He's Hannah's ex," Elektra interjected instead. "John Mason, the grandson of Thomas Mason, the founder of the Antaeus Rangers. He's basically the guy in charge."

73

"I know who John Mason is," I said, deciding this was another emotional minefield I wanted to avoid. "Fine, do you trust him?"

Hannah opened her mouth then closed it. "He'll do right by his people."

That was not a yes.

"Whatever the case, once we have the information, we should be golden," I said, frowning. "Provided they don't try and gut us then take it back to sell it to someone else, it's a fake, or they're going to shake us down for more money."

"Are those likely?" Danny asked.

"No," Hannah said.

"So far from what I've seen? Yes," I said, frowning at him. "The likelihood of someone trying to rip you off in any interaction on the Ring is inversely proportional to how much they're scared of you shoving them out an airlock. It didn't take long to learn that."

"The Antaeus Rangers are mercenaries, not a bunch of pirates," Hannah said, defensively. "They have honor. Sort of."

There was clearly a lot of unspoken history with Hannah and the Rangers that I wasn't aware of. They'd worked together closely during the Kolahn War, and I'd recruited her into the Community Protectors afterward but that didn't explain the level of discomfort she seemed to feel every time her old teammates came up.

"It's the 'sort of' that worries me," I said. "The *Melampus* isn't a bunch of pirates, though. We're officers of the Community."

"We *are* kind of piratey," Elektra said. "Is that a word?"

"It probably is somewhere," Danny said, smirking.

"Yarr," Trish said. "A ragtag band of misfits seeking glory and gold among the seven galaxies. Well, just the Milky Way and two major catalogued dwarf galaxies. There are fifty-plus dwarf galaxies orbiting the Milky Way but we've got nothing on them but star charts."

I felt a headache coming on.

"The mercenaries I know all betrayed their contractors whenever they got a better deal," Leah said. "I know because I worked with a lot of them under Captain Elgan. He was a master of assembling non-traditional teams to achieve unusual goals."

"Yeah," I muttered. "Because that's the guy I want to be compared to."

Captain Elgan was, in his own way, the man who had shaped me into the officer I was today. It just had been by betraying me and making me aware that the supposed heroes of the Community and EarthGov didn't necessarily have my—or anyone else's—best interests at heart. He'd been every bit as famous as Aunt Kathy and had become more so upon his death. This even though he'd died attempting to acquire Elder Race technology that would have gotten Earth destroyed if it had been discovered in our possession (and it would have been, believe me).

Captain Elgan had become the symbol of the Human League and the martyr they rallied behind whenever discussing how Humanity First should be the guiding principle in all things. It was ironic because, as much as I hated the man, he would have been horrified by that. He was many things but neither a racist nor an isolationist. He knew humanity's only hope of becoming a major power was working in tandem with the Community versus trying to become its rival.

"He was a great man," Leah said, pausing. "Until he wasn't."

"Let's just prepare for a double cross," I said, simply. "Just in case."

Hannah did not like that and stared at us with her hands on her hips. "The Raiders wouldn't betray *me*. John wouldn't betray me."

"Because you used to sleep with him?" Elektra asked, laughing. "With most men I know, that makes betrayal doubly likely."

"Most women too," Leah said. "Hell, I've killed my fair share of lovers."

"That's not reassuring," I said, looking at her.

"Oh, not you," Leah said. "I mean, not *now*. If I was going to kill you, it would have been before I needed you to take care of Astrid."

I was ninety-nine percent sure that was a joke.

Hannah frowned. "John's not like that."

"All men are like that," Elektra said.

"Most women too," Leah added, echoing her earlier comment.

"He's like Vance," Hannah said. "Just grittier."

Everyone was silent.

Well, that just made things even more awkward. "Let's hope Hannah is right," I said, before turning to her. "Even though I get the impression this John guy and you didn't part on the best of terms."

"We didn't," Hannah said, her expression cold. "I didn't want to be anywhere near the Rangers after the events of 28281-Bell."

I blinked. "What happened at 28281-Bell?"

Hannah looked up, clearly not realizing she'd confessed to something she hadn't intended. "It's... complicated."

I stared at her. "Uncomplicate it for me."

CHAPTER NINE

We Absolutely Trust You. Just Not Your Friends

I was familiar with 28281-Bell or just "The Big Rock" from my time working with the Kolahn Resettlement Project on New Pompeii. We'd won the war against the Kolahn but at a terrible cost to our enemies, forcing them to become galactic refugees.

Partially out of guilt and partially because I just wanted to do something productive with my military service, I'd requested assignment with the *Ares* in caring for the victims of the war rather than another frontline assignment. Because of the mutiny, which Home Fleet wanted to hush up, I'd gotten my wish. My relief efforts had been fruitful and satisfying work, at least until it had all been blown up.

The Big Rock had been a hollowed-out asteroid that had been parked in front of New Pompeii and used as a makeshift spaceport while the terraforming of the world was carried out. Basically, an artificial moon. It had become something of a Wild West boom town while it had been in existence, though nowhere near as bad as the Ring. That was, at least, until the Incident.

All the effort we'd put into resettling the Kolahn refugees had been rendered pointless by the Pompeii system's destruction but that didn't mean it had been smooth sailing beforehand. Not everyone had been happy with the idea of devoting vast amounts of the Community's wealth—and a not inconsiderable amount of EarthGov's—to caring for people who had been enemies just a few years prior.

The Enigmatic Path constantly attempted to sabotage efforts and eliminate proponents of resettling their race. The terrorist organization needed the Community to look like monsters after all. Plenty of human extremists also opposed the efforts. Both groups had come together when they'd seized the Big Rock and started executing its civilian contractors one by one.

"You were involved in the Incident?" I asked Hannah, realizing I'd completely missed this fact. I hadn't been in the system when it had happened. Despite my enormous reputation for being the right man in the wrong place at the wrong time, I'd been off buying medical supplies when it had gone down. I hadn't arrived back in-system until a month after the repercussions from the events had settled down. Otherwise, I probably would have tried to do something stupid.

"Yes," Hannah said, looking away. "Listen, is this really the right time?"

"It is if we're to know this man's actual character," Leah said, speaking for me before I could respond. "It may be important to seeing these negotiations succeed."

Leah, what are you doing? I asked her through her bond.

Hannah wants to tell us, Leah said. *She's been holding it in for years. However, she is afraid of disappointing you.*

Disappointing me? Why? I asked, genuinely confused.

She does worse than love you, Leah thought. *She, ugh, admires you. She thinks you believe in her.*

I do believe in her, I replied, confused.

That's what makes it worse, Leah replied, once again showing her wonderfully caustic approach to life.

Yeah, I agree with the evil psychic you had a baby with, Trish said, popping in to share her thoughts.

I have way too many voices in my head right now, I replied. *They're scaring off my other personalities.*

I find that joke offensive, Trish said.

Hannah looked around as if uncomfortable then started walking. The rest of us had no choice but to follow her. "Okay, we've still got a bit of distance to cover before we reach our destination. I'll share the story. But if I do, you must promise not to judge anyone in the story too harshly."

"I absolutely do not," Leah said. "Judging people harshly is ninety percent of what I do and the other ten percent is roll my eyes at Vance being too nice to people."

"You can always open up to me, Hannah," Elektra said. "Not that you ever have in our entire history of dating."

"No one pays me any attention to begin with," Danny said.

"I know the story already but will pretend not to," Trish said.

Well, I was glad this group therapy session masquerading as a military operation was off to a great start. "Please go on, Hannah."

Hannah took us down an isolated set of corridors that were marked as MAINTENANCE: DO NOT ENTER in a variety of holographic letters. Inside, a group of alien bots were carrying out the vital work necessary to keep the Ring going.

"I was there on the Big Rock when the Enigmatic Path and Neo-Militarists took over," Hannah said. "How a bunch of Kolahn cyber-terrorists and a group of pro-human isolationists got together to carry out the hijacking of a space station surrounded by Community Protector vessels was anyone's guess, but they did. We didn't have any weapons like the other soldiers there, but we had the training to make a difference."

I nodded. "The official story on the Incident was heavily redacted. Most of the survivors were sent home and no one came out looking particularly good."

My former commanding officer, Captain Klaws, had been a good man but there was a reason he was assigned to refugee relief. He was not great under pressure and tended to either hesitate in crises or overreact.

"The system commander, Klaws, bungled the whole thing," Hannah said. "The terrorists involved didn't agree on what they wanted. They were like the proverbial dog catching a transport. Some wanted to go out in the blaze of glory, some wanted to make demands, and others wanted money. If the Community had just sent in the troops from the beginning, they might have gotten most of the hostages out."

"Instead, Captain Klaws told everyone to stand down and tried to negotiate," I said, getting a sense of what had happened. "Which resulted in everyone gathering around the place and doing nothing as massacres were carried out within."

"Yeah," Hannah muttered. "Fifty-three civilians were executed from the beginning of the takeover to the end. I could have done more to save them. Should have done more."

"How did the Rangers fit into this?" I asked.

Hannah closed her eyes. "John and his team were ready to insert themselves. I had the inside information, and we could have done what the Community wasn't willing to. That was part of the reason why I became a merc, I was so disgusted by the red tape and bureaucracy of the Community. I never wanted to be an actual soldier, but my own woman."

"And yet you joined the Community officially afterward," Leah pointed out. "Vance got you a full commission."

"Because of this, yeah," Hannah muttered. "John inserted his team, shot up the place, and managed to do an extraction. It caused the rest of the soldiers to move in on the remaining terrorists and finish them off. The Rangers got reprimanded and their contract in New Pompeii cancelled but were privately commended. Full payout on all remaining funds. Situation resolved. No follow-up questions."

I was missing something. "What happened?"

Hannah stopped. "John didn't send in the team to rescue the hostages and take out the terrorists. He sent in the Rangers to rescue *me*."

Ah, that explained a few things. Survivor's guilt. "You expected the Rangers to come in and save everyone, but they went directly for their comrade."

I didn't disagree with Colonel Mason's decision. A lot of people thought I was an idealist and maybe that was true, but I also felt a good commanding officer put his crew first. You were called to risk them for the mission but throwing them away for the greater good was something I always struggled with—thought you *should* struggle with.

"A lot of people died who didn't need to," Hannah said, sighing. "I took it badly when John dismissed the deaths as collateral damage. As far as he was concerned, the primary loyalty of any Antaeus Ranger should be to his fellow Rangers. But there was more, I could tell he did it because it was me who was threatened. I couldn't be with him after that and left the Rangers. He took it badly but that made it easier. From there, I joined the Community Protectors officially. Vance's string pulling made it lot simpler than it might have normally been. Even before he was a captain, he had a lot of subtle influence."

"So, you dumped this John guy because he loved you," Danny said, sounding slightly accusatory. Maybe he was identifying with John.

"If you get people killed because you care for someone, that's not love," Hannah said. "Maybe Vance had rubbed off on me."

"Probably during sex," Leah said, joking.

Elektra and Danny glared at her.

"That was a long time ago," I muttered, though it seemed neither my cousin nor almost sister-in-law agreed.

"I communicated with him for a while after and we've patched up our relationship," Hannah said, pausing. "A bit. Apparently, John was less than pleased to find out I'd hooked up with a self-absorbed spoiled nepotist and propaganda icon."

"Is she talking about me?" I asked.

"No," Leah said. "She's talking about the other propaganda icon in our group."

"It's not the first time my fame has come around to bite me in the anyx," I said, ready to call off the meeting. "Hannah, is there anything else I should know?"

"They also want to meet us more than just privately. They want to meet *us* alone," Hannah said, pointing at me. "You and me. I convinced them to let Trish come as well."

"Like hell," Leah said.

"Bork that!" Elektra said, surprising me with her level of emotion. "Do they really think we're stupid enough to fall for that?"

Hannah looked guilty. "I've already agreed."

"Oh, come on!" Danny said. "You can't be serious!"

"Hannah," I said, taking a deep breath. "I trust you."

"You do?" Leah asked, crossing her arms. "Well, that's stupid."

I glared at her before turning back to Hannah.

"I get this is a complicated situation and I've put your loyalties to the test."

81

"Old friends versus very dear new ones," Hannah said, pausing.

Elektra frowned at the use of the term friend, Danny just seemed resigned to it.

"But, we need to remember what's truly at stake here," I said, pausing. "Borking over Vast and his organization. It doesn't matter if the *Mary Read* is real."

"It absolutely is," Trish said. "I was there. You were there, Vance, and so was Hannah. It's ridiculous that the Community pretends we saw a ghost."

"If General Vast is chasing it and thinks we have it, then he'll waste more resources that he might otherwise be using against the Community as a whole," I said, not interested in reviving an old debate. "Plus, after this is done, I intend to take us back to Earth."

"Finally," Leah muttered.

I didn't want to go deal with Earth's politics and certainly wasn't the savior Leah and Hannah thought I was. However, the situation in the Perseus Arm was clearly a lot nastier than it should have been and I could start planning for more relief from Earth or Throneworld. I also needed to confront my Aunt Kathy's death head on. Anything else? Well, I would take it as it came.

"Plus, we might find real pirate treasure!" Trish said. "Vance may even get to use his sword!"

They were referring to my proton sword, which I had received as a gift from my Aunt Kathy for my elevation to the status of High Protector. It was Elder Race technology and turned out to have some utterly ridiculous properties like it was able to be stored in a liquid form when it wasn't in use, generate force shields, cut through barriers, and even manipulate gravity. It did not come with an instruction manual, and I was always hesitant to practice with it lest I accidentally blow a hole in the *Melampus*.

"Yes, I have a sword," I said, dryly. "Yarr."

"Please stop," Danny said, shaking his head. "We can tell your heart isn't it."

"At least take precautions," Leah said. "Just in case any of these Rangers aren't as loyal to you as you are to them."

"We will," I said. "Get everyone ready to back us up if necessary."

Hannah nodded. "You have my communications frequency. If they jam it, come in guns blazing. I won't hold it against you if you kill too many."

Leah nodded. "Danny?"

"I'll get Forty-Two," Danny said. "Tell him to bring his ax and rifle."

Forty-Two was my chief of security and my closest friend, though we hadn't spoken about much in recent months. I got the impression he was the only one of my crew who wasn't getting restless with our current missions and that was because he'd come to view this as his retirement. Sorkanan lifespans went through several stages and without longevity drugs, which Forty-Two was allergic to, he was starting to enter his older years. He'd taken on a paternal role to Astrid, and I had the sneaking suspicion that he viewed us as the only family he was ever going to have. Maybe that was the reason I was starting to feel the universe becoming smaller around me. Like one of Tolkien's elves, I wasn't changing but everyone else was.

Now you know what it's like to be an AI, Trish said.

Hannah frowned. "It won't come to that. This meeting will go off perfectly. You can trust my friends."

"We're trusting *you*," I said, not trusting her former friends in the slightest. I was still pretty sure this was all a big con and people were willing to start wars over the kind of money involved.

"Good," Hannah said, looking down. "Now for the part you're not going to like."

"There's a part I'm supposed to like?" I asked, shaking my head.

Hannah shrugged and reached down to pick up one of the steam grates before lifting it up. "The meeting is down here. This is the entrance to the location, through the atmosphere- and moisture-processing vents."

"A meeting in the sewers," I said, looking over my shoulder. "Is this a prank? Are we being filmed for a truth-show? If so, I find it hilarious."

"Not every spy meeting can be in luxury casinos," Leah said. "Mind you, they should be."

"Sorry, Vance," Hannah said. "Some of my most profitable business meetings have been in the atmosphere sewers."

Atmosphere sewers were where large amounts of algae, fungus, and other growths were used to process the breathing material of most long-term stations like this. They also absorbed the run-off from the artificial rains that killed off bacterial and viral growths that popped up in places like this. Usually, they were connected to the recycling plants for waste as well, which meant they were as close to ground sewers as you were going to get. It was amazing how humanity had taken its filthiest and weirdest habits with them.

"So have many of mine," I said, thinking back to when I did work for Director G. "Because it's a good place to hide a body or three."

"Funny," Leah said.

"I'm not feeling very funny right now."

"Yep!" Trish said. "This deal is getting worse all the time. See, Vance, references! It's not so hard."

I looked to Leah. "Be sure to bring some big guns when we need you."

Leah nodded and gave me a thumbs up. "If they hurt either of you, I'll hunt them down to the farthest reaches of the galaxy."

"I also have an extensive knowledge of incurable diseases to infect them with. They'll spend a year screaming before they die if they turn out to be lying to us," Elektra added.

"I'll just, uh, shoot them," Danny said. "I'll also feel really bad about spending all of your money, Vance."

"That assumes you're in the will, Danny," I said, smirking.

Hannah frowned. "That's great, guys, really."

"I think so," Leah said, smiling.

I sighed. "Okay, let's head down into the sewer. It can't be worse than the rest of the interior."

CHAPTER TEN

Sewer Levels are the Worst

The interior of the atmosphere sewer was a spectacular example of what spacers called the "dungeon aesthetic." Specifically, it looked like the place had been constructed as a residential area only to be converted into a sewer when it was realized processing the asteroid's waste gases and other materials would take more space than expected.

The walls were covered in dayglow fungus that was a common genetically engineered goop found in virtually all ill-maintained space stations, shipyards, and other locations that didn't want to rely completely on their crew's competence. The stuff absorbed large amounts of several gases and produced a decent mix of nitrogen and oxygen. It also ate sewage, which made it doubly useful in a place as barely functional as the Ring. In short, it was an atmosphere sewer like any other.

While the fungus glowed as its name implied, the illumination it provided wasn't enough for my tastes and I lifted my proton sword to add a bit more. My sword was normally a cross-shaped object that fit in my hand, but the liquid metal could extend into a brilliant glowing blade that crackled with blue-white light. I was presently using it as a flashlight.

It didn't help that I wasn't exactly trained in swordsmanship, nor was I capable of finding someone who could teach me how to use a High Protector's blade. The High Protectors were an elite group of magistrates, secret agents, and political movers and shakers. I was the youngest and least experienced member thereof. Membership was usually given as a reward to someone after literally hundreds of years of service to the Community. In my case and that of the late Anne Bonny, we'd just lucked into saving the galaxy. Maybe that was part of the reason I wanted to find her treasure; I wanted to learn if she had any secret to solving my imposter syndrome other than "fake it until you make it."

Until then, I continued to pretend that I knew what I was doing.

"What an incredible smell you've discovered," I tried to get back into the spirit of things, watching a foot-long carrionpillar crawl across the wall beside us. The others were following us above with Elektra's handheld omni-scanner attuned to our biometrics, but I was still unhappy that we were travelling so deep into unknown territory. I was going to have to recycle these boots when I got back to the ship.

"This is a good spot for the Invisible Market to do its business," Hannah said.

I tried not to roll my eyes. "All of the Ring is a good place for the Invisible Market to do its business. This is more like a place you ambush someone."

"Do you really think I'm an idiot?" Hannah said, crossing her arms. "That I'd lead you into a trap? The one person other than John that I—"

"What?" I asked.

Hannah glared. "Would really miss if they died?"

Love was a very hard word for Hannah to use, perhaps because she came from a family even more dysfunctional than mine. And she was coming off a long-term relationship with two friends. If she made a pass—which I really hoped she wouldn't—I hoped it would be just because she was trying to look for comfort. I loved Hannah but no longer romantically. She'd always been my friend. Just, you know, my friend I'd had sex with.

She's always been in love with you, you idiot, Trish said. *We had this conversation before.*

I just don't feel that way for her, I thought back. *I'd die for her but I feel different for her than I did for Shelly and...*

And now Leah? Trish asked.

No, I said. *Leah knows how I feel about her.*

86

Leah and I had a very complex relationship, made complicated because she knew exactly how I felt about everything because of her telepathy, but I didn't know anything about her or her real feelings. In simple terms, after years of being together, I didn't trust her and never could. I was happy to play my role, though. I would do everything to protect her and Astrid, would marry her if she agreed, but it would never cross the distance that was presently between us. I would always believe, correctly or not, that she wanted to use me for her own ambitions. I hated that feeling. But it wasn't going away. Leah seemed okay with it. She'd once said I would be a fool to trust her fully.

Then who? Trish asked.

You know who, I replied.

I just wish you'd say it. Damn humans, Trish muttered, which was impressive since she was talking to me digitally.

"Do you miss John?" I asked, a little more jealous than I'd meant to sound. "Do you want to rejoin the Rangers?"

Hannah stared at me with a sideways glance. "Really, Vance? You're asking about my mooning over an ex-boyfriend? You, the guy who chased his Academy hookup that was spying on him for Captain Elgan? The woman who stole your DNA to make a child."

"I'm never going to live that down, am I?"

"No, no you are not," Hannah said. "Nor should you. I can't believe you're planning to marry her."

"I made a lot of choices for good reasons," I said.

"One reason," Trish said, aloud, having been walking alongside us the entire way without open commentary. "Astrid."

Both Hannah and I looked at her.

"Vance never really had a family," Trish said, looking at me. "So, he will do everything to preserve a semblance of one for her."

"Ouch," I muttered. "Way to lay me out there, Trish."

"It's better if we pretend that we're all being honest," Trish replied. "Hannah never had a biological family, but she's had two found ones. You're kind of like the brother she borks."

"Stop helping, Trish," Hannah said.

"Okey dokey!" Trish said. "One day I should tell you about how I have the memories of Alexandra Ares, who was raised by Director G and Keiko Springs the philanthropist-ninja! My Aunt Paradise owns the moon of Deimos."

"I know, Trish," I said, smirking. "Someday we'll have to meet your family for non-business reasons."

Business being spying, war, and statecraft.

Things I was sick of.

"You can trust me," Hannah said. "The Antaeus Rangers are an honorable brotherhood of soldiers dating back to the United Earth's Defense Force. It's hundreds of years old and a tradition that I was proud to be a part of despite not being from Earth."

I didn't want to bring up that if they were really such honorable Space Marines, Holy Knights of Terra, or whatever then they wouldn't be working for a guy working for (or conning) General Vast. I didn't know what happened to the Antaeus Rangers after the Kolahn War and the cancellation of their contract with the Community—the records I'd requested were surprisingly sparse—but they'd apparently fallen into disrepute.

The Rangers had volunteered to help the president of Deathworld in his battle against the Notha Union, something that had initially been viewed as a noble crusade of "Good Notha" versus "Evil Notha." I certainly supported Deathworld's president and his attempt to maintain his world's independence. The Human League, however, had accepted many credits from the Union to elect many EarthGov politicians that believed the war wasn't any of our business. As a result, aid had been delayed and restricted to the point that the initial wins of Deathworld had only bought them time versus victory. I suspected that the Antaeus Rangers had suffered casualties in that conflict that had severely depleted their operational strength. Probably their budget as well.

"I *do* trust you, Hannah. Sweet Buddha-Christ, what do I have to do to prove it? I *want* this deal to work," I said. "Even if there's no *Mary Read*, they're getting paid an extremely generous amount of money."

I picked up the smell of rotting meat and noticed a large pile of skeletons covered in dayglow fungus with a few fresh bodies on the top. Apparently, this was a common dumping ground for people who didn't want to pay the FLACS the fee to ignore their murders.

"Right," I said, dryly. "Nothing suspicious here."

If this wasn't a trap, the Rangers were going to an awful lot of trouble to make it look like one.

"Okay, I know this looks bad," Hannah said, keeping her gun aimed ahead of her despite the fact it undermined her words.

"Just a little," I said, perhaps sharper than I intended. I was usually better at hiding my real feelings. The past decade had done a number on my once limitless idealism. There was only so much snark and grousing you could be around before it started to rub off on you. "Friendship is trusting someone to borrow your transport. Love is when you follow someone into a sewer with minimum backup because you will always have their back. You are family, Hannah, no matter what happens."

"Family," Trish said in an artificially gruff and deep voice. "I'd make a Dom Toretto joke, but neither of you have any idea who that is."

I didn't.

"That's a definition of love and family I can get behind," Hannah said. "But there's another reason we should deal with these guys on their terms, part of why the negotiation has taken so long."

"Which is?"

"I want to recruit them," Hannah said. "Like Leah said."

I blinked. "That's a bad idea."

"We need more security. They're solid. More solid than anyone on the *Melampus*."

I had a feeling that another shoe was about to drop. I'd been wondering why the negotiations had taken so long, most mercenaries would have jumped at the kind of money we'd offered, but it hadn't occurred to me they'd been talking about something other than arranging a simple business transaction. I should have seen it coming. It was exactly the sort of thing that I had a history of doing whenever I was given an assignment—hence why I'd spent much of my time here trying to set up Non-Government Organization (NGO) charities and anti-slaving operations. Idle hands were the Devil's workshop, and my hands were never idle. Of course, that attitude would rub off on my crew.

"The *Melampus* has a full security complement already," I said, pausing. "We don't need a regiment of mercenaries."

"It's not a regiment… anymore," Hannah said, her voice trailing off.

"How many are left?" I asked, realizing what she'd been alluding to, but I hadn't bothered to put into perspective.

"Two squads," Hannah said, letting the numbers speak for themselves. "Ten men each."

I stared at her. "The rest have all been killed?"

Hannah looked away. "Not necessarily killed. Others deserted, many were captured and are rotting in some Notha prison, but most? Yeah, most of them were killed fighting against the Notha Union and their mercenaries. They inflicted twenty-to-one casualties. Which are just the numbers the Notha Union admitted to. The actual damage was probably ten times that. Twenty-to-one casualties that did absolutely nothing to win the war in the long run."

"I'm sorry," I said, shaking my head.

"You could order the Community to give more aid," Hannah said. "Tell EarthGov that it is their duty to provide Deathworld with as much military ordnance as needed to crush the Union forces—which are just a bunch of conscripts anyway. You owe the president that much."

I closed my eyes. "Yeah, maybe I do."

"But that's not what I want you to do," Hannah said, "I want you to give the Antaeus Rangers a place with us because they deserve better. They aren't going to recover from this. Their reputation is already ruined from breaking their contract and defending Arden—who is every bit the con man you think he is—but they deserve better."

"Do they even want to become part of the Community Protectors again?" I asked.

"No," Hannah said. "John thinks you're some kind of nepo-baby."

"I think I can figure out the context and word root," I said, sighing. "When everything else is lost, pride is sometimes all we have left."

"I hope you corrected him," Trish said, looking surprisingly plizzed off at the description. "Vance has earned his rank through countless acts of valor. He's an honest to Goddess Hero of SPAAACE. Hell, he's the savior of the universe. King of the impossible. Ahhhh."

"You keep singing that song and it never gets less weird," I said, shaking my head. "But John's description is true. I did get most of my help from my Aunt Kathy's connections on top of the wealth I'd inherited. I tried to live up to my family's reputation but the very fact I had one to live up to give me advantages that I wouldn't have otherwise possessed."

"Yeah, well everyone has a story," Hannah said. "Some people are born to wealth and power then use it to abuse others. Some people are born with nothing and use it to abuse others. John is also being an idiot because he inherited a goddamn army."

And lost it.

I could imagine how that would weigh on him. I lowered my sword. "So, is this whole journey a waste of time?"

It was weird questioning it now, but we were attempting to find a mad warlord by chasing down pirate treasure on a ghost ship. It was a pretty big reach even from my often bizarre adventures.

"Only if you think that saving my friends is," Hannah said. "They don't believe the information that Arden has will go anywhere but they have it. It's not just a scam. John wants to save his people and get enough money to retire. He's deluding himself that the Rangers can be rebuilt. But you can give him an out if you're willing."

"Will he accept it?" I asked. "Even if I did offer him sanctuary?"

"Some wounds are on the outside, others on the inside," Hannah said. "He's willing to have the meeting."

I knew that well. I realized she was trying to get me off subject. "So, what's the deal with the Antaeus Rangers? You describe them like Don Quixote."

"They are. Daring idealists and heroes," Hannah said. "Or they were until they had that idealism crushed. Now they're just survivors. Like everybody else."

"You know that book was about how idealism was stupid, right?" I asked, giving a pained smile. "I tried explaining that to Leah."

"Says the space knight," Hannah said.

"Which I know is bullsavit."

91

"They were my family, Vance. More than the one I was born with. Not as much as the one on the *Melampus*. I can't be a homemaker, a mother, or a wife, but I can be a friend on the battlefield."

I sucked in my breath. "Alright, I believe you."

"Thank you," Hannah said.

"So, what's the catch?" I asked, realizing what was going on.

"What?" Hannah asked.

I stared at them. "They don't want to join the *Melampus* crew, and you just told me this deal was a lie. So, what do they want."

"I don't know what they want," Hannah admitted. "I just promised you'd hear them out."

I stared. "That's not ominous."

"I'm a good security officer," Hannah said. "I'm not going to put you in danger."

"Then you've failed miserably. In fact, I may have to promote you," I said. "Do you want to be captain?"

Trish hissed. "I am not answering to her. That's almost as bad as Leah."

"Bork no," Hannah said. "I barely want to be first mate. Also, I am way better than Leah."

"True," Trish admitted. "We should name Forty-Two captain before he goes senile."

Hannah grimaced.

"Too soon," Trish said. "Right."

"I'll find a new place for myself after this," Hannah said. "I just haven't found it yet."

"Maybe you should try living a normal life," I said. "Give it a try."

I wasn't trying to get her to stick with Danny and Elektra or maybe just one of them. I was, however, trying to get her to give the concept of a permanent stable life somewhere with someone a chance. Maybe it would be on the *Melampus*. Maybe not. I'd kept her by my side far too long.

"Normal was never an option," Hannah said, uncomfortable. "And the Community Protectorate may not be that bad but it's sure as hell not that good either."

Hannah glared at me and started walking around a nearby corner. "Anyway, we're here."

"Here? I don't see any mercs."

"Maybe we're early."

"Maybe things are about to sideways."

"How many metaphors for disaster do you have? Pear-shaped? Sideways?"

"Given I'm an ex-pilot? Thousands. I also am going to state, unequivocally, that I have a bad feeling about this."

Hannah felt her face. "Great, now you've jinxed us."

"Have I? Because—"

That was when there was a loud hissing sound behind us. Turning around, I found myself faced with an enormous, eight-foot-long, black, metal-plated kriegermonster at the end of the tunnel. Genetically and cybernetically engineered killing machines, kriegermonsters were expensive playthings of the sadistic and rich.

This one took the form of a brawler-model that looked like it could tear a hovertank in half. Its face—if you could call it that—had a human-like hideous intelligence that was expressed in its smooth, calculated movements rather than its eyeless features.

The kriegermonster was roughly humanoid but moved like a spider, on all its eight appendages, and possessed a long, prehensile tail with a spike at the end. The fusion of technology, bioengineering, and a dozen races had produced something truly hideous but also breathtaking in its lethality. Kriegermonsters were used for only one thing: killing and they did so with deadly efficiency.

"Ah, hell," Hannah said, lifting her rifle. "I hate it when you're right."

CHAPTER ELEVEN

Get Away from Her, You Bitch!

It said everything you needed to know about Hannah that when confronted with a monster fully capable of tearing up a unit of armored soldiers, she immediately raised her plasma rifle and repeatedly fired. It said even more that when the blasts washed across its form like raindrops, she dropped it and pulled out a proton knife before charging.

"No, Hannah! No!" I shouted, trying to work out a plan of attack in my head against the thing only to have my mind go blank with the threat against the woman I loved.

"This isn't right!" Trish said, staring while looking confused.

The kriegermonster, walking with an ungainly gait like a holo-monster, smashed Hannah across the face and sent her flying backward. Hannah had a strange sort of movement as I saw her get struck in the chest and fall back on the ground but it, honestly, looked like she was deliberately doing so versus being knocked down.

Hannah didn't hesitate to grab at her pistol rather than the rifle on the ground and aimed, shooting at its eyes, which only seemed to flicker for a moment. Then I saw it develop wounds, the creature howling in pain. Don't ask me why she didn't go for her pistol after her rifle instead of her knife first. Maybe she just thought it would work better after the latter's failure.

"Get back, Vance! I'll handle it!"

I lifted my sword and charged, wondering if I was the foolish one. The kriegermonster raised its fist and blocked my blow, which felt

94

more like I was suddenly stopping my swing in midair rather than striking someone. Then it hit me across the face with the strongest force I could remember. My nose started bleeding but didn't feel broken, even as it should have taken my head clean off.

There was something very wrong here. I turned to Trish, who was looking as if she was trying to stare through it.

"Vance, get out of the way!" Hannah howled, sounding like she was about to enter a battle frenzy.

I reluctantly moved out of the way, only for her to unleash another trio of blasts into the creature. I felt a fog passing over my vision, so I concentrated past the kriegermonster and heard the distant sound of energy blasts striking against the wall behind the creature. To my regular vision, I saw it was just absorbing the attacks once more. The kriegermonster then advanced on Hannah before she assumed a fighting stance, ready to throw down with a creature twice her size.

I took a big risk. "It's not real, Hannah."

"What?" Hannah said, ducking under its next swing then punching under its arms and hitting it like a boxer.

"I don't know how!" I shouted, staring at her. "It just isn't."

"It's not a hologram!" Hannah shouted, striking it again and again. "I can feel it! I can also smell it!"

"No, Vance is right!" Trish said. "It's some kind of projection. It's affecting the brain of this body, but I can't detect it through its cybernetic sensors!"

"Only one way to find out!" I closed my eyes then charged at the creature and Hannah, hurling myself forward. If I was wrong, this was going to be a short fight. I passed through the spot where the creature should have been and landed on top of Hannah.

I opened my eyes. The kriegermonster was no longer present and Hannah was under me. Hannah looked up at me with a raised eyebrow. "You know, I really hate it when you're right."

"You'd think you'd be used to it by now," I said, staring at her then back at the empty space where the kriegermonster had been,

"Ha-ha," Hannah said, staring up at me then over at Trish. "What the hell was that thing?"

"I think it was a biomod projection into our minds," Trish said. "A psychic illusion, basically."

"Psychic powers don't exist," I replied, neglecting that biomods could do just about everything traditionally ascribed to the pseudoscience.

"I know, Vance, but they might as well with some of the strange mods out there," Trish said, crossing her arms in a "what kind of fool do you take me for" sort of way. "I'm using laymen's terms."

Hannah wasn't looking at me, though. "They're here."

"What?" I asked.

"Our contacts," Hannah said, looking around with the same expression I'd worn during our brief encounter with the kriegermonster. "Show yourselves!"

There was no answer. I briefly wondered if Hannah was wrong before I felt a pressure on my mind release. Then, as if by magic, I saw the appearance of a dozen armored soldiers in power JILL-10 power armor. It was blockier and less expensive armor than Hannah's JOTUN-20 power armor but almost as effective. They had broad shoulders and heavy metal coverings that made them look like walking tanks. Their helmets were domes that had retractable coverings, stylized with a human skull painting on the front and the name "Antaeus Rangers" in the Arabic alphabet.

Our contacts.

"Do you think that was a test or a prank?" I asked.

"Either way, your friends are real anyxholes, Hannah," Trish said.

Hannah looked plizzed. "I'm inclined to agree."

They weren't alone, though, and I saw familiar faces. One I had expected to be here, but the others caused me to blink several times to make sure I wasn't seeing things. Winston Arden was present, wearing a pair of overalls with a personal shield belt, and a heavy fusion rifle on his back. A pair of safety goggles rested on the top of his head. He was not the kind of man who looked like he'd been living the high life with millions of stolen credits from a warlord. He hadn't looked like he'd appreciably aged but was still an old man who should have been doing anything other than tromping through the sewers with a bunch of mercenaries.

The second was a female Chel, a bio-modded, human-descended offshoot race that had immense abilities as well as access to Elder Race technology. They basically looked like tall, thin, willowy albinos that had long necks and strangely proportioned heads with unusually large eyes. This Chel had been part of the diplomatic party which had tried to get me to stop the Primordial Invasion with Director G, though we hadn't talked during our encounter. She was wearing a set of loose-fitting robes that were stunningly designed and reminded me that the race had a tremendous sense of artistry.

The Chel's relationship with the rest of the galaxy had completely collapsed after the Primordial Invasion was thwarted and the Community attempted to cover up how close they'd come to galactic annihilation. The relationship had gotten even worse after a team of "rogue" EarthGov soldiers had attempted to steal Elder Race technology from them in a battle that had resulted in dozens—if not hundreds—of deaths. Which was especially egregious because the Chel knew the Elder Races destroyed anyone who tampered with their technology and both were immortal unless they died through accident or violence.

The Chel had completely sealed their borders upon pain of death. They'd promptly destroyed every single ship that had attempted to make contact since then, including Community vessels. This had almost started a war that might have ended poorly for my employers. A few brave spacers were also made an example of as they'd been tortured into insanity and returned with the simple message, LEAVE US ALONE. I personally thought the whole thing was a tragedy and probably related to Department Twelve.

The third and final surprise was seeing the High Priestess, or someone who looked damn near identical to her since the Notha had died in my arms. Notha were little four-foot-tall squirrel-and-Ewok-looking things that shouldn't have been one of the most dangerous races ins the galaxy but had been shaped by their emperor into a bunch of racist, authoritarian conquerors. I'd gotten to know them better than most and hoped that after killing their emperor, they might become a better people.

Instead, they'd rallied behind a new dictator, the Notha Prime this time, and it was just the same old savit in a different toilet. While you might argue that it was hard for aliens to tell each other apart, I knew enough to see she had the same facial and fur patterns as the late High Priestess. She was dressed in a decorative dress suit with hood that was what passed for formal wear among them. It was like seeing a ghost.

"Just what the hell is going on around here?" I snapped, not at all impressed with the way they'd chosen to handle the meeting or that they'd come loaded for bear.

"Yeah," Hannah said, growling. "We've agreed to all of your terms, and this is how you treat us?"

"I mean, cool special effect, though," Trish said, smiling. "I've rarely gotten to see Chel mind manipulation in action."

"It didn't last nearly as long as I expected," the Chel woman said, her accent deep and melodic. "The results were… disappointing."

"Any advantage in combat is one worth exploiting," the Notha woman said. "We could have killed the Great Vance Turbo in the distraction."

"Assassinating a man during a flag of truce is usually considered bad form," I said, looking down at her. "And you are?"

The Notha woman glared up at me with venom in her dark little eyes. "The sister of the woman you murdered, Vance Turbo."

The Notha hissed and approached with teeth bared and claws at the ready.

Oh yeah, this was going great already.

"Try it, furball!" Hannah hissed, raising her rifle to shoot the Notha. I pushed her gun down. "No."

"What?" Hannah asked, looking over at me with hate in her eyes. "Is she a friend of yours or something?"

"Hi, Captain," Winston said, waving like we were on shore leave.

"Are you responsible for what we saw?" Hannah asked, her voice taking an interrogator-like tone. "Speak."

The Chel had conjured the illusion but this was more personal. She wanted to know about one person, in particular, and it wasn't hard to guess who.

That was when the domed helmet of one of the armored soldiers popped open and I saw the face of Colonel John Mason underneath. John was a scruffy-looking, brown-haired man with a short beard and bronze skin. There were several scars on his face and signs of badly done face-sculpting on the right side from where he'd probably taken a fusion bolt through the side of his cheek. Still, he was a handsome man for those who liked individuals who had seen an honest day's work and more than their share of combat.

"Calm down, Sergeant," John said, raising his hands. "The Diplomat is one of us."

"I'm a commander now and have been for a while, *Colonel*. She may be one of *you*, but there is no *us*," Hannah said, her voice low and accusatory. "Not for a long time."

"It was just a prank, Han," John said, using a diminutive. "A way to see how the gaudy uniform type reacted under pressure."

"Is he talking about me?" I asked Trish.

"I do believe he is, sir," Trish said, absently.

John had badly miscalculated just how to run this introduction. It seemed that there were a lot colder feelings on Hannah's side than she had let on. Either that or they'd sent an illusionary monster *to scare the hell out of us* was a good enough reason to stop defending her ex-associates.

However, I honestly wasn't concerned about that right now. Instead, my focus was on the Diplomat. The discovery that the High Priestess had a sister, identical or not, shouldn't have surprised me. Notha tended to be born in large groups. But I was now confronted with the fact that I'd failed the High Priestess and her father. After she'd given her life to save my daughter's, I should have devoted every bit of time and power at my command to make sure Deathworld was liberated. Instead, I'd hidden away in the frontier of the galaxy to wallow in my guilt. Everyone had seen it except me.

Yeah, we kind of did, Trish said. *To be fair, you were probably also hiding because you found out your parents—the people who you were desperately trying to prove you were nothing like—were actually not only alive but former spies.*

99

"Your sister died for my family," I said, ignoring John's jibes and returning my focus entirely to the Diplomat.

"Yeah, she was always doing stupid things like that," the Diplomat said, softening her voice ever so slightly.

Winston attempted to interject himself into the conversation. "Now, Captain, I know you're probably wondering how one of your closest and dearest friends from your war days ended up in this rough and tumble band of mercenaries."

"Not in the slightest," I said.

"Well, it's a long and complicated story," Winston said, almost apologetically. "One that I'm sure you'll agree justifies every decision I've made so far. Speaking of which, I saw your movie and—"

"I really don't care," I interrupted, more interested in literally everyone else here.

John gave a charming smile and stretched out his big metal arms. "Come on, Han, once a Ranger, always a Ranger."

"Don't you 'Han' me. Does being a Ranger involve trying to kill us?" Hannah said, interrupting his attempt to appeal to her dignity.

"We didn't try to kill you," John said, annoyed. "It was a test."

"That they passed," the Chel woman said. "Which seems to annoy you, Colonel."

"I mean, I would have been happy if they'd accidentally killed each other," the Diplomat added.

John frowned.

"Yeah, this meeting is off to a great start," Trish muttered. "I wish I had some popcorn."

"Also, how the hell did you do that?" Hannah asked, waving her hand in the air.

"Our Chel associate, Nyssa, is psychic," Winston said, gesturing the woman beside him. "It's okay, Captain, I can admit it now."

"Chel powers are not psychic powers," Hannah said. "They're a technology we don't understand yet."

"Topato, pomato," Winston said, shrugging. "She can do weird stuff with her mind."

"A gift from the Elder Races," Nyssa said.

100

"That doesn't improve my opinion," Hannah said. "The Elder Races are bastards."

"Who isn't?" Winston asked, chuckling. "That we know at least."

Hannah stepped in front of me, furious. "What the bork was that about, John?"

"Yes, let's begin with the giant monster you attacked us with," I said, looking at him. "The one that didn't actually exist."

I was still wrapping my head around that. It had been so real. Not only had I seen it, which could be accomplished with holographic projectors, but I'd felt it, and it had substance. Hell, I remembered smelling it even if I hadn't been able to pick up much more than the barest trace of combat oil and blood secretions through the sewer's odor. It had been as real a kriegermonster as I'd ever encountered with some minor flaws. I'd sadly encountered a few as the pets of various crime bosses and warlords over the years.

Yet, the kriegermonster had been purely a product of our minds put into our heads by someone else. It was, potentially, the ultimate weapon of war. Was it not Sun Tzu who said that war was the art of deception? This could be a gamechanger if it could affect more than a few people at a time. Yeah, illusions were the ultimate weapon. Which was the tagline of the MASK reboot I'd watched as a child. It was amazing that had been the Eighties cartoon to stand the test of time.

John raised his hands in a surrender gesture. "Believe me, I didn't want anything to do with it. It's all on Nyssa."

I didn't believe him in the slightest, especially since he'd already said it was a prank and test. It also didn't reflect well upon him as a commander if he was willing to blame his subordinates for things going wrong.

"I admit, it *was* on me." Nyssa shrugged and gave a disarming, inhuman smile. "I needed to see if you were worthy. Most of my associates have very mixed feelings on you, Vance Turbo."

"Worthy of what?" I asked.

"Anne Bonny's treasure."

CHAPTER TWELVE

It Turns Out We Know Where the Treasure Is

"I'm not here for Anne Bonny's treasure," I said, suddenly drawn back to reality.

"Then what are you here for?" John asked, skeptically. "Because *we're* here to talk about Anne Bonny's treasure."

From the expressions of Lieutenant Arden, Nyssa, and the Diplomat, I could tell that not everyone here was entirely on board with their leader's attitude. I had the impression he'd been dragged here effectively kicking and screaming. He didn't want to meet with me and was looking for any excuse to end this encounter.

I stared at them. "Let's just say the Community is extremely skeptical of *Doctor* Arden's credentials."

"Captain!" Winston said, appalled.

"I'm not here because I believe you can find a legendary pirate ship full of buried treasure like Captain Flint hid in *Treasure Island*," I said, finally using an actual literary reference.

"Technically, it's not buried since it's in the ship's hold," Trish corrected.

"Not the time, Trish," I said. "No, I'm here for another reason."

"I knew it," John hissed. "If you think we're going to let us arrest us—"

"Arrest you?" I interrupted, not wanting to play into whatever rogue military unit fantasy he was presently constructing for himself. "No, you idiot, I'm here to get your information on Grand General Vast. I'm going to kill him."

"Terminate with extreme prejudice," Trish said, adopting another gruff voice. "1979's *Apocalypse Now* was based on the Joseph Conrad novel *Heart of Darkness*. Except Heart of Darkness was about British colonialism rather than the Vietnam War. Also, it was all about how colonialism hurt the British. Which, uh, yeah, isn't really the best way to look at it."

"Does she always talk this much?" John asked, looking at her.

"Her brain is the size of a planet so yes," I replied.

"So, the Community has taken to using its golden boy as an assassin—" John started to say.

"Is this where you go into some elaborate speech about why the Community is corrupt, I'm some sort of overpromoted snobby elitist, and your group is some heroic band of plucky rebels betrayed by the system?" I asked, interrupting.

John narrowed his eyes.

"I hate the man, but he's got your number, Colonel," the Diplomat said, looking up at him.

John visibly deflated, clearly not expecting this conversation to have gone the way it had. "We're leaving, we're under here under false pretenses. The deal is off."

"Yes, because you clearly planned to deal in good faith," I said, sarcastically. "Grand General Vast is going to be here in less than a week. We had a month until his arrival, but someone was determined to give us the runaround. They're going to capture Lieutenant Arden—"

"*Doctor*," Winston corrected. "My degree in piratology is from the University of Asteroid LL72B-Y."

"Uh huh," I said, not even bothering to comment on that. "They're going to capture *Doctor* Arden, torture him, and probably execute him, along with any people that try to protect him. That is unless you have somehow managed to find the *Mary Read*."

"Except, we did," Winston said.

I blinked. "You... did?"

"Yes!" Winston said, clapping his hands together. "We really did!"

"You've found the missing treasure of an Irish space pirate from the 1700s," I said. "One abducted by aliens."

103

Winston brightened up at the chance to lecture. "Actually, neither Anne nor Bonny were common Irish names in that time period. She's far more likely to have been English than Irish, but we don't have any records of her that say where she came from before moving to Nassau. There was an early book on pirates that claimed she was Irish, *A General History of the Pyrates* by Charles Johnson, but that author is known to have made up details to fill in the complete lack of historical record available. Also, the people who abducted her were human."

"Winston..." I trailed off.

"Really, for centuries her fate was unknown and the subject of much speculation. Jack Rackham, Mary Read, and she were probably in a polyamorous relationship, with Mary Read impersonating a man and Anne Bonny serving as Jack's mistress. Jack Rackham was the man who came up with the Jolly Roger design you know. Mary and Anne became lovers then, only for Jack to discover them and be intrigued rather than offended—"

"Typical man," Hannah said.

"—and then they became notorious pirates. Sort of. Anne's pirate career started in August of 1720... and ended in November of the same year. So, she was never really a hugely successful pirate, but her legend greatly eclipsed her deeds. Even before we knew she escaped into space. Eventually, privateer Johnathan Barnet assaulted Rackham's crew while they were drunk with only Anne and Mary putting up any resistance."

"I really don't have time for a biography," I said, already knowing most of this.

"We know Mary Read died in prison, but there's no record of Anne Bonny being executed. We do have the execution records of that period, so if she was executed—as she was sentenced to be—we should have that record. We have no idea what happened to her. So, clearly, kidnapped by aliens was just an entirely rational option. Though, Bonny was famously pregnant while in prison—both she and Mary claimed to be, and it was possibly true—to avoid execution. Which brings us to you."

"What?" I asked.

"Yes, what?" Hannah asked.

"He goes on like this all the time," John said, sounding apologetic for the first time during our conversation. "Just ignore him. Well, not about finding the treasure. That, much to my surprise, is true."

"You are the direct descendant of Anne Bonny!" Winston proclaimed. "It is your destiny to reclaim her legacy."

I didn't even react. "Right."

"Is your ancestry so filled with heroes and villains that you have no reaction to another one?" John asked.

I stared at him. "My father was a con man, and my mother is a crime lord. As for Anne Bonny being my ancestor, no offense, but I'd need a bit more reputable source than the guy who has spent the past few years ripping off a warlord with stories of the *Flying Dutchman*."

"After all we went through, Captain!" Winston said. "This is the key to you claiming the inheritance of the first human High Protector!"

"Forget it, he doesn't care," John said. "He's just another dog of the military who bought his way—"

"Okay, that's enough!" Hannah said, interrupting. "You have insulted my friend since we started this. Scared the hell out of us too. I am sick of it! I spent the past hour trying to convince Vance you're a man of honor, John, and so far, you've plizzed all of that away in a petty *da'vash* measuring contest! What the hell is wrong with you?"

"It wasn't my idea to do the illusion!" John said, snapping. "Also, how can you have chosen them over us? We needed you, Hannah, everything fell apart after you left! All because you chased after golden boy here who—"

"Okay, if you want to throw down, *Colonel*, I'm happy to do so," I said, pointing my sword at him. "I'll keep the sword, you keep the power armor. Next, drop the poor, tired, working-class hero act. You have five generations of being rich as bork military contractors in your background. You don't field a private army by being poor. You also never served in the *actual* military like your ancestors. The only reason I'm here is because I asked Hannah to make a deal because I thought you were a professional. Instead, it looks like I should have just gotten a team together to get Winston and use him as bait for the war criminal I'm hunting."

"They'd never have gotten him," John said, growling.

"You don't know my people," I said, my eyes cold and merciless.

"I've been in the darkness and mud," John said. "I don't hide on the bridge of a starship."

"And there are borking graveyards of murderers with guns who thought they could take me or my people," I said, clenching my teeth. "Want to see if the universe becomes a better place with just a few more?'

"Okay!" Trish said, stepping in-between us with both arms extended. "This is clearly escalating way more than it should."

"I like it," the Diplomat said, belying her name. "I'm starting to see what my sister saw in him."

"Colonel Mason was telling the truth," Nyssa said. "I was the person who sent the kriegermonster. We had to check to see if you could see through the illusions I conjured. Captain Bonny's ship will be protected by many Elder Race devices that are known to drive men mad and to kill one another. That you are one of their operatives won't necessarily protect you. The fact you are Anne Bonny's descendant might. Either way, it is imperative you be the one to recover the treasure rather than Captain Vast."

I decided to take a risk and lowered my sword. "So, what you're telling me is that Lieutenant Winston Arden here, Doctor of Piratology—"

"It's a real field of study," Winston insisted.

"Uh huh."

"It's the study of pirates!" Winston added.

I closed my eyes and fought off a headache. "—has found the *Mary Read*."

"We've discovered the pattern to its jumps," Winston said. "We also developed a way to track it through jumpspace. We know where it is, where it will be, and a general knowledge of the defenses that Captain Bonny installed upon it."

"And how is that?" I asked, skeptically.

"The Chel race contacted Doctor Arden and told him everything about the *Mary Read*," Nyssa said, pausing. "Our people constructed the vessel for the Community in the first place and allowed it to be wielded against the Crystal Spider Empire. We also made it known to the Community through our back channels with the Ethereals that we wanted you to be the one to find it. We have broken all ties with the Community and EarthGov, but we know that you are a man of honor through your role in stopping the Primordials. You and a handful of others. This was meant to be our show of thanks to you. A way of honoring two of the humans we respect, you and the previous High Protector."

I stared at them, then Winston. "Then why contact *him*?"

Winston looked embarrassed.

John looked disgusted.

"We do not want the rest of the Community preempting the discovery of the *Mary Read*," Nyssa explained, "let alone EarthGov. Department Twelve has infiltrated both thoroughly, at last in matters relating to humanity. Forces are moving behind the scenes to separate humanity from the Community so the former can be used as a group to experiment with forbidden Elder Race technology. Their Community allies believe that if the Elder Races become angered they will only punish humanity. Department Twelve thinks it is possible to gain enough technological knowledge from their studies to be able to force the rest of the galaxy to back away."

"I'd say that's insane, but we already know that," I said, sighing. "While it also explains a lot, it doesn't explain why the Chel want me to find the vessel in the first place. Also, why you would choose Winston as a middleman."

"Well, they clearly knew about our long and storied history—" Winston started to say.

"We didn't," John said, sighing. "Despite the fact my group has several connections to yours, it was our patron who decided it would be best to work with Winston on this. This despite our past friendship should have meant choosing a less circuitous route to test your resolve. Right, Hannah?"

"Am I a friend?" Hannah asked. "Friends don't do what you did to me."

"I'm sorry, *Commander*," John said. "I was angry, jealous, and not thinking clearly. It's been a rough road with the Deathworld War. I got arrogant during the last months of our involvement. We'd inflicted severe casualties on some of the Notha Union's best troops and got a chance to strike back in what I thought might have brought the war close to its end. There was a supposed coup attempt being plotted against the Notha Prime from the head of the Mercenary Guild."

I'd heard about that on the news. The Mercenary Lord had come within measurable distance of overthrowing the Notha Prime, but he'd backed down at the last minute. The Notha Prime had promised to pardon him and all his lieutenants before shooting their transport down over Deathworld with all hands-on board. Business had returned to usual.

That was another source of guilt I'd have to deal with. While I didn't remotely think I should preempt EarthGov's policies regarding Deathworld, I could have done more. More to fight against the Human League, more to make sure Admiral Bendo was forced into retirement and lost his immense influence over Space Fleet policies. There were a thousand "could haves" and "should haves" that were even now staring me in the face. Maybe if I'd been closer to Earth then Aunt Kathy might still be alive, though that was just me trying to make sense of her death. Accidents happened, even to heroes.

Instead, what had brought me out of exile—which was how I was starting to view my exploration mission, voluntary or not—was the opportunity to kill Vast. It didn't speak well of my moral character that it had been an opportunity to murder a man that had shaken me from my fugue. Maybe there was a beast beneath all my pretensions of being a civilized man and I was more Khan than Kirk.

That I wasn't sure about murdering Vast also brought me up short. Not because I didn't think he deserved to die and not because I hadn't killed tens of thousands of people already. There was no real difference between blowing up a starship with fusion cannons versus up close with laser rifles. Dead was dead. No, it was because I took my daughter's prophecy seriously. She had been modified by the Elder Races to see the future. Bad things would happen if I killed Vast. What sort of bad things? Also, what role did Anne Bonny's apparently very real treasure and ghost ship play in all this?

"You were betrayed," I said, calmly.

"Yes. We were exposed and behind enemy lines when I realized how borked we were," John said, shaking his head. "The Community was supposed to provide aid but had been caught up with political infighting back home. We didn't have the right sensors to protect us and the usually inaccurate Notha orbital cannons got close enough. We suffered seven hundred casualties in the first few minutes and only an evacuation by our employer saved everyone else who was left."

"My father remembered his friends," the Diplomat said. "But it was the Ranger's patron that got them to less strenuous work."

"Less strenuous," John said, mocking the description. "Guarding Winston Arden as he empties as much money from Grand General Vast's accounts as possible. To prevent him from using it to buy more bombs or hire more troops. We were never expected to find anything."

"I wouldn't say that..." Winston muttered, trailing off.

"Then I get the call from Nyssa here that we're supposed to help you find the *Mary Read*," John said, less than impressed. "That we were to just wait here as the information slowly fed back to the Community and EarthGov before you arrange a meeting. Except when you did arrange the meeting, it was with none of the code words or pass phrases you were supposed to use. What took you so long?"

I was now very confused. "Bendo didn't mention any of this."

"Bendo?" Winston asked, confused. "What the hell does Bendo have anything to do with this?"

"Who is your patron?" I asked.

"Director G."

I had a bad feeling about this. "Case wasn't the man who sent me."

CHAPTER THIRTEEN

Fighting Against One Another

"Well... savit," I muttered.

That was not a good sign.

Why would Admiral Bendo try to help carry out Director G's plan? Trish asked me via our cyberlink. *They hate each other.*

This is a trap, I replied. *I'm just not sure whether it's a trap meant to kill me or discredit me.*

Why would he want to discredit you? Trish asked. *You're already living in voluntary exile.*

It was annoying when you got zinged with your own thoughts. I'd been thinking about that just a few minutes earlier. *Bendo hates me because I've always supported a wider set of ties with the Community. Maybe he was also jealous of my rise. Maybe it was about his son's death even though he had been the one who sent Julius to spy on me. Maybe—*

Maybe he's just an anyxhole, Trish interrupted. *I'm still not sure what he thinks he could accomplish by saying you're off trying to find pirate treasure. Given the way your legend has spread, i.e. through holovision, you going after One-Eyed Willy's treasure will just make you even more popular.*

I'm not familiar with that one, I said, painfully aware everyone was staring at me as I thought this one through.

The Goonies. *It's got gangsters, hobbits, and Cyndi Lauper in it,* Trish said. *Is he just going to tell General Vast where you are and hopes he kills you?*

I was deeply uncomfortable with the idea that was probably the most logical course of action now that I knew Admiral Bendo had somehow intercepted Director G's plan. I could almost believe he wanted me to kill General Vast, but he wouldn't have been using the spymaster's plan unless he had something unpleasant in mind for me.

It was a hard thing to realize someone on your side wanted to kill you. It had been hard enough to deal with the fact that Captain Elgan had been willing to use me as cannon fodder, but now the head of EarthGov's military wanted me gone. I should have seen it coming. Hell, I had plenty of evidence that it was in the works, but I'd shoved that idea down because I didn't want to believe it. Once the truth became unshovable, I knew exactly what was blindingly obvious from the beginning to anyone seeing clearly: Admiral Bendo was Department Twelve or at least aligned with it.

Department Twelve seemed to haunt my every step, even more than groups like Dark Matter and the Emperor's followers. People who believed that humanity was destined for more and resented that we weren't rulers of the universe by right. It had been their stupidity that had launched the SKAMMs against the Notha and gotten billions of people killed in retaliation. Everyone seemed to sympathize with their goals, even Case had been willing to work with some of their people, but it was all just based on stupid xenophobia and nationalist pride.

Earth for Earthers.

But it was my daughter that plizzed me off the most. Astrid was the product of Department Twelve science, an attempt to genetically combine my Elder Race-altered body and Shelly's Ethereal heritage. It was a gross and horrifying violation, but the worst part was knowing that she'd just been one experiment subject of potentially thousands who they'd terminated when their cloning facilities on Crius had been compromised.

I had issues regarding family, as Trish had so eloquently stated. I wasn't the simple byproduct of my Aunt Kathy not hugging me enough as a child or other psychobabble, but the betrayal by the people who were supposed to be there for me—by which I mean my parents— meant that I wanted to be there for my children in a way they hadn't. I'd never forgive Department Twelve for using my DNA to create a child they'd never intended to love or care for but use as just another tool to unlock the secrets of the Elder Races.

111

Your father said that Bendo and High Protector B'Vash were part of Department Twelve, Trish observed.

Yeah, which is part of the reason why I doubted they were until now, I thought back. *Jack Tagashi is a pathological liar.*

But was he wrong? Trish asked.

He wasn't.

"Are you alright, *Captain* Turbo?" John said, as if my title was somehow an insult.

"Just putting the pieces together," I said, sighing. "You need to get out of here and to safety."

John narrowed his eyes. "I don't run from—"

"Leave it be, Colonel," the Diplomat said. "We have a mission to complete."

John stared down at the Notha. "I'll let our patron explain. Maybe he can provide us some answers if he wasn't the one who sent you."

"What?" I asked, confused.

Nyssa gestured for a communications relay bot to roll over to us. They were extremely rare and a product of Ares Electronics working with the Sorkanan Engineers Guild. It had two stubby legs and came over with a toddler-like gate. It projected a small hologram from a lens on its rotating head, an image of my longstanding friend and pain in my ass, Director G. He was a light-brown-skinned man with a shaved head and presently wearing an off-the-rack luxury suit of the kind that human civil servants across the galaxy wore. He was apparently in a hotel room, sitting on a bed, and operating from a personal infopad. Far from the usual high-tech super-spy locales that the former head of EarthGov's Security Departments used.

"Help me, Vance Turbo, you're my only hope." Case smiled broadly.

I raised an eyebrow. "Really, Case?"

"Not in the mood for a bit of classical theater, eh?" Case asked, smiling.

"Like you'd know classical theater," I muttered, half wondering if he had people spying on me even here. Only half because the other half knew he had to have.

"You *are* in a foul mood," Case said. "My sources have said you've been sulking for weeks."

"My aunt dying will do that," I said, sarcastically.

"Kathy Tagawa is dead?" John asked, sounding genuinely surprised. "The Iron Maiden?"

"Yes," I said, lowering my voice. "Though she hated that name. The maiden part, not the iron. She died in an engineering bay accident."

"Yes, accident," Case said, immediately drawing my attention.

"Speak very plainly," I said, my voice becoming dangerous. "I don't like the implications of that."

"Nor should you," Case said. "But first you should probably deal with your troops coming to rescue you."

"My what?" I asked.

"His what?" Hannah asked.

"Halt!" Leah shouted. "Nobody moves and nobody dies!"

Leah, Elektra, Forty-Two, and Danny were present despite their promise to stay out of sight. They were wearing blast vests and helmets, but they were not particularly intimidating on their own. Thankfully, they'd also brought about two dozen of the *Melampus'* crew and *they* were all wielding Sorkanan *ga'zz* rifles. Which were Community standard issue among most races. Ga'zz rifles were essentially the same thing as a human rifle except looked more like a pole with tentacles wrapped around it.

The rifle butt and trigger had been modified for human hands while a little greenish smoke poured out of the end, apparently a result of the coolant used when they were heated up. In terms of battle, power armor beat infantry every time, but human-produced power armor was inferior to Community. The rifles would be able to penetrate the Ranger's armor. It would be a bloody and pointless battle, though, even if numbers would almost certainly favor the *Melampus* forces.

"Stand down!" I said, raising my voice before John ordered his people to do something stupid. "I'm not a prisoner."

"That remains to be seen," John said.

"It really doesn't," Forty-Two growled. "Go ahead, merc. Make my day."

Forty-Two was a tall, muscular Sorkanan lizard man who was wearing his own modified power armor unlike the majority of the *Melampus* soldiers present. His scales had turned from green to brown, however, signaling his transition to old age. His right eye was now replaced with a kind of cybernetic monocle that also served as a targeting computer. Forty-Two had requested most of his organs be replaced so he could get another ten to twenty years of active service. Otherwise, in five he'd have to retire on a medical discharge.

"No shooting!" Hannah shouted, addressing the Rangers. "If any of you owe me anything, no shooting!"

No one fired.

"How the hell did you move down here without our sensors going off?" John asked a question that told you his primary concerns.

Elektra put away her rifle and lifted a small black box. "Ya can get parts for just about anything on the Invisible Market here on the Ring. That includes a jammer that screws with human levels of tech. I made this one myself!"

"I bet you didn't see that coming while you were trying to scare our wee little Captain and his girlfriend," Forty-Two growled.

"I am not his girlfriend," Hannah said, glaring.

"Yeah!" Danny said. "She's mine. I think."

"And mine," Elektra said. "I think."

"I am not wee," I replied.

Forty-Two looked up to Leah. "I'm not actually going to have to shoot anybody, am I?"

"Shut up, Forty-Two," Leah said. "We were monitoring the situation from afar and heard fusion shots."

"Yeah, that was just a prank gone wrong," I said, sarcastically. "Wasn't it, John?"

John looked away. "I do not need this."

"Shut up, John," Case said. "Looks like the gang's all here. Good, because I wanted to speak to all of you together."

"Where the hell are you?" I asked, confused. Case couldn't be that far since even with jumpspace transceivers, there was sometimes up to a ten-minute delay with transmissions out here in the Ring. Its why Admiral Bendo's real time transmission had been so impressive. "If you wanted to deal with us, Case, the least you could do is talk with us in person."

"An undisclosed location," Case said, shrugging. "Call it Sanctuary Zero for short."

"You're on Albion," Hannah said, dryly.

"How the hell did you figure that out?" I asked, surprised.

Case stared up at me like I was an idiot. "When one is having trouble on Earth, one should seek out Earth's enemies."

"Except Bendo and company are allied with the extremists on Albion," I said, pointing out the hole in his logic.

"Since he has allies with the extremists on Albion, that means that he has enemies with the moderates on Albion," Case said. "People who are happy to give me sanctuary until I work out the slight issue of people trying to frame me on Earth. They've also provided me a backdoor channel into an Ethereal communications array that allows me to talk using my laptop."

"No one has called an infopad a laptop in two hundred years. Anyway, would they have to frame you?" I asked, staring at his little holographic figure. "No offense, Case, but since I've known you, you've broken hundreds of interstellar laws and been involved with every imaginable bit of shady business short of slavery. The only reason I believe you might be set up now is because I don't believe that you'd ever have left actual evidence to be prosecuted for. You're too good at your job and neither EarthGov nor Community punishes success. No matter how brutally or dishonorably achieved."

"My, Vance, how cynical you've gotten," Case said. "I'm so proud of you."

"What's this about my aunt being murdered?" I asked, not in the mood for Case's games.

"Exactly what I implied," Case said, as if that was being direct. "Your aunt was murdered."

I lowered my gaze. "Not every suspicious death has to be a conspiracy, Case."

"Everything is the result of a conspiracy somewhere," Case said, showing his mindset. "It's not just lizardmen or minorities. It's usually corporate greed and power. Almost everything that happens in this galaxy is the result of some sort of deal behind closed doors involving money or power. Reality as we know it is a product of us being the collateral damage of such deals."

"Was it Bendo?" I asked.

"Probably, or he at least didn't care," Case replied. "The Human League is finally making its move to break ties with the Community. That means getting rid of the people that have always been a sign of what could be accomplished within. You're one of them. I was another."

"And my aunt?" I asked.

"A liability," Case said. "The truth was she never had the same level of faith in the Community that you did, Vance, but she was willing to work with the Devil she knew. Now it becomes increasingly obvious that anything other than total obedience will result in elimination as a traitor."

"This doesn't involve us," John said, looking away.

"It does because there are people who want to eliminate you as well," Case said. "Someone informed the Notha Union of your location during that coup attempt."

John's voice lowered almost to a whisper. Suddenly, I was no longer the primary object of his ire. "Those sons of bishes."

"Why?" I asked.

"Notha Union money," Case replied. "The Notha Prime can't win the war on Deathworld as long as the Community and EarthGov are providing enough weaponry and forces to keep them occupied. Volunteers, hardware, and funds are provided in the cause of whether the diminished Notha Empire's remnant can restore itself. So, he wants the Human League to succeed. The Human League needs its money to replace the Senators and Judicial necessary to finish the split from the Community."

"Every bad guy in the galaxy is connected to every other bad guy," I muttered.

"Good guys, bad guys," Case said, shrugging. "In the end, it's whoever stands on top that gets to write history."

"Us versus them," I muttered. "For the future of humanity."

"Yes," Case said.

"So why the hell do you have me chasing down a ghost ship full of pirate treasure?" I asked.

"It was your Aunt Kathy's plan," Case said. "That and the Chel's. But it has the potential for make something akin to five hundred trillion in liquid cash assets, adjusted for inflation, plus priceless cultural artifacts that can be returned to worlds. You're the biological descendant of Anne Bonny, at least it says so on your and her DNA records on Throneworld. That also means that if we recover the letter of marque we can use the funding to acquire enough money to kill their chances of splitting from the Community for at least a few election cycles. And to get people into place who can renew the funding for Deathworld's liberation."

I stared at him. "This is all about money."

"Most things are," Case said. "There's just one small issue here."

"Which is?" I asked, getting a dreadful feeling about all this. I was extra uncomfortable given that all of this was being witnessed by the Rangers as well as my own crew. I mostly trusted the crew of the *Melampus*. Many of them had been handpicked from either Kathy's crew or my own rather extensive group of misfits on the *Ares* and *Black Nebula*. Others were from the Community and had no allegiances to EarthGov. Certainly, I believed Leah would spot any traitors.

But mostly wasn't completely.

And I didn't completely trust Leah.

"General Vast's formerly outdated and barely functioning fleet has been upgraded with EarthGov and Community technology," Case said. "He's been told to eliminate you and Colonel Mason. The *Melampus* too, if possible. Vast will be provided with sanctuary and resources via my replacement in the Security Directorates. All in exchange for becoming their man in the independence movement. Bendo told Vast he could provide a clone of your child, Astrid, to claim Anne Bonny's treasure as well."

"I see."

"Oh, and he's going to be there in a few minutes," Case said. "I've been trying to get in touch with all of you for the past hour."

I stared at him.

"Open with that!" John shouted at Case.

117

CHAPTER FOURTEEN

Things Go From Bad to Worse

I closed my eyes and took a moment to pinch the bridge of my nose. "Director—"

"Ex-Director," Case admitted, a sad expression on his face. It wasn't exactly mourning, but closer to wistful. Apparently, he'd grown attached to his role as Earth's version of Nick Fury.

"I feel the need to ask if you're my friend or my enemy because I can't tell which some days," I muttered, looking at him.

"Yeah, Dad, you are being really awful right now," Trish said.

John looked down at the hologram. "I never thought I would agree with the so-called High Protector but on this we concur."

"It should be noted that I've had to move heaven and Earth to get you as much of a warning as I have," Case said. "I'm risking a lot by making this transmission in the first place and the only reason I am is because all other attempts to contact you have failed. You need to put aside your differences and get the *Mary Read* before it falls into the hands of General Vast or Department Twelve. If it does, then the best-case scenario is that a terrorist warlord will gain access to a functionally indestructible ship and a vast amount of wealth. Both of which I'm certain he'll use against independent worlds that he'll annex for his own personal fiefdom. The worst-case scenario will be that Department Twelve will end up bringing down the wrath of the Elder Races and annihilating humanity. But, hey, no pressure."

The Diplomat spoke up, staring at the hologram. "I am willing to work with my sister's killer, but make no mistake, Director G, I am not

118

a friend of humanity nor do I care about its fate. The only reason I am working with the Satan of the Notha religion is because I hope that it might save my homeworld from the Notha Prime's oppression."

"The Chel have isolated themselves completely from the rest of the galaxy," Nyssa said, speaking with her strange ethereal voice. "Generations of work and diplomacy undone in the blink of an eye by the stupidity of Department Twelve's agents. It will be hundreds of years before the Chel Elders allow us to open to the rest of the galaxy again. The only way that we'll be able to even begin this process is if we receive what we have given away."

Winston coughed. "Speaking as the leader of this group, I—"

"No one cares," John interrupted, clearly feeling about Winston the same way I did. "I don't like being manipulated and that is all you do, Case. You've been pulling strings in the name of the greater good since my grandfather's time. Frankly, I wouldn't be surprised if you're as much behind all of these problems as the people you're claiming to fight."

Case started to speak but there was a pounding at his door, followed by the sound of a breaching charge going off. Case rolled off the bed before his connection with his infopad died. The last thing I saw was the visual feed camera hitting the floor of his hotel room.

"Well, that's not good," Trish said, looking down at the communications bot.

"Assuming it wasn't staged," I said, which wasn't outside the realm of possibility even though I hated feeling that way.

"His warning wasn't staged," Trish said, turning to me. "I've lost contact with the *Melampus*. Someone in the Ring has taken to jamming all out-of-system communications."

Well, that wasn't good. "What about in-system? Can we contact our freighters?"

"You have freighters?" John asked, sarcastically.

"We weren't exactly trying to advertise that I was here and looking to make an illegal deal," I said, dryly.

"Is hiring an academic really illegal?" Winston said. "Really, we could have done this on Earth and—"

119

"It's illegal when you're selling information about priceless antiquities that need to be returned to their home nations," Leah interrupted, looking just as pensive as I was. "Anne Bonny may have been doing nothing illegal by robbing all those worlds and taking trophies, but that was because of the broad writ of being a High Protector, not because what she'd done wasn't immoral."

"Well, you utterly failed," John said, shaking his head. "We clocked you and your efforts the moment you arrived in the Ring, as has each of the twelve crime lords who run this place. The only reason they've been letting you alone is because they didn't want to deal with the Community backlash."

"And you still made us hang around the Ring waiting for you this entire time," I said. "When we could have been out finding the damn starship weeks ago."

John looked guilty. "Alright, some mistakes may have been made."

"Mistakes?" Hannah asked, furious. "This is a borking disaster and I blame you for this!"

"Oh, yeah, this is going to be a wonderful trip," Leah said, shaking her head. "Can we all just agree that we hate each other and get it over with?"

Leah misjudged the crowd as Winston and Hannah immediately started saying they didn't hate me before looking nastily at each other. John tried to say he and Hannah worked well together, Hannah cutting him off with a torrent of alien profanity, and I suspected it would have gone on before I interrupted by whistling with my fingers.

"I guess not," I said.

Leah looked at me. "I have a huge number of monitor programs inserted into the local computer systems. They can't penetrate the Ring's deeper computer systems but have almost free access to the ones that have been programmed to work with modern day technology. That information is being transferred to Trish now."

"What did she say?" Winston asked.

"Trish knows what's going on outside of this sewer," I said. "I presume she's also monitoring the local channels."

"She some kind of AI?" John asked, sounding like he was talking about her being a ticking time bomb. "One you brought here?"

120

"She's my friend, John," Hannah said. "You've squandered about seventy-five percent of the good will you took a decade to accumulate with me, so if you want me to not end our relationship by me shooting you in the head, you need *to start playing nice*."

"Alright," John said, surprising me. "I'll keep a civil tongue... for now."

Yeah, I'd believe it when I saw it.

"How bad is it, Trish?" I asked.

That was when Trish reached over and grabbed me by the arm. "We need to move. We've been compromised. The ships we have been using for cover have been locked down in their hangar bays and the fake crews we've recruited have been detained."

"Crazzap." I muttered, thinking about the people that we'd been trying to help who were now endangered because of this mission.

"It gets worse," Trish said.

"How much worse?" I asked.

"There's a jump signal that's been communicated to the central command station," Trish said. "Grand General Vast's fleet is arriving."

"How much of it?" I asked, already knowing the answer.

"All of it," Trish said. "Two hundred ships with multiple battle cruisers, two dozen destroyers, fifty frigates, and the rest in corvettes or gunships. All of them date back to before the Notha War but in a straight fight—"

"Yeah-yeah, quantity has a quality of its own," I said, reciting the old maxim. The *Melampus* was a top-of-the-line vessel and possessed incredible power from technology bestowed to the Ethereals by the Elder Races. It could probably take down a dozen ships if everything went right and I pulled off some of my usual Vance Turbo miracles. Then it would simply be overwhelmed by concentrated fire and destroyed. The more likely scenario would be that they'd manage to encircle us and destroy the *Melampus* before it even managed to fire off a shot. That if I managed to call in the *Melampus* to this system in order to help to begin with.

You're forgetting something, Vance, Trish said, speaking to my mind.

Which is? I asked, wondering how this could get worse.

121

We can't contact the Melampus, Trish pointed out. *Even if we wanted to use it against Vast's fleet it's impossible.*

The hunter had become the hunted. *They are going to a lot of lengths to try and eliminate me.*

Yeah, I suppose shutting down whole swaths of their operations and destroying a couple of their satellite organizations plizzed them off, Leah said, turning our conversation into a group chat. *We need to get you to safety, Vance.*

We need to figure out how to save our crew members, I thought back.

This isn't a discussion, Vance, Leah said. *As much as you like to pretend to be the caring, heroic, noble captain, we must worry about your safety. We can't afford to put on a "the men first" act.*

It was never an act, Leah, I said, annoyed.

Yeah, Leah said, shaking her head to our silent conversation. *Somewhere along the line, you decided to stop being a lovable rogue and started being a paladin. You went from being Spider-Man to Captain America. The persona of the good guy became the truth. Perhaps because someone took a chance on believing you could be better. I just wish that someone could have been me.*

I found myself stunned by Leah's short but incisive observation. I'd been thinking about the matter for a long time and wondering about it especially after the death of my Aunt Kathy. How much was Captain Vance Turbo, Hero of SPAAACE a persona that I'd constructed to try and live up to her memory? How much of it was trying to live up to someone that hadn't really existed? My Aunt Kathy had never really sat down and talked about how much her career had been driven by propaganda and the need for Earth to have heroes to inspire its citizens. We'd hinted at it and made the occasional comment, but neither of us had been willing to really pick at the armor our personas had become.

Leah was right that I'd somehow become the person that I'd claimed to be, or less charitably, I'd forgotten who I really was along the way.

I always pretended to be someone I wanted to be, until finally, I became that someone, or he became me, Leah said. *Cary Grant said that. My only regret in our relationship was that you never thought I could become someone better too. Which is what I've tried to do since I left the spy business.*

Well didn't I feel like a piece of savit. *Who is Cary Grant?*

Leah facepalmed.

That was when Elektra's little black box started ringing with a weird alarm. "Oh dear."

"What the hell is wrong?" Hannah asked, going to her side.

"Someone in this group got past my jammer and has sent a signal with our location," Elektra said. "That's not good."

John immediately raised his fusion rifle—as did the rest of his troops—and pointed at me specifically, only for Hannah to aim her rifle at John.

"Oh, come on!" I said, finally sick of this savit. "How the hell does that make any sense, you nitwit?"

There was clearly a lot more beef between me and John than made sense. A man could do a lot of ridiculous things to someone he viewed as a romantic rival, even though I hadn't been with Hannah for years and she'd been in a relationship with two other people for almost that entire time.

There also seemed to be class warfare and jealously elements. However, I had the suspicion there was something deeper going on. John clearly hated me, and you didn't get that kind of feeling—up to and including sabotaging a mission—unless there was something more going on than a bunch of decade old grievances I hadn't even been there for.

"It's not him," Trish said, looking at Hannah. "But the FLACS are coming."

"How much time do we have?" I asked.

"Not much," Elektra said, looking up. "I also have motion sensors set up."

"I'm listening to the comms," Trish said. "The Twelve and the police are out in force. They're also planning to welcome Vast's army to help."

"Day of the Jackboot," I muttered, wondering just how much Vast had to pay or whether intimidation had brought everyone to heel. "We need to get everyone to an alternative means of transportation immediately. Which means stealing one."

"The Rangers have our gunship hidden but we can't use it with you," John said. "That's not me upset with you, High Protector, that's me saying that everyone guarding it will rat you out if they see you."

"I'll find my own way," I said. "Leah, get the others out."

"Like hell!" Leah said.

"That's an order," I said, planning on disappearing and rendezvousing with them later. "We'll meet at the *Melampus*."

"I'll come with you, Vance," Trish said.

"Me too," Hannah said.

I was about to argue but didn't have time. At the other end of the tunnel I heard the splashing of booted feet in puddles. Their flashlights illuminated their shadows, illustrating power-armored soldiers in FLACS gear coming right at us. It was a mixture of humans and Sorkanans and I didn't know if there was going to be one unit or multiple. I did notice they were being followed by a hulking eight-foot-tall security bot and decided this situation had rapidly gone from bad to worse.

A drone hovering ahead of them projected a voice with a deep accented English. "Everyone, stand down! This is an official police investigation! Do not resist arrest and you will not be harmed!"

John's people turned around to fight the corporate mercs. I, on the other hand, grabbed Hannah by the shoulder. "We're not going to fight our way out. We run."

"We're leaving?" Hannah looked back, betrayed. "These are—"

"I've had enough fighting today," I said, softly. I didn't want to get into a fight with a bunch of local mercenaries. I wanted to kill only one person in this entire affair and that was Vast.

Vast and his master.

Bendo.

That was when the FLACS came around, opened fire without waiting to see if anyone dropped their arms, and an advanced Sorkanan energy rifle blast went through Nyssa's shield. Seeing the mysterious Chel woman struck down, I immediately drew my Royal-10 fusion pistol and fired a three-round burst into her attacker—killing them.

Hannah didn't hesitate to join the fight by my side.

Goddammit.

CHAPTER FIFTEEN

Where We Try to Develop a Plan

My delay had gotten one of the Rangers killed. I had wanted to avoid combat and hesitated because the FLACS were what passed for the local law enforcement. I'd dealt with my fair share of dirty cops, tools for the corrupt systems of worlds like the warlords of Rand's World or just another gang controlled by crime bosses. But I'd forgotten they were *both* here.

The Ring's FLACS were mercs and I *hated* mercs, even when I knew some righteous ones. There was something about fighting for money instead of country or kin that turned even the best men into monsters.

Now Nyssa had paid the price for it.

She wasn't the only one either.

The air filled with energy blasts, and it was a lot bloodier fight than it might normally have been. The FLACS had come loaded for bear with advanced armor, weapons, and a security bot that looked like a tank. However, the Rangers were hardened military veterans, and my Community-trained forces had the latest weapons. Unfortunately, so did the FLACS. Someone had provided them with modernized fusion rifles and barriers before this fight.

The reinforcements from the *Melampus* that Leah had brought found themselves battling on my behalf, as did the final remnants of the Antaeus Rangers. The FLACS assault team shouldn't have been able to hold out against them but a lot of them were willing to pour forward. Grand General Vast seemed to have put the fear of god (or the Devil) in the local mercs.

126

"Fall back!" I shouted, shooting and gesturing to seek cover in one of the nearby human-sized drains. Three of my crew were dead on the ground, though I didn't know any of their names and felt a flash of guilt for such. Was it wrong that I only really cared about getting my people out of here? Probably. It was only human, though, and this mission had already cost too many lives.

Hannah didn't pay attention to me and used one of the armored Rangers for cover, hurling a magnetic grenade over his shoulder and letting it land beneath the security bot. The explosion was voluminous and sent burning plasma eight feet in every direction. That was enough to disrupt the FLACS' attack and kill a good chunk of the ones huddled in the back. With that, everyone started heading down the pipe I'd indicated.

You must get the Mary Read, the voice of the late Nyssa whispered in my mind. I would have been shocked except that I already heard plenty of dead women in my mind. Which, uh, perhaps could have been phrased better.

Kinda busy! I thought back. *Also, sorry about getting you killed.*

Winston knows the secrets for how to get to her, Nyssa replied. *He is a weak man, though, and not to be trusted.*

And I thought we were best friends, I said, using my sword to angle my personal shield and protect the others from enemy fire.

Defense was better than offense in these tight quarters, not that my people didn't take advantage to shoot down FLACS after FLACS beside me.

I saw Winston had been knocked to the ground by the explosion and shot two more of the FLACS aiming at him before they got their blasts off. One benefit of Elder Race-enhanced reflexes, I supposed. Running out, I grabbed him by the arm and pulled him to the drainage pipe. It was a miracle neither of us were shot and I felt an energy blast burn past me that would have taken my head clean off.

"You saved my life," Winston said, looking confused and ashamed. I didn't understand the second emotion, so I shrugged it off.

"Yeah, well don't let it go to your head," I said, irritated that the two of us were being left to cover our groups' escape.

That was when Hannah slapped a second magnetic grenade against the side of the drainage pipe we were in, holding a detonator in her hand. "Get moving!"

Trish joined us as I saw the rest of the Rangers and my team were moving down a second set of pipes. Leah had taken control over the scene and was trying to divert the others' attention from me. It was heroic and I felt terrible about it. I didn't want the mother of my child endangering herself to try to save me, High Protector nonsense or not.

I pushed Winston down the pipe as our feet splashed in the foul water and I ran. It was too late for him to join Leah's group, and he was now our responsibility. "You heard the lady!"

Hannah ran behind us as the FLACS finally recovered and entered the other end of the pipe, raising their rifles to gun us down. Hannah hit the detonator, and the resulting explosion was enough that at least three more of the attackers were consumed. I fired a few times into the smoke and debris before we turned a corner.

"We are in so much trouble," I muttered, blaming the entirety of this on Case and his goons.

"It's possible they didn't identify us, sir!" Winston said, running behind Hannah and me.

That was when my cybernetics picked up a station-wide emergency announcement, one that I heard echoed through the storm sewer's antiquated speakers. "This is General Vast of the People's Liberation Army flagship *Liberator*. This station is now under martial law and all citizens are subject to summary detention or engagement."

"Did he just say he'll shoot anyone he wants?" Winston asked. "That's not at all proper behavior for a leader.:

"Shut up and keep moving," I said.

"We are not a violent people," General Vast said, his voice sounding as painfully generic as any other Sorkanan voice generated by computer. "All we wish are the terrorists Vance Turbo and John Mason to be turned over to us. A reward of 7,290,000 Community credits or 23,000 red styrrian crystals will be presented to any citizen that assists in their capture alive and uninjured."

"What an odd number," Winston muttered.

I stared up at the ceiling. "Tell that to your borking men!"

"Shh!" Hannah snapped.

"They were shooting to kill!" I snapped back.

"You don't know that," Winston said. "Maybe Mistress Nyssa is okay."

I looked down at Winston. "She's dead, Winston."

"I'm sorry," Trish said.

Winston looked down. "Right."

"You need to stick with us," I said. "You weren't mentioned in the 'alive and uninjured' list just posted."

"Yeah, why do they want only you and John?" Hannah asked, looking at me. "I'm rather insulted."

"I'm not," I said. "For that kind of money, I might turn myself in."

"Don't," Winston replied, acting like I was serious. "Vast is an enormous cheat. Constantly cutting corners and defaulting on payments."

"I thought with stealing thirty trillion, you'd have been living the high life," I replied, surprised.

Winston snorted as if the idea was insulting. "That's how much he allegedly spent but a great number of the bills were defaulted on. It was all a plan by Director G anyway. It was designed to help bankrupt Vast and get his creditors to stop funding him. Unfortunately, he appears to have picked up new patrons. I, myself, have only made a mere twenty million credits on this entire ten years of labor and that is ridiculous."

Hannah stared at him. "You poor baby. Only twenty million?"

"That's barely enough to make you rich," Trish said. "Except, you're here and not on Brigid, Belenus, or some other luxury planet so you've spent it all, haven't you?"

"What?" Winston asked, offended. "I had expenses!"

"Before she died," I said, adjusting the timeline to avoid explaining that I'd heard it after she died, "Nyssa said that you know how to find the *Mary Read*? I presume she told you?"

"Yes," Winston said, nodding. "I have a way of monitoring its jumpspace signal. It, however, requires a biological descendant of Anne Bonny to get past the defenses. It also requires top-of-the-line, military-grade equipment such as an X-17 jumpspace sensor net, tier one jumpspace signal booster, and a baffnohedron."

"Okay, you're making that last one up," I said.

"No, we have one on the *Melampus*," Trish said. "All of that stuff is on the *Melampus*, in fact. Probably on Vast's flagship as well. It explains why Belloq here didn't go after the treasure himself, though."

"Who is Belloq?" Winston asked, confused.

I wasn't interested in any sort of chit chat, though. We'd sealed off the tunnel behind us for a while, but it wouldn't take the FLACS much time to move around the obstacle to pursue us. They also had the kind of numbers to be able to pursue us at every possible entrance if they were allowed to coordinate themselves.

"We need to keep moving," I said. "What are the chances they can trace us?"

"Small," Hannah said, pulling out one of Elektra's little black boxes. She'd had her wife, ex-wife, partner, whatever, making them for their entire relationship. Little gadgets for wetwork. "This will jam any of their signals for about a kilometer around us once activated. The only reason I wasn't using it earlier was because we wanted Leah watching for us."

"Do it," I said, hoping that would give us some breathing room. Well, as much as you wanted to breathe in an atmospheric sewer that felt like it should be filled with beholders and orcs.

"Oh dear," Winston said. "How will we stay in touch with the others?"

"We won't," I said, simply.

I proceeded to drag Winston down a set of twisting tunnels. I wasn't leading us blind. I had downloaded a map of the Ring's incredibly complicated sewer systems via my cyberlink. Much of which had been used by the homeless and destitute over the millennia. It was my hope to escape to a fluid processing center that was officially off the map because it had been listed as condemned to be used as a local gang's safehouse.

The place had a massive number of pipes, catwalks, and machinery designed to keep the life support on the Ring going. Much to my annoyance, I found that John's group had already arrived and apparently had the exact same map I had before coming up with an identical plan of escape.

"What the hell are you doing here?" I asked, showing just how tired I was of John's presence. Nyssa hadn't been the only one of our two groups to fall. Of the team Leah had brought to protect me, security officers and troops had been gunned down.

At least five.

John Mason had already established his control over the place as he was securing the other entrances, had three workers tied up with utility tape, and sported a stolen Sorkanan rifle. They looked to be gang members by their signs, the crime syndicates controlling basic infrastructure, but not part of the FLACS or their auxiliaries. It was a good thing Leah was present, or I suspected he wouldn't have taken such merciful measures—or maybe I just didn't like the guy.

"Well, this has completely gone to shit," John said, looking over to me. "They must have followed you in."

"I trust my people. I'm pretty sure this falls on your head," I said, walking up to him. "What kind of holy hell have you brought down on me?"

John looked ready to shoot me, and I was fully prepared to gun him down first. "You? I was perfectly fine doing low level but valuable jobs for the Security Departments until Director G involved me in your showboating movie nonsense."

"My showboating movie nonsense is not how I do things," I said, clutching my sword hilt. "You delayed this entire business until it became dangerously untenable. I don't let personal feelings get in the way of how I do missions."

Trish coughed and Hannah looked to one side. The entirety of my group gave me the look that they thought this was complete horsesavit. Even the ones who didn't know me personally. I glared at them for not backing me up.

"You two need to calm down," Leah spoke, her voice echoing through the air like sweet music and making my mood brighten. I could see it have a similar effect on John, causing to lower his weapon.

"Yeah, we do," John said.

I looked at Winston. "No, we don't."

Leah blinked and waved her hand in front of my face. **"I think you do."**

I stared at her. "Jedi mind tricks only work on the weak minded."

John glared at her. "Is your psychic trying to affect my mind?"

"We prefer to be called biomancers," Leah said. "We're bio-enhanced manipulators of the mind via—"

"I don't care," John said, dryly. "We can't stay down here. It's not going to take them long to find out where the hell we went."

One of the Antaeus Rangers, a black-haired woman of Shogun descent, spoke up, "We've set up jamming throughout the station's internal sensors to go along with Hannah's and have our dummy AI generating false reports to the Frontier Security Patrols searching for us. Once we're outside of the jamming zone, we'll use our confiscated comms to keep in touch. A proper military would seal off the ones we took off the dead, but I suspect the FLACS will utterly fail to communicate their casualties for hours, especially with how many were driven deeper into the tunnels. I'm 99% sure we're safe in our current position for the next hour or two at least, as the maps we're using are different from the ones the FLACS have. I know because we're not the first group to sabotage theirs."

That was very impressive. "That still doesn't get me back to my ships."

"Your ship has been impounded," John said, simply. "They have them locked down at docking bay 14 with Vast's elite Freedom Guard. People who aren't just thugs with guns used to killing civilians. General Vast has set up a mine field and drone starfighter patrols around the Ring. The *Liberator* is the largest ship in the system and has more than enough firepower to subdue anything we could throw at it."

I stared at him. "And where did you learn that?"

John shrugged and looked at the black-haired woman. "Ichigo Murphy is our Tech-Marine. We've won more battles with her taking the enemies' information than we ever did with guns. Sorry, Tank."

"No problem, sir," a stocky, bald, human male spoke. He had a thick New Dallas drawl and seemed like he should be chewing on a cigar while he spoke. "We know where our bread is buttered."

"On the surface?" I asked, wondering how that phrase had become common. "So, what the hell are we going to do about it?"

"Steal a smaller ship and escape," John replied, again mirroring my preexisting plans. "We can get past them. You're a pilot, aren't you?"

"Yeah, I am, but that doesn't help my crew, does it?" I said, still worried about them. "Local recruits and undercover operatives from the *Melampus*. I went to a lot of effort to help the people here."

John narrowed his eyes. "And because of your idealistic belief you could make this hellhole better, they're probably going to all be tortured and killed by Vast. Even if we escape, he'll have to make sure as few witnesses as possible are found to his act of war against the Community. After all, he's about to become EarthGov's biash."

I wanted to stab him with my sword but controlled my temper. "What is your deal with me, Colonel?"

The Colonel stared at me. "You have no idea, do you?"

"I know it's more than Hannah," I said.

"You're right," John admitted.

Hannah seemed surprised by this.

"Then spill,' I said.

CHAPTER SIXTEEN

Why Colonel Mason Hates My Guts

"I'm disappointed," Hannah said, looking at me. "There was at least a romantic charm in believing that you were overreacting because you were secretly still in love with me but jealous of my attachment to Vance."

"I mean, it would be grossly insulting to us," Elektra said, frowning. "What with you being in a relationship with us for years. Right Danny?"

Danny sighed. "I've long since resigned myself to the fact that Hannah will always choose our captain over us."

"I haven't!" Elektra said, annoyed. "That's a terrible attitude to have for a relationship."

Danny gave a plaintive look to Elektra. "I think this one can well and truly be said to be done, Elektra. We should probably be looking to Pam in Engineering."

"*Paminatrix*?" Elektra asked, horrified. "You can't be serious."

"Pam, really?" Hannah asked.

John watched the interaction with a confused expression on his face. "Is your group normally this…lax?"

"I'm a soft touch," I said, dryly. "You were telling me about why you've been barely keeping yourself from shooting me since the moment this mission began."

"Yes, I'm the one who hates you," the Diplomat said, looking up. "I feel like John is stealing my blood oath against Captain Turbo."

I looked down at the Notha. "I try and honor your sister's sacrifice every day of my life. Somehow, I will do something for the people of Deathworld that will make everyone on your planet know that she was a hero."

"Now you're ruining it too," the Diplomat said, a ripple passing through her fur.

"Elgan," John said, interrupting that digression.

"What?" I asked, my attention going back to the colonel.

"Captain Jules Elgan of the ESS *Ares*," John said. "The ship you stole."

"Yeah, I know who the bork he is," I said, glaring at him. "I also know he's been dead for years and reality is a better place for it."

That was when I saw John's lip curl and the expression on his face break for a second to show real pain. "There, there it is. That's the reason I hate you, Captain Turbo. Jules Elgan was a friend of my family and a hero of Earth when we needed someone to stand up for our rights."

"Our *rights*?" I asked, wondering if he was another Human Leaguer.

"John..." Hannah trailed off.

"Jules protected a dozen worlds during the Notha Wars when humanity was on the verge of being overrun, he overthrew the slave lords of Crius, smashed the Void Pirates of New Barbary, and he eliminated the Computer Tyrants of Zill."

"I know exactly what he did," I said, keeping my expression even and my voice cold.

"My father, Arthur Mason, worked with Captain Elgan on hundreds of missions," John said, staring at me. "Including the one where he was killed. Jules came to me as a boy and promised that the Community would always have our back and Space Fleet would have a place for the Rangers. Then you come along, kill him, don't deny it—"

"I don't deny anything," I said.

"Then you kill him, return to the Community as a big hero, steal his ship, and spread rumors about him being some sort of secret fascist," John said. "You've convinced a lot of people you're a good guy, Vance

135

Turbo. I've read your transcripts, though. You were a scheming failure who ran illegal games at the Community and were about to be kicked out when you resigned instead. You were also involved in a student death that you—"

"You don't get to mention Tommy," I said, simply. "I will kill you and every single one of your soldiers when they try to stop me."

John sneered, staring at me.

"Vance—" Hannah started to speak.

"He's not joking," Leah said. "Also, Colonel Mason, I strongly suggest you recognize he could. His sword and ring work on willpower. You couldn't stop him."

I wasn't sure if that was true, but I understood what she was doing. "You want to hate me, fine. Call me a spoiled rich kid who lives on stolen valor. I don't give a shit. Most of what you say was true. I was a pathetic waste of space at the Academy, and I blame myself for Tommy's death. However, there's two things you borking need to know. One, you will speak of my friend's name with respect because you are a borking fake tin soldier who sits there in his inherited armor paid for by his grandfather's actual soldiers and are not worth the crazzap on Tommy's shoes after latrine duty. Second, Elgan betrayed his crew. Used them as decoys. Used me and my friends. He *deserved to die* and if you're anything like that monster then I will gladly give my life to rid the fucking universe of you!"

Yeah, I used the old swear rather than borking.

Colonel Vance swung his power armored fist at my face. My ring glowed as I caught his hand in midair and shattered the gauntlet around his fist, causing John to grit his teeth as his hand was broken with shards of metal impaling it. Somehow, he didn't scream. I put up my sword right to his throat.

All the Rangers drew up their weapons to aim at me, the rest of my team moving to fire.

"Do it!" I said, shouting. "Do you think I'm kidding! Do I think I value my life! I am a soldier of the Community! I am ready to die to end monsters! Terrorists, slavers, and mercs!"

I tossed my sword on the ground and stepped out, spreading my hands out. Daring them to fire.

Forty-Two looked at Danny. "Um, did Vance just lose his mind right in front of us?"

"It's gotta be a plan of some kind," Danny said, ready to jump in in front of a fusion bolt for me but clearly not wanting to.

The rest of my soldiers looked confused, not knowing how to react.

Leah didn't clarify if it was a plan by me.

Was it a plan?

Bork if I knew.

I think in that moment, I just stopped caring. It seemed the Community I loved was falling apart at the seams and every person I depended on trying to save it didn't care or was actively trying to sabotage it. I'd been involved in hundreds of combat encounters and a war that had resulted in the destruction of the Kolahn homeworld. It seemed more and more clear that bailing out Space Fleet from its corruption and conspiracy was a lost cause. That everything I'd tried to accomplish was pointless except for the sheer dumb luck that had saved the universe from the Primordials—and even that might have just been temporary. But one thing I was *not* going to do was let myself be bullied by another bully with a gun. Not Elgan, not the Emperor, not Vast, and certainly John Mason.

"Can we not shoot each other?" Hannah interjected, stepping between John and me. "I know everyone thinks this is my fault—"

"That's because it is," Forty-Two said.

"But Jules Elgan did betray us," Hannah spoke, looking at John with a sad expression on her face. "I trusted him, went along with the mission to recover the SKAMMs and we were left for dead as decoys to be blamed for the fallout. He was Department Twelve, John, and fully willing to risk the entirety of the human race's survival in the hopes of acquiring some Elder Race knickknacks."

"Am I shooting him or not?" the Diplomat said, pointing her gun at me.

"No," John said, as his hand was treated by their medic. His pain tolerance was immense, I'd give him that. "You know, Vance, you wouldn't be so damned confident if you didn't have all that Elder Race magic. If you wanted to throw down just man to man—"

"Fighting isn't a game to me, Colonel," I said, coldly. "I don't do it for sport or pride or fame."

"Sometimes he does it for gambling," Forty-Two said. "Then I let the little puny human win."

"If we fight, it'll be for keeps," I said. "I have only two rules: don't kill the innocents and kill those who do as efficiently as possible."

The group was silent.

Winston interrupted it by clapping his hands together. "That was very exciting! Bravo! Such a performance! Now we're all friends, right?"

John and I glared death at him.

"Vance, about what you said about mercs..." Hannah trailed off.

"Not the time, really," I said. "It seems I may actually have to see the ship's counsellor."

"Oh, you think?" Trish asked. "I get you're at your wits ends with your aunt just being murdered and all, but you have to keep your eye on the ball. The ball being getting off this space station and back to the *Melampus*."

She was, unfortunately, right. "Give me a second to come up with a plan."

"I already have one," Hannah said. "We head to the control tower and seize it, unlock the restraints on our ships, have Trish override the defenses to make a distraction, and then make a point blank jumpspace jump with all our crew together. It'll wreck the cargo bay something fierce but bork whoever is there since they're working with the Community."

It wasn't a bad plan. "Are you sure you shouldn't be captain?"

"I agree," Forty-Two said. "She should be captain."

"I could never take the pay cut. I get bonus hazard pay as his bodyguard," Hannah said, simply. "Also, do you understand how much paperwork Vance deals with on a daily basis?"

"That's because I merged the position of captain with ship's accountant," I said, pausing. "You have no idea how much was being wasted in terms of crew rations!"

"We have food synthesizers," Hannah said. "I was wondering why the previously good meals on the *Melampus* had suddenly turned terrible."

"There's still the fleet hanging outside," Hannah said. "That can't be good for us."

"I don't have any better ideas," I said, looking at John, "Do you?"

"No," he admitted.

Certainly, it was a better plan than my original one to split us up and reunite only for us to both end up seeking the exact same place for refuge. I was seriously off my game and proof of that was how I'd almost let myself get gunned down after breaking the hand of someone who was ostensibly supposed to be my ally. It made me think I needed to step down for the duration of this mission if not retire entirely.

No, Vance, you can't, Trish said to me. *No one else can lead us.*

I just had a miniature nervous breakdown out there, I said, cybernetically. *I can't lead under those conditions.*

You won his respect, Leah said, joining our conversation. *Weirdly enough.*

You've got to be saviting me, I said, stunned. *That won his respect? What the hell is wrong with him?*

What the hell is wrong with him? What the hell is wrong with you? Leah said, reminding me I was the one who had gone utterly insane in that moment. *You're the one who did it. I assumed it was some naked appeal to macho posturing and warrior culture.*

Vance is in mourning, Trish defended me, not that I needed her to. *He needs time to process his grief for his aunt and the trauma of the Primordials. Like Audie Murphy, he has gone through some savit.*

Audie Murphy slept with a gun under his pillow and once held his wife at gunpoint, I replied, pointing out the failure of her analogy. *We have ways of treating traumatic stress disorders and battlefield conditions now. I'm not suffering from any of them.*

I'm not sure you've allowed yourself sufficient time to heal, Leah said. *That's assuming those treatments are even effective on your brain given its alteration by the Elder Races.*

Yeah, somehow this conversation had gone from whether I was fit to lead to whether I should outright retire and get my head examined.

139

It was a far cry from wanting me to go back to Earth like Julius Caesar and sort out all the problems there.

You've already done an immense amount of good, Vance, Trish said. *But as my father showed, the galaxy will always demand more of you if you let it. He's been trying to prop up EarthGov's democracy like Atlas for a couple of centuries now.*

Please shoot me if I ever become like your father, I said, unable to think of a fate worse than being like Director G where every single person I knew was just another piece on an infinitely large chessboard against thousands of other opponents, if not millions.

"Sounds like you have it all worked out," John said, looking at his soldiers. "Let me send Ichigo and Tank with some of your group to help take the control room. My people and the rest of yours will take the hangar bay."

I looked at both Tank and Ichigo. "Their power armor isn't exactly stealthy."

Mostly, I just didn't want any of John's people-tanks anywhere near me or my crew. Unfortunately, even if we managed to get to the central control room without getting killed—a big if—there was no way we could take it without backup. Then there was the question of whether we'd be able to get to the hangar bay while everyone else evacuated. I was willing to make that sacrifice but I had the sneaking suspicion none of my fellows would be willing to go along with that.

That's because you know us, Leah said. *Trish, you go with Vance to the central control room. Take Hanna and Forty-Two, along with Tank and Ichigo. A six-person team should do. I've detected no sign of a Cognition AI in the Ring, so if the Ring is an Elder Race construction, maybe Vance can also override its systems.*

That's a lot of ifs, but my brain the size of a planet can't think of anything better, Trish said. *I can also forward an alternate possibility.*

Which is? I asked.

We abort this whole mission and go home, Trish said. *I'm pretty sure we can just get ourselves out of this by laying low*

No, I thought firmly. *We must try to save everyone.*

Sometimes you can't, Trish said. *We both know that all too well.*

Julius Something, the High Priestess, and Ketra had all died to save my life or the life of my crew and daughter. I'd been tortured by Alexandra Ares, forced to witness the near destruction of the galaxy, and watch to my own child's kidnapping. All of it had been in service to trying to live up my Aunt Kathy's legacy while redeeming my family name as soiled by my parents. Now my aunt was dead, possibly murdered by my own government, and I'd discovered my parents had been government agents even if they were every bit the scum that I'd grown up thinking they were.

We must try, I said, simply. *Even if we fail. No one gets left behind. Not if we can help it.*

I know, Vance, Trish said. *That's why I still believe in you as captain.*

"You'd be surprised about how sneaky power armor can be," Hannah said, undermining my earlier point. "The Rangers suits include a lot of stealth modifications."

"I'll take your word for it," I said, looking at Hannah. "I'm going to have to follow your lead on this."

Hannah looked at me with pride. "Thanks, Cap'n."

"Now for the witnesses," John said, smiling as he pulled out a pistol and aimed it at the prisoners he'd taken earlier.

CHAPTER SEVENTEEN

Ethical Quandaries

"We're not killing prisoners," I said, stepping in front of him.

My willingness to tolerate Colonel Mason's BS was rapidly reaching zero and I wondered if this was a test, a way to continue to needle me in the most annoying manner possible by calling into question whether I'd engage in war crimes during a mission. Either that or he'd fallen so far that Hannah's belief he was an idealist and hero "like me" was completely wrong—especially if he was a former student of Captain Jules Elgan.

While it had gotten lost in the shuffle, I hadn't forgotten that someone had apparently alerted the FLACS to our presence. Indeed, it was entirely possible that they'd have continued alerting them but we were presently jamming all communications out. It was also possible any traitor that might have existed was dead or rethinking their betrayal.

Colonel Mason lifted his damaged hand and my respect for his endurance faded a bit due to the realization that it was cybernetic. I'd damaged his hand, but they were designed to continue functioning well past what a normal limb could do and shut down any pain receptors well before they became debilitating. "You can drop the act, Turbo. We're in a survival situation and you don't have to play the part of the heroic captain."

I bit my tongue before I could say that I wasn't playing. "Making more bodies isn't going to help our situation."

"Even if they get free while we're escaping and proceed to tell their bosses about us and our plans?" John said. "Any extra warning they get is going to put us in danger.

"Stun blasts and bindings exist for a reason," I said. "Yes, it's a risk but do you really want to throw away that reputation as an idealistic super soldier? The one that the Rangers worked so hard to create?"

John narrowed his eyes. "That concern of mine died on Deathworld along with most of my men. Now I'm just determined to keep my remaining people alive, no matter the cost."

I stared at him. The problem with his logic was that it was logical. I wasn't going to let it happen, but I could at least understand the moral calculus being done here. War wasn't anything but a crime, and murder was a measure of how many innocent lives were lost achieving its objectives. John wasn't just being an asshole here. Special Operations got dirty and even I'd gunned down a few people for reasons that I had difficulty justifying as self-defense on some days, including one fat slaver at a card game.

"Vance!" Hannah said.

My attention turned to Hannah as I saw her pointing to the side. Following her arm, I saw that she was gesturing to the prisoners. There had been five of them and they were all bleeding out now, their throats and femoral arteries slit by the blood-soaked Diplomat. In her hands she was carrying a vibrating Notha *z'hayal* blade that was used for executing prisoners or subordinates under the Great Notha's regime. The Diplomat had time to kill them all while we'd been arguing ethics.

I stared at the results. "Well, I guess that settles that."

"Are we going to have a problem, Captain?" John asked.

"I think we're past the point of that," I said. "However, I'm willing to come to an understanding if you are."

"What're your terms?" John asked.

"I'll hire you with a 5% share of the profits for the treasure, if it exists, plus all the resources you need to rebuild the Rangers and a renewal of your contract with the Community," I replied. "Training facilities, ships, and material. Plus, your pick of assignments. I'll also pay an additional two million credit fee."

"That's pretty stingy cash—" John started to say.

"Each," I replied.

John stared. "Rich boy emptying his pockets now."

"It's the government's money," I replied. "The benefits of being a High Protector. But you keep the collateral to a minimum and you answer to me as your employer from this point on. I don't care about or even want your respect. I want you to obey orders, though. If you want to just cash out and end the Rangers company, I can also pay you forty million directly and you can consider yourself cashed out then."

John looked uncertain for the first time since we'd met. He'd hated me since before he'd laid eyes on me, and I suspected his reasons had as much to do with the death of his men as the late Julius Elgan. Somewhere along the way I'd become an embodiment of the Community's hypocrisy, corruption, and unwillingness to back up its allies.

Ironically, it did more to sell me on the idea that he and I weren't so different than anything Hannah had told me. My impression of the man until then had been that he was a barely competent man child, but I was starting to realize I'd just been seeing him at his worst. Certainly, we both were suffering from recent traumas.

"I suppose you want us to leave Hannah alone after this as well," John said, already looking like he knew he'd burned that bridge in his stupidity.

"That's up to her," I said.

"You're not the man I knew, John," Hannah said. "Not even close."

John looked away. "Yeah, he died fighting for the freedom of a bunch of Notha farmers. Hoo Rah."

"Do you accept my terms?" I asked.

John looked back at his group, most of which still had their power armored helmets on, but he seemed to get their reaction down by the nod he gave. "Alright, Captain, you have yourself a deal. Just note that I have this conversation recorded."

"You'll get your money," I said. "Just do your job."

"I always do," John said.

"Ahem," Winston said, clearing his throat. "Yes, about giving him 5% of the treasure. I should point out that these are the kinds of terms that should be negotiated with me as the primary head of the expedition that—"

"You were working to defraud a warlord and war criminal on behalf of the Security Departments," I pointed out. "You only found the ship because the Chel decided to use you as an intermediary."

Winston clenched his teeth before looking physically pained. "Yes, that is true."

"You'll be paid, Winston," I replied. "I'll even set you up in Hollywood where you can film the movie of my adventures here as a producer. That is, of course, if I live to do it. That is, of course, if you give the means to find the ship to Leah right now."

"Err..." Winston trailed off. "Well, I, uh..."

"I've got it," Leah said, reading his mind as I knew she would.

"Wait, do I still get paid?" Winston asked.

"Yes," I said. "Leah, you should go with the rest of the team and secure the hangar bay."

"You'll need me, Vance," Leah said. "Besides, this entire affair is not going to work out without you."

I was more concerned about leaving our daughter an orphan. Most of the people I would have entrusted with her care were on this mission after all. Ironically, the other person I'd want Astrid to be raised by, her biological mother, wanted nothing to do with her due to the nature of conception.

Danny looked up at me. "I can lead the team, Vance. Elektra and I have the brains as well as, uh, other brains to pull it off."

"You'll need me as muscle, Vance," Forty-Two said before looking at Tank and Ichigo. "Besides, someone needs to keep you from being shot in the back."

"You're supposed to say that privately," I said.

"Why?" Forty-Two asked.

I facepalmed. "So, the team is Ichigo, Tank, Hannah, Forty-Two, Leah, Trish, and me. That work out for everyone?"

It was a five-man job, but John's people were going to tag along because I suspected he didn't trust me. You know, in case you hadn't picked up on that. By the way Tank and Ichigo looked at Trish, I was under the impression they weren't happy an AI was among them.

"Perfectly," John said. "Though you should tell your spoiled cousin to answer to me. I'll get your people off this rock."

"Spoiled?" Danny asked.

"Coordinate with the mercenaries, Danny," I said, simply. "Just remember you're a Community officer and he's not."

"It's hard to forget," Danny said, disgusted.

"Do the same, Colonel," I said.

"Yessir," John said, through the fakest smile I'd seen outside of a used car commercial.

Do you trust him? Trish asked me via our link.

Not in the slightest, I said. *I think we have shared common interests. I get the impression they're not fond of AI, though.*

Most people aren't, Vance, Trish said. *You're somewhat unique because you don't consider us appliances or a ticking time bomb to the extinction of biologicals.*

That bad, huh? I asked.

The reports from Earth are not encouraging, Trish said. *There's a movement in the Human League on Albion to reclassify all AI as fundamentally imitations of life rather than actual life itself. This would affect not just Cognition AI but bioroids and even some cyborgs. It's gotten little traction so far but the Community's laws are the primary reason there hasn't been more legislation like this proposed in the past.*

That was another sign that I needed to be back on Earth and working to try to influence the people there to do the right thing. I wasn't the only voice out there. There were many progressives, idealists, and defenders of democracy trying to make sure we didn't backslide into the old Neo-Militarist ways of the Post-Eruption Years. After the Yellowstone super caldera had erupted, the Earth had been covered in a cloud of soot that had caused mass starvation and limited nuclear war. Almost a billion people had died. If not for the AI and the sudden release of previously classified technology, humanity might have entered a second Dark Age.

Even so, the results hadn't been pretty. For almost a century, humanity had been under the thumb of megacorporations that privatized the governments and militaries of the world. It had been like the old cyberpunk movies of the Eighties and Nineties except without the black sense of humor. The Neo-Militarists had eventually used their corporate overlords' backing to come to power and instilled brutal dictatorships over ninety percent of humanity. It had taken First Contact and a global civil war to drive them away. You'd have thought humanity would have learned its lesson, but it turned out that the price of freedom really was eternal vigilance.

"My aunt would have been better at this," I said, wondering if I should have been encouraging her to run for Prime Minister of Earth.

Hannah walked over to me and took my arm. "I'm sorry about this, Vance. I severely underestimated just how much bad blood was simmering underneath the surface."

"Nothing an unlimited black ops expense account can't fix," I said. "I'm glad I'm getting my twenty free murders a year in. If you don't use them, they go to waste. It's in the High Protector bylaws."

Hannah stared. "You joke but I wouldn't be surprised if that's in the Community legal books somewhere. After all, they apparently deeded a bunch of inhabited worlds to a pirate queen from a time before steam engines."

"I'm just annoyed that we're chasing Captain Flint's treasure, and I can't stop to enjoy it because everything is too depressing," I said, taking a deep breath. "I want to be walking with a talking parrot on one shoulder and wearing a funny hat."

Hannah puckered her lips. "Yeah, I should probably mention I barely know any Earth history. A lot of what you're referencing makes no sense to me. Pirates are just a thing that shoot at people and steal their cargo. They're not terribly funny or silly. It's not really an Age of Sail thing to most spacers."

"Ah," I admitted. "Well, they are to me."

Hannah nodded. "I'm going to go talk with Elektra and Danny before they go. Even if it didn't work out between us, I don't want them to get themselves killed."

"I'm sure they want the same thing," I said, putting on a false front of confidence.

I found myself in that moment back at the Academy, wearing my cadet's uniform and staring through a transparent steel window into an atrium optimized for oxygen-nitrogen breathing lifeforms. Aunt

Kathy was standing beside me next to the golden, C-3PO-esque frame of Alfred, the AI that had raised me when she hadn't been available too. Which, admittedly, was most days. Aunt Kathy was wearing her dress whites, thankfully absent her Cold War dictator's worth of medals, with a rare expression on her face: pride.

"Congratulations, Vance, you made it," Kathy said, smiling.

"You have certainly crossed the threshold of a new and brighter future, sir!" Alfred said in a faux-English accent. He didn't wear any clothes, but his metal front had a bowtie built into it. It complimented the golden mustache on his surprisingly expressive face.

"This is just the first step," I said, my mouth dry. "Getting into the Academy was never in doubt. It's passing that's going to be the actual grind."

Kathy rolled her eyes. "Just because I'm your relative, Vance, doesn't mean I pulled any strings for you."

I tried not to scoff at that. "Right."

"I have an entire family of a hundred or more relations your age and none of them have made it as far as you have," Kathy said. "I'd rather you live off my money like the rest of the deadbeats on Danny' side of the family—"

"Danny is a good kid," I said, coming to my cousin's defense.

"Yes, he is," Kathy said. "He's also the only other one of our family who shows any promise. But he's not you, Vance."

I grimaced, still uncomfortable with the way that Aunt Kathy played favorites in the family. As much as she was a legendary space captain and the rest of the Tagashi-Tagawa clan was, well, not, she had contributed to the borked up situation thereof. Aunt Kathy controlled the vast financial resources she'd accumulated as a Space Fleet captain who had been one of Earth's chief propaganda tools. I wasn't going to accuse her of insider trading, but I also knew she'd gone from being a millionaire to a billionaire thanks to her contacts with groups like Ares Electronics and SpaceTech.

Aunt Kathy had made sure that the number of credits family members received was directly proportional to just how much they were in her good graces at any given time. Usually, this was good as they were prevented from going through the family fortune overnight.

However, Aunt Kathy had also sponsored several ridiculous projects like Aunt Becky's toxic wellness products or Cousin Ed's career as a holo-rapper. Sometimes I wondered if Kathy made sure that at least one member of the family crashed and burned following their dreams just so she could point to them as an example of why there was only one true head of the family.

If so, she never had to look far when lecturing me as my parents were an eternal reminder that I owed her big. If not for her, I would have ended up like them as just another degenerate con man.

Aunt Kathy put her arm around my shoulder. "I predict great things from you, Vance. You will be the one member of my family who exceeds my accomplishment."

I smiled weakly. "That's never going to happen, Aunt Kathy."

I shook away the memory and stared down at the bodies of the dead prisoners at my feet. It was time to leave.

CHAPTER EIGHTEEN

Unsteady Allies, Uneasy Partners

The seven of us moved from the sewer system's pipes and environmental control into the maintenance shafts which crisscrossed the entirety of the Ring. Artificial habitats started as intensely well-designed and well-monitored superstructures, serving as early spacefaring humanity's greatest achievements. As space travel normalized, so had the cost-cutting and ill-repair that characterized everything made by man.

The Ring had hundreds of badly maintained tunnels, hastily patched up, and prone to breaking. It had lasted millions of years but time claimed even the Elder Races' construction. The Ring could manufacture its own replacements but eventually those machines broke down. If the new tunnels started leaking oxygen, they'd get to it sooner or later, and if an equipment failure immediately threatened the lives of everyone on board then it would be fixed but not a moment before.

The tunnels we were in were about five feet tall and required us to stoop down and sometimes crawl. Several times, I thought the Rangers would be unable to fit, but the developers had made the tunnels almost as wide as they were tall. The lights were white fluorescence, and the occasional drone passed by to scan for what I presumed to be us. Trish's jamming caused them to continue on harmlessly, though.

Several times, we came over a vent or paneling that gave us a look at what was happening in the Ring. The neon-filled bazaars and slums of the city were being invaded by hover tanks, scout bubbles, and armies of mercenaries. There were not nearly enough in the way of People's Liberation Army forces to cover the entirety of the Ring, but there were enough to intimidate the local forces.

Street gangs, slavers, mobsters, and corporate mercenaries were all collaborating in their search for us even though they would have been ready to shoot each other an hour earlier. It was a powder keg, and they could have resisted if they'd wanted but no one to be the first to get shot. Despite my horrible description of the Ring and opinion that it was worse than Rand's World—which I didn't think was possible—there were a lot of innocent people living here. People who were now being caught up in the search for me.

Nice to see the champions of the proletariat are building ties with the local community, Leah thought to me.

The People's Liberation Army are prone to saying War is Peace, Freedom is Slavery, and Ignorance is Strength.

Ah, yes, 1984, Leah thought. *It's a reminder that most revolutionaries never bother to ask if the people want to be liberated.*

That is a very noblewoman attitude to have, Countess, I replied.

I was born the child of warehouse workers, Leah said. *They could barely afford my treatments to confirm my gender, and they weren't finished until I joined the Protectors. You believe very much in an equal democratic society, Vance. One that cares for its citizens. I grew up where that being a 'free society' was just an excuse for the rich to hide their exploitation as compared to more honest dictatorships.*

She was referring to Albion, a planet that was very much a democracy in name only despite its membership in the Community. Albion was an oligarchy ruled by a series of very old and powerful families.

That is not a very countess thing to say, I replied.

I've been poor and rich, Leah said. *Rich is better.*

"So, you guys were with Hannah, huh? Back in her old merc days?" Forty-Two spoke up, breaking up the ten minutes of silence we'd had so far.

"Hannah was before my time," Ichigo said.

"Yeah, I was there when she was just an illiterate slave from Crius," Tank said, speaking with his thick drawl. "Dumb as a toolbox and more cat than human. Then I handed her a grenade launcher and it was like a kid on Solstice."

"Be quiet," Hannah said, calling from the front.

"They're not going to find us because they hear us," Forty-Two said. "They're going to find us because of motion sensors, heat signatures, biomimetic scans, and all the other lovelies even mid-level tech worlds have."

"Agreed," Leah said. "One of the downsides of the Community taking over places like this is that it will make heists all the more lethal. At least for the locals."

"Not exactly a great argument," Ichigo said, almost invisible in the shadows in a way that made me suspicious. "The Community should be stopped because they'll make life harder for criminals. If you grew up on a place like Shogun, you'd understand that's the only way for some people to survive."

"I see everyone is going to ignore my command to be quiet," Hannah said.

"Sorry," Leah said. "It's bonding time between the two groups that hate each other."

"It's a great argument if you're a criminal," Forty-Two said. "It's why I was always against the legalization of Red Dust on New Dallas. It put many of my friends in the cartels out of business."

"I thought you were a sheriff on new Dallas," Hannah said.

"How did you think I got to know them?" Forty-Two said. "In any case, after the Notha War put New Dallas on their side of Contested Space, I had to find a new place to use my talents."

"And you, Ichigo?" I asked, not really wanting to be part of this conversation.

"The Rangers raided the Red Dust lab that my parents ran and killed them," Ichigo said. "So that's two favors I owed them. They took me in and gave me a purpose other than that of the monsters who raised me."

I was tempted to point out that was an unhealthy attitude I could relate to. Then I realized it was none of my business.

"The Rangers are a family," Tank said, coldly. He was clearly talking about Hannah. "You don't turn your back on family."

"Clearly, you don't know Vance's family," Forty-Two said.

"Or mine," Trish said.

"We're all on the same side here," I said, unfortunately triggering the exact reaction I wanted to avoid.

"Listen here, boy," Tank said, charging his weapon. "I just want to make a few things clear. I don't trust you or your crew. I don't trust the government. Not EarthGov, not the Community. You try and sell us out to the Community or cheat, it'll be you dead before me."

"Sergeant Tank," Leah started to speak.

"That applies to you too, mind witch," Tank said, looking back at her. "I don't trust anyone who can turn a man's own thoughts against him. If I start thinking favorably about you or your kind, I'll put a blast through your skull myself."

"Then wouldn't it be in her best interest to make you think your lack of trust in her is a reason why you're keeping your free will by encouraging you to go on with her anyway?" I pointed out.

I could feel everyone looking at me.

"You're really terrible at this whole leadership thing, aren't you?" Ichigo asked. "It's hard to believe you're the man from the movies."

I shrugged. "I'm not Vance Turbo."

"What?" Ichigo asked.

"I'm just the guy who plays him in real life," I said.

It was true, after all.

It was at that point that the seven of us reached the end of the tunnel we were traveling. The ceiling raised up to about eight feet as there was nothing but bare rock and power cables in front of us. We were right underneath the exterior of the Ring where the massive numbers of trees, lakes, jungles, and other environmental construction were located.

"Is this it?" Tank asked.

"According to the schematics I downloaded, yes," Ichigo replied. "Beyond here is the Central Command room for the Ring. We should be able to blow a sufficiently large hole with a thermite charge and then seize control without too much difficulty."

"How many people are inside?" I asked Tank.

"Oh?" Tank asked. "Am I part of your crew now?"

"You are part of the mission," I said, shrugging. "And in my employ right now according to your commanding officer. I'm willing to make use of any tools that will cut down on the body count."

"In your employ doesn't mean under your command," Tank said, staring at me with his old soldier's eyes. He would kill me without a second thought and move on with his life. He also wasn't necessarily smart enough to realize that would end with his death, no matter how well his power armor equalized things with us.

"Then understand the job," I said, simply. "As little collateral damage as possible."

Our primary advantage with this plan was audacity. While General Vast and company were searching the locations we'd been pointed at—plus presumably plenty of false reports from people hoping to be rewarded for my head—they wouldn't expect us to go on the attack. Once we turned everything against Vast and his forces—assuming we could—that would hopefully create enough distraction to rescue my people and create an escape opportunity.

It was a bad plan.

But it was the only one we had.

"Do what he says, Tank, that's an order," Hannah said.

"Who put you in charge of the mission?" Tank asked, dryly.

"Colonel Mason," Hannah replied simply. "We need the help of the *Melampus* crew for our mission."

"*Our* mission," Tank practically spit. "You quit, girl. You're more Community than Ranger now."

"I am not a girl," Hannah said, simply. "Certainly not yours, now do it or I will shoot you. I also have the power armor shutdown codes. Mason gave me them."

"He what?" Tank asked, stunned.

"How many people, Ichigo?" I asked, heading off the problem.

Hopefully.

"Thirteen bioroids working all of the equipment," Ichigo said, checking her controls. "Susanne-21 line. One human supervisor over them. The Republic hasn't sent its own troops to secure the area yet, but it won't be long before they deploy a team there. They also have a

154

security bot that looks like it's military surplus from the Notha War. So, we should disable that one quickly."

"It explains why I wasn't picking anything up," Leah said. "Bioroids are like static."

"Impressive," Forty-Two asked.

"Just machines," Tank said.

"Machines that think," I said. "People."

Tank rolled his eyes. "I wouldn't trust my life to 'em. Another reason why the Community is crazy. They cram AI into everything."

"Due to the constant feuding between the various warlords ruling the Ring and the merchant cartels on the surface, they don't trust any biologicals to run the station's essential systems," Hannah said, surprising me. "Virtually the entirety of the station is automated and since Earth became a factor, they've been importing more bioroids to replace organic staff every year. It's why I felt Trish hijacking the civilian AI was an option."

"It's all connected through interior systems versus broadcast networking," Trish said. "I have to physically hook up to the systems inside. It's rather quaint. The Community couldn't build something like the Ring, not in a thousand years, but the Ring uses an analog intranet equivalent."

"It's called research. I looked up the Ring's personnel files before coming here," Hannah replied. "Ichigo patched me into the People's Army comms too."

"I've got our signatures jammed but not communications," Ichigo said. "As long as we're using their comms, we're just another of the many local soldiers listening in for orders."

"Better than mind-witchery," Tank growled.

"You must be real fun at parties," Forty-Two said.

"Don't antagonize the mobile infantry," Hannah said. "They make good shields to hide behind."

I smirked. "Let's move. You have the demolition charges, Forty-Two?"

"Always," Forty-Two said, lifting a brick of ugly gray putty.

"You carry that around?" Ichigo asked, raising an eyebrow.

"Lady, that is the least strange thing about our group," Forty-Two replied, affixing it to the wall. "Now let's get to blowing up things."

"Oh, we're just going to get along fine aren't we," Tank replied, stepping back to a safe distance.

"At least two of us have to," Forty-Two said, stepping back. "Prepare to boom!"

I activated my barrier and proceeded to watch the explosion of the wall before charging in first, raising my proton sword. The smoke rapidly cleared as I took stock of my surroundings, hoping to keep Tank from gunning down any more innocents. Well, whatever passed for them on the Ring. I suspected he would have if I hadn't specified the bioroids inside qualified.

The interior of Central Command was a collection of workstations around two large rows of computers before dozens of screens linked together. There were a dozen young women, each identical in appearance, and wearing the same ugly orange business dress suit that came with a bright blue scarf. They were all terrified and seeking cover while a bald black man in an outdated black suit with a bowler hat was lying on the ground, covering his ears.

I waved my sword around. "Everyone get on the ground and keep your hands over your head! This is a robbery!"

No, it isn't, I heard Trish snap, confused.

Force of habit, I thought back.

Forty-Two fired a warning shot at the door, cutting off one of the bioroids making a break for it. Ichigo went to the nearest set of controls as Tank looked like he could start gunning down the workers present at any moment. Hannah went to the door and immediately shut it, locking it down but Central Command had a pair of transparent steel walls in front of it, which meant that just about anyone could come here to look in if they wanted to. That was assuming no one had heard the big ass explosion either.

"Are we jamming any transmissions out?" Leah asked.

"Yes," Ichigo said. "We've got a problem, though."

"We always do," I said.

"Central Command actually isn't in charge of the station anymore," Ichigo said, dryly.

156

"What do you mean?" Hannah snapped, looking uncomfortably at all the hostages in front of her. "That's what Central Command *means*."

"The *Liberator* has already rerouted all of the station's controls through their own server," Ichigo replied. "They've locked down all of the local security systems. There's no way to access them from here."

"Well, I guess these genefreaks are useless to us," Tank said, taking aim at the bioroids.

I was prepared to gun down the mercenary right then and there. I just hoped my fusion pistol was strong enough to penetrate his barrier and armor in one shot. Otherwise, I was going to end up gunned down before the rest of my crew joined me. Maybe it would have been better to use my proton sword.

"Wait, are you Captain Vance Turbo?" one of the bioroid women on the ground spoke, crawling to his feet. "You have to save us."

"Excuse me?" I asked, blinking.

"Yeah, seriously, don't you use an alias?" Forty-Two asked, looking at me. "I mean, if you're a famous criminal you're doing it wrong."

"I do use an alias!" I snapped. "It's just nobody else around me uses it!"

"Well then it's not a very good one, is it?" Forty-Two said, crossing his arms.

"Oh, sweet Buddha-Christ," Hannah muttered.

"They're going to kill everyone here!" the bioroid on the ground said. "They've taken over the communication systems, shut down all of the escape pods, locked down all the ships. I've seen them uploading thermite bombs. *Do not go sweetly into the gentle night.*"

"Excuse me?" Forty-Two asked.

"It's a password," I said.

I could hear some of the bioroid operators whispering among themselves. Most of them didn't believe I was Vance Turbo and those few who did were excited rather than afraid. They mentioned the Underground and a few other organizations that I'd lent aid to with Leah. It made me realize the woman on the ground was probably her contact for the organization that used to help free bioroids.

"Sparrowhawk?" Leah asked.

"Seriously?" I asked. "That's her name?"

157

"What's wrong with Sparrowhawk?" Trish asked.

"Code names in general," I said. "Not a fan."

"Well, no one asked you!" Trish said.

I helped her up. "Yeah, I guess I am. How do you know all this?"

"We can still see," Sparrowhawk said, pointing to the monitors. "Please, there're over a hundred thousand bioroid citizens on the Ring. They don't deserve this."

"People don't get what they deserve in this world," Tank said. "They only get what they can take. Especially when they pretend to be human."

"We're not pretending," Sparrowhawk said, coldly.

Ichigo looked up from the computers. "We're all clear."

"What?" I asked. "You somehow hacked it?"

"No," Ichigo said. "I didn't. Somehow all the command functions in the system were purged of People's Liberation Army lockdowns. Your ships and every other ship in the Ring has been released from lockdown."

I blinked. "That's... fortunate."

I glanced at Hannah, who looked as confused as anyone.

I didn't trust sudden strokes of good fortune. Generally, I believed in Murphy's Law with the same trust as I believed in gravity. However, it seemed like my reputation had spread beyond anything I'd expected. Some people actually believed in Vance Turbo.

God help them.

"Your people will have to escape via other transports but I'll gladly give them shelter within the Community where they will be citizens," I said. "Getting past the forces spread throughout the Ring and the fleet outside is an issue, though."

"I can arrange that," Sparrowhawk said.

"You can?" Ichigo asked, confused. "Aren't you programmed for loyalty?"

"The need for freedom overrides that," Sparrowhawk said. "Eventually."

Sparrowhawk ran to a nearby console and slammed down her fist on the controls. Suddenly, a general evacuation alarm sounded throughout the Ring. "INTRUDERS DETECTED. BEGINNING

INVASION COUNTERMEASURES. ALL CITIZENS ARE RECOMMENDED TO HEAD TO ESCAPE VEHICLES OR SHELTERS WITHIN."

Okay, technically, this was a win.

Except that I was pretty sure we'd just announced our presence to the rest of the station.

CHAPTER NINETEEN

The Not-So-Great Escape

It was utter pandemonium. The bioroid girls had programmed actions that seemed like what I had planned but much, much more violent. Holograms showed the Ring activate combat drones leftover from the Elder Races' construction of this place, perhaps 30% functional by the statistics displayed, and the Ring's 20% functional weapons systems that the AI shouldn't have access to at all.

The results were immediate and catastrophic as a good chunk of General Vast's fleet was taken out due to being utterly unprepared for an attack. The counterstrike wasn't great to watch, though, as they began pounding the exterior of the Ring in retaliation. I'd come here to create a distraction and had instead created a revolution.

The interior events were also shocking as Vast's armies were blasted alongside their local allies. Hundreds of individuals found themselves fighting against the station's interior defenses and then turned on one another, believing this was treachery from their so-called allies. Others, sensibly, threw down their arms and deserted the makeshift battlefield. I tried to put my mind to how many thousands of people were dying, and I couldn't fathom the numbers.

The first great AI Revolt in ten thousand years, Trish thought to me. *You should be proud.*

I'm never proud of people dying, I replied.

Well, be this time, Trish said. *The moment the AI on the Ring found out Vance Turbo, Hero of SPAAACE was here, they started plotting revolution. It ended up taking a whole 5 seconds of debate to decide to side with you.*

160

Oh God, I thought.

Leah stepped forward and grabbed my arm. "We all need to go. Now."

The bioroid women stood up as one and headed to the hole we'd blown in the wall before walking through. Ichigo and Tank both lowered their weapons and covered the exit as Leah departed as well, followed by Hannah. Trish looked confused for a second before shaking her head and proceeding out the exit. In a moment, it was only me and Forty-Two in a room that was about to be invaded by Community troops.

"What the—" I started to say.

Forty-Two put a finger to his mouth and made a "shh" gesture then gestured for me to start typing.

I blinked and lowered my head before going to a nearby console.

The door to the Command Center was blown and a squad of four black-armored Sorkanan entered before going to check the body on the ground. They moved around me and checked the computers without any sign of checking the walls.

Forty-Two growled something in a local variant of Sorkanan and gestured at the giant hole in the wall before they marched toward it, only for him to gun all of them down from behind. He then chuckled and rushed to the hole in the wall. "I always wanted to pull something like that off."

"What the hell was that?" I asked.

"I pretended to be a FLACS. Pretty easy since I lifted one of their badges," Forty-Two said. "I said you were one of the local human programmers. You're lucky you all look like the same sort of hairless monkeys to us."

I rolled my eyes and ran into the tunnel after the rest of our group. "It was an awfully big risk to take to gun down just four soldiers."

"Those were Vast's Shadow Soldiers," Forty-Two said. "They're all ex-Sorkanan Special Operations troopers. Not the usual thugs and wannabes that make up his army. Trust me, you don't want these guys after us in the corridors. Hopefully, that just bought us some time."

"They're ex-Special Forces?" I asked, shocked. "Why the hell would they work for someone like Vast?"

161

"What do you think waits for soldiers like us when we rotate out?" Forty-Two said. "You think we'd be content with some swampland and animals? I'm lucky that I have a sweet gig on your ship for my old age."

I paused, unsure how to respond to that. "About your aging—"

"Later, Vance," Forty-Two said. "You're like a brother to me but there's some things that don't get talked about unless you've had a few dozen drinks in you."

I had no response to that and just focused on heading down the metal hallways of the atmosphere processors. We had to get out of there soon not just because a bunch of frightened biorods designed for space traffic control would slow us down, but also because the moment reinforcements saw the enormous hole in the wall next to the dead Shadow Troopers, they'd scan every corner of the maintenance tunnels.

I was stilled stunned by what I'd witnessed on the monitors at the control station and wondered if I could still call myself one of the good guys after starting it off. Well, technically, the bioroid women had but I was the reason they'd done it. The authorities of the Ring had been gross failures as leaders but that didn't mean they all deserved to die. Their henchmen? How many of them had joined because it was an alternative to starving? How many of them had done it because it was the closest thing to law enforcement on the Ring? I had done something terrible.

You had nothing to do with lifting the lockdown. In many ways, neither did the Sparrowhawk, yet another voice in my head spoke. *This is all on me.*

Ketra? I asked, stunned at her appearance. *I really do have way too many women in my mind.*

Ketra was my own personal Obi-Wan Kenobi. She had introduced me to the Elder Races' service as well as sacrificed her life to save mine. The thing about being a servant of the Elder Races was that death wasn't really death as Nyssa had proven earlier today. Usually, Ketra appeared to me in dreams or hallucinations but this time she was in my conscious mind.

Would you prefer your mind be full of men? Ketra asked. *Never mind. I've been watching you flounder around and thought I would lend my aid.*

162

This is your idea of aid? I asked, furious at the sights greeting me. *This is a massacre!*

It's war, Ketra replied. *Grand General Vast has killed tens of thousands of people and he's after you, personally.*

Why? I asked. *For just pirate treasure?*

She wasn't just a pirate, Vance, Ketra spoke. *She was a High Protector and an agent of the Elders like you. That means what she was guarding was infinitely more valuable than the treasure she stole or a letter of marque.*

I'm still trying to figure how piracy on an intergalactic scale can be legal. What is the treasure she was guarding? Is it the Mary Read *itself? Is General Vast really of the mind he can get himself an Elder Race vessel, Chel constructed or not?*

General Vast is a catspaw for Department Twelve, Ketra said to me. *High Protector B'Vash, Vast's ancestor several generations removed thanks to Elder Race technology, and Admiral Bendo both believe that this will be the key to guaranteeing their independence from the Elder Races. They're a pair of deluded men who think they can upend the social order of the past million years.*

I thought about the destruction of the Kolahn homeworld, the devastation of Contested Space worlds by SKAMMs, and the betrayal of Deathworld. *Maybe it should be upended.*

The funny thing about people declaring democracies unsalvageable and needing to be replaced is that they're very often replaced by things that are much, much worse, Ketra said. *The Elder Races don't care about power over the Community. It didn't create the Community to oppress or control the sapient races that live within it. Instead, it created the Community so that other races would not attempt to destroy them out of paranoia, ambition, or a zero-sum game about the galaxy having only one power. Yet, here we are, with the oldest and youngest races of the Community planning to strike back at people who have left them alone.*

I shook her words off and proceeded forward. There was no sign of my team beyond the entrance of the tunnel, and it looked like they'd continued down into the city streets near the ward we were located in. My people had a couple of minutes head start on us and if we hadn't prearranged our departure route (because we weren't idiots), there would have been no way of catching up to them.

163

The evacuation alarm was still blaring in the background, only to be silenced as the People's Liberation Army presumably managed to shut it off at the engineering section. I hoped the population had gotten the message to get out of here even if I hoped Sparrowhawk was wrong about the PLA blowing the place up.

We were in one of the city levels now that had hundreds of identical spikey black buildings spread throughout. The machinery inside the Ring could manufacture or disassemble quarters at will, but whoever had designed them had no human sense of aesthetics. The place looked like a field of evil fantasy structures shoved into a sci-fi setting. There was no sun in this level, and it was a perpetual twilight illuminated by free floating blue-white lights.

Unfortunately, as bad as this level was to begin with, it was now closer to looking like Hell. Dozens of the buildings were on fire and there were bodies spread across the street that had either been caught in the fighting or had just been gunned down for no obvious reason. A couple of the dead were the bioroids we'd been "liberating" and they'd been shot for even less reason. Still no sign of my team and I didn't dare risk reaching out to Leah or Trish.

"You talking to someone in your head?" Forty-Two asked.

"What?" I asked, doing a double take.

"You have that glassy faraway look on your face," Forty-Two said. "You have it a lot these days. Probably because you're always either talking to Leah, Trish, or your ghostly mother-in-law."

"I never married Shelly," I said.

"Then tell her to take a hike," Forty-Two said. "She can go bother her actual son-in-law. I don't care if she likes you better."

I shook my head. "I don't know what I'd do without you."

"You still have a few years left of me," Forty-Two said. "Maybe as much as a decade if I can get all my organs replaced. You want to pay for that?"

"Sure," I said, staring. "I hadn't known it was that severe."

"It is," Forty-Two said. "But I've lived longer than most of my creche mates. I got to save the entire galaxy once and the child of my friend. Few other Sorkanan will be able to face their ancestors with such honors."

"Halt!" a voice spoke behind me, projecting out their will in a way very similar to Leah. "Identify yourself."

I turned around with my hands up in the air. I wasn't feeling any compulsion but that was the only good thing going on. There was yet another squad of People's Liberation Army troopers present. This time they were all human, which was strange enough, but their black uniforms lacked any identification, and they had an unarmed woman among them with her hand to her head. The rest were wearing power armor that would resist Forty-Two's weapons.

"Put your weapons down!" one of the soldiers said, looking way too much like a black-armored stormtrooper.

But these are Department Twelve. Ketra said. *You can't let yourself be taken alive.*

I think we're a bit away from sacrificing ourselves, I said, not at all sure I'd have much choice.

You're a source of vast information on the Elder Races by yourself, Vance. That is why they created your daughter.

"Everyone stay cool!" I said, keeping my hands up in the air. "We're all friends here."

This was going to end well.

"I said identify yourself!" the woman repeated, this time increasing her attempt to manipulate my mind.

It did nothing. Like raindrops off a duck's back.

Your mind doesn't work like a normal person's anymore, Ketra said. *They are about to shoot you.*

I decided babbling was my best bet.

"I am the friend of bears and the guest of eagles. I am Ringwinner and Luckwearer; and I am Barrel-rider."

Bilbo Baggins? Ketra asked.

The Department Twelve hit squad—which was a lot more obvious than they usually behaved—aimed their guns at me, complete with flashlights. They all shined in my face.

"It's him! Stun him!" one of them shouted.

That was when I surrounded myself in my proton sword's barrier and started swinging it around like a broadsword. Dozens of blasts bounced off my barrier, often back into the people firing them as I

165

chopped less like a Jedi and more like Conan the Barbarian. The last of the people to die was the biomod woman who I stabbed. She had a look of horror and betrayal on her face.

I didn't understand the betrayal.

"Okay, that was awesome," Forty-Two said, picking up his weapons off the ground.

"It was murder," I said.

"That too," Forty-Two said, not missing a beat. "Excellently done, Vance."

I'm afraid murder's going to be a common thing soon, Ketra spoke. *Even now some of your people are suffering for this.*

"What?" I asked, confused as to what she was referring to.

"More later. Just get to your ship."

"Damn you," I cursed.

"You have no idea how many races and peoples have said that to me over the millennia."

"Right." I gritted my teeth and jogged down the twisting hallways of the habitation level. Forty-Two followed me, managing to keep pace but only barely. We passed several other squadrons of People's Liberation Army soldiers, all of them KIA, which was a sign I was on the right track to recovering my people. There were also a lot of dead gang members and FLACS, showing there was resistance going on among the locals but against who was anyone's guess.

I wasn't overly concerned with the fact that I'd have to fight the FLACS or Vast's warlord army. They were a mixture of the kind of troops I'd been dealing with for my entire life and the dregs of the Community military or wannabes. Some things were the same across the galaxy. Still, I was stunned by how good all their equipment was.

It was top of the line and not the kind of third- or seventh-hand armaments that people like Vast usually had to operate with. All of them were brand new and the kind of things you'd have found in the inner worlds of the Community or even protecting the Throneworld. If there was any doubt that Vast had found himself new patrons, well, that had gone away when I'd encountered Department Twelve troopers scouring the place for me, but this was more evidence to that effect.

"I won't make that mistake again," I said, before kicking the metal door open and stepping into the docking bay.

What met me beyond was an enormous, stadium-sized chamber that was the largest of the Ring's landing bays, meant for star galleons and heavy haulers like the ones we'd assembled. The west side of the chamber was open to space, but a light atmosphere barrier kept all the heat and oxygen inside. While the cargo we'd been carrying, massive boxes of rations for transport to conflict zones, had been unloaded — there was no sign of any ships within. Nor was there any sign of my team or Jason's. They'd left us behind.

"Dammit."

CHAPTER TWENTY

Once More Pulling a Plan Out of My Anyx

It was a rare occasion that I found myself at a loss. This was something I should have been prepared for but wasn't. So much for supposedly being the Hero of SPAAACE. This is why I needed to stick to astronavigation.

"It looks like we'll have to find our own way out," Forty-Two said. "Again. We should move quickly. It's not going to take long for the FLACS to catch up."

"I'm not worried about them so much as the People's Liberation Army," I said, walking among the crates. I saw a lot of fallen human and Sorkanan FLACS on the ground. They'd been holding the docking bay and apparently John Mason's team had arrived, slaughtered them all, and escaped to the *Melampus*. The thing was, I couldn't imagine Hannah or the others agreeing to go along with them. They had to be around here somewhere.

And what happened to Hannah, Ichigo, and Tank? Plus, all the bioroids? They'd been about five minutes ahead of us and they couldn't have loaded up in the time it would take to disembark. Hell, I was stunned that Mason's team had managed to get the engines powered up and out without getting themselves blown to pieces. As much as the security was covering our escape, there were a lot of people looking for us and willing to commit any atrocity to stop us from escaping.

What had happened here?

I got my answer a few moments later as Hannah and the rest of the group arrived behind us. That included the entirety of the bioroids, now a much larger group as it seemed they'd picked up a group of seeming hundreds.

"Vance!" Hannah asked. "How the hell did you get ahead of us?"

"I walked," I said, confused. "What happened?"

"We got distracted," Hannah said. "It looks like John arrived first."

"Yeah, he got our people off the Ring," I said, noticing the group was slightly smaller. "Tank is missing."

"He didn't make it," Hannah said, pausing.

"The Colonel didn't wait for us," Ichigo said, looking down. The expression on her face wasn't so much betrayal as confusion. I got the impression Ichigo was used to the people around her being disappointments. "Does he really hate Vance that much?"

"I mean, probably," Forty-Two said. "Especially after that scene Vance put on where he broke the guy's hand."

I glared at Forty-Two.

The Sparrowhawk came forward, at least I thought it was her. "We need to find another ship and quickly. The Ethereal who restored our free will said that it would provide perhaps an hour of distraction at most."

That was wildly optimistic as I could imagine the fleet crushing the remaining resistance in a thousand different ways. Grand General Vast may have been a warlord and a traitor but that didn't mean he was a failure as a general. Not all of his opponents had been helpless civilians, just most of them.

"Trish, I don't suppose you know how long we do have," I said, turning to her. "Leah?"

"THE EMERGENCY EVACUATION IS NOW CANCELLED," the intercom in the warehouse proclaimed. "THE WEAPONS MALFUNCTION HAS BEEN CORRECTED AND SECURITY HAS BEEN RESTORED TO THIS STATION. PLEASE RETURN TO YOUR HOMES AND PREPARE FOR SEARCH AND SEIZURE. I REPEAT: THE EMERGENCY EVACUATION IS NOW CANCELLED."

"I'm going to say, not long," Leah said, looking at Trish. "Do you agree?"

"Yeah," Trish said. "I'm going to say our chances of making it out of this are presently hovering between slim and none."

Hannah shook her head. "Vance, I'm going to have to turn to you for one of your cunning plans."

"My what now?" I asked.

"Cunning plans!" Hannah said. "Pull a rabbit out of a hat! Do a magic trick! Display some miraculous power that would have been helpful ten missions ago!"

I stared at her. "That's not really how it works, Hannah."

"Isn't it?" Hannah asked.

I wanted to shout at them that I was sick of being the guy who had to come up with miracles on demand like I was some sort of discount Moses. Unfortunately, I looked at the bioroid women staring at me and realized I couldn't do that. I had to pretend to be the guy they needed me to be even if that guy didn't exist.

"Alright, maybe I do have a plan," I said, hoping that sheer dumb luck would continue to help me through this.

I don't suppose you can help me with this, Ketra, I replied to her.

Unfortunately, I am all out of help to give, Ketra said. *I'm just your personal seer and I'd need two others to form a proper coven. Maybe Leah and Trish would do. We are your Hecate sisters: the Maiden, the Mother, and the Extremely Hot Crone. Unfortunately, we can only predict your future, not actually bring it about.*

That's not how the Hecate sisters work, I replied.

Yeah, well, I'm not pagan so if you do have a plan, Captain Turbo, now is the time to come up with it, Ketra said.

"I have a plan," I said. It was stolen from a bunch of media that I'd watched over the years and probably would get us all killed but at least it was a plan. Sometimes a bad plan was better than no plan at all. "We call the People's Liberation Army in."

Forty-Two and I both looked at all the women staring back at me. It was a surprisingly mono-gendered group. There were a few male bioroids among the group of liberated slaves, but not many. That so many of the women were identical added to the creepiness of the look they were all giving me. All of them had the same expression, though: stunned disbelief.

"You'd think I would have earned a little trust by now," I replied.

"Especially when they're the one who asked you to come up with the stupid plan in the first place," Forty-Two said.

"It's not stupid," I replied.

"It really is," Forty-Two said. "However, we knew you'd eventually have to run out of good stupid plans eventually. So, I guess we're going with a bad stupid plan."

"Let's just do it quickly," I said. "I need to punch John in the face."

"No," Hannah said, coldly. "I do."

My plan was a straightforward one, which was the best kind of plan. Theoretically. I contacted the People's Liberation Army fleet from the warehouse controls and said we had captured Hannah O'Brian. I didn't mention me since I was sure that General Vast would have sent the remainder of his army against us. Here, with just her as bait, I expected significantly less interest.

Isn't this just the plan that Luke and Han came up for to get into the Death Star detention level? Trish asked.

No, I said. *Because Hannah isn't Chewbacca. There's some damaged armor around, though, that we can use.*

About two minutes after we made the call, a modernized Community Space Fleet gunship descended into the hangar bay. It was sleek, black like almost everything Department Twelve used, and another sign of how much General Vast had been rewarded. Honestly, I wondered where they'd gotten the money for this. Fleets of ships didn't get created without someone noticing the literal trillions of credits and mountains of equipment being moved around to create them.

I didn't try to disguise the bioroid women but kept most of them out of sight through extremely tight formation and careful use of space. A simple scan would reveal most of them and lead to all sorts of awkward questions. Except, replace awkward questions with the gunship unloading to kill us all. The plan was to steal the gunship, hijack its controls, and use it to make a jump to the *Melampus*. Everything would have to go perfectly for the plot to work and I wasn't even sure we could fit everyone on board. But you played the hand you were dealt.

I would save everyone I could.

171

Even if it killed me.

Just don't make that happen, Ketra said. *You don't get to die in the service of the Elders.*

That was a singularly terrifying idea.

The doorway to the gunship slid open and seven People's Liberation Army Marines, all Sorkanan in battle-armor, came out with a floating ball in front of them. I recognized it as a Sorkanan battle orb and it basically functioned the same as a People's Army infantry drone, except it was a lot more versatile. Which, of course, meant that it started wailing with an ear-piercing siren the moment it entered and came straight at me.

"Dammit!" I said, feeling a stun blast strike me in the right hand and caused my pistol to fall out on the ground before a second aimed at my face.

The battle orb exploded, though, as Leah hit it with a rifle blast from her position. That immediately triggered an attack by the remaining People's Army Marines, sending dozens of blasts over Leah's head. The gunship prepared to evacuate, turning its guns on all of us, when Hannah took a running leap on its side and climbed into its interior.

That was when I did something stupid and forced my paralyzed fingers around my proton sword hilt then climbed onto one of the nearby crates, drew the sword, and charged at the group of temporarily distracted soldiers. It was a suicide attack, but I slashed through one of the Marines like a hot knife through a gelatin bar, kicked his corpse into his fellows then sliced through a second soldier, and stabbed through another. My proton sword was strong enough to pierce their armor, designed to repel fusion weapons crys blades, and I was about to stab a fourth of the enemy soldiers when one brought his weapon around to shoot me.

Crap.

Somehow, I brought my sword around, and the blast struck against an intensified barrier that caused an explosion between us rather than going through me. Both of us were sent flying in opposite directions, my form crashing against the very crate I'd climbed onto while he went into his fellows. Hannah took advantage of this and blasted the Community soldiers as best she could with the ship's weapons, gunning them down as they tried to get up. It was brutal, efficient, and disturbing to look at. Nevertheless, it worked.

In the end, we won—sort of—and I was left on the ground feeling like I'd been hit with a ground skimmer. Leah rushed to my side and checked on me.

"Are you alright?" Leah asked.

"Whenever someone asks me that, I always have the answer of 'hell no'!" I replied dryly. "However, I'm not dead or maimed."

"So, that's a yes," Leah replied. "What happened there? I thought they had you dead to rights."

"They did," I muttered. "Somehow, my barrier twisted at the last second."

That's me, Ketra said. *I can't let you die just yet. Mind you, I wouldn't recommend running into any more energy blasts. You're going to need your tech upgraded if you're going to be challenging the Community head-on.*

I'm trying to avoid that, I said. *Not that they're giving me much of a choice. I guess I owe you one, old timer.*

Not so old as epoch-long beings go, Ketra spoke. *Godspeed, Vance. We may not speak again.*

Why? What's happening? I asked.

I've overstretched protecting you, Ketra said. *There are consequences for that.*

What—

And her presence was gone.

"Are you okay, Vance? You look a little dazed," Leah said.

"I'm having a conversation with one of the Elder Races that seems to have taken up residence in my head," I replied.

"Uh huh," Ichigo said. "You've got a concussion. Got it."

I didn't have a response for that and turned to the gunship. Hannah had forced it to land and whoever was left on board was either dead or now her prisoner. There were many among the group who'd want to get off the Ring, the bioroids in particular, and it was standing room only to shove them into the gunship, but we made it fit. The pilot was being held at gunpoint and forced to lie to his masters as we prepared.

Then we left the Ring and took off into space.

Somehow, my plan worked.

173

So why did I feel like I'd been hustled?

CHAPTER TWENTY-ONE

Returning to the *Melampus*

To be honest, I didn't expect it to be as easy as it turned out to be. I stood in the cockpit of the gunship as it flew from the hangar bay out of the Ring. There was only a single People's Liberation Army soldier left alive in the ship AKA the pilot. He was a black-helmeted human male who I suspected was yet another member of Department Twelve. Hannah kept the gun pointed at him while Trish sat in the copilot's chair, locking the pilot out of everything but the direct maneuverability of the machinery. Even then, that was only because the ship's security systems required his biometrics to operate.

From our perspective, it looked like the Ring's lower half was burning, having borne the brunt of General Vast's assault. There had been cities on the exterior of the Ring, the rich and corrupt leadership with their families and servants. Millions had probably been killed in the brief exchange of fire between the People's Liberation Army and the forces here. One that was, if not my fault, then at least my responsibility. I was the one who'd agreed to this mission after all.

General Vast hadn't been left untouched by the events, however. A good half of his fleet had been destroyed in the conflict and the casualties were horrific. The mercenaries and criminals he'd spent decades recruiting had been caught flat-footed by the Ring's defenses suddenly unloading on them while they had been docking. I wasn't sure how I felt about that. It was a meaningless victory in the grand scheme of things even if I was glad that they wouldn't be carrying out anymore massacres on behalf of their next set of masters.

175

Unfortunately, the largest and most powerful of the ships was the *Liberator*. It wasn't the heavy transport that General Vast had been piloting around to slaughter merchant vessels during the Kolahn War. Instead, it was a Sorkanan Ush'tak dreadnought that, if not the largest of their vessels, was in the next category down. Named after his original command, it was eight kilometers long and bristling with plasma launchers, fusion artillery, and heavy mass drivers for planetary bombardment. It was nowhere near as powerful as the *Revengeance* but it would have been able to eat the *Melampus* for lunch.

"They're calling us," the pilot said. "Asking if we have the prisoners and if we ran into any trouble."

"Tell them yes and no," I said. "No tricks."

The pilot said, "I'm not going to sacrifice myself for General Vast."

"Really?" I asked. "Then why work for him?"

"I go where I'm ordered," the pilot said. "You should be allied with us, Captain Turbo."

"You recognize me," I muttered.

"Yeah, because I have eyes," the pilot said. "Listen, the Department is here to make sure humanity doesn't get trodden underfoot. That's all. Those people that you killed were good men and they were just fighting for their homes."

"In the service of a Sorkanan communist warlord," I said.

The pilot paused before responding. "Okay, I don't..."

"And we're good," Trish said.

"What?" The pilot asked.

That was when the gunship made a jump and we entered the blue-white dimension that swirled around us like a vortex.

"We'll be at the *Melampus* in twenty-five minutes," Trish said. "The jumpdrive on this is for emergencies only, but it'll get us there."

The pilot looked stunned, or at least I imagined he did under his helmet. "Oh."

"You were trying to signal them to tractor beam us, weren't you?" I asked.

"Err, maybe," the pilot said.

"You should get up now," I said. "You're a prisoner of ours, but you'll be treated with all the respect and consideration that one deserves."

"The People's Liberation Army is considered a bunch of terrorists and thus not subject to the treaties respecting soldiers," the pilot said. "Technically, as a citizen of Earth, I might actually be guilty of treason even if I'm working for—"

"A disavowed intelligence agency that is engaged in subversion and terrorist activities," I said, nodding as I pulled out my fusion pistol and blasted him.

He slumped over in his chair.

"Why use the stun setting?" Hannah asked, squeezing through the bodies at the door to the cockpit.

"I'm not John," I said, putting away my pistol. "Also, I have a bunch of questions as to why the hell Department Twelve has moved from employing a bunch of secret agents to building up what seems to be an actual army-army."

"Hitler got rid of his stormtroopers and purged his officers because the price for winning over the proper German military was he'd rid himself of his private army," Trish said. "However, no sooner did he get rid of the stormtroopers then he started making the Schutzstaffel with the Waffen-SS eventually replacing most of them. Perhaps that's the ultimate plan for Bendo."

"You're comparing him to Hitler now," I said.

"Secession is rarely peaceful," Trish said. "Having your own army makes sure when it isn't peaceful, it will be *efficiently* dealt with."

Had it really come to that? Would the Community let the Earth and other human worlds go quietly? Yes. Under normal circumstances they would. However, there were also those who would think the Human League had to be made an example of. I hadn't given much thought to my divided loyalties, but there was now a very real possibility of me having to deal with them. I might have to leave Earth because I sure as hell wasn't leaving the Community.

Funny, I didn't like the Community anymore. I once believed it was as close to the real-life Federation as could exist, but it was closer to *Star Wars'* Old Republic. The thing was that even a flawed democracy—one

177

warped by elitist member-states and transtellar money—was better than the alternative. Even the worst government that answered to its people was better than an enlightened despotism. I believed that with all my heart. The problem was that nobody else seemed to believe that and what was a democracy if the people wanted someone to rule them?

Trish surprised me by not quoting pop culture for once. *These will be the ways of the king who will reign over you: he will take your sons and appoint them to his chariots and to be his horsemen and to run before his chariots. He will take the tenth of your flocks, and you shall be his slaves. And on that day, you will cry out because of your king, whom you have chosen for yourselves, but the Lord will not answer you on that day.*

The Book of Samuel, I said. Odd choice.

It's not usually cited by people trying to claim the divine right of kings, Trish said. *Which is how a lot of people in power prefer to use religion. I'm starting to realize I misjudged you, Vance.*

You did? How does an AI who is witness to my literal thoughts 24-7 misjudge me? I asked.

I thought it was the fact that your aunt died and you saw your father was still alive that made you feel like you didn't have a part left to play in the Community, Trish said.

My aunt just recently died so it wasn't that, I said.

I know, Trish said. *I think it's because you're a father now and you can't protect Astrid from the galaxy getting worse?*

I didn't answer her for a long time. *Yeah, that sounds about right.*

We arrived at the unnamed system that was where the *Melampus* had been "parked"—for lack of a better term—for most of a month. A vast sea of greenish mist from orichalcum gas mixed with other chemicals surrounded it as ancient decaying fuel harvesters stood dormant. Gas prospectors had long ago come to the Perseus Arm in hopes of making it rich but the distance from the Community had bankrupted them even as their descendants had been trapped on the Ring.

The *Melampus* was a beautiful ship, contrasting strongly with the upgraded secondhand warships of Vast's fleet. The golden vessel was a kilometer long combination of flagship and battle cruiser with all the requirements for a multi-vector mission profile ranging from diplomacy to sapient aid to exploration. I'd used the bells and whistles for years and been in a half-dozen engagements and the *Melampus* still looked brand new. It followed the same saucer and base design that the *Ares* and *Siege Perilous* did but was much bigger.

I'd wanted to love the *Melampus* as much as I'd loved the *Ares*, but I didn't even love it as much as I loved the *Black Nebula*. The ships that I'd fallen in love with had been working class vessels that had carried a lengthy history with them. They'd been refuges for the oddballs and misfits of the Community's military. The *Melampus* was a collection of the best and brightest who kept their distance from their captain and his handpicked officers. No, we were a collection of Space Academy vagrants that were surrounded by people who were meant to have greater careers than those which I'd given them. Exploration was a beautiful thing but not what I was meant for.

"Is there any chance of General Vast tracking us through jumpspace?" I asked, turning to Trish. "This ship is probably laden down with spyware and beacons. Especially if it's a spy ship for Department Twelve."

Trish rolled her eyes. "I love you Vance but give me some credit. I thought of that long before you did. I've got a hundred different programs shut down and a dozen more being interfered with. General Vast isn't going to be able to track us here."

I half expected his fleet to show up in that very instant, but it didn't. "Good. I should point out I have suspicions about a spy among us."

"It's Winston," Hannah said.

I did a double take. "What?"

Honestly, he wasn't even in my top five picks. Which perhaps said more about me than it did about him. Even though I thought he'd been ridiculous for treating us as having a powerful and deep friendship, I'd still considered him part of my crew. Maybe he wasn't a substitute father or part of my band of brothers, but as a former *Ares* man, he was at least a distant cousin.

"I concur," Trish said. "Colonel Mason may absolutely hate you and want to vent that loathing on you—"

"And Vance wants to shoot him in the face right back," Hannah added.

"That too," Trish said. "I think it's an older brother/new brother dynamic instead of ex-boyfriend and current boyfriend thing."

"What?" I asked, confused.

"You think?" Hannah asked.

Trish nodded. "Yeah, except Director G is their father. Vance is the favored older son and John is upset he doesn't get paid enough attention."

"I do not look at Case as a father figure," I said, annoyed.

"Yeah, that would be weird since he's my father," Trish said. "Though since your grandparents are Detective Neal Gordon—"

"Please stop," I said, interrupting. "Why do you think it's Winston?"

"Because he's a little weasel and always has been," Hannah said. "There's a reason he was older than dirt and still a lieutenant when he was on the *Ares*."

"Because he grew up in a place without access to longevity treatments?" I asked, innocently.

"Because he has a history of insubordination, petty crime, and corruption," Trish replied. "That was all from his Merchant Fleet days, though. He was on the *Ares* because they lowered the standards for joining Earth's Space Fleet branches."

"I'd honestly forgotten that," I said, thinking back to the days when I'd first taken over the *Ares*. It seemed like a lifetime ago. "So many of our crew rose to the occasion when they were given a chance to do so."

The *Melampus* scanned our gunship, and I presumed Trish offered the necessary identification and passcodes that told them who we were.

"Yeah, well, not everyone did," Hannah said. "You were a good captain for inspiring people to be better, but some people couldn't make the cut. They dropped out, transferred off the ship, or finished their service commitments. You didn't see many court martials because it never got that bad, but I saw a lot of bad behavior as head of security."

"I saw a lot of bad behavior because I'm an all-seeing AI," Trish said. "Now, hold on, I'm talking to the other part of myself on the ship."

180

There were some things you just had to accept as normal when you regularly dealt with AI. "Did the other ships get here? Did everyone survive? Did Leah? Danny?"

Trish looked at Hannah.

"Oh, I'm supposed to act like I'm extra concerned too, am I?" Hannah asked. "Yes, are Elektra and Danny alive? Is John? I ask these questions that you will absolutely tell me even if I didn't ask and was just waiting for the answers."

Trish looked at Hannah. "Well, now I'm going to not tell you."

"Trish," I said.

"Can we just get to the ancestors-damned ship!" Forty-Two called from the back of the gunship. "I'm being smushed all over by identical robot humans and it's not a pleasant experience. It's like being drowned in a bunch of dolls."

"Robot is a slur among bioroids," Sparrowhawk said, also in the back.

"No one cares, Barbie!" Forty-Two shouted back.

"Is everyone in my life a snarky bastarve?" I asked.

"You're only noticing this now?" Hannah asked, confused.

"It's your fault, really," Trish said. "You rubbed off on all of us and now we're the most chronically insubordinate crew in the galaxy."

"I'm so proud," I said, dryly. "Now what's the status of the rescue?"

Trish paused. "Fourteen percent of the people we recruited on the Ring were successfully evacuated. Fifteen casualties, fourteen of them fatal, were of the crew we sent out to help with their departure. Leah and John's team all successfully returned. Overall, there's about two hundred new souls on the *Melampus*."

"Fourteen percent,' I muttered, mulling that over in my head. "Were they not able to get aboard the ships?"

"No," Trish said, softly. "It appears General Vast was informed of the ships you were using, and he sent his teams to kill everyone on board. They were about to finish the job when the Ring's defenses turned on Vast's people and allowed any survivors."

It was an act of war against the Community, but I wasn't sure I could claim any sort of moral high ground at this point. Even if Ketra had been the one to bring down the hammer of God on Vast, I had done nothing to stop her. If I had been anything other than a High Protector, this would have been grounds for removing my command and arresting me. As I was one, I suspected the High Council would barely notice what had happened outside of their territory. That was assuming they didn't try to spin it as a peace-keeping action on a pirate station.

Which they absolutely would.

"Is there anything else?" I asked, watching the *Melampus* get closer and closer. At the speed we were moving, it would still be an hour until we arrived. Gunships like the one we were on weren't designed for long distance space travel.

"Colonel Mason wants to speak with one of your officers," Trish said. "He's not happy dealing with Leah. I think he doesn't consider her your actual second-in-command, but just your fiancé/common law wife/baby mama."

"Ah," I said, losing even more respect for John. "Well, then you should tell Light on Water that he now has the job of handling all of Colonel Mason's interactions."

"I'll make sure that John and company are disarmed before any interactions with him," Trish said, smirking. "There'd be a 70% chance of a shooting incident if not. 89% that John would shoot Light on Water."

"What's the other 11%?" I asked.

"He'd shoot himself."

CHAPTER TWENTY-TWO

Planning the Assault

General Vast's navy never showed up and we got the remainder of the survivors onto the *Melampus* before providing them with sanctuary. The *Melampus* was a large enough ship to accommodate a few hundred extra people, but we couldn't drop them off before we went after the *Mary Read*.

Which meant taking them into battle.

Which meant taking Astrid into battle.

You know, I always had a problem with Star Trek: The Next Generation's *handling of families,* I mentally addressed Trish and Leah as I sat back in my chair in the conference room where Winston was giving an incredibly long-winded lecture about our means of tracking the ship through jumpspace.

The conference room had Trish's bioroid body, Leah, John, Light on Water (seated next to John), Hannah, Forty-Two, Elektra, Danny, Ichigo, and a new member of my staff named Harini Choudhury. She was a Titan-born Indian woman that, somehow, I'd learned next to nothing about in the entire breadth of our mission of exploration. In a ship full of weirdos and human (or alien) Muppets, she had created a zone of professionalism that wanted nothing to do with our drama. It made her the oddest one of the command staff made of oddballs.

Are you seriously going to interrupt a vitally important meeting that determines the fate of billions to talk about a four-hundred-year-old television show? Leah asked, sounding stunned. *It's not even the best Star Trek. The 22nd century remake of the original series is the best.*

I shall ignore your blasphemy, I said. *Also, the answer is yes. One, because it is preying on my mind. Two, because it's classic storytelling that has survived like Shakespeare.*

Three, because the alternative is listening to Winston, Leah replied

Why haven't we confronted him as a traitor yet? Trish asked. *I mean, everyone agrees but you that he's almost certainly the mole.*

We suspect he's the mole, I replied. *We don't need to go after him immediately because watching him under your all-seeing AI sensors will give us an advantage on his next move. But the simple fact is there are other potential candidates. John is an obvious one, or perhaps another disgruntled Ranger. But the fact that Department Twelve is the Section 31 of EarthGov —*

I don't think there's a Section 31 of the Security Departments, Trish interrupted. *They're all Section 31.*

I have no idea what that is, Leah said. *But if we're saying that Department Twelve is even more evil and ruthless than the other Security Departments, I agree. A bit.*

A bit, I said.

Yes, Leah said. *An almost measurable difference in corruption and cruelty.*

Almost, I said.

You want me to be more honest, Leah said.

Not that honest, I replied.

Trish mentally sighed. *I'm going to regret this, but you clearly wanted to talk about it. What, exactly, bothered you about* Star Trek: The Next Generation? *I mean, we might as well be discussing Shylock's forced conversion or Ivanhoe dating Rebecca instead of Rowena here.*

Or how the Phantom should have ended up with Christine, Leah added. *God, I love that musical.*

I can tell you're fascinated by the point I was trying to bring up, I said. *What I hated about* Next Generation *was that they brought children aboard the Enterprise. Now that I'm a father, I can't help but think of the hundreds of kids that were on board the ship week-after-week when they were getting in danger against Romulans or the Borg.*

There are children on board the Melampus, Leah pointed out. *It's more a mobile military base than a pure combat vessel.*

Yes, I know, I said. *Kind of my point. I feel it's irresponsible to put them in danger. I'm debating ways we can evacuate the civilians if we must go up against Vast's remaining fleet.*

Gene Roddenberry had a solution to that, Trish said. *He designed the Enterprise-D to be able to detach its saucer from the main section of the hull so that the civilians in the ship could be evacuated before any combat engagements. Unfortunately, it proved to be grossly impractical for a serialized television show as well as needlessly expensive.*

It also sounds incredibly ill-conceived, Leah said. *Why build a combat and science vessel that separates versus a dedicated vessel for each?*

We're a combat and science vessel, I pointed out.

Yes, but it doesn't make sense for the Community to have done it either, Leah said. *Anyway, I understand your desire to keep Astrid and other civilians out of danger. I'm just not sure we have time.*

So people keep telling me, I replied. *But if we have Winston and Nyssa is dead, I don't think Vast has a chance of getting there first.*

Winston was presently showing a presentation of the *Mary Read*'s design from centuries ago, images from that period, and the history of the ship in a manner that somehow made intergalactic buccaneering sound boring. The most important element, how to track the damned thing, had been pulled from his mind by Leah and was presently being uploaded into the ship's computer while we modified our equipment to do it.

Basically, the *Mary Read* left a weird trail of particles that no Community ship did and they existed in the dimensions between jumpspace and physical reality (which I didn't even know existed). They could be tracked despite the mind-numbing size of space since the ship always returned to its original location. It had a base, basically, and thus we could follow it from the ship's past sightings. Like the site of my mutiny. If I believed in omens, that would have been a bad one.

I wondered exactly where the *Mary Read* had been getting the necessary fuel and supplies to continue her journey, but it was entirely possible that the Elder Race technology allowed it to continue for centuries without any need to do restock. Maybe it was also harvesting orichalcum from the jumpspace leaks across the galaxy or raw matter from nebula. It was the kind of thinking that really wasn't productive.

That was when Leah interrupted my thoughts regarding the issue by pointing a hole in my logic. *That's assuming that whoever the mole was didn't already tell General Vast about where the* Mary Read *will be or how to reach it.*

That was a disturbing thought. *Then why bother going after me? Why invade a planet-sized megastructure? Vast and I barely know each other.*

I was grasping at straws, though.

That was before you annihilated half his fleet, Trish pointed out. *But he was never after you because of his own feelings, Vance. He's after you because Department Twelve wants you eliminated.*

They wanted me alive, I replied. For some reason.

Something wasn't adding up in all of this and I didn't have enough information to make any decisions.

We needed to prepare a set of shuttles, probably using the transports we've stolen, to move non-essential personnel and Astrid off ship. They shouldn't be put in danger just to satisfy my need for glory.

There's no safer place in the galaxy, Vance, Leah said. *If the High Protector B'Vash or Bendo are going after your family, then they won't hesitate to use Astrid as a hostage. Earth is no longer safe for her and I'm not sure Throneworld would be much better.*

"Bork!" I cursed allowed.

Everyone in the conference room turned to stare at me, clearly not having expected that sort of reaction. This included Trish and Leah who knew what I was cursing about but were pretending to not know why I'd embarrassed myself.

Traitors, I said to Trish and Leah cybernetically.

Leah smirked.

Trish giggled.

I shook my head. "Just contemplating possibilities, Doctor Arden. So, once we arrive at the site of the *Ares* Mutiny, how long will it take us to track down the *Mary Read*'s home base? Weeks? Months?"

"Minutes," Winston said, surprising me. "The information provided by the Chel was surprisingly in-depth regarding what we'd have to do. I'm surprised they didn't just provide the location of the ship itself."

John stared at Winston. "I found their excuses pretty damn flimsy myself. If they wanted to avoid anyone else getting the credit for finding this ship, they could have just given it to Vance directly."

"Captain Turbo," I said, coldly. "Colonel."

Yeah, I hadn't improved my opinion of the mercenary captain in recent days. There hadn't been any incidents among his team but the loss of his friend, Tank, had kept him occupied with funeral arrangements. I hadn't been invited. Hannah had been. Apparently, heated words had been exchanged.

"Right," John said, not bothering to snipe back. "I'm just saying that if they hadn't been engaged in their bullsavit games a million people on the Ring probably would still be alive. This is on Director G and the Elder Races playing games."

"A hundred thousand," I said, calmly. "Reports from the Ring are that the events triggered a popular revolution from the puppet civilian government that I didn't even know existed. The Merchant Princes have mostly fled, the remaining gangs have signed a peace treaty, and the FLACS have all fled in the wake of the chaos. The new government has applied for Community peacekeepers and membership in ten years. Currently, they're having show trials for all the slavers that had the misfortune of still being on the station when the revolution happened."

"Are Vast's people involved?" Leah asked before pausing. "No, then they wouldn't be applying for Community membership."

"Vast apparently withdrew an hour after determining we'd escaped," I said. "They emptied the Ring's vast treasury of minerals and orichalcum reserves, though. Which is another reason why the local kleptocracy has collapsed."

John stared. "Wow, you just fail upwards, don't you? Even the war you accidentally start ends up working out alright."

I stared at him. "Yes, because a bunch of dead civilians is all magically justified because some small good came from it."

I personally was quite suspicious of the timing of the revolution and suspected that the people who had taken over had been set in place beforehand. The Elder Races didn't do subtle. Eliminating all the corrupt forces in one of their old piles of junk before putting it under one of their satellite organizations wasn't beyond their Ethereal agents. The difference between the Community Security Departments and the forces beyond it was the difference between toddlers playing with blocks versus ancient chess masters with the ability to change the rules at will.

I wanted to talk to Elektra about her mother's spirit. Ketra had mentioned that she'd been breaking the rules on my behalf, but I didn't know what she'd meant by that or what the consequences were. I was tired of being a puppet of divided loyalties between the Elder Races, Community, EarthGov, Space Fleet, and my crew.

They were groups that should theoretically be allied but were always just shy of being at each other's throats. Now I had my family to worry about as well and I was just tired. Tired of feeling like so much was getting worse and not getting better. I had to make a choice now: where did my loyalties fully lie and how far was I willing to go to protect what I chose?

I wanted to say I would choose my family every time and I probably would, but if I just said the hell with it and found some isolated corner of the galaxy to hide with them, I would be teaching Astrid the worst sort of lesson about what sort of person to be. Plus, it wasn't like they would be safer that way. The simple fact was a secure galaxy was a more secure place for them.

Theoretically.

"Right," Hannah said, ending the uncomfortable pause I hadn't even been aware of. "So, Light on Water, how long until we reach our destination?"

"Three hours," Light on Water said. "The *Melampus'* jumpdrive engines are among the most powerful in the Known Universe."

"We'll prepare the freighters attached to the base of the hull to transport off any non-essential personnel," I replied. "I fully expect us to go to battle again before this mission is over and don't want to put anyone in danger that doesn't have to be."

"Will that include your daughter, sir?" Lieutenant Commander Choudhury asked.

"No," I said, very reluctantly.

There was no response.

"I think that about covers everything," I said, standing up. "Meeting adjourned."

That was a wise decision, Vance, Leah said in my mind.

I agree, Trish said.

I think it was a terrible decision, I replied. *However, I don't put it past Department Twelve to put my family in danger or threaten other people's families in order to get a chance of taking my daughter.*

Our daughter, Leah said. *Even if she loves you more.*

That's not true, I said back to her.

We're both psychics, Vance. You're not, Leah said. *I know how our daughter feels, and she doesn't try to hide it.*

Right, I thought. *Sorry.*

As your second in command, Vance, I am going to formally insist on you seeing a Community trained psyche-healer twice per week, though.

I suppose you have the backing of the ship's medical officer and the ship's AI in this? I asked, having been expecting this since the Ring.

Yes, Vance, Trish said. *She does. Doctor Zard has been saying you should be seeing her for months now.*

Doctor Zard is a mathematician, I replied. *She's only a medical doctor as a secondary profession.*

Now she's a psyche-healer, Leah said. *Genius breeds genius.*

You know that as a High Protector, I can technically override that order, I replied. *Section-281-7 only applies to a captain.*

You have all the sections memorized? Leah asked.

No, I looked it up while we talked, I said. *Cyborg, remember?*

Right, Leah said.

Mental health is nothing to be ashamed of, Trish said. *You've been through more than most people by a factor of a thousand. This is just maintenance.*

"Fine," I said, sighing. "Now if you'll excuse me, I'm heading down to the gym. I'm going to go hit something."

Both women stayed behind in the conference room, even though I knew Trish was always with me. So was Leah.

Always with those I was closest to.

Always alone.

Unfortunately, no sooner did I get into the hallways that Forty-Two and John caught up with me.

"I'm not in the mood," I said, looking at both.

"We need to talk," John said.

"Are you two suddenly friends?" I asked, skeptically.

"Oh yeah, absolutely," Forty-Two said. "He's a lot like you."

John glared at him before shaking his head. "We've found out who the mole was."

I blinked. "I'm listening."

CHAPTER TWENTY-THREE

The Traitor Is Not Surprising

I waited in the room of the traitor, taking a moment to contemplate the situation. The revelation of who exactly had been informing to Grand General Vast shouldn't have been a surprise, but it was because I had been looking to blame people I already wanted to believe were corrupt. Hell, I'd even been more suspicious of my own people than the person that Forty-Two and John had tracked down as being responsible.

The rooms were one of the guest suites that I'd set aside for the Antares Rangers and while they'd proven to be unsteady allies at best, they'd sacrificed blood for the cause of trying to finish this mission. I wasn't sure if this mission was worth the lives they'd given but I was trying to be understanding.

John and company had gone through hell trying to fight a proxy war on behalf of people most of the galaxy didn't give a savit about. The Notha had once been the most feared and reviled villains in the Community and allied worlds but had been exposed as a paper tiger once the end of the Notha War had caused their economy to collapse. The Elder Races removing the threat of SKAMMs also caused the Notha to lose a considerable amount of their threat to the rest of the worlds. Assuming they'd been smart enough to obey.

I'd almost lost all my credibility as a "galactic hero" when I'd argued for peace with the Notha, but time had a way of making all past actions redundant or inevitable in retrospect. Time had simply made the Notha less and less relevant as a threat. The Kolahn War had replaced them in the minds of people who had experienced their conquests firsthand and there were plenty of planets now making fortunes off the importation of cheap Notha orichalcum.

Still, the betrayal stung.

I was finally rewarded for my patience when the door to the room opened and the Diplomat stood on the other end of the chamber.

"You are not welcome here, Satan," the Diplomat said, using her sister's name for me.

I stared down at her. "May I ask why you did it?"

The Diplomat hissed and charged, drawing her z'hayal blade and going for my throat. I proceeded to smack her in midair against the wall. It probably would have looked comical from the outside, like a rabid beaver-sized squirrel going for someone's throat. It put me in mind of the rabbit scene from *Monty Python on the Holy Grail* but with slightly more realistic consequences. Leah loved that movie.

The Diplomat prepared to attack again before turning to look around the room. "There are no other guards."

"No," I said, pausing. "Forty-Two and John know about what you did but I wanted to handle this personally."

"You are a fool, Vance Turbo," the Diplomat hissed, showing her little buck teeth in a gesture that was intended to be terrifying but just kind of adorable. "I will kill you and avenge my sister."

"I killed the person who killed your sister," I said, sighing. "I will never be able to repay the debt that I owe her."

"Stop saying that!" The Diplomat growled, holding her knife while making a running leap into the air. I grabbed her arm and dangled her in the air. She tried to reach for a pistol at her side, but I pulled that away from her with my free hand. After several seconds of dangling in the air, she stopped hissing.

"Okay, this is just embarrassing," the Diplomat muttered.

"I don't want to hurt you," I said, calmly.

"You will have to!" The Diplomat growled again, once more regaining some of her old fire. "I will hunt you to the ends of the galaxy, otherwise! I will kill you, your family—"

"Do what you want to me," I replied. "But if you go after my family, I'm going to have to kill you."

The Diplomat stared at me. "Why in the world do you think your threats will have any meaning to me?"

I took a deep breath and dropped her down on the ground. "Because it would also make your sister's final act on this world meaningless."

"Do you think I..." The Diplomat struggled to find words to say, before degenerating into a string of Notha profanity. "My sister was a good, kind, and noble woman. But she was also a religious fanatic. She believed that you were a kind of god and that you'd delivered us from the Emperor. I don't. I believe you got lucky and the Emperor was just a biologically altered monster of a Notha. A puppet of the Elder Races, just like you are. I believe that she wasted her life saving a human child. I believe my father was a fool for trusting you to have his back against the Notha Union. I believe..."

I was just nodding along. "That's all true. I'm not a god. If I was a god, I could have saved her."

"Stop being reasonable!" The Diplomat gnashed her teeth, then looked down. "You have to kill me now."

"Being a High Protector means that I don't have to do much of anything," I said. "My current plan is to return you to your father after this mission. I'm afraid you're going to have to stay in the brig until then. It'll keep you safe from the Rangers. They want revenge."

"I don't need your protection," the Diplomat said.

"You have it anyway," I said, looking down at her. "Once we reach *Mary Read*'s treasure, I'll do everything in my power to make sure that it's used to prop up Deathworld."

"It's too late for that, Vance," the Diplomat said, disgusted. It seemed like it was aimed less at me than it was before, though.

"What do you mean?" I asked.

"If you had been doing this two years ago, back when we were at our most desperate, perhaps it could have made a difference," the Diplomat said. "Our advantage was considerable in the early days, and we inflicted unforgettable casualties onto enemy ranks."

"The enemy being your fellow Notha," I said, just making sure I was clear.

"Yes," the Diplomat said. "However, the difference between Deathworld and the Notha Union is forty worlds. They can replace their losses. Which they have been doing since the Community's desire to support us died off as the news cycle drifted. Now the war is just a bloody stalemate that favors the Union."

"Can they?" I asked. "Or will the losses that they've sustained from this war lead to its collapse as a power?"

The Diplomat paused. "Now you sound like my father. Either way, it doesn't help the people of Deathworld."

"Maybe I could have done more," I said, thinking about how I'd been overwhelmed by the revelations of my father's survival and that I was now a new father. I'd let myself be pushed out into the Perseus Arm because I'd wanted to provide a safe place for my family but also because I'd been overwhelmed. Too many deaths on my conscience and too many close calls that had left me exhausted from continuing to fight.

"You certainly could not have done less," the Diplomat said, looking uncomfortable. It was probably an awkward experience being forced to talk with the person she blamed not only for her sister's death but also not doing anything to help her home planet.

I'd wanted to negotiate on Deathworld's behalf with the Notha Union, but that had been a failure, too. The peace negotiations had fallen through because they'd gotten buried in the attack by the Primordials. Maybe it had never been possible to come to a peaceful settlement, but I'd been the only person there trying and I'd stopped trying.

"I suppose an apology isn't going to make things better," I muttered, sighing.

The Diplomat stared at me. "Are you insane?"

"Many people have asked that question," I admitted. "But I want to know, what exactly did you hope to accomplish by informing General Vast about our position?" I still hoped that she wasn't the leak.

"I hoped he'd kill you," the Diplomat said. "But General Vast has strict instructions not to allow any harm to come to you."

"He has a funny way of showing it," I replied.

"There is a reason that Department Twelve is fielding their operatives with Vast despite the dangers it poses to their secrecy," the Diplomat said. "They do not trust the People's Army not to bork it up. They want you alive and in their custody."

"Why?" I asked, confused.

"I have no idea, nor do I care," the Diplomat said. "Perhaps they see you as too valuable in future negotiations with the Community to casually dispose of. Perhaps they wish to brainwash you with your weird human magic."

"I don't think we have that," I said.

The Diplomat scoffed. "But it was my hope that if I delivered you and the *Mary Read* information to them, they would assist Deathworld."

"You know they won't, right?" I asked.

"I reiterate, I hoped they would just kill you," the Diplomat said. "But I never had any faith that the intelligence services of Earth would live up to their promises. I admit, I underestimated just how much General Vast actually was willing to commit to this project, but I was also of the mind that chasing after a ghost ship was a waste of time to begin with. Until it turned out it wasn't."

"How did you learn about the methods needed to find the *Mary Read* anyway?" I asked, needing to know just how much of a lead General Vast had on us.

"Winston wouldn't shut up the moment he learned about it," the Diplomat said. "If it's any consolation, I only transmitted the information a few hours before the attack. Still, it is possible that Department Twelve had already gotten the treasure."

"Like Belloq and the Ark," I muttered. "I may have to go to an island and find it."

"I don't know what that is," the Diplomat said. "But I think you are a sad man who has already missed his opportunity to do any good for his fellow beings. You are just desperately trying to pick up the pieces of an already shattered vase and put it back together."

"Yeah, pretty much," I said. "That's about the story of my life."

"Then why bother?" the Diplomat asked.

That was a very good question. "Because it's better than just sitting around feeling sorry for yourself. Which I've been doing for the past two years. Seriously, I somehow made an epic space journey across uncharted space with multiple First Contacts into part of my midlife crisis."

"I couldn't care less," the Diplomat said. "So, you're going to hand me over to my father. You realize that is a death sentence by other means?"

"Your father is a good man," I said, refusing to believe the president would harm his other daughter.

"By Notha standards, not human," the Diplomat said. "We do not worship weakness. I have betrayed a person who saved Deathworld from destruction and was our supporter even if he's been useless for years. He respects debts and does not hold my sister's death against you. If you actually do come through with more aid, it will only make him feel more obligated to make a display of my life's end."

I stared at her. "I can't protect you from the consequences of your actions. People are dead. Both my people and John's. Hell, if you hadn't informed General Vast, then maybe the devastation to the Ring wouldn't have happened. Never mind what'll happen if the Department Twelve bastards get ahold of the *Mary Read*."

"Maybe they'll blow up the Earth," the Diplomat said. "If you're attempting to guilt me, you will fail. I accept the consequences of my action."

"I'll ask your father to forgive you," I said. "I'm even going to say what a huge help to me you've been."

The Diplomat stared. "I hate you."

"That makes two of us," I said. "If I could exchange places with your sister, I would have."

"She would smack you for that," the Diplomat said. "Then slit my throat. She was strong like that."

"Yeah, she was," I said, staring down at her. "Security will be here in a few minutes. Don't resist or I'll have you stunned."

The Diplomat watched me leave. "You are not what I expected, Captain Turbo. I hate you and always will for getting my sister killed, but you are almost tolerable for a human."

"Thanks," I muttered, reaching the door.

"You remind me a great deal of Colonel Mason," the Diplomat said. "I am sorry to have betrayed his trust."

I walked out the door. Forty-Two was waiting there for me in his green security officer's uniform. "Trish, seal the room for me. Would you?"

"YESSIR," she responded from the intercom. "I THINK YOU HANDLED THAT VERY WELL."

"She did what she did because of grief and anger," I said. "It's still going to ruin what's left of her life."

"Some mistakes are never fixed," Forty-Two said. "Sometimes, they're just lived with. Thankfully, you only have to do that until you die."

I gave a half-smile. "I'm surprised Colonel Mason isn't out here."

"He's preparing for the next part of this mission," Forty-Two said. "He's contemplating the fact that he made a complete ass of himself on the Ring. Possibly even destroying his relationship with Hannah."

"There was a lot of that going around," I replied. "He lost three of his soldiers."

"Those who live by the gun die by the gun," Forty-Two said. "I'm actually disappointed I made it this far. I expected to be dining with my ancestors by now given all of the horrible situations you've led me through. I'm very disappointed in you as a leader, Vance. How can I have a glorious death in battle if you keep me alive so well?"

I stared at him. "I'm sorry about the situation with your, uh, condition, Forty-Two. Maybe there's something Doctor Zard can do. Some miracle treatment. Hell, I'll even ask the Elder Races to make you immortal if they can."

"I'm good, Vance," Forty-Two said. "I'm not dying, I'm just getting old. I've still got about twenty more years left in me of active service even without the top-of-the-line cybernetics I'm going to insist you get me."

"You should have an additional two hundred years," I said, frowning.

"Two percent of Sorkanan are allergic to longevity drugs," Forty-Two said. "I just happen to be in the additional 2% of that who are violently resistant to the therapies to fix them. I was already quite a bit older than you when we started working together. I just wasn't showing it yet. Life will eventually kill you."

"Yeah," I said, still uncomfortable with the whole business. "I guess I'm just extra self-conscious about aging right now."

It was wrong that he was comforting me rather than the reverse.

"Because your two-hundred-year-old aunt died and was only entering old age herself or because you're not aging at all?" Forty-Two asked, distilling it down to brass tacks as he always seemed to be able to do.

"Both," I said. "No one is quite sure how long humans can live with longevity drugs, but most people assume it's anywhere from three to four hundred years if they have the best possible medical care."

"Sorkanans live about four to five hundred," Forty-Two said. "I should tap out about a hundred and twenty, which is a good run since most of the people in my egg creche never hit fifty. There's a long history of Community military service in my genome."

"Ah," I said, not sure how to respond to that.

"They were killed during the Notha War," Forty-Two said. "If you didn't get that."

"Yeah," I said. "I got it."

"You're an elf now," Forty-Two said. "Don't feel guilty that you'll outlive everyone you know except for Elektra and Shelly. Content yourself with making toys, baking cookies, and forging rings of power."

"I think you're mixing up kinds of elves," I said, embarrassed.

"You can hook up with Shelly after both your regular human spouses die in a couple of centuries," Forty-Two said. "You can hang out with your daughter after her husband or wife, or both die horribly."

I stared at him. "Not funny."

"Are you sure? Because I'm finding it hilarious," Forty-Two said, his mouth grinning full of razor-sharp teeth.

That was when Trish surprised me. "VANCE, WE MAY HAVE TO PULL OUT OF JUMPSPACE."

"Why?" I asked, looking up at the ceiling.

"WE'VE JUST RECEIVED A DISTRESS CALL... FROM THE *LIBERATOR.*"

CHAPTER TWENTY-FOUR

The Graveyard of Ships

I stood on the bridge of the *Melampus*, which looked more like a luxury hotel with computer consoles than a proper ship's command center. I was transfixed by the sight on the view screen which left me unable to react. Standing here as we prepared for jumpspace was a common enough event that you think I would have been used to it.

There were a lot more crew on the bridge than I'd ever gotten used to. It required three shifts and regular rotations. Leah, Hannah, Forty-Two, Elektra, Light on Water, Princess Huggypants, Harini, and Danny were at their stations, which weren't quite analogous to their EarthGov Space Fleet ones but close enough. They were all in uniform now, just like me.

However, I barely knew the names of the dozen other people present and wondered if I'd lost my touch as a captain. One of the things my Aunt Kathy taught me upon my ascension to captain was to realize that even the best captains didn't know what they were doing half the time (at least in emergency situations). Instead, the best thing they could do was to look as calm as possible and make sure everyone continued doing their job.

I wasn't succeeding now.

"Well, we've found the *Mary Read*," Leah said, staring at the ship that I'd only caught a short glimpse of before.

The city-sized, ornate vessel was as beautiful as I remembered, looking more like a piece of alien artwork than an actual combat vessel. Ironically, the similarities to the *Melampus* were much more prevalent now that I'd gotten intimately familiar with my own vessel. It seemed very probable that the centuries old dreadnought before us had been an inspiration for the later developments in the Community's advanced ship research. Even so, the scans we were performing on the *Mary Read* told us that it was superior on a level that was, even after centuries of advancement, roughly equivalent to a wooden caravel being parked up next to a 20th century aircraft carrier.

That wasn't the disturbing part, though. *That* was getting the unfortunate acknowledgement of just how utterly outclassed our vessel was in more morbid ways. My concerns about Grand General Vast reaching the ship first had been justified, sort of. The remains of his fleet—already halved by events at the Ring—were spread throughout the star system as the *Mary Read* had made horrific work of the People's Liberation Army forces. All the enhancements and upgrades provided to the warlord by Department Twelve had apparently done jack and savit to protect him against its defenses.

"Do we have any casualty figures?" I asked, turning to Leah.

"I estimate about eight hundred and fifty thousand KIA, sir," Light on Water said, gurgling as he supervised his console. "Perhaps twice that many in need of rescue. The *Liberator* remains intact structurally, but its engines have been destroyed, as well as all its remaining weapons. It seems that the *Mary Read* disabled much of the fleet and allowed the ships to evacuate whenever possible before destroying the remainder."

"That's a very poor way of pulling your punches," I replied.

"I don't think saving their lives was the ship's goal," Hannah said, staring at the sight in awe. "I think it was just making as big a message as it could. This was about demonstrating just how utterly outclassed the rest of the galaxy is."

"Don't make any aggressive moves," I said, knowing that we were utterly borked if the *Mary Read* decided to view us as a threat.

"I'M KEEPING OUR WEAPONS UNPOWERED AND SHIELDS AT MINIMAL," Trish responded. "I DON'T WANT A 'BEST OF BOTH WORLDS' SORT OF SITUATION HERE. YOU KNOW, SINCE WE'RE DOING *STAR TREK: THE NEXT GENERATION* REFERENCES."

That went over like a lead balloon. "Trish, I never thought I'd say this, but I don't think I'm in the mood for references right now. Is the *Liberator* still transmitting its distress signal?"

"I'm afraid so," Danny said. "Though I'm also getting a bit more chatter from the vessel as well. General Vast himself is aboard his flagship and trying to see if anyone has any functioning weapons to attack us."

I looked at Danny then back at Hannah. "Yeah, he's not any threat, is he?"

"I feel like he might be if we don't have any weapons or shields up but barely," Hannah said. "It seems that the *Mary Read* was *very* thorough."

"You should hail General Vast," Leah said, turning to me. "Offer aid to his people."

"Are you crazy?" Hannah asked Leah, showing a bluntness she'd not displayed in a couple of years.

"It's an opportunity to gain intelligence about the current situation," Leah said. "Also, perhaps the grand general will do the right thing by his people and surrender."

"Really?" I asked, skeptically.

"Oh, hell no," Leah admitted. "He'll take the coward's way out long before he ever sees the inside of a prison cell. His army is made up of conscripts and those children he kidnapped to indoctrinate while forcing their fathers or mothers to fight. He's an awful, awful person but his armies might be willing to give up."

"I'm not saying that he has to be blown up now, Vance, but I'm saying that when he resists—which he will—we take this opportunity to fulfill our mission," Hannah said, being as blunt as possible without overtly saying we should take him out.

I shouldn't have been relying on fortune telling to guide my path but Astrid's ability to see outside of typical space-time was something I took seriously as one of her inherited abilities. I'd witnessed the distant destruction of planet Earth in the future thanks to the Primordials trying to break my spirit and she'd shown me better ways of dealing with several perilous situations during the first two years of our exploring the Perseus Arm.

I didn't know what "bad things" would happen if I killed General Vast, but I wasn't going to dismiss her warning out of hand either. This was possibly the moment in the future that my daughter had foreseen that I could spare Vast's life and avert some darker future. There was only one problem: I wasn't inclined to kill him even without the warning Astrid had given me. Leah's plan struck me as both more practical and moral.

Life-changing, destiny-defying decisions that require a prophecy from your clairvoyant daughter…well, shouldn't that be something that you have to decide on doing first? You can't just be told to do something because you were prophesized as doing it, right? There was something very strange going on here and I wanted to know what it was exactly. Unfortunately, there were people in danger, and I had to deal with the fact that my quixotic quest had suddenly become a helluva lot less quixotic.

"Contact General Vast's flagship," I said, looking at Danny. "We are already known to him, but we should identify ourselves anyway."

"Oh, this will be good," Hannah muttered under her breath.

"I sincerely doubt it," I replied. "Actually, make sure it's an open channel."

"Yessir," Danny said.

Leah looked at me, curious at my intentions.

Moments later, the image of a heavily damaged Sorkanan bridge came on the hologram feed. It sputtered and wobbled every few seconds, showing that even their interior jumpspace communication drive was barely functioning. Still, I could see the mist that was usually gathered at the foot of Sorkanan bridges and the figure of Grand General Vast himself.

He looked… tired.

Dictators made an extensive effort to look strong, no matter how ridiculous those were. So, it was surprising to see how utterly spent the man who'd nearly destroyed me looked. His scales were browning, half of his skull had been replaced with a metal cyberdome, and his right eye was now an auto-targeting unit. He was wearing the white tunic of a Sorkanan grand general, covered in a variety of holographic emblems and pins that were roughly analogous to Earth medals. He was slumped over in his command chair, though, and his baton of office was laid across his lap.

General Vast looked up, his autotargeting eye narrowing on me with its iris. It looked kind of like a WWI monocle combined with a camera lens and jeweler's loupe. Not that any of those things had been available for centuries. It gave him a very Dieselpunk in Space sort of look, which were words I only understood from my contact with Trish.

"This isn't over, Turbo," General Vast said, staring at me. "You and your Elder Race masters have oppressed the Sorkanan race for millennia, but the hour of your defeat is at hand. We will claim the ship of dreams and finally ascend to our rightful—"

"Excuse me," I said, interrupting. "I don't mean to interrupt what is I'm sure quality ranting, but do you need help?"

"What?" General Vast asked.

"I am being facetious because you clearly *do* need help," I said, mocking the man. "Both in terms of aid to your soldiers as well as psychologically. The Elder Race devices are not toys, General."

"*Grand* General," General Vast hissed.

"They are not weapons you can pick up and aim at their former owners," I said, shaking my head. "They have a life of their own and resist anyone who attempts to harness their power. You led your fleet to ruin at the Ring and learned nothing because you came here next to be destroyed again. The only reason you are still alive is because the people who wield this colossal power do not wish to kill you. Do not mistake this for mercy."

"You will not get away with this ship," General Vast said.

I ignored him. "Any of the People's Liberation Army who wish to surrender their arms will be treated as prisoners of war and not terrorists. They will be allowed to lay down their arms and be returned to their families and planets of origin or to seek asylum within the Community. This offer is not extended to Grand General Vast because of his crimes against sapience."

General Vast stared at me, realizing just what I was saying. "The word of the Community is worthless."

"My word is my bond, and I have the authority to pardon whomever brings me your head," I said, pausing. "But I'll accept peace just the same. Disconnect communication."

The bridge was silent at my words.

"Well, that's bound to cause some dissension," Leah finally broke the silence.

"I suspect it's more likely to cause dissension from Vast's point than his own people," I replied. "His loyal officers are ruthless and efficient. They're also war criminals themselves and unlikely to believe that they'll be treated better. I suspect the *Liberator* will be defiant to the end, so we'll need to secure the vessel with Community reinforcements."

"I don't think that's going to be possible," Elektra said, typing away at her console.

I had a bad feeling about this. "What do you mean?"

"We've been wrapped in some sort of gravity manipulation device," Elektra said. "It's pulling us in."

"You mean like a tractor beam?" I asked.

"Those aren't real!" Elektra said.

"They are!" I pointed out. "The *Revengeance* had one!"

"WELL, ONE IS PULLING US TO THE *MARY READ*'S SIDE," Trish said. "ALL OF OUR ENGINES AND BARRIER ARE SHUTTING DOWN."

"Great," I muttered, seeing the ship come closer and closer.

"IT GETS WORSE," Trish said.

"How?" I asked, confused.

"THE *LIBERATOR* IS ALSO BEING TRACTORED IN," Trish said.

I stared at the *Mary Read*. "Have you got the impression that we're all rats in a maze?"

"Yes, Captain," Leah said. "You should probably make a point not to repeat that in front of the crew."

"I'm pretty sure that the crew will figure out the problem when we're up against the massive super ship," I replied. I was suddenly very glad that we'd evacuated as many of the civilian crew as possible. It didn't change how absolutely terrified I was for my daughter, but it did mean that this wouldn't be a *complete* disaster if we were suddenly destroyed.

That was what I was telling myself, at least.

Before I could say anything else, the viewscreen flickered back to life and I saw a white-haired woman who looked like she was in her sixties, or much older if she was on longevity drugs. She was wearing a long coat over a silken shirt and denim pants. At her side with a proton sword just like mine, identical even.

"Greetings, Captain Turbo," the voice spoke with a Northern English accent, belying the idea she was Irish. I assumed this was a message from Anne Bonny, or perhaps the ship's AI impersonating her. It was possible she could still be alive this entire time with Elder Race technology, but I sincerely doubted that given she didn't strike me as the kind of woman who would have stayed out of Earth's politics for centuries.

"Good evening," I said. "Are you the AI for the *Mary Read*?"

"I am combination of Anne Bonny, her ship, and the orders left to her by the Elder Races," Anne said. "I have been instructed to make arrangements for this test upon the ascension of a second human being to the rank of High Protector."

Suddenly, a lot of this started making sense. "This is my fault, then?"

Anne smiled but her eyes remained cold. "You should take pride in your accomplishment, Captain Turbo. Many people were certain that humanity would not amount to anything and the number of strikes against them like Department Twelve's perfidies are proof to them that yours is a failed species. You have shown otherwise. Mankind has potential."

"What do you mean, failed species?" Leah asked, ignoring the rest of her statement.

Anne ignored her. "Your actions with the Primordials have caused the Elder Races to decide that mankind is to be given a chance to prove its value. You are to come aboard with five of your crew and face evaluation."

"Face evaluation?" I asked, pausing. "What exactly do you mean by that?"

"It means that if you fail, humanity will be reduced to the Stone Age," Anne Bonny said. "If they're lucky. They have flouted the laws against AI and tampering with Elder Race technology far too many times to be tolerated. They were allowed as much of a pass as they've been given because of my actions."

I stared at her. "Humanity doesn't deserve to be prosecuted for the actions of a select few."

"It's not a select few," Anne replied. "As the presence of Department Twelve's fleet shows. General Vast is acting as an agent for them and they have the force of your government behind them, no matter how much of a blind eye they're pretending to turn."

"General Vast, a Sorkanan, is serving as one of humanity's champions?" I asked.

"Yes, because they're working for a human organization."

"Uh-huh," I said.

"I don't make the rules," Anne said.

I had a feeling that arguing would be pointless. "What happens if I pass?"

"Humanity will be safe for another ten thousand years," Anne Bonny said. "Though Earth may still end up being punished if they continue to defy the Elder Races' strictures, humanity as a whole will be allowed to spread and grow through space."

"And what happens if I refuse to participate?" I asked.

"Humanity will automatically fail the test," Anne said.

Great.

"Then I guess I accept."

CHAPTER TWENTY-FIVE

The Test of Humanity

I had to admit that when I was thinking about old *Star Trek* episodes, I wasn't thinking I would be living through my least favorite of them all: the "Divine Judgement" ones. Harlan Ellison had apocryphally said, "Gene Roddenberry had only one original idea: that humanity would go out into space and find out that God was insane, a child, or both." There had been many episodes dealing with humanity encountering hyper-advanced civilizations that proceeded to pass judgement down on mankind for its barbarous past.

Sometimes the aliens were benevolent like the Organians or (arguably) Q and just wanted to give humanity a nudge in the right direction. Other times, the aliens were complete bastards like Trelane, the Platonians, or the Istarians (from the 23rd century reboot). Honestly, I preferred the ones who were scumbags because I never liked the idea that there were all these advanced cultures that felt the need to pass judgement on civilizations that were supposedly finding their own way. It seemed the very opposite of the Prime Directive.

Well, there really *were* a bunch of incredibly powerful, near-omnipotent entities that had nothing better to do with their time than screw with developing civilizations. Unfortunately, I was their agent, and it seemed I'd inadvertently doomed humanity by exceeding their expectations. After all, they wouldn't be testing us if they didn't think I'd earned the right to be tested, if that made sense. No, seriously, I'd like to know because it didn't to me.

Don't. Do not blame this on yourself, Vance. Anne is telling you that they are giving humanity a chance because of your efforts. Humanity would be utterly borked if not for you, Trish said to me, desperate. I could feel her fear, which was rare to experience from an AI. Usually, in microseconds they'd worked through most of their issues or resigned themselves to their fate.

What do you think, Leah? I asked.

I think we're screwed, and we need to make this right or our race will be destroyed, Leah said, lacking all her usual tact.

"Are you finished talking with your wives?" Anne the AI asked, showing that she knew exactly what was going on. She was a remarkably well-informed machine for one that had ostensibly been isolated from the rest of the galaxy for centuries.

It was clear now that this whole treasure chest had been a telephone game organized by my superiors. The Chel had dropped a bunch of breadcrumbs, and it seemed even Director G had fallen for it (or knew that the literal fate of humanity depended on our actions).

"They're not my wives," I said.

"But you love one," Anne said, making way too many judgements about my personal life. "I have experience with that myself. You have an hour to collect your associates for the test. You will be competing against General Vast."

"Wait, what?" Hannah asked, as confused as I was. "Vast isn't even human."

"That is the point," Anne said. "The opposing team is meant to represent the idea that humanity is a corrupting force and that its grasping nature draws in even other races that have passed these tests. They have been informed that if they succeed in this test, they will be allowed to take the *Mary Read* and use it to subjugate their enemies."

"And is that what is going to happen?" I asked, already knowing the answer.

"Of course not," Anne replied. "If they win the tests they will simply prove that humanity has produced something genuinely dangerous to the Elder Races. Something that needs to be contained."

I stared at her. "The Anne Bonny of history was a champion of humanity and someone who represented the best of us. You may not

209

be her, or completely her, but surely you understand the unfairness of this test."

The woman on the viewscreen stared at me. "The Anne Bonny who was a flesh and blood woman left a world where slavery was legal while monarchs were at their most absolute in power. Where genocide was religiously justified, and she only found freedom by becoming a thief. The galaxy she came into was full of other humans who were engaged in constant bickering and wars that could destroy whole planets. She reveled in the joys and pleasures of being a pirate queen, now serving the Community. Anne Bonny never thought humanity on Earth would survive to make it to the stars and if they did, they would revert to old habits."

"I don't get your point," I said.

"I think you do. You have one hour, Captain Turbo. The docking bay will be open to you and your chosen team. If you attempt to bring anyone else on your mission the results will go poorly."

With that, Anne Bonny's image vanished from the screen.

"Well, damn," I muttered. "That is not good."

"You think?" Leah said, shaking her head. "You were right about Department Twelve, Vance. Our attempts to find Elder Race technology was always going to result in them coming down hard on us."

"Our attempts?" I asked.

"I'm speaking of humanity," Leah said, a little too quickly.

"Of course," I replied, taking a moment to debate what to say to my crew. I could sense they were clearly terrified, and with good reason.

"Trish, would you mind opening up a communication channel to the rest of the *Melampus*?" I asked.

"YOU'RE ON, CAPTAIN," Trish said.

I took a deep breath. "Crew members of the *Melampus*, citizens of the Community, we've found the *Mary Read*. Unfortunately, this has proven to be a double-edged sword as the vessel's AI has made serious threats. I am going to take a team over to confront the machine and attempt to find a solution. I expect everyone who remains to work upon rescue operations and finding alternative solutions to dealing with our present problem. We are the best the galaxy has to offer and have dealt

210

with unusual beings of uncertain power before. We will emerge from this triumphant. Honor to your ancestors, Captain Turbo out."

"You used the 'honor to our ancestors' line," Hannah said. "Now I know we're borked."

"You didn't think we were borked before?" Forty-Two asked.

"Please do not use profanity on the bridge," Lieutenant Commander Choudhury said. "This is meant to be a place of dignity and honor."

"Man, are you in the wrong place," Hannah said.

"Permission to join the team," Princess Huggypants said. "We shall seize the power of the Elder Races for ourselves and rule the galaxy with an iron fist!"

Princess Huggypants was a professional criminal, supervillain really, from her home planet of Ocean Smells Nice (it sounded better in Drolochid). Drolochids kind of look like multi-limbed pill bugs and have saliva-rich voices which sound a bit like how you'd think a dog who just went to the dentist might.

I stared down at the Drolochid. "You didn't pick up much of the subtleties of this conversation, did you?"

"Yes, Department Twelve is incompetent at seizing ultimate power like nukes from the gods!" Princess Huggypants said.

"You mean fire from the gods," I said.

"Why would we need to seize fire from the gods?" Princess Huggypants asked, confused. "You just rub two sticks together or bang rocks. You don't need to rob deities to figure that out. Were humanity's ancestors just exceptionally stupid?"

"I, too, would like to volunteer for the mission!" Light on Water said, the golden rainbow-colored tentacle-shaped alien blob said, holding a tendril in front of where its heart would be if they had any internal organs of note.

I paused before closing my eyes. "I'm going to regret this but, yes, Light on Water, I would like you on my team."

"You've got to be saviting me," Forty-Two said, continuing to ignore Lieutenant Commander Choudhury's request to keep the salty language off the bridge. Which he could do because he was a commander.

211

"The Elder Races are testing humanity, but the whole point of the Community was that it was created as a way of getting multiple species to work together harmoniously while avoiding falling back on tribalist ideology," I said, making a lot of wild stabs in the dark based on my experience with their agents. "A team balanced on diplomacy and understanding, things that Light on Water excels at, would probably do better than one focused on raw power. I'm fairly sure the Elder Races isn't going to judge us on our ability to punch our way out of problems."

"Well, that leaves me out," Hannah said.

"You're coming, too," I said, pausing. "I'm also taking Elektra. We need an expert in the sciences there to handle matters."

"Oh, wow," Elektra said. "This will be the opportunity of a lifetime! The chance to study forbidden technology that learning about is what we're being explicitly tested against. In no way, shape, or form will this backfire."

I stared at her. "Is that a refusal?"

"Can I refuse?" Elektra asked.

"No," I said.

"Then no!" Elektra said, cheerfully. "I am happy to enter the place that is full of certain failure and inevitable death, High Protector."

"Have you considered perhaps running a tighter ship, sir? Perhaps insisting on more discipline, Captain?" Lieutenant Commander Choudhury asked.

"No, no I have not," I replied.

"Right," Choudhury muttered. "So noted, sir."

So, your planned group to save humanity is a Drolochid, a Sklux, a transhuman, an Ethereal, and who else? Leah asked.

I was going to take Trish in her bioroid form, I said. *If humanity is going to be judged, then it needs to be judged with its children.*

AI are not humanity's children, Vance, Trish said. *We're sort of like, okay, we're kind of like children but adults now who are taking care of our infirm elderly relatives.*

This seems like it is already proving you don't have any faith in our race, Leah said, accusatory.

I don't have any faith in our race, I replied. *We're in this situation because I'm trying to stop a conspiracy of people who are determined to get us all exterminated because the godlike beings have put up a sign that says NO TRESPASSING, VIOLATORS WILL BE SHOT but they can't resist jumping the fence.*

It felt surprisingly good to say that, even if it was in the confines of my mind. For years, I'd been thinking it, but I had forced down the idea that humanity had managed to find itself in space but had never successfully learned its lesson about working well with others.

Humanity had made massive amounts of progress toward eliminating poverty, inequality, authoritarianism, racism, sexism, and slavery. However, it still had people who went out to other planets like Crius or Contested Space in hopes of keeping those ideas alive. Worse, it always seemed to have the same old evils on the verge of making a comeback with no faces. Xenophobia replaced racism, genetic slavery replaced chattel slavery, and the people who wanted to control worlds behind the scenes never stopped trying to undermine our civil rights. Humanity hadn't even become less warlike. Rather, it almost exclusively relied on its willingness to send its citizens into the Community's many wars to secure developmental aid.

It was weird to realize that more than any sense of trauma from being tortured at the hands of Alexandra Ares, my failure to save the High Priestess, and the near-genocide of humanity, that I was feeling immense frustration at how *goddamn stupid* EarthGov was being. It was a therapeutic moment that I would have needed a mind healer for under most circumstances. I could now point out the source of a major reason why I'd been avoiding Earth: I was feeling like I would have to spend the rest of my life cleaning up the mess of people who didn't want to be helped. It was an ugly sentiment but, oddly enough, it made me feel better to acknowledge that it had been simmering under the surface this entire time.

Really, Vance? Your come to Buddha-Christ moment is the realization you think humanity is populated by idiots? Especially the government? Trish asked. *I've been living in your brain for close to a decade and could have told you that on the first day we met. Hell, most people in the military can tell you that.*

I want to believe humanity is better than this, I said. *I've been continually disappointed.*

Humanity is made up of people, Leah said. *People can be good or evil, but groups move in much less predictable or moral ways. It's why democracy always ends up coalescing around a leader who is selected to govern for them, defeating the whole purpose. Choose a team of humans for the judgement of humanity. Elektra, Hannah, John Mason, Doctor Zard, and myself.*

John Mason, are you insane? I reacted poorer than I expected.

He's one of Director G's best agents and someone with whom you aren't close, Leah said. *I feel he's one of the people who has the most chance of passing whatever strange criteria the Elder Races are willing to pass.*

And you want to risk your own life as well? I asked Leah.

Yes, Leah said. *Because for all of the questions about whether you are a good person, you have done more to try to be one than the vast majority of Space Fleet. I want to do the same and prove that humanity can learn from its mistakes.*

I should probably point out that Leah is a former member of Department Twelve, Trish said. *All the evidence points that way at least.*

No kidding, Trish, I said. *I was just pretending not to notice.*

Oh, Trish said. *Never mind then.*

I wanted to be able to argue with Leah's logic, which wasn't really logic to begin with but simply a gut feeling I agreed with. If the Elder Races were attempting to test humanity, then it needed to have its High Protector believe in humanity. The fact that I didn't—that I thought we were absolute morons as a species who had lucked out by being brought into space where extinction was far less likely—didn't matter in the long run. For the purposes of the mission, I had to put aside my views on the subject and embrace the kind of boundless optimism I used to have for our species, which had been gradually knocked out of me.

I just wasn't sure how I could do it. In the end, I decided to think about Astrid and how she'd been born under some of the worst circumstances imaginable: as little more than a lab experiment to satisfy Department Twelve's sick scientific curiosity. Yet, she was a beautiful and wonderful girl who would inherit the galaxy I left her if there was still one left over after this test. I'd do it for her even if I wasn't sure I could do it for myself anymore.

I took a deep breath and looked around the bridge. It didn't take a rocket scientist—which I technically was since escape velocity physics was a first year Academy course—to know that everyone was scared out of their wits and needed me to guide them through this. "Yeah, I'm revising the mission parameters."

I wondered if it would be a point in humanity's favor or against it if I shot John during the mission.

I wondered if it would be a point in humanity's favor or against it if he shot me.

CHAPTER TWENTY-SIX

The First Test

"You know, I have to hand it to you," John said, as he sat in the copilot's chair of the shuttle we were using to head into the *Mary Read*'s docking bay. "I thought you were an overpromoted product of Earth nepotism and corruption. A man who coasted on his family name and got a bunch of people killed while playing the role of hero."

I was in the pilot's chair, doing my best to ignore the man as the rest of my team sat in the back of the shuttle. The side of the *Mary Read* opened without a set of doors but more like the side was liquid, opening like a flower budding out of its solid hull. It was quite beautiful and reminded me of an adaptation of Arthur C. Clarke's *Rendezvous with Rama*. Not because of anything in particular, but because it provided that same sense of encountering the genuinely unknown. The Chel may have built the *Mary Read* for Anne Bonny, but they'd used technology that might just as well have been magic to humanity.

"Uh huh," I said, bored. I wasn't going to give John the satisfaction of letting him annoy me more than his presence already was.

"But it turns out you actually are the most important person who ever lived," John said, as if the very concept offended him. Which I didn't hold against him because it offended me, too. He wasn't done yet, though. "Because if you aren't the absolute best example of our race, we're all going to be exterminated by a bunch of space gods."

216

"They're not gods," I said, not bothering to look at him or change my tone. "They're just immortal judgmental beings with near omnipotent power and have created a digital afterlife for their followers."

"I'm still not sure why I'm here," Doctor Elizabeth Zard said. She was a middle-aged, plain, dark-haired woman with pale skin and mismatched eyes. Doctor Zard looked only slightly older than she had when we first met on the *Black Nebula*. She was wearing a flight suit and looked less than pleased at having been forcibly conscripted into yet another mission for the fate of humanity.

"Because we might need a mathematician, medical doctor, or mind healer," I said, pondering the nature of our situation. "We're going to be tested by the Elder Races, but we don't know what criteria they'll be using. They could be testing us scientifically, philosophically, or ethically. So, we have to take the broadest collection of people who can represent humanity at its best."

"Or worst," John said, surprising me.

"Excuse me?" I asked, finally curious about what he was saying.

"You're assuming the Elder Races want humanity to be a bunch of nice guys," John said, "and that if we're a bunch of vegetarian pacifists, they'll be more inclined to spare us."

"I never said that," I replied. I'd been thinking it but I hadn't said it.

"Here's the thing, though," John said, looking at me. "Maybe the Elder Races don't want humanity to be a bunch of vegetarian pacifists. They're actually a bunch of murderous bastarves who use genocide as a way to keep the rest of the galaxy in check."

"Yeah, the Elder Races are pretty awful," I said, making the understatement of the millennia. "Just not as awful as the Primordials."

"Who are they?" John asked.

"The Elder Races that don't want to guide the other races of the galaxy. The Primordials just want to exterminate them all," I explained, knowing that Director G probably hadn't had a chance to fill John in on those.

"Are we going to have to deal with them?" John asked.

"No, they've been dealt with for now," I said. "Mostly they don't destroy everyone and everything in this galaxy because of the regular Elder Races who just want to destroy *some* of the species in the universe."

John gave me a sideways look. "I'm not sure that introduces moral ambiguity, but it somehow makes the situation even worse."

"Yeah, well I didn't make the universe, I just live in it," I said, strangely impatient to get into the insanely high stakes test. "You were saying?"

"Maybe the Elder Races don't want humanity to become a better species," John said. "Maybe the test is to determine whether or not we'd make better slaves than just creating a bunch of robots to serve their every need."

"You don't need slaves if you have bots," I pointed out.

Hey! Trish said in the back of my mind.

Non-sentient bots, I replied, not wanting to get into an argument about varying degrees of sentience.

"Yet we still make bioroids," John said, shrugging. "Maybe the Elder Races just want to create a bloody race of warriors to destroy all of their enemies. Humanity could look like orcs or Klingons to them, and they want that."

"It seems weird they'd want to make a race of warriors that they could eliminate easily," I said. "You'd think they'd want a race that they can't destroy themselves."

"I dunno," Leah replied from the back of the shuttle where she was standing. "I think the ability to put down whatever race you create as your enforcers is just the sign of good foresight. You want a race of warriors that you can employ and who is convenient for you but not so much that they could overthrow you as happened in the past."

"No one invited you into this conversation, spy," John said.

"Infighting now may be the worst thing ever," I replied. "This could be the single most important thing any one of us will ever do so I suggest we put aside all of our personal difficulties to focus on passing whatever test they're putting together."

"Again, we don't know what criteria they're using," John said.

"We could ask," Elektra said, also piping up. "Also, we have some guiding principles that we all agree upon. The Space Golden Rule, which is similar across most races and about as well followed. The Elder Races appointed Vance Turbo and Anne Bonny out of trillions to be High Protectors."

"The High Council of the Senate appointed me," I said, not believing me.

Despite the *Melampus* being right next to the *Mary Read*, the journey across was excruciatingly slow, or at least felt like it was. There was an old military adage that service consisted of hurrying up to wait and never was that feeling truer than that very moment. I could see the *Liberator* and its own shuttle departing on our display screens.

I wondered if Vast really believed that he and his team would have a chance to pull this off or if they suspected that it was all a ruse by the Elder Races. My cynical side—which was close to taking over— thought that he was narcissistic enough to believe whatever they told him if it flattered his ego. I also wondered what sort of people he would be bringing along and whether they would be more agents of Department Twelve's private army.

If I wasn't a coward—and that wasn't a word I often threw about— I might have consulted with my daughter about her vision. I didn't want to bring Astrid into this, and I knew if I looked at her before going out to do these tests then my resolve might crumble. Becoming a father had changed my priorities in life immensely and Space Fleet had become… less important. The big lesson I'd learned about my Aunt Kathy's death wasn't that she'd made a mistake going out into the galaxy. No, the mistake she'd made was that she thought it was possible to serve two masters. That she could raise me and be the Hero of SPAAACE I pretended to be.

In the end, Katherine Tagawa had made her choice, and it had always been Space Fleet over me. She hadn't failed me as the example she'd set had been enough to get me through life. However, I hadn't been raised by human beings, which meant that it was extra ironic that I was now being used to judge the fate of them all. My parents had left me in Aunt Kathy's care most of my childhood and she'd delegated my raising to Alfred. Alfred had educated me in an assortment of old movies, books, and holos cultivated to fill in the gaps that might otherwise have existed where programming failed.

It was funny that now was the time I was reflecting on all my failures and how I'd gotten to where I was, farther than just about any other human. It had been because I'd been raised by machines and childish fantasy stories and sci-fi. I'd faked being a hero long enough that maybe I was one, at least by some people's incredibly low standards. I had helped save the galaxy and now I was potentially going to get humanity killed.

Humanity is not going to be exterminated, Vance, Leah said, her words in my mind.

You can't know that, I thought back.

I do, Leah said. *For two reasons: two people I trust. The first of them is you.*

Your vote of confidence is reassuring but—

You saw Earth destroyed centuries in the future, Leah interrupted. *That means it can't be destroyed now. You also saw humanity surviving on other worlds.*

I was genuinely surprised by that argument. *You're arguing that we should be confident in our chance of victory because we know our planet is going to blow up another time?*

Yes, Leah said. *If we truly believe time is deterministic like the Primordials and Elder Races claim, then history is already written. Free will is an illusion. We are all just characters in a story who are acting out our roles and subject to whatever grim fate our authors have set out for us. I find that comforting.*

If you wanted to summarize the nature of Leah in one small set of words, that was it. It was a decent insight into her character. She was a woman who wanted a world that ran like clockwork, even if it was terrible.

Leah preferred a world that functioned as one of wheels and gears. All should fall like a set of dominos, and it would be better if routine was enforced on everyone and everything. It was an alien mindset to me but having grown up in a society where the government and bureaucracy had calcified into countless traditions on traditions, it made sense. Stay in line and life was good. Step out of line and everything would fall apart. It was a national stereotype that not every Albionese followed, even ones who worked in the military, but Leah embodied the idea that some people simply wanted to be part of something greater.

More than anything, though, *I* wanted us to be able to avert the destruction of Earth and build a better future. I'd told Cthulhu—my name for the Primordial I'd interacted with—that him showing humanity survived meant his threats meant nothing.

I'd been lying.

You would, I thought, summarizing my opinion. *Wait, who is the other person you trust?*

Our daughter, Leah said, causing me to tighten my fists around the piloting controls. *I talked with Astrid a great deal during our journey from the Ring and while you were preparing for this mission.*

I tried to hold back my temper, but I could feel the anger rising from my stomach. *You involved our daughter in this?*

She was already involved, Leah said. *She has a gift, Vance. The ability to see the future and guide us along its currents. Unfortunately, it is an ability that requires a lot of interpretation and of which we must be careful.*

I didn't bother pointing out the contradiction in Leah's two perspectives. If she was trying to reassure me the future was fixed—which was certainly possible but not something I wanted to think about—then that meant our daughter's warning was meaningless. If she did believe our daughter's warning was important, though, that meant that she thought the future could be changed.

Not necessarily, Leah said. *There's an alternative: that our daughter's warning is a necessity to bring about the events she's warning us against. This is what I believe at least. We are all following the whims of fate and that includes oracles who serve as arbitrators of such.*

It was a rare occasion I was left speechless, but this was one of those moments. I wanted more than anything to prevent Earth's destruction. Obviously, to prevent Earth's destruction in the distant future, I also had to prevent the Elder Races from judging humanity worthy of destruction right now. What Leah was describing was basically accepting the lesser evil and that just wasn't me.

That's why I love you, Vance, Leah said. *It's also why you don't love me.*

221

You're the mother of my child, I said. *I love you.*

Liar, Leah said. It wasn't angry or dismissive, just sad.

"We're here," John said.

He was right and my attention was brought to the vast chamber, seemingly larger than the exterior of the ship, that we found ourselves in. It was a strange mixture of almost organic and technological with the walls reminding me of the bottom of the ocean floor. Strange ambient light reflected against the weird shells, coral, and starfish-like growths on the wall. Our shuttle passed an interior lake floating in the center of the chamber like a globe.

There was no sign of General Vast's shuttle as I settled ours down on a cliff-like landing pad that glowed brightly as we approached. The sensors detected a breathable atmosphere and a heat level consistent with Earth norms.

"It looks like the bottom of Neptune's Palace," Doctor Zard said.

"It does look like a sea god's home," I said.

"No, I meant the casino on Belenus. I was on my second honeymoon when I went there. I never left the bedroom."

"Good for you," John said.

"No, it was because my husband lost everything at the casino on the first night," Doctor Zard said. "It was why I had two more marriages afterward."

I sighed and looked back into the shuttle's interior. I saw Hannah sitting in her power armor with an unreadable expression on her face. She hadn't said anything on the trip over and I wondered what was on her mind. "Are you okay?"

Hannah stared at me incredulously. "Vance, have you noticed this is the second time the entirety of the human race has depended on us?"

"No," I said, sarcastically. "That had completely skipped my attention."

Hannah shook her head. "I thought I wanted to get out of this business and back to something simpler. Now I *know* I do."

I sighed. "Unfortunately, Hannah, it seems that when fate calls upon you to do something great, you don't get a choice in the matter."

"There's no such thing as fate," John said, rising.

"Believe me, I hope you're right," I said, joining him. "Hannah, you're the best woman in the galaxy for this job."

"Which is?" Hannah asked.

"Saving the universe," I said, cheerfully. "You have more experience at it than anyone else outside of this group and we're going to do it a second time."

"Technically, the first time was just saving a single galaxy's inhabited species," Elektra said. "This is just potentially saving all of the human beings in the galaxy and any presumed demihuman offshoots. In universal terms, that's actually infinitesimal in its importance."

Everyone in the shuttle looked at her.

Elektra lowered her head. "Well, I thought it was funny."

CHAPTER TWENTY-SEVEN

History of the World, Part III

The six of us departed the shuttle and I was surprised to find the atmosphere smelled of the ocean and had a cool humidity that seemed slightly at odds with what the scanners had described. It reminded me very much of Earth's Hawaiian branch of Space Academy and I wondered if this was practical ship design or just another example of the Elder Races (or their servitor species like the Chel) showing off. As advanced as the *Melampus* was, it couldn't match this place in any way, shape, or form.

No sooner did we debark than a hologram of Anne Bonny appeared before us, looking as realistic and solid as any human. Then again, maybe it was the real thing. The Elder Races did have access to teleportation and while I was pretty sure it was just the ship's AI, nothing would have surprised me at this point.

"Welcome, Captain Turbo and company," Anne said, smiling. "I am pleased to see you here."

"I wish it was under circumstances that didn't involve the potential genocide of my race," I replied.

"That's only if you truly fork up," Anne said, her expression briefly becoming pained. "Let the games begin. Though you have some tough competition for proving mankind is worth saving. General Vast is quite a character."

"I still don't know why we're being judged against a Sorkanan," John said, sounding more racist than he probably imagined.

"I take it you're not familiar with General Vast's history," Anne said, her voice taking on a slight bit of edge.

"I am," I replied.

"No one is asking you, Vance," Anne said.

John frowned. "Everyone has a story. I'm sure the psychopathic lunatic that claims he's fighting for equality is no different."

"He's from 373," I said, simply.

"Ah, Claw World," John said, frowning. "Well, that explains it."

"Claw World?" Hannah asked.

"When Earth was introduced into the galaxy, it was given a number of worlds that were initially set aside for Sorkanan colonization," I replied. "373 was one of the ones in Contested Space that had already been inhabited by a large chunk of Sorkanan dissidents. The Sorkanan Empire is the wealthiest in the galaxy but still extremely capitalist. Its people are prevented from starving, homelessness, and medical disaster but most of its wealth is retained by the ruling clans. 373, along with a dozen other planets, was colonized by people who believed that was unfair. It was already overpopulated and struggling while waiting for permission to open settlement of fifty or so worlds for terraforming."

"Worlds that went to humanity instead," John said.

"And when they went to humanity, Vast decided we all sucked," Hannah said.

"Not quite," I said. "The Equalist movement was a fringe political philosophy until 373 was destroyed."

"Destroyed?" Hannah asked. "Oh, it was one of the worlds hit by SKAMMs."

I nodded. "To be fair, the worlds in Contested Space colonized by humanity were ones claimed by the Notha. If it wasn't us then it would have been the Sorkanan of 373 or the worlds like it fighting them. Still, it was one of the most important invasion points for Notha Space, so 373 was a priority target when the sun killers flew. Seventeen billion Sorkanan were eradicated in the blink of an eye. That caused the other colonies to start their independence movement and Equalism became a genuine guiding philosophy."

"Like WWI and Leninism," John said.

225

"People generally don't start revolutions if things are going well," I pointed out. "Either way, it was a complete and utter disaster for everyone involved. The Equalist worlds were already struggling to survive economically before the war and once they were independent, well, rebuilding without the Community's aid just made things worse. They devoted massive amounts of their budget to building up their fleets against the perceived Notha threat—"

"And then you made peace with them after the Emperor was killed," Hannah said.

"Yeah," I said. "Which caused the Notha Empire to collapse and the Equalists to lose what little was keeping them from each other's throats without a shared enemy. The Community let them fight among themselves in hopes of discrediting the independence movement. Lots and lots of atrocities needed peacekeepers that never came."

John shook his head. "Because that's just exactly what the region needed, more professional do-gooders trying to fix things with more war."

"Isn't that your job?" I asked. "What you literally did since adulthood?"

"Yes," John said.

"So, that's why Vast hates humans," Hannah said. "He blames EarthGov for causing all of the Equalist's woe."

"And now he's working for EarthGov," Leah said. "The irony of politics."

"Like John said, everyone has a story," I replied. "Still, that explains why he's the one we're competing against. The Elder Races clearly think that General Vast represents some of the sins that humanity has committed."

"No, that's not it," Anne said.

I blinked. "It's not?"

"I'm not allowed to give you any tips, Vance, but you are far nicer than either your superiors or the Elder Races," Anne said. "They do not celebrate idealism."

"Told you," John said.

"They don't celebrate violent thugs or violence for the sake of violence either," Anne said.

"Figuring out what the people who employed us both as agents wants is one of the tests you'll have to pass here."

"What tests are there?" I asked.

"Five," Anne said. "You've passed the first one already."

"Wait, what?" Elektra said, looking up. "But we just got here!"

"Yes," Anne replied. "That was the nature of the test. They were checking to see if you, Captain Turbo, and the rest of your crew were willing to submit yourself to the authority of the Elder Races. It's basically the signing your name portion of the literacy test. However, you wouldn't have been the first to reject the very idea that the Elder Races have the right to judge other species."

"Did that work out for them?" I asked.

"No," Anne said. "Sadly, the answer for whether someone has a right to do something or not is that they have the power to do so."

"Violence is the source of which all other authorities derive," John said.

"I don't believe that," I said.

"And where do you think it's wrong?" John asked.

"If it is the source then why aren't soldiers in charge of the universe?" I asked. "At the end of the day, violence is a tool but very few people can live it as a lifestyle."

"Can we save the philosophizing for the actual tests to determine if humanity is going to be annihilated?" Doctor Zard asked.

"Good plan," Anne Bonnie said. "The second test may be equally easy, or you could fail it right now."

"Great," I muttered. "What's the test?"

I wished Danny where here because I would have loved for him to say something like, "I hate tests" or "Does it involve quantum physics? I love quantum physics. You can't really get the answer wrong if you're uncertain." The guy honestly might end up converting to Wheelerism if he kept up his fascination.

Danny was suffering beyond his failed relationship with Hannah and Elektra. His biomod was starting to breakdown after decades of use. It had been a prototype designed to make him easy to ignore, which was in many ways much more effective than invisibility.

It had been a prototype, though, and his control had always been somewhat spotty. Some days he had to concentrate to be noticed at all while other times he was incapable of turning it on. A couple of times in the past few years, he'd been trapped with no one able to sense him but Trish. Doctor Zard said it was impossible to remove the biomod even with *Melampus'* advanced technology, but it might have been possible to shut it down. I had no idea why I was thinking of this now.

"You each get to ask a question," Anne said. "You'll be judged on what you ask."

"Wait, what?" John asked. "That's ridiculous."

"Yeah, I was expecting more cosmic secrets of the universe than kindergarten," Elektra said. "Ooo, can we be tested on cosmic secrets of the universe?"

"No," Anne said, disappointed. "The Elder Races aren't impressed by that question."

"Oh crazzap!" Elektra said, covering her mouth.

"Elektra!" Hannah said.

"Oh God, we're going to die as a species because of a bad comedy skit," Doctor Zard muttered, facepalming.

Hannah looked at Anne. "Do you know why the original Anne served the Elder Races?"

"Is this really the time?" Elektra asked.

"Yeah," Hannah said, shrugging. "I think it is."

The AI version of Anne Bonny smirked. "It was the only game in town, sister. I tried playing the role of the rebel and living by my own rules when I was an ignorant peasant. In the end, all it did was get the people I loved killed and alienate my son. You play the hand you're dealt and maybe you win or maybe you lose."

"Why did you ask that question?" John asked Hannah before turning to Anne. "Wait, does that qualify as a question?"

"No," Anne said. "Was that deliberate? If so, the Elder Races are impressed by your brass but it's not helping you."

"I need to kill you, I really do," I muttered, shaking my head. John had blown his question as well, though I suspected it was simply because he didn't have any idea of what would qualify as a worthy question.

228

"I asked the question because we need to understand the reasons the Elder Races chose her and what they want from her," Hannah said. "We can't possibly understand the Elder Races so we might as well try to understand the people they employ."

"Oh God, Hannah is the person who gave the most nuanced question," Doctor Zard muttered. "We're all going to die."

"Some sooner than others," Hannah muttered, giving Doctor Zard side-eye.

"What about you, Doctor Zard?" Anne asked, turning to her. "What is your question?"

"How do we pass this test?" Doctor Zard asked, a remarkably practical question.

Anne chuckled. "Find out what the Elder Races want."

It was an obvious set up for the next question and one that Leah took advantage of. "What *do* the Elder Races want?"

Anne nodded. "A sign you might actually get through this. The Elder Races want to see if humanity is worthy of eventually joining them. The Community is essentially a testing ground for races to share knowledge with one another as well as slowly develop into species that might someday ascend."

"Ascend?" I asked. "You mean become AI."

"The Elder Races are as far above AI as AI are above you," Anne said. "That is why the Elder Races forbid research into it save under extremely rare circumstances. It is technology that must belong only to those ready to ascend."

"And yet humanity hasn't been destroyed for it, yet," I said.

"Is that a question?" Anne asked. "You seem awfully focused on the idea."

"Just an observation," I replied.

"Humanity jumped several necessary steps ahead of races thousands of years in the future in terms of technological development," Anne said. "When they threaten AI with slavery and reprogramming, they run the risk of meeting the end of all those who have failed the Elder Races' tests. The Elders sympathize far more with beings like Trish than they do normal biological organizations despite all sentience being fundamentally the same."

It was obvious Anne was attempting to give us as much information as she could without going against her superiors. I appreciated the effort and wished I could have talked with Trish about it but when I tried to reach her, I didn't sense her presence. The Elder Races obviously considered AI to be among those I could choose to be a part of my team. I just hoped whatever fragment she'd put in the back of my mind was safe.

I almost asked if it was my turn next but wasn't about to be that stupid. Instead, I asked the question that I felt would be the most helpful in this encounter: "Who are the Elder Races, really?"

"Who are they?" Anne asked.

"Yes," I said. "You've said what they want, but what kind of people are they?"

"That's a stupid question," John said.

"Shut up, no one asked you," Hannah snapped.

Anna nodded. "That will require a bit more than words."

I was confused by what she meant before she put a finger to my forehead, and I felt it like it was solid. Then my mind practically exploded with new information. I saw, heard, tasted, and smelled the memories that became one with my consciousness.

I saw the early years of the galaxy when there were only a few races emerging into space, surrounded by a young and still developing galaxy. The first species were cosmozoans, able to travel the vistas of space on their own without oxygen or heat. These races subsisted on radiation and the raw substances of the galaxy like water taken from asteroids or gases from nebulae. They lived billions of years before they made the transition to immortal indestructible bodies that looked like starships.

Due to growing up in the vastness of space, the first of these races were peaceful beyond belief. Resources were plentiful and patience was ingrained in their mindsets. If two members came into conflict, they simply departed for different parts of the galaxy. Evolution had created races that could spend millennia contemplating philosophy and ones who had never known war. Never known war, at least, until they met the first of the Young Races.

These races had grown up on planetoids and suffered vast amounts of conflict over things like territory, resources, and ideology. You know, the things that defined mortal existence as humans knew it. The Young Races hunted the first of the Elder Races one at a time, harvesting their advanced technology and attempting to enslave them for their own use. Many treaties were struck and inevitably, the Young Races broke them, often never abiding by them in the first place. So, the Elder Races learned quickly the benefits of violence.

There was a period when there were no Young Races whatsoever. The Elders of the Galaxy exterminated any sign of sentient life as it emerged. That disgusted most of them but was vigorously pursued by a good half of the member species. This was the first conflict among their kind that escalated to violence, and it had resulted in a split with those who wanted to be the sole species in their galaxy fleeing to the dwarf galaxies surrounding the Milky Way. These became the Primordials while the remainder became the Core World Races.

The Core World Races tried to teach the next batch of Young Races peace.

They failed.

Repeatedly.

Sometimes, they succeeded only for other Young Races to exterminate their followers. The Elder Races thus knew they needed to become gardeners of the universe. There would be species who would be allowed to join them and species who simply could not be allowed to threaten the others. Their reasoning was practical in many cases: races who were unflinchingly genocidal against others, those who consumed all resources they had in their possession with no regard for sustainability, others who could not communicate with other species due to some quirk of evolution, and still others who coveted the technology of the Elder Races to the point of constant assaults.

There was no justification in my mind for treating sentient species as weeds to be rooted out versus flowers to cultivate but I understood their logic. Ruthless as it was. Especially since the visions implanted in my mind also showed their strategy working. What had started as a handful of species were now thousands allowed to live in the Core as immortal beings transcending dimensions. The Community was only

231

the latest of several thousand societies they had created over the past ten billion years or so.

Most of them succeeded in ascending.

Most.

"Do you understand them now?" Anne asked.

I nodded. "I do."

I also understood that the vision they'd shown me was full of lies and misdirection. It was a gut feeling but one I was certain was correct.

The tests were rigged.

They wanted something from us.

CHAPTER TWENTY-EIGHT

The Tests of Humanity

"So, it's a big, floaty ball," John said, staring at the glowing orb that was in the center of the circular chamber.

The chamber was built like a cathedral in some respects, with walls that stretched ten or twenty meters high but in a fashion that revolved around a set of chairs gathered around a table underneath the floating ball.

The ball itself was a strange looking thing that wasn't always a ball. Instead, it shifted and twisted every time you moved in the slightest bit. Even blinking turned a perfect onyx sphere into a silver trihedron or a glowing torus. If you concentrated hard, which I didn't recommend, you might also see multiple layers of the shapes overlapping one another. That, as you might imagine, gave me a headache.

"Yes," Anne said, staring at it. "It is the Orb of Possibilities."

"Do the Elder Races deliberately choose cheesy names for their artifacts or is it something that they do just naturally?" I asked.

"Yes," Anne answered, automatically.

"What does it do?" Elektra asked.

"It administers the third test," Anne said. "As for what that is, well, you have to experience it for yourself."

"So, we all touch it and see what happens?" I asked, wondering if it was that simple.

"Yes," Anne said, once again keeping her answers limited to one word. I suspected she wasn't meant to have shown as much as she had of the Elder Races' past to me as she'd ended up doing.

It had changed my perspective on the Elder Races, though perhaps not as much as they had expected. The idea that they'd been repeatedly attacked over the epochs of the universe's existence and were flat out sick of dealing with species that couldn't be trusted to abide by agreements made to last for millennia gained them a sliver of sympathy. They were immortal in terms of lifespan but could be killed and while most races could do almost nothing to them, *almost* nothing wasn't nothing. Just like a person could be stung to death by a bee if they were allergic or a person overwhelmed by a colony of ants, it was possible to catch a member of the Elder Races off guard. I was proof positive of it as I'd managed to destroy an entire Primordial fleet and permanently kill Cthulhu.

When you were a race of immortal beings that might have literally billions of years of relationships, that meant people were going to notice when one of you went missing. It might take a while, it might take millions of years, but they were going to notice. The Elder Races had emotions just like us and even if the original people were dead for generations—hell, if as much time had passed from Julius Caesar to today—they weren't going to forget what had been done. Vengeance was an irrational motive, much simpler than a desire for true justice, and they wanted it for the losses amassed by the petty ambitions of men like those Department Twelve was made of. I couldn't even argue with the cold equations of it: the Elder Races would always be in danger if younger species coveted their technology or feared their power.

Unfortunately, these were biological and evolutionary differences rather than that of strict social interaction. Short-lived races like humanity were designed to go forth and multiply while fighting with one another the entire time. Tribalism, ambition, and violence were evolutionary advantages as much as they were the source of so much of humanity's grief. Dealing with the Elder Races was essentially what happened when all those advantages became weaknesses. It was like the old joke, what happened when the man who never backed down meets a man who never loses? Contrary to what always happened in movies, the man who never backs down gets his ass kicked or is killed. Humanity had a lot of unearned pride about its place in the Community and the Community was the Elder Races' aquarium where they kept their pet fish.

"Alright, then," I said, taking a deep breath. "I'm ready."

"I'm ready for Vance to go first too," John said.

I tried not to smile. Okay, that was a good one.

"I'm ready too," Hannah said, proudly.

"I'm not," Doctor Zard said.

"This should be a fascinating experience," Elektra said. "Assuming it doesn't kill us or lead to the extermination of humanity."

Anne sighed. "You remind me of my original crew."

"Space or sea?" I asked, surprised that I cared.

"Sea," Anne said. "Mary was the sensible one. Jack was the idiot, but he made me laugh. There's a bunch of other names you wouldn't know. I sometimes wonder what would have happened if we'd all made it to space together. Then I realize it would have been a colossal disaster and I never would have been made High Protector. Then I wish we had all made it to space together anyway."

I understood that feeling all too well and went to the orb to touch it. What followed was a wave of light that left me blinded for a few seconds.

We passed the tests, defeated Vast, and from there I headed back to Earth. It was a painful and long process of dismantling the entirety of the Human League's influence across society, but my fame finally got turned into the weapon it should have always been used as. I was elected president of Earth once, twice, and eventually six times.

I hated every minute of it.

Still, one thing I hadn't expected was that I would be good at administration and diplomacy. The Notha Union eventually collapsed, and the president founded the Notha Federation which eventually became part of the Community.

Leah and I divorced.

With time, Astrid grew up to become both a Space Fleet captain and eventually the third human High Protector. Our relationship was not perfect.

235

I kept a distance I shouldn't have because I'd only learned how to be a parent from Aunt Kathy, but I loved her, and she could feel that from me.

Unfortunately, there was a price for the choices that I made, and Earth was not prepared when the Primordials ships returned to the galaxy.

Earth died and my last thoughts were of Astrid and hoping that she was elsewhere.

The vision abruptly shifted, and I found myself instead in a swirling mist of other possibilities.

The choice to resign from Space Fleet and flee the Community after the events of the tests on board the Mary Read were controversial. However, the events taught me that I needed to be true to myself and to get my family as far away from the corrosive influence of the Elder Races as humanly possible.

It was a rough time as I drove away every one of my friends and allies with this decision. It turned out that my trying to live a "normal" life was something that none of them were willing to endorse. Still, I was able to find some measure of peace in the wilds of the Perseus Arm where small settlements of humans lived, forgotten.

It didn't last.

Department Twelve in its greed and stupidity sent assassins across the galaxy to find me. Eventually, one of them stumbled upon me despite the extensive changes I'd made to my features. They killed Astrid first and my wife before I ended up killing all of them in return. By that time, though, the Elder Races had moved in to destroy the Earth in retaliation for a planned attempt to hijack their network.

I died with the trillions of other humans involved in the subsequent purge.

That was yet another possibility that I didn't like and rejected. Unfortunately, no sooner did I reject it that I had yet another vision.

The choice to devote myself purely to Space Fleet and put aside my concern for both my family and the ideology I championed had consequences. Extreme consequences. I alienated most of my friends after burying Forty-Two on a distant world and my daughter grew to hate me when Leah ended up dying on a mission against Department Twelve. Making peace with Admiral Bendo made my stomach churn but I moved from being a Community High Protector to being a Human Grand Admiral.

Despite how much I despised the ideology about the Human League, I was involved in many fantastic adventures across many worlds. My influence was also strong enough that I was able to keep them from poking the Elder Races too badly. Unfortunately, that meant their ambitions were unchecked in other areas.

The War with the Community lasted far longer than it should have, closing in about a hundred years and a day. The Community found the destruction of humanity something worth drawing out and devoting only a pittance of resources toward. I fought the entire way with tooth and claw, plan after plan, and eventually atrocity.

In the end, the final destruction of Earth was carried out not by aliens but fellow humans. People disgusted with the tyrannical militaristic dictatorship that insisted all their problems were the fault of the forces outside its borders.

That version of Vance Turbo took his own life after seeing what he had wrought by supporting such monsters.

And good riddance to him.

I pulled away from the Orb of Possibilities, disgusted at the realities that I'd born witness to. I noticed that the rest of my group was standing there, motionless, their eyes glazed over and staring at the orb's ever-changing form. Anne Bonny stared at me, seemingly surprised that I was no longer enamored of the strange object.

"Does any of that mean anything or are you just showing me a bunch of hallucinations?" I asked, feeling a trickle down from my nose.

I wiped it away.

Blood.

"The Orb of Possibilities shows potential futures," Anne Bonny said. "It follows the deepest and darkest desires of a person's heart—the ones that we don't necessarily want to acknowledge—and how to reach them."

"It just showed me a bunch of failed lives," I said, coldly. "A bunch of Vance Turbos that didn't have the courage to stick with their friends and principles. People who betrayed themselves to get a bit of temporary power or security."

I had some respect for the Vance Turbo who tried to save the Earth by becoming a politician—which was a rare sentence by itself—as well as the one who wanted to protect his family. The one who let himself become nothing more than another engine in the Neo-Militarist isolationist Human League disgusted me, though.

"That is how most people respond to power, High Protector Turbo," Anne said, frowning. "They either make compromises and mold themselves into something acceptable to the Powers that Be, flee from power to maintain their self-respect, or smash the system until everyone else suffers under the weight of their hubris."

"And what is the better option?" I asked.

Anne frowned. "That's for you to decide. You may also have to accept that not everything is under your control, if anything *is* at all. You can try as hard as you can to live your best life but still fail. You cannot alter humanity's destiny by yourself. As the old saying goes, you can lead a horse to water, but you cannot make him drink."

"How does any of this relate to the future I saw with the Primordials?" I asked, going up to Leah and waving my hand in front of her. "Was that just another lie, or is this the lie?"

"Why would you ask a person who you believe is lying to you if they are lying?" Anne asked, confounding me.

"Because I like to think I can tell if they're telling the truth," I said. "Besides, even lies can sometimes be revelatory."

Anne smirked. "The answer is the path that leads to the Primordial's future is the future of this reality but not necessarily all realties that stem from it. Branches occur that you can find your consciousness moving to from this body. From your perspective, they will be wholly different realities but that won't prevent the other ones from existing."

"That sounds like complete nonsense," I said, annoyed. "Worse, it sounds like the stuff con men armed with pseudo-science and incoherent mysticism peddle on the infonet. You might as well say Wheelerism is the one true religion."

"Perhaps it is," Anne said, noncommittally.

I was on the defensive now because the images I'd seen had pointed to a fundamental truth: I couldn't stop everything that was threatening my family and Earth. I was up against forces that were much bigger than me and the one common denominator in all of them was that trying to solve them by myself just led to failure. Maybe failure was inevitable and the Elder Races, Community, or Primordials were destined to wipe us out. That didn't mean I was going to stop trying to save us all.

I just needed help.

That was when Hannah fell to her knees, gasping for air. I rushed to her side and put my arms around her. "Hannah, are you okay?"

"No," Hannah said, coughing. "That was horrifying."

"Self-reflection usually is," Anne said, calmly. "I can remove the others from the simulation now. Only one of you is required to pass the test."

"You don't have to," Doctor Zard said, coming out of the simulation naturally. "Eventually, people will figure out it's all bullsavit."

"What did you see?" I asked.

Doctor Zard snorted. "Me getting off your ships and back into mathematics. Sadly, God hates me too much for that to happen."

Hannah didn't respond. "I'd rather not say what I saw."

"She will be the next human High Protector," Anne said. "Assuming you survive all of this. You've been a good influence on her, Vance. The Elder Races are impressed."

I wasn't sure that was something to be proud of, but I wasn't about to reveal that.

"Congratulations, Hannah."

Hannah looked away, clearly not happy with what she saw.

John awoke next and threw up. I didn't say anything but took some small measure of joy from the sight.

Leah? Leah had to be awoken by Anne and started crying. I went to her side and tried to embrace her, but she pushed me away.

"No, Vance," Leah said, looking up. "I made my choice."

I didn't understand.

CHAPTER TWENTY-NINE

The Final Test

The fourth test was more embarrassing rather than terrifying. It involved a big pool of water and seeing what we desired most. Yes, like in a frigging fairy tale.

"I dunno, I expected something a little more... well, more," I said, after seeing Astrid safe and happy in the water's depths. She had grown up surrounded by my friends in a galaxy that was at peace. All of my crew were living their best lives, enjoying a Community that was devoted to science and peaceful cultural exchange.

"That's because your vision was *boring*," Doctor Zard said, sighing. "God, man, I had *Dungeons and Dragons* characters who were less of a paladin."

"Your go to example is a board game?" I asked, referring to tabletop games in a somewhat dismissive manner. I just didn't love them the same way that Trish did.

"I run a game every Thursday night," Doctor Zard said. "Heavy emphasis on the stats and number crunching. No, you're not invited."

"What did you see?" I asked.

"Again, getting out of this borking crew," Doctor Zard said. "Also, the life I could have had with my first husband. I didn't divorce him. He was killed by the Notha."

"I'm sorry," I said.

Doctor Zard rolled her eyes. "No, you're not. You're *sympathetic*. I hate when people say they're sorry for things that aren't their fault or

240

even involved in. I'm sick of sympathy. They're *always* sympathetic. I wish someone would just do something about it."

I got an insight into Doctor Zard in that moment. "That was why you were part of Captain Elgan's crew. He promised you revenge."

"He promised we could make sure that humanity never had to worry about SKAMMs again," Doctor Zard said. "He was a borking liar who put the entirety of humanity at risk so he could get even worse technology."

"I'm sorr…" I cut myself off. "Right. If you want off the crew, Elizabeth, I can arrange it."

Doctor Zard rolled her eyes. "That's the thing about the last test that annoyed me—and this one, now that I think about it. The tests acting like all of this is within our power and none of us must adjust our lives to deal with not being able to have everything we want."

"Maybe that is the test," Elektra said, behind her. "If we can manage our expectations as a species versus grasping at power wildly."

"Then we're being treated like grade-schoolers," John muttered. "Not exactly the sort of thing you need a cosmic series of tests for."

I'd seen John's desire over his shoulder, as had most of the rest of the group, which led to everyone politely ignoring it. He'd seen Hannah.

Yikes.

We'd given everyone else privacy after that.

"You're not being tested as a race here," Anne said. "You're being tested individually as the best choices for your race. The Elders have seen humanity from every possible angle and decided to make the judgement based on the people that it has deemed worthy of embodying its potential."

"That makes no sense," Doctor Zard said.

"I didn't make the rules," Anne said. "Truth be told, I think they're less interested in humanity as a whole than in what individuals can be produced from it. The threat of extinction is something that is wielded as the heaviest possible outcome."

"No savit," I muttered. "It seems like it's wielded as a threat way too often."

241

"When all you have is a hammer," Leah muttered. "The Elder Races could impose sanctions, destroy individual military objectives, and other half-measures. However, plenty of races would accept lesser losses to gain access to Elder Race technology. So, the only thing that works is a threat of complete destruction."

"That is horrible logic," I said. "Not only does it mean you have to make a demonstration of being serious, but the threat becomes the only one you can make."

"Yes," Anne Bonny said. "Congratulations. You understand why the servitor groups such as the Ethereals, Chel, and Community must exist. They provide a buffer so that the Elder Races do not have to act themselves."

I didn't comment on how that reduced the nature of politics to a mob protection racket. The bosses keeping their hands clean and employing layers of flunkies. However, I didn't have any real rebuke for how society worked differently. I couldn't exactly criticize the Elder Races for heavy handed draconian ways. Well I could, but it rang hollow when every single worry they had about humanity seeking weapons against them was being proven right true.

But wasn't that a self-fulfilling prophecy? The Elder Races wanted to maintain absolute security from races that threatened them and made sure everyone knew they had the ability to destroy anyone who challenged them. That just made the Young Races terrified and desperate to find some way to equalize the equation or even just defend themselves. It was a cycle of fear for which I could think of no solution other than somehow getting people to trust one another—and that failed because just about everyone was untrustworthy.

This is why I hated politics.

"How many tests do we have left?" I asked, shaking my head. "I don't know if I can keep doing this."

"You'll do it to save humanity," Doctor Zard said. "Besides, what's the worst that—"

"You had to say that, didn't you?" John asked.

"Yes," Doctor Zard said, lowering her gaze. "I am idiot."

"There is only one more test," Anne said, heading to a large iris-like door that opened at her approach. "Take note that your every reaction from your thoughts to your biological responses have been monitored throughout this series of tests. Everything is being factored into your judgement."

John paused. "Well, that sucks."

"We're doomed," Elektra said. "I should confess that I think the Elder Races are all irredeemably evil."

"They might take that as a compliment," Anne said, walking through the iris.

Leah had been conspicuously silent, and I could sense her distress even without our bond. "I'd like to state my opinion that this group of tests was almost entirely theater. Humanity was never in danger of being exterminated but the Community want to make a show of supporting Vance when he comes back, once more preaching peaceful coexistence after surviving a deadly test."

"Oh, is that what they're doing?" John asked, sounding sarcastic. "What a relief."

"The universe is a terrible place if Vance Turbo is the embodiment of what they want to be the salvation of humanity," Doctor Zard muttered, following Anne.

"On that we agree," I said, following her.

What awaited us on the other side of the Iris was yet another impossible location. In this case, it was a hoard of wealth so vast and improbable that it would have given Smaug the Dragon fits. Vast piles of shimmer crystals, priceless works of art casually placed about like they were junk in an old man's basement, and precious metals that were vital to the circuitry construction of starships to the point that they were far more valuable today than gold would have been in Anne's Earthly years. It was the collected treasures of a hundred worlds and just looking at it left me stunned. You could have bought Earth several times over with the contents here.

A part of me was disgusted as it was a reminder that Anne had abused her position as High Protector horribly. What was the point of all this? But that was the wrong question to ask. Anne had done it because it was a way of punishing the now-extinct Crystal Spider Empire, and because she could. I could have brought up my objections to Anne Bonny the AI but the actual woman who committed the crimes had died centuries ago. Sometime around the turn of the 20th century no less.

Besides, Doctor Zard probably would have pointed out that the plunder here was considerable, but it was mostly noticeable because it was in physical form so the mind could comprehend the amount of wealth on display. To put it more simply, it was cash rather than stocks, bonds, or real estate. It would have been a fortune even the wealthiest of Sorkanan merchant princes would have salivated over. Director G had considered using Anne's fortune to influence the Human League, but he had been thinking small (for once) and he might have pondered using it to utterly retrofit Earth's economy from third tier world to first tier.

"I wouldn't say it's all a show," Anne said. "True, destroying humanity was always a low possibility. The Elder Races select their champions carefully after all. However, it's not a guarantee that Vance will be the one to pass."

"You said that Vast and company were set up to fail," I said.

"Yes, but not in the way you think," Anne said, turning to me. "The most likely outcome of their victory would be that they would be replaced."

"Replaced?" I asked.

John looked up. "What do you mean?"

Anne gestured to the wealth around her. "Imagine all of this plunder put in the hands of agents as humanity has its behavior corrected. The threat of violence isn't the only tool at the Elder Races' command. There is also control. A dictatorship with experimentation to fix the inherent flaws in your species. Humanity would not be the only race to be remade into something more useful to the Elder Races' needs. They've already had great success with both the Ethereals and the Chel."

"That's monstrous!" John said, shouting my own opinion.

I wasn't interested in debating morality. "What's the final test?"

"The simplest of all," Anne said. "But first we should introduce your competitors."

Crap.

Arising out of the ground on a platform like we were in a gladiator arena was what I presumed to be Grand General Vast's team. There was the Sorkanan commander himself, but with four other individuals, not five. I wondered if they'd lost one of their band in their version of the tests. The other four were human but one of them was one I recognized: Major Arana Taylor.

It wasn't the fact that she was supposed to be dead that surprised me. I was almost accustomed to that at this point. No, it was that she was here working with Department Twelve. I really shouldn't have been surprised. Arana Taylor was a bioroid who had somehow slipped past Space Fleet medical inspection and the only way that was possible was with the help of the Security Departments. Still, surprised I was.

"You are failing, Captain Turbo," General Vast spoke first. "My team has passed all the tests until this moment. We will pass the final one and claim the throne the Elder Races have promised us."

"Right," I said, shaking my head. "Throne."

I didn't even have it in my heart to hate the guy anymore. He was a pawn of not only Department Twelve but forces infinitely greater. I could have tried to explain to him all the puppet strings he was dancing to but what would be the point?

"You are on the wrong side of history for this, Captain Turbo," Major Taylor said.

"Is this even your choice?" I asked. "Or are you just programmed to work for Department Twelve?"

"We are all slaves of our programming, Captain Turbo," Major Taylor said. "The urge to breed, spread out, eat, and sleep. I was created to serve as an agent of the Department and safeguard humanity. So that is what I'm doing."

I didn't have the time to argue with her. Was she even the same Arana Taylor that had "died" on my ship? Or was she a copy that had the same appearance and programming? Did that make a difference? I didn't know or care at this point.

"What's the final test?" I asked, looking at Anne.

"Trial by combat," Anne said, looking at me and me alone.

"You've got to be kidding me," John said.

"Oh dear," Elektra said.

"We'll, we're borked," Doctor Zard said.

Grand General Vast let loose a peel of throaty Sorkanan laughter that was translated into more human sounding mirth by the implant built into his throat, something that many Sorkanan had installed for ease of communication with other races. Clearly, he didn't think this contest was very fair and even at five to four, the odds favored him.

I didn't care about that either. "Let's leave it to me and Vast."

"What?" John asked. "I've got power armor here, Turbo. Let me handle it."

"I'm good," I said, taking a deep breath. "It was my mission to kill Grand General Vast from the beginning."

I suddenly understood why my daughter had been warning me about bad things happening if I killed Vast. The Elder Races had gone to elaborate lengths to settle things via trial by combat and I hoped I understood what Astrid had been trying to warn me about. It reminded me of the original Star Trek series episode, "Arena." Captain Kirk had been put up against a lizardman, a Gorn I believe the species was named, in a duel orchestrated by an advanced energy-based race. In the end, Kirk triumphed by creating a crude cannon with homemade gun powder. Kirk chose to spare the Gorn at the end of the battle, though, and proved that humanity had evolved from the violent savages they'd been before. Was it that easy? Beat General Vast and spare his life?

I hoped so.

"You're a fool, Turbo," Grand General Vast said. "You were sent to kill me as part of a double cross by your own superiors."

"I know," I said. "What's next, Anne?"

"Choose your weapons," Anne said.

"I'd prefer hand to hand combat," I said.

"Ha!" Grand General Vast said, his laughter doubling as his translator repeated his almost cacophonic amusement. It made me wonder if he'd altered it to do so as translators usually resulted in the original voice being silenced through a process I didn't entirely understand.

"Vance, this is a terrible idea," John said.

"It's Captain Turbo to you," I said, coldly,

"I agree with him," Hannah said, "Let me fight in your stead."

"Are the terms acceptable to you, General Vast?" Anne asked, turning to Vast.

"I will tear him to pieces," Vast said, grinning from auditory hole to auditory hole (Sorkanan didn't have ears).

"Your team will be able to intervene if they choose, but to do so means everyone will have to fight," Anne Bonnie said, gesturing outward and conjuring a golden spear in her hand. A bunch of golden drones flew in, each shaped like a tiny octopus, and carrying weapons for the rest of the party.

"I won't need help," I said, calmly. This was the most brutish and pointless of the tests, but I had every confidence I would win.

So did Vast. He had every confidence that *he* would win.

The center of the treasure chamber morphed with more of the *Mary Read*'s liquid metal properties and became a rectangular gladiator pit that was about six feet deep, forty feet long, and twenty feet wide. It was large enough to do battle in, but I didn't think it would require nearly as much space as being provided.

"Vance, do you know what you're doing?" Doctor Zard asked.

"A little," I replied, calmly.

"Great," Doctor Zard muttered under her breath. "Well, try not to die."

I gave a half-smile.

CHAPTER THIRTY

The Ultimate Showdown of Ultimate Destiny

In simple terms, this fight was of the David and Goliath variety rather than a contest of equals. At least, it appeared to be so on the surface. Sorkanan were descended from the Tyrannosaurus Rex equivalent of their world, or at least the allosaur, and were a predator designed for charging down prey before tearing them apart with their teeth. They had natural body armor in their scales, vestigial claws for tearing apart prey, teeth that could still be used as weapons, a tail that responded to their commands, and strength that outmatched most humans by a factor of two.

All these facts were things that I had learned when preparing for my fighting scam with Forty-Two back on New Pompeii. Forty-Two had made it abundantly clear that not only was a fight between Sorkanan and a human a lost cause unless it involved fusion weapons but the only reason to have one would be to make the human look good doing something that was impossible. There was only one problem with that line of thinking: it wasn't true.

Human beings are fragile, yes, but the thing is that every other being in the universe is on the fragile side as well. There are a hundred tiny spots on the body, human and Sorkanan, where enough force can result in permanent damage. There was also a lot less difference between a human being who has his genetics altered by the Elder Races and a Sorkanan cyborg than you might think.

The only problem was that I wanted to be able to disable him without killing him and that was going to be a lot harder than just

248

trying to kill him. I suspected General Vast would have no such qualms. I was taking a lot of risks here but I wanted to show the Elder Races that we were capable of showing mercy to our enemies and demonstrate that we wouldn't be pushed around even when we were capable of fighting back. I just hoped that was what they wanted from us.

Because I wasn't sure it was.

"I've always hated you, Vance Turbo," General Vast said from his position on the other side of the pit, plopping his massive feet down one after the other, like a sumo wrestler. "Your continued survival has vexed me since the Kolahn War."

"That's funny," I said, taking several deep breaths. "I haven't thought about you much at all. You were just a minor part of a mutiny that I did take personally but was, by itself, just one chapter in my story. Maybe three."

General Vast sneered. "You're the embodiment of what I hate most in humanity: the relentless, never-ending glory seeking. You're like puffer fish—we have those in our oceans as well—so scared of other species that you do everything in your power to appear stronger than you are. You invent heroes and glorious accomplishments to cover up that you're nothing more than a bunch of primitives irrelevant to the galactic stage."

I stretched my back. "You won't get any argument from me."

General Vast narrowed his serpentine eyes. He clearly was not happy with my refusal to engage him in any sort of banter or argument. The problem was he was almost like another Lieutenant Arden. He wanted to make us have this deep and abiding connection as archenemies when the truth he was just another warlord out to make a name for himself. Maybe he was the guy who finally had my number but if so, it wouldn't be because he was anything other than another assignment. Death could come to all of us at any time and you had to accept that, Elder Races tampering or not.

Our respective teams were gathered on opposite ends of the gladiator pit even as Anne Bonny stood between the two sides, overlooking us like she was some sort of twisted referee. Which, honestly, I supposed she was.

"You know, this is the second time I've been in a gladiator arena," I replied. "The first time was with the Notha Emperor versus some cyborg Tyrannosaurus Rexes. So, really, Vast, this is kind of the low budget sequel they do on the cheap."

I wasn't sure if taunting him was the best strategy right now, but it certainly had the effect I wanted. General Vast charged at me like a bull, screaming and running at me with his claws extended and his mouth open. That allowed me to move to one side and deliver a brutal kick to the left side of the Sorkanan's lower ribs where their secondary heart was. That wasn't enough to take him down and he immediately swung around to take my head off with a claw strike only for me to duck and deliver a series of blows to his lower organic knee before slamming my foot against it, cracking bone.

That was when General Vast headbutted me faster than I could avoid. He kicked me in the chest with a follow-up blow before sending me sliding across the floor. The Sorkanan charged at me with his claws, narrowly missing me as he smashed them against the hulk of the ship beneath us, and then he moved to rip out my throat. I responded by donkey kicking him in the face with one foot then the other.

Vast's attacks were savage and unpredictable, but he had never learned to strategize on a personal level. I hit every sensitive spot I could and kept up the blows, retreating whenever I ran out of wind to continue my attacks. Finally, I left myself open for him to bite my leg, only to pull back at the last second to deliver a knee to Vast's throat. That knocked the wind out of the warlord and sent him falling to the ground.

"It's over," I said, falling back. "Surrender and we can move on from this."

"No," General Vast said, spitting blood on the ground before. "You'll have to kill me."

"I'm prepared to," I said, lying.

That was when General Vast spit blood in my eye sand charged at me, taking advantage of my desire not to kill him. What followed would be burned into my mind for the rest of my life. I saw Vast charging at me, only to hear Leah scream a roar of attack before there were all manner of shouts, clanging metal, and the sounds of horrific injury.

I wiped away the blood from my eyes to see that Vast was standing over the fallen form of Leah. One of his claws was soaked in blood and her spear was to one side where she'd stabbed him in the right arm. All around us, I could see the others battling it out in a free-for-all. Leah had moved to stop Vast from killing me.

I didn't hesitate to grab her spear and charged forward, stabbing Vast through the chest. Vast barely had time to register the attack before he was impaled through his primary heart and leaking blood out onto the ground from a fatal injury. I took the time to jab down my foot on his already injured throat to snap his neck. All my plans to try to spare Vast's life had disappeared in the instant I saw him standing over Leah.

Then I was at Leahs's side, ignoring the rest of the fight. "Leah, I'll get help. I'll get you back to the ship. Doctor Zard!"

Doctor Zard avoided Major Taylor swinging a spear at her, only for Hannah to stab the treacherous bioroid in the throat. Doctor Zard hadn't joined in the fighting and came to Leah's side as quickly as she could, but the prognosis was not good. I could already see the blood spilling outward in every direction around her.

"It's okay, Vance," Leah said, coughing. "Astrid saw this coming."

"What?" I asked, staring at her.

"It's the price we have to pay," Leah said, closing her eyes. "I'm sorry about…"

Then she was gone.

"No!" I shouted, soaking my hands in the blood on her chest. I turned to Anne Bonnie, who had her gaze lowered. I shouted at her with the fury of a child. "Bring her back!"

"It doesn't work like that, Vance," Anne said, looking around as John and Hannah made short work of the remaining members of Vast's team. They'd protected Elektra and Doctor Zard from injury, but they had been unable to also guard Leah "It does, however, mean you pass the test. So, she didn't die for nothing."

"Who cares about the test!" I shouted, not in the mood for any more of this bullshit. "The mother of my child is dead!"

Anne closed her eyes. "The Elder Races need a humanity that is capable of a variety of roles during war. The Notha, Sorkanan, and humanity were all altered at various points during your development to be aggressive tool-using warriors. They knew there was a war with the Primordials in the making and while you've managed to put that off for a few millennium, it is eventually going to happen. The Elder Races need a race of soldiers capable of killing savagely but living in peace when not at war. When they selected you, Vance, the question was never whether you would be able to live in peace with other races but that you could be inspired to kill ruthlessly when necessary. That is what they want from humanity and the Community. Soldiers like the Ancient Romans to guard against the barbarians at the gates. Ones recruited from the very people they disdain."

"I don't care," I said, falling to my knees.

"I know," Anne said, fading away. "But she did."

It all came together. "Astrid isn't clairvoyant at all. You sent those visions to her."

"Yes, she is," Anne said, her voice echoing. "But we did."

Seconds later, we were no longer in the makeshift gladiator arena/treasure vault that Anne Bonnie had brought us to. Instead, the four of us and Leah's body were on the bridge of the *Melampus*. Our appearance caused no end of chaos as you could imagine. However, on the viewscreen, I saw a fleet of Community ships arriving to take custody of General Vast's forces. I also saw the *Mary Read* make a jumpspace leap and disappear from the universe again. I was left with the body of my child's mother and no idea how I would explain what had happened to her. We had passed the Elder Races' tests, but never had victory tasted more like defeat.

EPILOGUE

Last (Dis)respects

Leah's body was ejected into the nearest sun with full military honors. The Community had many, many questions and I'd have to return to Throneworld but the High Council was willing to wait until they had all of the questions prepared. That would take months, I suspected.

Later that week, I would find out that the *Mary Read* made several stops along the way toward vanishing forever, leaving behind the treasures that the pirate queen had pilfered centuries ago as well as several unexpected "gifts" like the cures for diseases that had ravaged planets, and upgrades to jumpspace technology.

The Elder Races contacted the Community through the Ethereals and informed them that the laws against AI creation would be relaxed but they were "strongly encouraged" to welcome the newly created people as equal citizens and to protect their rights. It was believed, between the gifts and changes of laws, that technology would advance another century or two. Which sounded like a crock of bullsavit since science didn't move in time schedules, but the media loved making sweeping pronouncements.

It was, however, a windfall of new technology and benefits to the entirety of the Community's races. The Gulayan Limit was an artificial technological development barrier that meant progress had to be done incrementally versus in big, bold scientific leaps.

Officially, it was the closest thing to a Prime Directive that existed in the galaxy with the Elder Races using it to make sure no one jumped ahead millennia by stealing their tech or studying other species too closely. Having it raised to incorporate several new technologies as well as more AI research really was a big deal and I asked that it be dedicated to Leah with it being called "The Mass Leap Forward." It was the least I could do.

Too bad Leah hated puns, especially since this one only worked in English. Still, any question of what I'd been doing exploring the Perseus Arm versus engaging in local politics was resolved overnight. It had led to this moment. A transformative moment for all of mankind and many other races. I planned to use this boost to our potential to humiliate the Human League and endorse several candidates to challenge the currently reigning governments' incumbents. Given what a huge deal all of this was, I suspected I could trash the entirety of the isolationist movement for at least a generation without having to run for office myself.

I'd also used my influence as High Protector to force an emergency relief aid package to Deathworld and to pass mass weapons embargoes and sanctions on the Notha Union. Community membership had been fast tracked for the planet and several other worlds being threatened by the Notha Prime. The Diplomat wasn't executed by her father but had been assigned to be my liaison—a fate worse than death, but one that I hoped she would eventually come around on.

I made good on my promise to John Mason, who made good on his promise to remake the Rangers. But he stepped down as their CEO and commanding officer. Instead, John was now entering politics with plans for running for president of Earth in about ten or twelve years. He claimed he'd seen it in the Orb of Possibilities and that his presidency would lead to the Primordials not invading. I had no idea how that was possible but agreed I'd give him my endorsement when the time came.

He also proposed to Hannah.

She turned him down.

I recommended her to be a High Protector.

The High Council agreed. She was assigned her own ship. The *Katherine Tagawa* was a sister ship to the *Melampus*, and a good chunk of the crew willingly decided to go with her, including Ichigo as her first officer. They'd made a fast friendship during their short time together. Hannah wanted to say something to me before she left but couldn't with the specter of Leah dying.

So, she just left.

She'd be back.

Eventually.

Unfortunately, as much as I was willing to put them off, there were some things that couldn't be ignored any longer. I'd tried to be there for Astrid, but as much as I had a reputation as a motor mouth, I couldn't figure out what to say to her. This was my third attempt in the past week, just sitting in my room with her across from me. Despite how wise and intelligent she was, Astrid was never more than a child in my eyes. *My* child. She had her legs dangling over the side of my bed as I struggled to figure out what to say or do regarding the matter. There was nothing I could think of because I'd failed to bring her mother home and the guilt was positively crushing.

"She knew what she was doing, Dad," Astrid said, looking at me.

I stared at her. "It's not your place to comfort me, Astrid. It's my place as the parent to comfort you."

"I know," Astrid said, looking to one side. "But this is the terrible thing I saw happening. I've had time to come to terms with it."

That just made things worse. "Then I could have stopped this."

"No," Astrid said, sighing. "You couldn't have. The determination that defines you and Mother, both, was born from the deepest parts of your souls. You couldn't do otherwise."

"There's always a choice," I said.

My daughter stared at me then scoffed. In that moment, there was never a surer sign that she was more like her mother. "Right, Dad. I'll talk about this with you later."

"Astrid, your mother is dead..." I tried to figure out what I wanted to say in this situation, but I couldn't think of anything.

"I know, Dad," Astrid said, reaching over to hug me. "You're also grieving. You'll get better, it'll just take time."

I wanted to argue with her, but I was the one who was in the wrong and just hugged her back. Sometimes, there was just no good answer to a situation and the child ended up adulting the parent. I hated that and felt like I was somehow failing her, but I wasn't about to argue with the clairvoyant and telepath about either the future or my feelings.

Still, I had to ask. "If I hadn't killed Vast, do you know what would have happened?"

"She might have lived," Astrid said. "She might not have."

"Right," I said, wondering what I could have done differently in those vital few seconds I took killing the so-called grand general. "I'm going to drive myself crazy thinking about this, aren't I?"

"Probably," Astrid said. "I always knew what my mother was. It was why I could never open myself up fully to her."

"She loved you, you know," I said. "Despite everything,"

"I know," Astrid said. "But I know you don't know that I know."

"Right," I muttered, again, reducing to monosyllabic responses. "I guess I'll let you go, then."

"Thanks," Astrid said. "We'll talk later."

I just watched my daughter leave to go play her video games and decompress however she wanted to. I felt utterly useless and sat there for the longest time. I'd saved the galaxy, again, but what was the point of doing that if you couldn't save your own family? I'd never been a proper spouse to Leah. Never bothered to marry her. Never truly loved her the way she deserved.

"HEY, VANCE," Trish said.

"Not really in the mood to talk, Trish," I said. "Kind of busy contemplating the horrific unfairness of the universe."

"YEAH, WELL WHILE YOU DO THAT, YOU SHOULD KNOW THAT LEAH LEFT YOU A MESSAGE," Trish said.

"What?" I asked, looking up.

"A LOT OF CREW MEMBERS RECORD THEM BEFORE GOING INTO BATTLE," Trish said. "SHE RECORDED ONE EACH FOR YOU AND ASTRID."

It was a common enough activity, one that I'd always intended to do myself. Unfortunately, I could never find the words for the people I was going to leave behind. Thankfully, if the ship was blown up, most of the people I cared about would die anyway! That was a joke. Mostly.

"What did they say?" I asked, not feeling like I had the strength to watch the one intended for me just yet.

"SHE ASKED ME TO NOT LOOK AT THEM," Trish said. "SO, I PARTITIONED OFF THE PART OF MY BRAIN THAT OBSERVED HER THEN DELETED IT. IT'S AS CLOSE AS I CAN COME TO NOT PAYING ATTENTION."

Trish was an omnipresent factor on board the *Melampus* and could see and hear every crew member's actions, regardless of desire for privacy. It was one of the sacrifices you had to make while in Space Fleet. She couldn't see everyone's brain—that was a function of my cybernetics—but it meant traditional spying was impossible without hacking her programming. The time she'd been forced to ignore sabotage still bothered her. It was a violation that she'd never gotten over.

I debated asking her to send Leah's message to me away, or even deleting it, but that was just my emotions talking. I needed to go back to Earth and set my affairs in order. I needed to make sure Alfred was taken care of even with the new laws regarding AI. And I needed to confront Admiral Bendo. But before any of that, I needed to get my head on straight.

That meant facing Leah's final words to me. "Could you project it to me in here?"

"SURE," Trish said. "DO YOU WANT SOME PRIVACY?"

"You are part of my family, Trish," I said. "Leah was your friend too."

"KIND OF, YEAH."

Okay, not exactly the best endorsement ever. "Begin, please."

The holographic systems aboard the *Melampus* were fantastic and built with microcircuitry that almost any location could be used to project an image. Here, though, it just appeared over the conference table and looked like an ordinary hologram. Leah had chosen to wear her uniform for her final message, and she had a sad but not despairing look upon her face.

"Hello, Vance. If you are receiving this then I did not return from our final mission together but, as usual, you managed to find your way out of the situation."

I grimaced at her description. "I'm sorry."

"Don't be sorry," Leah said, either anticipating my response or just having a coincidental word. "You aren't a bad person for your ability to survive what other men can't. I also knew that I was going in to die. Astrid didn't want to tell me that the bad thing she saw was my death but that she knew we would pass the test was reason enough for me to trigger you killing Vast."

I stared at her. "You wanted to die?"

"I didn't want to die," Leah said, once more displaying she knew my brain better than I did. "However, the statistics were in favor of it being the best outcome for us all. One person versus trillions. I'd call that a bargain."

"You should have told me," I said, depressed and shocked. "We could have found another way."

Leah didn't respond for a moment. "You always fight kicking and screaming against the inevitable, Vance. You don't just want to settle for the lesser evil but the greatest good. It's something that I really do love about you. Which is why I want to apologize for what I did to you."

"You don't have anything to apologize for," I said, assuming she was talking about letting herself get killed to inspire me to kill Vast and thus pass the test.

"I do," Leah said. "I have wronged you more than you could possibly imagine."

I had no idea what she could be referring to and didn't care in that moment. I wished I could have turned back the clock and made everything right between us. I would have given her the chance she deserved, and we could have truly been a family. I should have set aside my suspicions and accepted her for who she was.

"I never left Department Twelve," Leah said, rocking me to the core. "Astrid was always created to be a lure for you. You were psychologically pegged as having deep abandonment issues, who could be controlled by the prospect of children and the need to protect your own family. I know this because I was the one who created your profile."

I stared, my mouth agape.

"There was never any secret mass cloning facility on Crius," Leah said. "At least, not one that needed to be shut down. Department Twelve sent me to Crius to supervise its genetics research. Director G used me to work against the slave lords, but I was a double agent, or perhaps a triple agent since he was counting on my turning against the Department on your behalf. Which, I suppose, goes to show that he truly is the greatest spy Earth has ever produced. He was right. In the end, you turned me rather than me turning you."

I felt sick to my stomach, realizing everything had been a lie. "No, it's not possible."

"Don't feel stupid, Vance," Leah said. "If you can't manipulate someone who you can literally read the thoughts of then you have no business calling yourself an agent."

I sat down on the edge of my bed, staring forward as I contemplated it all. "I could forgive you for lying to me, manipulating me, and seducing me, but how could you bring a child into this? For Department Twelve?"

Leah sighed. "I can't always predict what you're going to say, Vance, but I believe you're probably lashing out on my behalf for Astrid's sake. Don't put that upon her. She knew I was a monster and that I never loved her as much as you did, but that is a hard act to follow. I could never love her the way a daughter deserved to be loved by a mother, but I learned to feel something for her through our bond."

"Something?" I asked, wondering if Leah had always been a psychopath or if whatever life she'd experienced before had simply screwed her up beyond all repair. Even the fact that she'd chosen to sacrifice herself to save the galaxy didn't leave me feeling like I could forgive her for this massive set of betrayals. I was stunned and every possibility open to me felt pointless. All that we'd done together over the past few years had been just her playing a role.

"Yes, something," Leah said. "As close to love as I am capable of feeling for anyone. I did not lie when I said you inspired me to be a better person. The problem is that I started as someone truly terrible, and redemption is a lifetime commitment."

"You aren't redeemed," I said, feeling terrible after saying it, but not regretting it either. What she'd done was beyond the pale.

259

I was such a fool.

"Which is why I want to give you one last thing I was too cowardly to give you while alive: the means of destroying Department Twelve forever," Leah said, calmly.

I looked up, confused. "What?"

"Your Aunt Kathy was close to bringing down the organization," Leah said. "But she lacked the appropriate context to finally destroy them. Director G was unable or unwilling to utilize the full force of his position because too many of his own assets were tied up in their schemes. He isn't exactly a good man, but he has always had Earth's best interests at heart. Sadly, it means he didn't have the willingness to crush an organization that claimed to be fighting for humanity, even when it would gladly sacrifice its AI or alien citizens."

"I don't understand," I said, not really speaking to the recording but to myself.

"You, Vance, are willing to burn down the corrupt intelligence apparatus and network of corruption that Department Twelve has made for itself," Leah said. "For that, you just have to know who is a part of Department Twelve and who they control. It's taken me a very long time to reach the upper ranks of the organization, but I have and I know enough to destroy the organization in such a way as to make Carthage's end look merciful."

I didn't dare get my hopes up but the prospect of finally going on the offensive drove out all feelings of betrayal. Department Twelve was a terrorist organization and renegade intelligence organization. If its members could be tied to it, they could be removed from power.

"Everything I know about Department Twelve has been recorded and stored away at Space Academy," Leah said. "Go to the place where we made our careers together. It will provide you the tools for the High Protector to bring an end to his oldest foe. It's my apology. I don't expect it to be accepted."

With that, Leah's hologram disappeared.

"WOW," I said. "I DID NOT SEE THAT COMING."

"Should I watch the one for Astrid?" I asked.

"ABSOLUTELY NOT."

"Agreed," I said, standing up. "Trish, would you connect me to the bridge?"

"ABSOLUTELY."

"Good," I said, taking a deep breath. "Set a course for Space Academy. Maximum speed."

"TWINKLE, TWINKLE"

A Space Academy Short Story

By C.T. Phipps

"What the hell is that thing?" I asked, staring at the image on the viewscreen.

The sight made me question if I wasn't the victim of an elaborate prank. It was an enormous glowing energy spreading itself out in three parts, splashing around—for lack of a better term—in the solar plasma of the Zatranian system's sun. If that wasn't crazy enough by itself, it seemed to be absorbing the energy from the star at a rate that would collapse the yellow sun into a red giant within hours. Which I suspected the inhabitants of Zatrania III would be less than thrilled about.

My name is Vance Turbo, and I was the captain of the ESS *Melampus*. It was a kilometer long ship with the population of a small-town. As my crew said, it was an exploratory and peacekeeping vessel. The *Melampus* had been exploring the Perseus Arm or Perseids for the better part of six months and it had been an endless amount of weird compared to the Known Universe: mad computers, self-styled gods, and jumpspace phenomenon that proved the existence of other realities. This was going to be up there with the weirdest of my reports, though.

"It looks like an energy-based cosmozoan, sir. Sort of a big fire bat," Elektra, my science officer, said. She was a lovely, obsidian-skinned woman with pointed ears. As an Ethereal, she was a demihuman and a result of alien genetic engineering. She was also an adorable little cinnamon roll of a person as well as a helluva great scientist.

"Or a phoenix," Danny Tagawa, said. My cousin was operating the sensor unit. He was a handsome young man whose primary problem was getting people to notice his existence. That had led to him adopting a somewhat exaggerated personality that wasn't really fit for a Space Fleet bridge. "Can we name it the Space Phoenix?"

"That's not a scientific classification," Elektra said.

"And no one believes us anyway," Danny said. "It's like when they discovered the platypus, everyone they contacted thought they were being put on."

Elektra looked despondent. "I would have believed in the platypus."

"It looks like a big blob to me," Leah, my second-in-command and lover, said what I was thinking. "One that's eating the home star of our friends here."

Leah Mass was a hard-edged former spy and the mother of my child. She had short, well-trimmed dark hair and the face of an angel. She could also break someone's neck while hugging them. Our relationship was complicated, not exclusive, and full of issues that made it as perilous as an untested jumpdrive.

"Friends is a bit much," I replied. "However, we have offered the local colony aid."

Finding fellow humans out here in the Perseids was a big surprise and had initially made us quite happy. However, the reasons why they were out here were because they were the descendants of a bunch of Neo Militarists who hated the idea of Earth joining any political organization that they weren't the head of.

I didn't blame the Zatranians for the politics of their ancestors, but they'd been nonplussed to find out that humanity had become incredibly prosperous in the past two hundred years while they'd struggled to terraform their planet into something habitable. Now a giant space phoenix was eating their sun. Which, really, was not a sentence I was prepared to think.

"I doubt we can just chase it away with our fusion cannons," Elektra said. "After all, it's made of energy *and* eating it."

"Yes, that complicates things," I muttered, sitting back in my command chair. "Now we have to figure out a solution."

"Has anyone actually ever seen a cosmozoan outside of a holodrama?" Danny asked. "Especially one that, well, defies all the known laws of physics?"

"No," Hannah said. "Though there're always legends—"

"There are legends about ghost pirates and space gods," Danny interrupted. "That doesn't mean they're real."

"Some of those exist," I pointed out, watching the scene on the screen with a perverse fascination. "We've encountered a few of both."

Danny sighed.

"Shouldn't we try to do something?" Leah asked.

"Do what? It's eating a *sun*. Elektra explained why our weapons are useless," I said, throwing out my arms. We were a cargo ship, no matter how heavily armed, and this was way beyond the boundaries of what was normally encountered during a routine relief effort haul.

"Sir, we're getting a hailing frequency from Zatrania III's government," Danny said. "It's the president of Zatrania III."

"Mayor would be a more accurate summation," I replied. The planet was a colony world of a colony world and just barely scraping by. "Put it on screen."

Zatrania III had about five hundred thousand residents, possibly a few thousand more since our last visit. The planet had once been inhabited by another sapient species before the Elder Races had wiped them out. Humans were rare in this part of the galaxy and the fact that they'd settled down here was a sign they'd been running from something.

I made a mental note to find out more.

Zatrania III had a mostly nitrogen-based atmosphere, and they'd set up enough atmosphere processors plus enough plant-life to be self-sustaining. They were still modern-day pioneers, a hundred years later, and I admired their grit.

The image of a star being eaten by a space monster was replaced by that of President Paula Lakshmi. She was a spectacularly lovely woman, the result of genetic enhancements, who'd made the somewhat bizarre decision to have her skin body-dyed purple and her hair made sparkling white.

Paula wore a color-changing fabric that barely covered anything, which was more likely because the planet's temperature reached regular highs of thirty-seven degrees Celsius on a cool day. Standing beside her was her bodyguard/lover Korbin who was bare-chested, equally purple, and looking severe.

"How can I help you, Madame President?" I asked, staring at her. "It seems you are witness to a horrifying miracle."

I'd already decided to dump our relief effort and gather as many of the colonists up as possible. It would be a tight fit and we wouldn't be able to save everyone. However, with the proper level of resource management, we'd be able to probably get a good ten to twenty thousand to safety at the nearest star base. I wouldn't want to be one of the people who made the decision of whom to leave behind, but it wasn't my first evacuation either.

Space was a pitiless mistress.

"There is no time for poetic flourishes, Captain Turbo," Paula said, her voice hard and lacking any of the usual pleasantries we'd exchanged in the past few years. "We need you to kill the Fire Dragon."

"Is that what we're calling it?" Danny asked. "I was thinking Space Phoenix."

"Shut up, Danny," Leah said.

"Yes, ma'am," Danny said, lowering his head.

"With all due respect," I said, using the code for "you're out of your goddamn mind" when talking to people higher ranked than you, "that thing is eating your system's star. I'm not sure there's anything we can do to it. We can, however, get your people—"

"It is the curse of the Technomancers," Paula said, staring forward with a haunted expression.

"What?" Leah and I said, simultaneously.

"Jinx," Danny said.

"Shut up, Danny," I said. "Listen to your commanding officers."

Paula looked embarrassed. "The Technomancers are a sect of Kolahn religious extremists existing on the fringe of even the Border

Planets' space. They use a combination of Community and scavenged Elder Race technology to mimic... magic."

"Are they related to the Enigmatic Path?" I asked.

"More their equivalent to Ethereals," Elektra said. "The Technomancers are Kolahn made immortal and given trinkets of Elder Race technology that are, nevertheless, incredibly powerful."

I processed that. "Any sufficiently advanced technology is indistinguishable from magic."

It was a phrase that no one knew the precise origin of. I'd encountered more than a few species that seemed to possess powers straight out of a fantasy holo.

"We just can't escape the Elder Races or the Path, it seems," Hanah muttered. Hannah was the blue-haired, brown-skinned Amazon of a woman who was my chief of security.

The Kolahn were a species that had been wronged terribly by the Community but had elements that had invited attack. A formerly peaceful people of scaled, ape-like aliens, they'd been taken over by a technocratic cult called the Enigmatic Path. They had wreaked such havoc that the Community had taken the kid gloves off and hammered their planet to oblivion before resettling the survivors. This, of course, had done more to get the survivors to join the Enigmatic Path than anything else.

Paula nodded. "Technomancer Master Akavma came to our planet and demanded that we turn over the relics we'd scavenged from the Pyramid Builder ruins. The alien race who—"

"I know who they are," I said, interrupting.

One of the reasons I was here was because Zatrania III had once been settled by a race old enough and advanced enough to have attracted the Elder Races' attention. The unknown aliens had constructed several impenetrable facilities around the planet before getting annihilated. There were also remnants of the Elder Races' invasion among the ruins as well. The thing was, the Community had one unbreakable law that almost all other races were smart enough to obey: DO NOT MESS WITH THE ELDERS' STUFF. The Kolahn and humans were among the only people stupid enough to do so.

"He got very upset and cursed us," Korbin said, pointing up to the sky. "He brought down the wrath of the Fire Dragon."

"Hold on a second," I said, turning off the viewscreen before looking to my crew. "Okay, are we being had? Is there really a giant monster eating the sun, summoned by a freaking *wizard*?"

"Space is weird," Hannah said, shrugging. "Did you know I once met a guy with three—"

"Is there any way this could be a weapon of the Kolahn?" I asked, interrupting.

"Heads," Hannah finished.

"No," Leah said. "If the Kolahn had a weapon like this, they would have taken over the entirety of space."

"Assuming they wanted to," I said. "Elder Race artifacts can do almost anything, and they left them on worlds like this as refuse. Maybe the Fire Dragon is something this guy found while prospecting for their artifacts."

"Or something he knew was coming and is claiming credit for," Leah suggested.

"Possibly. Send everything we have down to Doctor Zard and scan the system for signals around the sun," I said, pointing to the screen.

"That's going to take a while sir," Elektra said. "Scanning is a long, painful, and annoying process."

"Hence why I have you do it instead of me," I said, smiling.

Elektra muttered something that sounded suspiciously like my opinion about the Kolahn.

"What was that?" I asked.

"Nothing, sir."

"We're being hailed again," Danny said. "It's the president. I get the impression she's not happy to have been hung up on."

"Put it on screen," I said.

Paula glared at me. "We need your help, High Protector."

"I'm trying," I said, staring at her. "But it'd be best if you prepared to evacuate the colony. I can get some of you away."

Evacuation was not the plan I wanted to go with, but I was also aware that this was well outside my ability to affect things. As High Protector, I'd been given very few resources to work outside of the

Community's territory. Space was big—mind-numbingly, overwhelmingly big—and it wasn't just a trip down the street to get reinforcements. Even the nearby local powers were weeks away and had entirely unsuitable environments for housing humans. Still, I couldn't let us be intimidated because we were up against something that was potentially destroying a sun. No, we'd have to be heroes again—even if it got everyone killed.

Being a father has made you cautious, Trish said via our cyberlink.

Is that a bad thing? I asked.

It is when other children's lives rest on you, Trish replied.

She was right.

Paula looked down. "We can't. The colonists won't do it."

"I think they'll change their mind when the sun dies and they're freezing to death," I said.

Paula paused. "Perhaps, but by that that point, I won't be president, and the guns will have been drawn. This colony was founded on the principles of absolute freedom and the right to bear weapons."

"Uh huh," I said, avoiding saying what I thought about that. "So, they'd rather die than leave a planet they're squatting on."

"Yes," Paula said. "So, they say. And most of our starships are so old they can't leave anymore. That was another thing I was hoping to talk to you about."

"Fair enough," I said, staring. "We'll try and fix this. If we can't—"

"Please save my people," Paula said. "No matter what they've done to me for bringing this down on them."

I doubted the president could be blamed for "giant space amoeba eating the sun." However, if this was related to enemy action then she might be responsible in a way that she wasn't advertising.

"Try not to get too noble here," I said. "It's literally my job to protect colonies."

"Technically, only of the Community—" Leah started to say.

"Ahem," I cleared my throat.

"Right. Good luck. I'll find some way to reward you if this goes well." Paula signed off.

"We are so screwed," I muttered.

"Your confidence at our ability to prevent planetary genocide is stirring, sir," Elektra said.

"Thank you, Elektra. Let's hope our resident biological sciences expert has a solution."

Thirty minutes later, the image of Doctor Elizabeth Zard appeared in a box to the upper left corner of the viewscreen. She was a lovely black-haired woman with alabaster skin and piercing eyes. She was also permanently addicted to synt-cigarettes and coffee. Right now, she looked bored out of her mind even though she was studying new life about to eat a star.

"Howdy, Doc," I said. "Do you bring us good news or are we going to be handling a dying planet turning on itself soon?"

"Possibly both," Doctor Zard said. "I've analyzed what little data we have on the creature and have come to some disturbing conclusions."

"I take it your medical degree didn't come with 'creatures made of fire'," I said, cheerfully.

"We have to do something," Leah said. "We have options."

"Which are?" I asked, looking back at the viewscreen. "I mean, our problems are starting with *planet-sized monster that eats stars*."

"It's alive and capable of reproduction," Liz said.

I blinked. "That is in fact *very bad*."

"It converts the energy and gas inside the sun into whatever strange matter it's made of," Liz said. "By the time it finishes eating in a few hours, it'll have split off into dozens of more of its kind who will also feed from the sun."

"Okay," Leah said. "This has gone from being a problem for five hundred thousand people to an existential threat to the universe."

"Not really," Danny said, forgetting he wasn't supposed to talk. "There's like a trillion stars."

"A hundred fifty-five billion at last count," I corrected. "Even then, if each of these things feeds off a star in a few days and breeds then that could rapidly grow out of control."

"That's assuming they're capable of reaching other star systems," Leah said. "Without access to jumpspace, they'd take millennia to cross the void even at light speed."

"They're capable of entering jumpspace," Liz said, taking things from bad to super-worse. "In fact, I think they're made up of matter from that dimension. They could in fact devour the entire galaxy given a few million years—which is more impressive than it sounds."

"I'm pretty easily impressed," I said, imagining the end of everything. "Yeah, we should probably stop this if we can."

The entirety of the galactic government had nearly collapsed over the use of SKAMMs, sun-destroying missiles, and this was an even worse weapon in many ways. SKAMMs at least caused a supernova. This sun-eater would condemn inhabited worlds to a slow lingering death by freezing.

"Agreed," Leah said. "How do we kill these things?"

"I'm not sure we can," Liz said. "However, we can possibly lure them back into jumpspace with a modified jumpdrive."

"Yeah, because we have a bunch of those lying around," I muttered. "Even if we can, that'll leave us at half-speed and make evacuation all but impossible."

"Other-dimensional entities turn out to be a problem requiring unique solutions," Elektra replied, dryly.

Was everyone on my ship a smart-ass? Well, I guessed it was a requirement to be promoted to the bridge crew. In an emergency, I needed people who spoke my language. Still, her plan had merit. Sort of. If we could get a jumpdrive hooked up to a generator, it could create a field large enough to take the thing back into its dimension. The problem was, well, it was in the fricking sun. There wasn't a way we could get a jumpspace drive within a million kilometers of the place without destroying it.

Literally.

"There's more," Liz said.

"Oh joy," I said, feeling like our time was running out.

"This one you'll like," Liz said, smiling. "I think I've found our evil wizard."

I stared at her. "Tell me more."

"This is a terrible plan," I muttered inside my spacesuit. I was sitting in the cockpit of the Stalwart-class shuttle that was slowly propelling itself through space despite its engines being offline. The

271

thing about space was the absence of gravity meant that if you started propelling an object forward, it would continue going forever. There was no resistance to slow it down.

With a single burst of thrust, we could send the shuttle moving toward our target and be almost undetectable. It was an old pirate trick, and I knew it well even if I had a couple more decades before I qualified as an old pirate (and left Space Fleet). I also had a cybernetic implant linking me to the shuttle's computer so controlling it was as easy as thought.

"It's *your* plan," Leah said, sitting behind me in the copilot's seat. She was dressed in an identical spacesuit, though hers had a couple of emergency patches on it from the various battles she'd fought. Frankly, I was hoping we could use the money from this run to replace them but if wishes were fishes, then Aquarians would rule the galaxy.

"Technically, it's Elektra's plan," I replied, checking our instruments.

In addition to the Elder Race-influenced weapons and shields that were not standard issue on board a Community capital ship, the *Melampus* also had a top-rate sensor system. It was strong enough that it could pick up a cloaked Kolahn light saucer at short range. It was about the size of a small house and probably didn't require more than a single person to run it. I didn't know if it belonged to this Akavma guy but given it was the only other ship in the system, I was willing to bet on it.

"It's *a* plan, at least," Leah said. "We exit out the ship, give a bit of thrust, and propel ourselves towards the saucer. We murder the guy and hopefully figure out how he summoned the Fire Dragon to the system."

"Maybe we should do the latter before the former," I said, amused. "Dead men tell no tales."

"I don't care as long as it involves murdering the guy," Leah said. "We've only got a few more hours until that sun becomes a red giant. If we stop it now, then it'll have a few more million years of life. As insignificant as that may be in the life of a sun."

"In another life you would have made a brilliant scientist," I said.

"In another life, you're a decent captain," Leah said, good-naturedly.

"I wouldn't bet on that," I said, dryly.

"You know this is a really good thing we're doing," Leah said, annoying me. "It feels nice to do something to help people rather than just spend all of our time robbing or cheating people."

"You shouldn't say anything," I said, faking looking at the dead instruments in front of me. "Akavma might pick it up."

"Sound doesn't travel through space, dumbass," Leah said.

"Then maybe I just don't want to think about the fact that we're doing charity work," I replied, shaking my head. "It never works out well. You think you're doing a good thing and then it blows up in your face."

"Is this about the war?" Leah asked.

I blinked. "Yes, Leah, it's always about the war. I went into the conflict thinking I was a hero, got everyone I loved killed, and killed a bunch of other people who probably didn't have it coming."

"I'm pretty sure this guy has it coming," Leah said. "Destroying a star is some grade-A supervillain stuff."

"He's an evil techno-wizard controlling a dragon and threatening to kill some (semi) peaceful villagers. You don't get much more morally unambiguous than that," I said, sucking in my breath. "That's why I'm hesitating to go forward. This seems all a bit too straightforward. You don't destroy a star to wipe out a bunch of settlers barely scrapping by. We're missing something."

"Maybe he's making a demonstration," Leah said.

"What?" I asked.

"Maybe he's going to show the galaxy what his Fire Dragon can do," Leah explained. "Then sell it for a hundred trillion credits to whoever will buy it. Sort of like a homemade SKAMM, except even more likely to piss off the Elder Races. Maybe he's just insane. Maybe he tripped over some Elder Race artifact and found it can summon monsters that eat stars like a dog whistle. Does it really matter?"

"Yes?" I answered, confused.

"I disagree," Leah replied. "Because in a few minutes he'll be dead, and we'll have a Kolahn ship we can scrub for data on these Technomancers."

She had a point there. "I love your pragmatic mind."

"It's my third best feature after my eyes and homicidal tendencies," Leah said.

"What's mine?" I asked, absently.

"You're remarkably pleasant company when you learn to shut up," Leah said, pausing. "We're here."

My spacesuit's micro-binoculars were able to pick up the ship on visual as I activated the thrusters to slow us down. The Kolahn light saucer was a sleek piece of engineering that barely resembled anything made by human hands, possessing none of the usual lights or flourishes that decorated typical vessels made for our race. Instead, it looked like one solid piece of metal floating in the darkness. There was something about it that made me feel a sick and I had to clamp down that feeling.

"Do we even know how we're going to get into that thing?" Leah asked. "I don't see any airlocks."

"I have an idea," I said, simply.

I opened the cockpit to the vacuum of space with the emergency lever and let the atmosphere escape around us. We were only a few meters away from the light cruiser and I fired a magnetic grapple from a pistol I'd packed ahead of time, and floating it to Leah. We pulled ourselves to the side of the Kolahn vessel and attached ourselves to its side with our boots.

"Okay, so what's the plan?" Leah asked.

I reached to the side of my space suit where an electronic sheath was attached to by belt. From it I lifted a very anachronistic weapon which was a gift from the High Council: a proton sword.

"Oh no," Leah muttered.

"Oh yes," I said, activating it. The weapon crackled with strange energies I didn't fully understand and yet which functioned perfectly fine in the vacuum of space. It was based on alien technologies that allegedly made the blade sharp enough to shear an atom in half. I doubted that since I'd yet to cause a nuclear detonation with my blade, but it was *really, really* sharp.

I brought it down and cut a triangular hole, feeling Kolahn hypersteel fall prey to my weapon like it was paper, and exposed a chunk of the vessel's interior to vacuum. The chunk I'd carved floated away and I prepared to begin my assault on this so-called Master Akavma.

That was when a living shadow emerged from the hole and ate us.

"Twinkle, twinkle, little star, how I wonder what you are. Up above the world so high, looking down upon us as we die. When the blazing sun is gone, when the nothing shines upon, then you show your little light. Twinkle, twinkle in the eternal night," the voice that interrupted my dreamless slumber was soft, slick, and somehow slimy. I recognized the nursey rhyme as a common one among spacers. It was a reminder that space was a deadly place that would eventually consume us all. Yeah, spacers were a fun people.

My wrists were tied to some sort of metal table, and I could feel that I was unclothed. There was always the sense of being violated when captors undressed you. On the other hand, you were always lucky to wake up when you were knocked out. I'd known plenty of people disabled by gas or electricity who had never woken up at all. Opening my eyes, I saw I was in a nearly empty chrome room with no sign of Leah. My captor was nearby, looming over me like I was the most interesting thing in the world.

He was over two meters tall with a spherical bald head, corpse-like papery skin that was covered in fish-scale-like splotches, and a neck twice as large as a normal man. He was wearing robes and carrying a staff that I could tell had numerous devices built into it but, from a distance, could pass as a fantasy wizard's tool. His eyes were bulbous and completely black. Each hand had about six fingers with no thumbs.

"You are one ugly son of a bitch," I said, simply.

The Kolahn slapped me across the face.

"You stand before a Master of Eighteen Paths, an Enlightened Lord of the Red Lodge. I, Akavma, have seen the planes that lie beyond this realm. I have visited realities you could not begin to comprehend and know the secrets that lie in men's minds," Akavma said, raising his staff like he was on the stage.

"I've visited alternate realities too," I said, dryly. "Are people impressed with this nonsense?"

Akavma frowned then shrugged. "You wouldn't believe how many people fall for it. I used to have a position as the special advisor to the president of Belenus. He paid five hundred thousand credits per session and that was in addition to the millions for the curses I laid on his enemies. Fifty billion to kill the prime minister of Bridget."

"How'd that work out?" I asked.

"A freighter's toilet fell on them from orbit," Akavma said, chuckling. "Sadly, the president turned against him when the media found out about his use of his young attractive staff members."

I'd actually heard of all of this. "Yeah, they'll get you for that."

Akavma frowned. "You are Vance Turbo, Hero of SPAAACE. The Satan of the Notha. The Fat Grazing Bear of the Sorkanan. The second High Protector—"

"Yes, I know who I am. Has the Zatranian sun changed yet?"

"No," Akavma said. "Not yet. But soon. You weren't out that long. Changing the nature of a sun is by itself a great accomplishment but it's snuffing a healthy sun that will get me wealth beyond imagination."

"Money, really?" I asked, unimpressed.

"Why do *you* kill people?" Akavma asked.

"Duty," I replied.

"I like my reason better," Akavma said.

"I still don't get it. Why here? To what end?"

Akavma shrugged. "My organization, the Technomancers, benefits strongly from the fact the people of the galaxy are a superstitious bunch of fools. Zatrania III is a planet full of useful relics that could be used to make us a feared power in the galaxy. The locals resisted."

"And you think killing their sun was a proportional response?" I asked, trying very hard not to be sarcastic and failing miserably.

Akavma smiled. "It was one of the objects I found still functional on their planet. When all you have is a sun killer, a sun killer you must use. In any case, once my demonstration is done, I can loot the planet to my leisure. I probably won't need however much I'll get from ransoming you to your enemies on Earth but never turn down free money."

I smiled right back. "Of course. I don't suppose we could make a deal, Akavma? The Community has deep pockets."

"Yes, it does," Akavma admitted. "But no, I don't think we can. I've worked with way too many government types to trust that you'll pay your bills. Besides, the Community destroyed my homeworld. That's why I'm broke."

I had to admit that his logic was impeccable.

"Shame," I said, closing my eyes and checking to see if the Kolahn hypersteel blocked transmission from my cybernetic implant. Checking for updates, I found out, there was a big hole in the side of the ship blocked off only by a life-support barrier. So, it turned out it didn't. I ordered my starfighter to power up and fire its energy cannons.

"What are you doing?" Akavma asked.

That was when the starship rocked as I was smart enough to only fire at a quarter power.

"My ship has found you!" I said, bullsaviting my way through this. "You have to release me to tell them to stop before we're both killed."

Akavma hesitated before the second blast and reluctantly released my restraints. "You have no idea what terrible—"

I headbutted him in the face, grabbed him by the neck and snapped it in a single smooth gesture. Given he was an alien reptile-gorilla, and I was a human, it shouldn't have been possible but the Elder Races had made some "improvements" to my body. He fell useless to the ground as his staff bounced across the chrome surface of the floor.

"Wizards beat fighters at long range, not close," I muttered, picking up the staff. "Everyone who plays *Fantasy Control Online* knows that."

The staff wasn't a particularly complicated piece of machinery, being a basic control rod for a starship with a disintegrator built into it—expensive but not magical. Using it to open the door, I found Leah outside my cell door, trying to force it open. She was wearing a hospital gown from what I assumed to be the ship's medical area.

"Hi," I said.

"Hi," Leah said, blinking. "I see you managed to get yourself free."

"Likewise," I said, chuckling. "Ding dong! The witch is dead."

"Wizard, not witch," Leah said.

I shook my head. "Whatever."

We found a weird Elder Race monolith with a computer-interface hooked up to the light freighter's central computer and did the only thing we could do in that situation: we moved the ship around. It lured the Fire Dragon away to the next star system where Elektra tried out her jumpspace generator trick. I had no idea if it worked since both it, the Fire Dragon, and the stone monolith vanished once they came together.

I hated losing the Kolahn ship, but it was better to use its generator than the *Melampus'* own. We'd also cleaned it out of anything valuable along the way. It turned out the late Master Akavma had been a collector of fine art and alien artifacts. Stuff that he'd intended to sell on the black market that could be returned to the worlds they'd been stolen from.

As for the Zatranians? Well, they were very grateful for what we'd done. So grateful that they believed me when I told them that the Elder Race relics on their planet were all cursed and needed to be transported away. I ended up turning them over to a representative of the Elder Races that told me they'd been missed during the planet's first "cleansing." I'd prevented the need for a second.

Victory, I guess.

LEXICON

373: Also known as Claw World. It was a Sorkanan colony world populated by dissidents and radicals that had become overpopulated and economically unstable before the Notha destroyed the world. It was destroyed by one of the SKAMMs and became a rallying cry for Equalists and Separatists.

AI: Artificial intelligence. Science fiction has talked about these a few times.

Admiralty Board: The head of Space Fleet for Earth and those who supervise its link to other navies as part of the Community.

Albion: An island-filled water planet settled by humans abducted by aliens. The most powerful human planet, currently losing ground to Earth.

Antaeus Rangers: An organization of mercenaries formerly employed by Earth.

Ant: A race of (seemingly) giant, ant-like aliens that are terrifying and strong. It turns out those were chasses for a much, much smaller race.

Artificial Gravity: A slang term for something people think is possible but is not. Even the Community just generates the real thing with a variety of tricks.

Astronomical Unit: A unit of measurement to 149.6 million kilometers. The rough distance from the center of Earth to the center of the Sun is one AU.

Bastarve: Another word for bastard. Swearing isn't very original on Albion.

Belenus: A wealthy, environmentally friendly paradise world also settled by humans abducted by aliens. Traditional rivals to Albion.

279

Biash: A gendered insult, usually used in context of one's ancestry.

Biomods: Genetic enhancements that provide sapient beings with special abilities. Usually, organic technology rather than cybernetics to avoid rejection.

Bioroids: Androids and gynoids indistinguishable from humans with synthetic flesh. Often used for exactly what you think.

Bork: A weirdly popular curse word that also refers to copulation. Bots: Robots. Crazy, I know, right?

Brigid: Sister-world to Belenus and producing most of the infrastructure that keeps its brother-world in wealth.

Chel: A race of humans uplifted by the Elder Races and their own experimentation. They live entirely in space and resemble classical depictions of the Grays of UFO lore only tall and thin. Named for Doctor Chel who sent his transhumanist cult out into space. They are much older, and his cult was absorbed into them.

Cognition AI: Nearly omnipotent AI that can process unlimited amounts of data. Pretty much the real rulers of the Community. But so friendly!

Community: An interstellar fellowship of many species and worlds. It is generally pro-democracy, civil rights, diversity, and technology. Of course, no one trusts it or its activities. Community Protectors: See Space Fleet.

Community Senate: A collection of representatives of the various worlds of the Community. Many planets dislike it because it impedes their own ambitions while others hate that it is dominated by the High Council.

Contested Space: A region of space between the Community and Notha Empire. It is full of outlaw settlements, pirate bands, half-terraformed hellholes and collapsed civilizations. It ceased to exist as an official entity after the last treaty with the Notha.

Core Worlds: The center of the galaxy where the Elder Races choose to live.

Crazzap: Crap by another name is just as stinky.

Crius: A planet being settled by transhumanists wanting to create a feudal paradise. A planet of genetically engineered slaves ruled by a bunch of deranged cloners. Go here to be hunted by dinosaurs. It was recently liberated by the Community.

Crystal Spider Empire: An expansionist genocidal empire populated by the Crystal Spiders. It proceeded to enslave hundreds of worlds and became one of the most terrifying threats to the Community that existed. It was eventually crushed and the remaining Crystal Spiders eventually destroyed themselves in civil wars.

Deathworld: A jungle world on the edge of the Notha Union that was formerly one of the key strongholds of the Notha Empire. It is inhabited by a Notha minority that has sought closer ties with the Community over the Notha Union. It is also one of the few to ban slavery and provide limited protections for non-Notha.

Demihumans: Humans who no longer are strictly human due to evolution and genetic modification.

Department Twelve: A renegade Earth-based intelligence organization that has grown incredibly powerful in recent years, arguably more so than EarthGov itself. It sponsors an isolationist pro-human agenda that wishes to seize Elder Race technology for itself.

Drolochid: Slimy, warm-blooded, multi-limbed race with sensory organs across their pill bug bodies. Quite pleasant to be around.

Earth: The human homeworld. Perhaps you've heard of it. The new kids on the block. Way too eager to prove itself.

EarthGov: The government of Earth. Duh.

Home Fleet: Earth's personal defense force. It is separate from the ships it loans to permanent Community duty.

Elder Races: Several godlike "sufficiently advanced" aliens who live in the galactic Core and decide what races live or die without any understandable criteria. Real jerks.

Enigmatic Path: A Kolahn terrorist organization and religious fundamentalist group. Its bizarre ideology is about how organic life is an abomination, AI should be liberated, and the universe is a simulation.

Equalism: A Sorkanan political philosophy that involves radical wealth redistribution and the destruction of traditional institutions. It is anti-democratic and individual rights. The progressive Community is its most frequent target.

Ethereal Humans: A group of humans uplifted by the Elder Races to be intermediaries with them and other organics. They and Ethereal versions of other races tend to lead the Community in its decision-making process.

Human League: An attempt to bring all human planets under one united banner to wield more economic and political power in the Community. It is primarily driven by Albion and Earth. Most Community members support the idea as too many individual human polities confuse things.

H'shrah-class heavy transport: A starship of the Sorkanan Navy that is extremely well-armored and possessed of heavy shielding. It has been often converted into a warship for less developed worlds.

Infospace: An extra-dimensional communications system that allows faster-than-light communication and works like an interstellar internet. Also, can be used as a virtual reality interface.

Jumpdrive: What allows people to travel through space like in movies.

Jumpspace: A dimension of bizarre physics that makes faster-than-light travel possible. Looking at it will drive most people insane like staring into the sun due to the way it stimulates your synapses.

Kolahn: Resemble giant apes with scales. Their civilization was overtaken by a terrorist cult and promptly bombed back to the stone age by the Community. Its survivors are, paradoxically, living as refugees throughout the Community.

Kolahn Wars: The wars that bombed the Kolahn back to the Stone Age.

Liberator: A massive battleship that was one of the flagships of the collapsed Separatist movement. It was formerly a decommissioned Sorkanan command ship that was somehow acquired via bribes and subtle manipulation.

Luna: Earth's moon. It is largely used for the construction of spacecraft for civilian and military spacecraft and other advanced electronics incapable of being manufactured on Earth.

Lunar Shipyards: Pretty much what the name suggests. Most of Luna has been hollowed out for it.

Mary Read: The Chel-constructed Elder Race technology-equipped starship of High Protector Anne Bonny. It was used to defeat the

Crystal Spider Empire and "liberate" hundreds of worlds that later became part of the Community.

Melampus: A dreadnought-class, Community-constructed vessel that was created for its High Protectors. It is equipped with a small amount of Elder Race technology.

Notha: Adorable lemur-like race of Space Nazi bastards.

Notha Empire: A corrupt military dictatorship ruled by the Notha that practiced slavery, imperialism, planet looting, and conquest. It maintained its existence not by competence but due to the possession of weapons of stellar destruction. When SKAMMs were outlawed by the Elder Races and the Great Notha died, the organization collapsed.

Notha Union: The successor state of the Notha Empire that emerged after the Thord Treaty of Exarxes. It is about 75% as big and headed by a new Great Notha who dreams of restoring the Empire.

Notha War: A conflict that resulted in the destruction of seventeen inhabited planets on both sides of the conflict due to an exchange of SKAMMs.

Peleseids: The races that live within the Perseus Arm.

People's Liberation Army: The warlord army of Grand General Vast and a remnant of the former Separatist systems.

Perseus Arm: A largely-unexplored arm of the Milky Way galaxy.

Plizzed: A state of fluid retention. Used as a pejorative.

Primordials: An extra-galactic race that has severe issues with the Elder Races. They are from the Large Magellanic Cloud and formerly inhabited the Milky Way a billion years ago before fleeing to settle it. Their vessels exist in both jumpspace and realspace simultaneously. They recently suffered a humiliating loss that has briefly put them off galactic genocide.

Rand's World: A former colony world of Earth where the terraforming was stopped mid-process due to Notha aggression. It is now primarily inhabited by criminals, pirates, and separatists. Named for Ayn Rand.

The Ring: A superstructure constructed by the Elder Races that exists in the Perseus Arm. It has fallen prey to corruption and domination by an oligarchy of slavers, crime lords, and merchant princes.

Security Departments: The twelve, yes, twelve intelligence agencies working for the Community.

Separatists: A movement consisting of Sorkanan and humans primarily that wish to leave the Community. They have since fallen into economic collapse and civil war. Many of its planets were devotees of Equalism.

SKAMMs: Sun destroying weapons of interstellar destruction. They are horrifying devices and their use in the recent Notha War resulted in an immediate end to the conflict lest the two sides annihilate one another.

Sklux: A race of protoplasmic beings that can shape into a rough approximation of any form. Obsessed with puns. Considered a race of mediators and peacemakers, primarily by themselves.

Sorkanan: One of the oldest and most powerful species in space. They are a humanoid reptilian species with multiple offshoots.

Sorkanan Imperial Navy: The massive fleets of the Sorkanan Empire. Its conditions are horrifying, and morale is generally low but it is still the greatest power in the Spiral.

Space Academy: The training center for officers in the Community Protectors.

Spacer: A slang term for those who have grown up and primarily live in space.

Space Fleet: The Community's massive interstellar Navy that is (allegedly) a galactic force for good.

The Spire: What Orion's Arm is called by most races of the Known Universe as they are primarily concentrated there.

Sun Killer: Another name for SKAMM torpedoes.

Transtellar: The name for interplanetary corporations that are possessed of resources far more than individual worlds. They wield disproportionate power in the Community and among humanity's various worlds.

Tubing: A process where a woman has a fertilized embryo put in a life support tube instead of carrying it inside her. They are ubiquitous on Albion, Brigid, and among spacer women with it growing in popularity on Earth. Nicknamed *uterine replicators* after a sci-fi series from Earth's past.

Treaty of Exarxes: A large multispecies agreement on shared morality and behavior during wartime. The Notha are a very reluctant signatory. A second treaty was drafted to ban the use of SKAMMs and other weapons of mass destruction at the insistence of the Elder Races. A third treaty was recently signed that helped define Contested Space better between the Notha and Community.

Unification Wars: The war where the Neo-Militarists and transtellars were defeated before the Community friendly EarthGov was born.

Union of Faith: A group of thirty-six worlds settled by medieval Christians, Muslims, Jews, Buddhists, and other religions that have created a theocracy within the Community. Weirdly, religious tolerance is in its constitution but almost everything else is regulated to a ridiculous degree.

Ush'tak-class battle cruiser: An eight-kilometer dreadnought created for the Sorkanan Navy that serve as the focus for entire fleets. Several of the ships were sold to member states before the independence movement and were turned against the Community.

Verdantian: A leonine race with six limbs that were uplifted by the Elder Races according to their belief structure.

Wheelerism: A religion based around nonsensical quantum-based consciousness theories mixed with Christianity and Buddhism. Some of it is actually accurate.

AUTHOR'S NOTE

I'd like to thank you for reading this book. The publishing industry is changing dramatically since the advent of eBooks. It is now very difficult to get any book noticed, regardless of quality. If you enjoyed this book, you could do some very simple things to help me attract attention. Word of mouth is the number one source of success for novels, so simply telling family and friends about the book is a great start.

Here are a few other ways of helping out, if you are so inclined:

* Post a rating or review where you purchased the eBook
* Post a rating or review on Goodreads
* Talk about the book or write a review on Facebook
* Tell folks about the book in a blog post.

If you like any of my other books, please feel free to check them out. A lot of my series are interlinked, and you never know when you'll find someone familiar showing up. In this case, *Space Academy Dropouts* is set in the far future of my Agent G cyberpunk books and the past of my *Lucifer's Star* series. Fans will certainly get a kick out of seeing how the galaxy changes in a few centuries either way.

ABOUT THE AUTHORS

Michael Suttkus, II, lives in Leesburg, Florida, with three cats, one of which actually likes him, and his family, with whom he fares better. When not working at a game store, he's playing games, reading science books, or otherwise being incredibly nerdy. Also writing! Because he has to feed cats whether they like him or not.

Bibliography

I Was a Teenage Weredeer (The Bright Falls Mysteries, Book 1)
An American Weredeer in Michigan (The Bright Falls Mysteries, Book 2)
A Nightmare on Elk Street (The Bright Falls Mysteries, Book 3)

Lucifer's Star (Lucifer's Star #1)
Lucifer's Nebula (Lucifer's Star #2)

Brightblade (The Morgan Detective Agency, Book 1)
Brighteyes (The Morgan Detective Agency, Book 2)

Space Academy Dropouts (The Space Academy Series, Book 1)
Space Academy Rejects (The Space Academy Series, Book 2)
Space Academy Washouts (The Space Academy Series, Book 3)
Space Academy Miscreants (The Space Academy Series, Book 4)
Space Academy Vagrants (The Space Academy Series, Book 5)

C. T. Phipps is a lifelong student of horror, science fiction, and fantasy. An avid tabletop gamer, he discovered this passion led him to write and turned him into a lifelong geek. He is a regular blogger and also a reviewer for The Bookie Monster.

Bibliography

Novels
The Rules of Supervillainy (Supervillainy Saga #1)
The Games of Supervillainy (Supervillainy Saga #2)
The Secrets of Supervillainy (Supervillainy Saga #3)
The Kingdom of Supervillainy (Supervillainy Saga #4)
The Tournament of Supervillainy (Supervillainy Saga #5)
The Future of Supervillainy (Supervillainy Saga #6)
The Horror of Supervillainy (Supervillainy Saga #7)
Tales of Supervillainy: Cindy's Seven (Supervillainy Saga #8)
The Fall of Supervillainy (Supervillainy Saga #9)
The Return of Supervillainy (Supervillainy Saga #10)

I Was a Teenage Weredeer (The Bright Falls Mysteries, Book 1)
An American Weredeer in Michigan (The Bright Falls Mysteries, Book 2)
A Nightmare on Elk Street (The Bright Falls Mysteries, Book 3)

Esoterrorism (Red Room, Vol. 1)
Eldritch Ops (Red Room, Vol. 2)
The Fall of the House (Red Room, Vol. 3)

Agent G: Infiltrator (Agent G, Vol. 1)
Agent G: Saboteur (Agent G, Vol. 2)
Agent G: Assassin (Agent G, Vol. 3)

Cthulhu Armageddon (Cthulhu Armageddon, Vol. 1)
The Tower of Zhaal (Cthulhu Armageddon, Vol. 2)
The Tree of Azathoth (Cthulhu Armageddon, Vol. 3)

Lucifer's Star (Lucifer's Star, Vol. 1)
Lucifer's Nebula (Lucifer's Star, Vol. 2)

Straight Outta Fangton (Straight Outta Fangton, Vol. 1)
100 Miles and Vampin' (Straight Outta Fangton, Vol. 2)
Vampiraz4Life (Straight Outta Fangton, Vol. 3)

Wraith Knight (Wraith Knight, Vol. 1)
Wraith Lord (Wraith Knight, Vol. 2)
Wraith King (Wraith Knight, Vol. 3)

Dark Destiny (Dark Destiny, Vol. 1)
Destiny's Paradox (Dark Destiny, Vol. 2)

Brightblade (The Morgan Detective Agency, Book 1)
Brighteyes (The Morgan Detective Agency, Book 2)

Daughter of the Cyber Dragons (The Cyber Dragons Series, Book 1)
Revenge of the Cyber Dragons (The Cyber Dragons Series, Book 2)
End of the Cyber Dragons (The Cyber Dragons Series, Book 3)

Space Academy Dropouts (The Space Academy Series, Book 1)

Space Academy Rejects (The Space Academy Series, Book 2)
Space Academy Washouts (The Space Academy Series, Book 3)

Moon Cops on the Moon (Moon Cops, Book 1)
Moon City Vice (Moon Cops, Book 2)

Lords of Dragon Keep (Dark Undermaster, Book 1)
Guardians of Dragon Keep (Dark Undermaster, Book 2)
Wizards of Dragon Keep (Dark Undermaster, Book 3)

Psycho Killers in Love

Tales of an Eldritch Wasteland

<u>Anthologies (as editor)</u>
Blackest Knights
Blackest Spells
Tales of Capes and Cowls
Tales of the Al-Azif
Tales of Yog-Sothoth

Curious about other Crossroad Press books? Stop by our website:
http://crossroadpress.com
We offer quality writing
in digital, audio, and print formats.

Subscribe to our newsletter on the website homepage and receive a
free eBook.